# A GIFT OF THE STARS

### BOOK 1

# M. L. DUNKER

Publishing Services provided by Paper Raven Books LLC
Printed in the United States of America
First Printing, 2021

Paperback ISBN= 979-8-9850536-1-6
Hardback ISBN= 979-8-9850536-0-9

*Dedication: For anyone who has been stuffed in a box, labeled, and buried. Break the box!*

# TABLE OF CONTENTS


Chapter 1: On the Road to Aldi . . . . . . . . . . . . . . . . . . . . . 1

Chapter 2: The Storyteller of the West Islands . . . . . . . . 9

Chapter 3: A Story of the Great Smith and Mother Earth 19

Chapter 4: Puzzles and Mysteries . . . . . . . . . . . . . . . 31

Chapter 5: Willow . . . . . . . . . . . . . . . . . . . . . 39

Chapter 6: Red . . . . . . . . . . . . . . . . . . . . . 49

Chapter 7: Kereki Metal Poisoning . . . . . . . . . . . . . . . 59

Chapter 8: A West Islands Constellation Tale . . . . . . . . . . 77

Chapter 9: A Conrosan Fairy Tale . . . . . . . . . . . . . . . 87

Chapter 10: A Grand Adventure . . . . . . . . . . . . . . . 105

Chapter 11: A Flower and a Weed . . . . . . . . . . . . . . . 117

Chapter 12: Trouble on the Coast Road . . . . . . . . . . . 127

Chapter 13: An Unwelcome Truth . . . . . . . . . . . . . . . 143

Chapter 14: A Gift of the Stars . . . . . . . . . . . . . . . 157

Chapter 15: Titiro Mai Ki Ahau . . . . . . . . . . . . . . . 169

Chapter 16: The Orphan Master . . . . . . . . . . . . . . . 181

Chapter 17: Matasi and the Kindness of Strangers . . . . . . 195

Chapter 18: Unexpected Gifts . . . . . . . . . . . . . . . 213

Chapter 19: Dancing with Trouble . . . . . . . . . . . . . . . 233

Chapter 20: Anarkio . . . . . . . . . . . . . . . 247

Chapter 21: Choices. . . . . . . . . . . . . . . . . . . . . . . 257

Chapter 22: Salisport . . . . . . . . . . . . . . . . . . . . . 271

Chapter 23: Weapons Training. . . . . . . . . . . . . . . . 287

Chapter 24: The Ambassador's Reception. . . . . . . . . . . . 295

Chapter 25: Secrets Revealed and Kept. . . . . . . . . . . . 307

Chapter 26: Goodbye. . . . . . . . . . . . . . . . . . . . . 317

Chapter 27: In the Tender Care of Viklanders . . . . . . . . 325

Chapter 28: Lost and Found . . . . . . . . . . . . . . . . . 335

Chapter 29: The Matasi Missionaries . . . . . . . . . . . . . 347

Chapter 30: Back to Kerek City . . . . . . . . . . . . . . . 357

Chapter 31: Softfooting . . . . . . . . . . . . . . . . . . . 371

Chapter 32: Best Laid Plans . . . . . . . . . . . . . . . . . 383

Chapter 33: Song Yao and Kern the Softfoot . . . . . . . . . 395

Chapter 34: Raumati of the West Islands . . . . . . . . . . . 409

Chapter 35: The Fate of the Lost Children . . . . . . . . . . 421


Reading Guide. . . . . . . . . . . . . . . . . . . . . . . . 422

Bonus Story: Men of Power . . . . . . . . . . . . . . . . . 428

Sneak peak of Book 2 Manumina. . . . . . . . . . . . . . . 439

Kerek City
SALT CLIFFS
Aldi
KEREK
Sion Inn
Ribelo
Tenro
Kairo
Subversiva
MATASI
Anarkio
Salisport
Alenti
Otalport

## CHAPTER 1

# ON THE ROAD TO ALDI

I opened my eyes against the pain to see another pair of deep brown eyes looking at my arm. I hurt everywhere. My face hurt, my shoulder hurt, and my body sprawled on the hot dry road hurt.

The boy, clean cheeked, dark skinned with thick black curly hair, pursed his lips. He then gently touched my face along my jaw, and I felt the rising bruise underneath his fingertips. He looked up, smiled at my opened eyes, and spoke. I didn't recognize the language. He shifted to Keresh. "Hello, there! You've taken quite a beating. Can I help you?"

I licked my dry lips. "Water."

The boy lifted a beautiful metal flask to my lips, and I drank the cool water. Before letting it go, I let it wash down my face.

He laughed easily. "We'll get you cleaned up in a moment. Can you tell me how you came to be on my road to Aldi?"

I started to reply, and then realized the boy in front of me could help me. If I was careful. If I could hide the knowledge that I had a face which would not let me lie.

I frowned at him and spoke slowly, "I truly...I truly don't remember."

"Let's start with your name and work back from that," he offered.

Again I paused. I told myself I wouldn't be lying—I truly didn't know my name. Everyone in Lowertown called me "Red" for the color of my skin, but that wasn't my name. I looked at him and panicked, thinking he would know what I had done. The boy saw my fear and mistook it for something else.

He said gently, "You took quite a blow to the head. No doubt it will come back to you, but for now, just gather yourself together." He paused, and then, "Are you hurt anywhere but on your head and your arm?"

I blinked again. "I hurt...everywhere."

"May I touch you?" He carefully started at my neck and slid his hands down my arms, my legs, and patted down my torso. He paused while he pulled the bag of coins from under my shirt and the dagger from my boot. "Well, you obviously weren't left here long—you still have your purse and your life, and your face has only been kissed by the sun and not ravaged. I know you don't feel like it right now, but you're a very lucky lordling."

He raised himself from his knees and settled into a crouch. "Can you stand? Walk? I would like to move you off the road before someone else happens by." I slowly rolled to my hands and knees, and then a wave of nausea hit, and I emptied my stomach onto the sand. The boy jumped back out of my way as I fell over on my side.

He sighed. "Well, I suppose it can't be helped, we certainly can't stay here." He looked to the left and whistled. A whistle came back, and I heard light steps running towards me. I opened my eyes and turned my head to see a pair of feet clad in worn leather boots covered in dust. I looked up and only saw a dark outline against the sun. I felt another stab of pain in my head and closed my eyes again.

"Will, my friend cannot rise. Can you take his feet and I will take his shoulders?" I tried to keep my stomach calm as I swayed between them. I felt the coolness of the shade as we shifted off the road, and then even the footfalls ceased as they carried me deeper into the trees. I kept my eyes closed as I was propped up against a tree trunk. My two rescuers moved away before they began speaking. Not Keresh, not Mata. The words swooped and danced almost as if they were set to music. I opened one eye just in time to see someone slip between the trees away from me.

I tried to push myself up. "What's happening?"

"You're in no shape to travel, so we are going to take you to our camp a little deeper into the trees. We shall spend the rest of today here and see how you feel tomorrow." The boy paused. "You didn't have any travel bags, and your boots don't have any dust on them so you haven't been walking a far distance. You have no food or drink with you. Do you think you were traveling on a horse and were thrown? Or riding in a wagon and your horses ran away? Do you think you were heading towards Aldi or away from it?"

I tried to focus on his face as he asked his questions. He wasn't as young as I first thought. There were lines by his eyes. He was shorter than I was and I had always been mocked for being undersized. It was why I had confused him for a boy. His fingers were rough and callused as he pulled a blanket from his pack and tucked it around my shoulders. He looked at me.

"Nothing? If I say 'Aldi' your heart doesn't leap with excitement for your arrival, or desire to be beyond the town?"

I shook my head carefully and it pounded in protest. "I can't remember if I know how to ride, where I was going, or what I was going to do when I got there." I squinted up at him. "Did you tell me your name?"

The man smiled. "Koanga."

"Koanga…not from Kerek then."

He laughed. "Not with this face. And the King's walking stick is taller than I am. No, my friend, Willow and I are from the West Islands. Here on an adventure and ready to go home. And you, lordling, you speak castle Keresh like the King, but I think, you are neither Kereki nor prince." He stood up and dusted his hands. "Never worry. We shall find your name and your home and deliver you safely. Your parents must be concerned."

I heard then what he had and tried to turn my head. Willow had returned.

Without a word, they picked me up as before and I swayed gently between them as they backed deeper into the trees. The woods thickened and then cleared. There was already kindling and branches gathered for a fire. I saw two travel packs tucked under an oilcloth draped over a rope and tied between two trees. Here Koanga and Willow gently laid me down.

"Ah, better?" Koanga sat down beside me and looked carefully at the unlit fire. I had the distinct impression he was deliberately not meeting my eyes. "My friend, in the great stories, this is where you discover you have been rescued by magical creatures who lay out a feast before you and whisk you off to their castle. Or at least by skilled hunters and talented healers who walk off into the woods with nothing but their sword and return with a brace of rabbits and basket of plants to cure your every ill." He gave a shy half smile. "Unfortunately, or perhaps fortunately, since you still have your life and your purse, you were found by Willow and me, who were on our way to Aldi to find work and supplies. I think you are too young to travel on your own, especially in Kerek, but to travel with us, you need different clothes and food and a pack of your own." He paused, still refusing to look at me, waiting for me to save him from begging.

I waited. Not because I wanted to see him squirm, but truthfully, I had no idea if the coins in my purse I carried were a fortune or a pittance. I didn't want to look foolish opening it up in front of someone I just met, smiling like a man without sense, as he robbed me with kind words.

I considered him closely and wondered how I could have thought him a mere boy. He was slender, but not the gawky skinniness of a half-grown man. His forearms, bare under his rolled sleeves were not fleshy and soft, nor were they corded with muscle. I noticed again his heavily callused fingers, now drumming on his thighs, so at odds with the rest of his body.

I looked down at my battered and torn clothes, and noticed the scrapes and cuts on my own cinnamon-colored skin. I am small and thin, but not as young as Koanga thought. There aren't a lot of birthdays celebrated in Lowertown. I think I am about seventeen, but truly? I could be convinced of any age someone wanted me to be.

I reached up to my aching head and felt curls, not as tight as Koanga's, but my dark brown hair touched the back of my neck. I wondered when my headache would end, and if my eyes would stop blurring. Koanga may not have known who I was or where I belonged, but I knew beyond a shadow of a doubt, Koanga and his friend couldn't leave me behind. I had danced with Trouble.

I touched his arm and waited until he faced me. "I pay my own way until I recover myself and our paths part. Let me buy food for our journey in gratitude for your help today." I fumbled in my purse without taking my eyes off him. I opened my palm and showed him three large coins.

He glanced at my hand and then looked me straight in the eye. "This will buy you food for the day or a change of clothes. I think you should dress a little less conspicuously." I pulled out more coins and offered them to him. The smile he flashed me was so full of relief and joy, I was stunned by how it transformed his plain face. "Thank you, we will also get you a traveling cloak to sleep in and food for all of us in the next town."

Well, then. I wasn't as rich as I thought, or Koanga could lie to my face without a flicker of unease.

## CHAPTER 2

# THE STORYTELLER OF THE WEST ISLANDS

The first thing I noticed when I woke up was the headache was mostly gone. I tenderly moved my head from right to left—no nausea, but I felt like my belly was rubbing against my backbone. I slowly opened my eyes, and no longer squinted in pain against the morning light. Morning? Where had yesterday gone? I turned my head to the other side and caught sight of Koanga pulling his shirt over his head. I turned quickly before his head popped through the collar.

I listened to the rustling near the unlit fire. Soon I heard the sharp snap of a lucifer and smelled the kindling catch and burn. Low voices, then the clunk and thunk of two metal pots set to boil. I listened for a while, trying to pick out bits of words, but Koanga had said they were from the West Islands, and Wester wasn't a language I knew.

Now that the pain had mostly left, there was room for more memories in my head, and I wondered how much I should tell them. The headache was replaced with the knowledge that I had escaped my pitiful existence in the dregs of Kerek City, and I had been dumped by the side of the road because of a fight, and perhaps a few other small details I didn't think Koanga and Willow would be happy to know.

I decided I would keep silent about what I remembered and when I remembered it. Yesterday was the first day I had been treated with kindness since, well, since a very long time. And although I had a face which would not let me lie—a problem where I grew up—I thought I could keep my past from them, at least for a little while longer. I stirred loudly, giving the pair time to finish their conversation. When I opened my eyes, I saw Koanga on his knees before the growing fire and the back of Willow heading deeper into the woods.

"Good morning!" He began softly, "How's the head?"

"Still attached, so I consider it a good morning indeed." I winced.

Koanga laughed and spread his arms wide. "You see my small stature? You are a far greater threat to me and mine, then we will ever be to you."

I wondered who had taught Koanga his Keresh—obviously not anyone from Kerek. He spoke with a lilted accent and used such old-fashioned words. It sounded odd to me because he wasn't much older than I was, but then I decided I liked it. It was no different than the many variations of words I had heard every day in Lowertown with its neighborhoods of immigrants, sailors, and travelers. I could understand him well enough. I smiled back at him. "We are no threat to each other at all. I am grateful for the shelter," I assured him.

He used a curved iron rod to pull one of the pots off the fire. From a cloth pocket, he pulled dried plants and dropped them in. "This is soapwort and lavender. Once the water cools a bit, you can wash yourself. We don't have medicine for your scrapes and cuts, but Will is looking for willow bark by the stream to ease your headache." He said nothing more but dropped oats and berries into the second pot.

I took the pot and the small piece of worn cloth Koanga handed to me and walked back to the canvas lean-to—out of sight of the campfire. It felt good to wash my face and neck. I hesitated for a moment and then pulled off my torn and dirty shirt, trousers, and small clothes. As I washed, I carefully examined the new cuts and scrapes and old scars on my body. I looked up as Koanga approached. "Here you can dry yourself with this, and these are the clothes for you, Will bought yesterday in the village past."

I smiled at his words, did anyone else talk like him? Then I realized what he said.

"Mmmm. How long did I sleep yesterday?"

"Most of the day. After you gave me the coins, I tended you while Will went to buy supplies. You can thank yourself for your breakfast."

The shirt I pulled on was a lightweight billowy shirt the farmers and country Kereki favored, with full long sleeves to protect against the sun and brambles. It was meant to be worn with a rough belted sleeveless tunic with pockets and openings to hide bits and pieces one would carry about with them. It fit well, as did the small clothes and the baggy trousers. I stepped back out near the fire and Koanga examined me critically. "You're too dark to pass for a Kereki, but perhaps your fine talk will convince people not to look closely. Wash your clothes while we wait for Willow. I can mend them well enough for our use, we will need them in the future."

I looked at the pot and my shirt. The look on my face must have showed my confusion. Koanga heaved himself up, took the shirt from my hands, and stuffed it into the pot I had just washed in. "Such a lordling!" he sighed. "It can soak while we eat and then you can beat it clean in the stream while we tear down camp." He grabbed the iron hook by my feet and pulled the other pot from the fire. After ladling a portion in a wooden bowl, he fumbled in the food bag for a piece of honeycomb and jammed it in the oats. He handed it to me. "Eat. The honeycomb is your spoon. Willow didn't buy dishes for you to conserve your coin. It's possible we could find your home as soon as today." He shrugged. "And if not, Willow and I can share."

There was a rustle behind me and Koanga pulled the breakfast pot from the fire, filled another bowl, and carried it into the woods. He came back empty-handed.

"Willow won't eat with us?" I lifted an eyebrow.

Koanga didn't respond but took the pot with my dirty shirt. "I'll wash this while I wait for Willow." He stood and walked easily out of the clearing and down to the stream humming tunelessly.

I looked around trying to see Willow in the woods and wondering about his shyness. I knew he was small, smaller than Koanga. But obviously not a young child, since Willow had been the one entrusted to do the shopping for food and clothes. The glimpses I had were of light or white hair fanned out in a nimbus about the head. His clothes were the same brown colored Kereki trousers and tunics with a dusty shaded shirt as Koanga and I wore. Obviously, Willow had observed me far better than I had been able to observe him, as the clothes were nearly a perfect fit and larger than either of them would have worn. I finished my oats and walked down the same path to the stream to wash out my bowl and give it to Koanga.

I turned the corner and nearly ran over Willow. My face must have shown my confusion and surprise, but Willow's showed only consternation. While Koanga was dark, as dark as the deepest almonds of the Matasi orchards, Willow was light, so light even the brows and lashes were as white as his hair floating about the face. I could see his eyes were the same deep brown as Koanga's and the facial features were so similar it was easy to see the West Islander in them. But that's where the similarities ended. I looked up and down and noticed a black cloth glove covering his left hand and up the arm underneath a worn shirt.

Willow recovered first. "Good morning, lordling. I am glad the clothes fit." Nodding at the empty bowl, "You've finished? Koanga is still at the stream, he can show you how to wash your bowl and shirt." He tried to brush by me.

I finally found my voice. "What are you?" I blurted out. "I mean, who are you?" Willow was dressed as a Kereki male, wearing the same type of dull baggy trousers, shirt, and tunic as I was. His pant legs were tucked into worn leather boots, and there were two Kereki ties wound around and tied about the ankles and calves. In Lowertown, we told strangers the ties were to keep out dust and insects. In actuality, they were used as distractions by the pickpockets, bindings by the robbers, and makings of riatas— those rubble filled weapons—by those inclined to violence.

Willow bristled and looked me in the face. "It doesn't matter, but you should know I carry a dagger of West Islands steel."

I stepped back. "No, no. I mean you no harm." I stared a little longer and stood rooted on the path, trying to make sense of all the pieces that didn't match up in front of me. His Keresh words sounded as harsh as Kerek City, not like Koanga at all. Footsteps approached and now Koanga appeared on the path behind Willow. "Bah! We had really hoped I could prevent the two of you meeting face to face until you regained your memory or your manners, lordling."

"You fear for nothing. There will be no harm from me." I held up my hands open-palmed.

"That's good to know. Willow is ferocious, but even a wasp can be swatted by a big enough foe." Koanga walked me back to camp and filled Willow's fresh-washed bowl with the oats and berries and a honeycomb. He asked me to bring the rest of my clothes, and we walked back to the stream together. Perched on a rock, he taught me to wash my clothes and alternated between eating his breakfast, mocking my efforts, and telling me stories of the West Islands. I looked up and down the stream, but Willow was nowhere in sight. When I asked about his traveling partner, he instead started another story. I threw down my shirt and rested on a rock. In Lowertown, I wore my clothes until they fell apart. I didn't see the sense of this and truthfully, I still hurt everywhere.

After another story of the West Islands, I asked, "You obviously loved it there. Why did you come to Kerek? You have no friends here."

Koanga shrugged. "People are people. How will the people of Kerek learn how wonderful the West Islanders are if they never meet us?" He flashed a huge grin. "Actually, I came to retrieve Willow. She was working in Kerek City. When the West Islands ambassador was murdered in the street almost a season ago, her father sent me to bring her home."

"She?" I said slowly. "You said 'she' and 'her.' I thought I was traveling with...I mean...when she carried me yesterday she was as strong as you, Koanga...she bought my clothes...great stars! I washed naked in front of her this morning!"

He flopped back on the rock and looked up. "I am not meant for this life of secrets," he announced to the sky. He pulled himself to a sitting position and looked at me. "You, lordling, are far too concerned with labels. Willow is Willow, and more ferocious than either of us. She will tell you what she wants to be called. She carries West Islands steel, so you better be more careful than I am."

I squinted up at him. "She has Kereki skin and a West Islander face." If Willow was a West Islander and a female—which I still wasn't so sure about—she should have been dressed in shirts and skirts heavy and awkward to move about in. She certainly wouldn't be carrying a weapon of West Islands steel.

Koanga laughed. "Now that secret I can keep. For someone who has as many secrets as you do, you sure ask a lot of questions."

He looked at me thoughtfully. "So tell me, lordling, what do you know of your own beginnings?"

"Nothing." I ducked my head away so he couldn't see the lie in my face. There was little that could be worse in Lowertown than a child who could not spin a tale. My honest face called me a liar faster than anyone who heard the words from my lips.

Koanga said slowly, "You remember something? Interesting. You are recovered to yourself then?"

"No." I ducked my head down further. Not every memory, but enough to know they would not be happy to know what I was, or where I was from. I was going to have to be much more careful with the words that fell from my lips. I *needed* them to take me with them.

I wanted to change the conversation, and I thought back to something Koanga said earlier. "I heard the ambassador was inciting treason against the Kerek King." I shrugged. "And that's why he had to die."

Koanga gave me a long look but answered me anyway. "Murderers, traitors, victims. All are people, and those who could tell us what truly happened that day are dead." Koanga slid off the rock and helped me gather my clothes from the bushes. "When such a thing happened, all of the West Islanders fled or went to ground. Willow hid, got word to her family, and now we are working our way to and through Matasi to take a ship back home."

I raised an eyebrow. "I know the West Islands do not allow ownership of another person..."

"Don't worry so much about it. Not everything needs to be named and labeled. She has my back and I have hers, and you know the lawlessness in Kerek as well as I do. It is always better to travel with another...especially in Kerek."

We walked back to the campsite. Or what had been our campsite. While I had been washing and drying my clothes and Koanga had been telling stories of the West Islands, Willow had taken down the canvas lean-to, rolled up the bedding, doused the fire, and bundled all the belongings into three tidy packs. She picked up one, and without saying a word pointed to the largest one. I settled it on my back, Willow took the lead, and we set our face to Aldi.

## CHAPTER 3

# A STORY OF THE GREAT SMITH AND MOTHER EARTH

We walked for decons. Willow walked ahead, occasionally veering off the path and rejoining us down the road. Sometimes Koanga told some of the great stories of the West Islands to pass the time, or he would finish a story and ask if there was anything like it in Kerek. For all of his easygoing manner, he said nothing more about Willow, my lack of memories, or himself.

Just as I was beginning to think we were not going to stop for midday, I heard a robber bird screech. Koanga grabbed my arm and rapidly pulled me into the scrub bush by the side of the road. "Down, down, down." He slammed his palm in the small of my back and laid me out flat. His light brown traveler's cloak drifted over the top of me and I felt him scramble in.

"What—" I began, and his hand covered my mouth and nose. I struggled to free myself so I could breathe and then, I heard it too.

A whip cracked, horse hooves pounded, a wagon swayed by, wheels creaked in protest at the speed. Only three heartbeats later, and I counted four more horses riding hard. A rear guard? Bandits? A hunt for outlaws, or by outlaws? The hoofbeats had long faded into silence before Koanga would lift the cloak. He rolled over onto his back and closed his eyes against the sun.

"I tell you, my lordling, I cannot get back to the West Islands soon enough. If one of the magic wielders of the Great Tales appeared before me, it would be difficult to resist any bargain to see me home in front of my fire."

I pushed myself up to my knees, hands still on the dry earth when I caught a movement across the road.

"Koanga," I hissed, "in the brambles ahead of us!"

Koanga rolled over, pulled a knife from his boot, and jumped to his feet, all in one fluid motion. I gawped in surprise. He looked down and laughed. "Lordling, if you could see your face." He gestured across the road with his knife. "Never mind. It's only Willow. We are safe."

She raised her hand and crossed the road to join us. "Sorry about the short warning, I saw the dust, but Trouble was traveling too quickly."

Koanga shook out his traveler's cloak. "We are alive and unhurt. Those who would harm us are gone like smoke in the night."

Willow took a drink from her metal canteen and passed it over to me. The water was still cold and clean tasting. I handed it to Koanga and waited until he tipped it up to his mouth before I asked Willow, "A water carrier like that is not found in Kerek, or to my knowledge, Matasi." I looked directly at Willow waiting for her to answer. She shrugged and turned her face to the road.

Koanga capped the container and handed it back to Willow. "Metal working in the West Islands is far beyond what I have seen here. Willow's flask is common for all at home. We do not often trade our metal workings with other countries, especially those countries such as Kerek who are not welcoming to West Islanders." He grinned. "You don't like us; we don't share."

I felt the sting of Koanga's words. Kerek didn't play nice with any of its neighbors as far as I knew. I shouldered my pack again and followed Willow out to the road. The rest of the afternoon we passed in easy silence and a long loping stride that ate up the distance.

* * * * *

We had walked late into the evening, and by the time we stopped for the night, Willow could only find a waterless scrubby bramble of shrubs and stunted trees. Koanga mixed and measured out of our food supplies and remaining water, and we ate well on rice and lentils and stonebread. Willow watched me eat. After I asked Koanga for a third bowlful, she silently got up by the fire, gave me the almost empty pot, and told me to finish it. Now, the two lean-tos were on opposite sides of the fire and the three of us contentedly watched the low flames.

"Are you inclined to hear another story, my friend?" Koanga started conversationally. "I thought I would tell you one of our great stories of the West Islands. Do you know our Great Smith?"

"I know there is a constellation called the Smith, but I do not know where I heard it, or why I know this."

"Ah, we make progress every day." Koanga pursed his lips, thinking. "The Great Smith lived among the darkness in the night sky. He was not given to idleness so he captured starlight and built a forge, a hammer, an anvil, and a water bucket. Do you know these constellations, my friend?"

I looked up at the night sky, stars pinwheeling towards dawn, and shook my head.

"Truthfully, I would be hard pressed to find the Smith."

Koanga smiled, and began,

"Once upon a time, the children of the West Islands lived very differently than they do today. Their island was beautiful, this has always been true, but to live in that beauty was hard work. Water had to be carried from lakes and rivers, houses were built of fallen trees, and fences for the animals were made of twisted brambles. Searching for food and medicinal plants took everyone farther and farther away from their homes as the meadows and woods were depleted of their bounty.

Now the Smith lived among the stars dancing across the sky night after night. He watched the children of the West Islands and wondered why they let life remain so hard for themselves. At last, he understood. The children would not make life easier because they could not—they did not know how.

So, the Smith flung his hammer from the sky in a shower of stars, he dropped his anvil, and tumbled his forge down to the West Islands. As they landed, his tools turned from stars to metal. At last, he leaped. But Mother Earth was ready for his descent, and she called her son, the North Wind, to come quickly and cradle the Smith gently down to Earth. When his feet touched the soil, he looked like a man.

The Great Smith explained to Mother Earth how he wanted to help the children of the West Islands. He wanted to show them how to mine the earth for metals to build plows and homes and wells and buildings. As he described it all to Mother Earth, she just grew more and more sad.

*Mother Earth drew her shawl about her more tightly. "Your cost is high, Smith, and perhaps more than a mother should bear."*

*The Smith thought about how all of his wonderful plans to harvest copper, tin, bronze, silver, and gold from deep in the earth would cause her harm. He looked at his hammer, his anvil, and his forge laying on the ground. He thought of the West Islanders, of their need and greed and how he could balance the two. He looked at Mother Earth in her tree-bark skin and her mossy robes.*

*Finally, he came to a decision. "Let us work together, you and I. Call metals to the surface I can work into tools. Mark trees by bark and leaves so the Islanders will know which should be felled for a purpose, and which ones must stand as sentinels and guardians for the future. Use color and taste and texture, so the children will know which plants are to be cultivated and medicines can be gathered. We can build waterways and wells to offer pure water, and fire from my forge will provide heat and help. What say you?"*

*Mother Earth considered and gave a wry smile. "I think you have lived too long among the stars. But I would like to believe my children could live up to your expectations of goodness. It shall be as you say."*

*For 3 x 3 years, the Smith labored on the West Islands. He traveled along the coast; he climbed among the foothills; he wandered in the woods and in the meadows. Each time he rested, he built a village forge and a fire, and built plows and axes, fishhooks and anchors, nails and knobs. He showed the islanders how to build home and hearth, barn and boundaries.*

*At last, the Smith grew homesick. He walked to the center of the biggest island and asked the mountain to raise him closer to the stars. He called to the moon, the Queen of the Night, to throw down her rope of pearls that lay nestled deep in a long shallow bowl in the night sky. First, he tied his anvil and anchored his forge on the rope. Then he threw his hammer high into the stars. He climbed the rope of pearls to the crook of the moon and then hauled up his forge and his anvil. These he placed carefully among the stars because a good Smith always takes care of his tools."*

Koanga looked at me, and his voice shifted from the rich storyteller cadence. "And that, my friend, is the story of how the Great Smith gave the West Islanders their metal workings."

I poked at the fire. "You're quite a storyteller." I heard a snort and looked over to see Willow smiling back at me.

"If you want to hear stories of the great constellations, Koanga has enough to last our journey to the southern lands of Matasi and the farthest ports," she said quietly.

I looked back to Koanga and held his gaze. "Are you truly going to Matasi to ship out to the West Islands? Kerek is lawless, true, but I have heard the Matasi people despise anyone who do not worship as they do. I can't think you, or I for that matter, would have an easy time traveling in Matasi."

Koanga carefully looked away from me. "Truthfully? We tried to leave from Kerek City and lost all our possessions and nearly our lives. Leaving from the Matasi ports is our only option at this point. Willow knows those who have traveled to and from Matasi. It is not as the stories in Kerek say."

My ears perked up. "Truly? That is a tale I would like to hear."

Willow hissed faintly. I think she only meant for Koanga to hear her warning. But when Koanga saw my head turn to her, he smiled. "That my friend, will have to be a story for another night. Tomorrow morning we will reach Aldi, and we will learn who is missing you from their table, or their bed."

I blushed, took myself to the closest lean-to, and laid myself down on my traveler's cloak. Through half-slit eyes, I watched as Koanga and Willow packed away their cooking and food packs. Finally, Willow doused the fire. Only as I heard them pass by me on the way to the other lean-to, did I realize they hadn't spoken a word since I had left the fire.

* * * * *

In the morning, Willow said she would stay behind with our tents and other belongings to make us less of a target for thieves and pickpockets. I was happy to hear it, the packs were heavy. Koanga and I left carrying only empty cloth bags for our shopping and walked the remaining decon into Aldi.

Aldi was more than a village and less than a town. Located on two major crossroads, Aldi had a greater mix of nationalities, languages, and cultures than I had thought there would be. Not that I had ever been anywhere else, but even in Lowertown, people talked and traveled. Lowertown, Dockside, Sinner's District—my neighborhoods—were all parts of Kerek City, the King's stronghold. Just not its wealthiest districts—more like the mud on the skirts of the city.

In Aldi, there were a few West Islanders, but none with Willow's coloring, all were the deepest almond color of Koanga. He told me they were looking for a West Islander who owned a printing press, and Koanga pointed out the shop to me. But we didn't go in, and I wondered about that.

We saw notices on crude handmade paper nailed to an old market cross in the village center. It had been generations since Kerek had venerated anyone but the King, but in the farthest and most remote towns, the old market crosses and round buildings of the Lost God remained. Together we walked over there.

Even with the crush of cultures, the notices were all written in Keresh. Not that it mattered to me, I couldn't read any of it. I watched as Koanga read the notices carefully. I muttered under my breath, trying to imagine what Koanga was looking for and how I could make myself useful. The farther away from Lowertown, I was convinced, the better my life would be.

Koanga looked at me in surprise. "You can't read this?"

I gave him a harsh look, and then looked back at the scraps of paper and cloth. "I don't see my handsome face, and I don't recognize a ship's schedule. Do you see something to cause you concern?"

Koanga turned back to the cross. "There is quite the reward for the ambassador's lost children," he said nonchalantly. "Perhaps the Kerek King would like to raise them for his own?"

I snorted. "The Kerek King just wants to find them before Matasi, the West Islands, or Vikland does." I looked down the alleys by the stables. "I wonder if the children are old enough to know how valuable they are?"

"They are little," Koanga muttered absently. He scanned the papers again. "Your King is arrogant. Those born and living in Kerek come in every shade and every tongue, yet those in power assume one language can be understood by everyone. Some of these rewards might have success if they were written in more than one tongue." He gave me an odd look. "You are right, there is no one crying out for a lost lordling, straying son, or an escaped thief."

"There you are then. I am a nobody who was meant to be on the road a little longer. No one has had time to miss me." I looked about the square. "What business should we do next?"

We stopped at shops along the square and down the narrow streets: bakery, apothecary, green grocer, and the rag and bone man. Koanga stopped at his cart and picked through his garments, finding another tunic, one in better shape than the one I had on, and two more pairs of pants.

He pawed through the dresses and finally sighed deeply. "There's no help for it then. We'll have to go back to the toggery."

"What are you looking for, lad?" The rag and bone man pushed himself off the tongue of his cart to crowd us close.

"I need a dress for a child. She is well-fed and ill-mannered and comes to his chin." Koanga pointed to me.

The man looked us up and down and scowled. "And what would the two of you be doing buying a dress for a girl child?"

"No sir, we are only the carry boys. This is but a dress for her to wear berry picking. She is such a careless child it will be once and done. Her mother despairs she will ever grow as gracious and well-mannered as your daughters must be," Koanga explained.

"You have a Westerman's honeyed-tongue. Hold on, I may have something." He dug through a barrel behind him and pulled out two dresses, both dated and worn through at the elbows. The blue one was tattered deeply along the hem. Koanga laid them out carefully and examined every seam, tested the cloth for strength, and sniffed at collar and cuffs, armpits and hem.

The bargaining was fast and lively. In the end, Koanga put back the smaller of the two pairs of pants and carefully poured the last of his coins into the man's outstretched hand. Koanga bundled the clothes together and handed them to me. "I can carry the food bag, it's heavier." I shrugged and took one last look around. I followed Koanga to the road and the long walk back to Willow.

## CHAPTER 4

# PUZZLES AND MYSTERIES

The clearing was deserted. Even the stones around our morning's fire had been tumbled apart and the ashes scattered. All the packs were gone, also both canvas lean-tos. Koanga walked in an ever-widening circle about the clearing. "Footprints are swept clean," he muttered.

I wanted to scream, to throw something. The whole point of leaving Willow behind, I thought, was because we didn't know what kinds of thieves we would find in Aldi. Now she and everything we owned was gone. Just gone.

Koanga paced off another three long strides and continued his concentric circles. "Stop!" I snapped at him. "Will you stop running around in circles and give me something that would tell me where my things are? Where to look for Willow?" I hastily corrected.

"I'm right here."

I spun around, and Koanga looked up as Willow slid into our campsite. Again I was struck by the pearl grey white of her skin, her white hair, her Kereki clothes, and her West Islander face. After spending the morning in Aldi, I realized next to another Kereki, she would attract notice, next to me? Or Koanga? Someone's eyes would slide right over her. She would be an excellent pickpocket in Lowertown—if she had fingers quick and light.

"I found a watersource—a bubbler in the rocks—just east of here. I thought since we needed to stay another night we should be where we have fresh water and farther from the main track."

I sighed in relief. "We left you here to be safe—not to wander."

"No, we didn't," Koanga interrupted. "We all have parts to play tomorrow, and she didn't want the townsfolk of Aldi to see three of us today and make assumptions of what they will see tomorrow. We didn't know how big the town was, who lived in the town, and how much strangers like us would stick out. Know this, my friend, Willow has better survival skills than you or I. Know this now, and hope that knowledge will never hold your life in the balance."

I looked at Koanga steadily and realized he believed it to be true. I considered how a woman in Kerek was treated as the property of her father, husband, or brother. Even where I had lived or maybe, especially where I lived, women either had a protector or exceptional knife skills. Clearly, things were different in the West Islands. I was going to make a nasty remark, but then I remembered I had not yet told Willow and Koanga how much of my memories I had recovered. I still needed them to think me too helpless to leave behind.

"Fine," I blew out a noisy breath. "Let's head to the new camp."

Willow took the carry bags from Koanga and gave him the cedar branches she had been using to wipe the tracks clear from the old camp to the new one. We followed a small game trail east into the shrubs and low trees. I turned once to watch Koanga walk crabwise, erasing our tracks into the dust.

To be fair to Willow, the new camp was much better than the old one. We had spent far too long on the road yesterday and then had taken the first available clearing when darkness caught us out. This camp had water, better shelter, and more privacy, which meant safety from Trouble passing on the main track. Willow had set up both canvas lean-tos, built a fire ring of rocks, and filled it with kindling. She had gathered larger chunks of wood and had filled both metal pots with water. It was only early afternoon, but we hadn't eaten since we had stonebread at daybreak, before Koanga and I set out to Aldi. Koanga unwrapped the food we had purchased, and we dug in eagerly to ruskies, camu camu berries, tree nuts, and bakery bread.

Koanga kept up a steady monologue of things we had seen and impressions of Aldi. I was surprised to hear his level of detail of buildings, people, even the content of the notices on the market cross. He described the layout of the streets, which businesses we had entered which had Matasian shop owners, West Islanders, or Kerekis. He noted the Justice office just south of the village green, and how the most prosperous houses seemed to wander off streets to the east of the center of the village. He said there were West Islands metal workings in some of the shops, not prominently displayed of course, since they had most likely been purchased on the sinner's market or taken in trade from destitute travelers. He mentioned the pushcart vendors and the rag and bone man who had been helpful, if not quite trusting, of their story. When he finally stopped to cram another hunk of bread in his mouth, Willow interjected, "The lordling?"

Koanga chewed thoughtfully and looked me straight in the eye. "Nothing. Not a notice, not a whisper in the shops, not a second glance on the street."

"That's a welcome truth." Willow gave me a smile. "A boy with no name, no destination, and no one to miss him when he disappears into the wind." She kissed her fingertips and let them flutter in the air.

Until now, I had been biddable and compliant—traveling where I had been told to go and eating what had been placed in front of me. While I spoke and understood Keresh, both the language of the docks in Lowertown, and the formal castle Keresh, I had never learned to read or write. Every one of those notices could have been a plea for me to come home and I would not have known it.

Except I did. Willow and Koanga may have just realized I had no one waiting for me. But I knew I had been abandoned on the streets for years. It made me fast, it made me wary, it made me fierce if I had to be.

"So tell me," Willow began, just a little too casually, "how did a boy with a cinnamon hue end up in the land of the dough-faced Kereki? You're not from Matasi with their curly brown hair and skin that looks like koa bark toasted in the fire, and you have none of the beauty of the West Islanders," she gestured to Koanga. "You have no woodsmen skills or traveler's knowledge. It's pretty safe to say you have never been on the frontier or much outside of Kerek City before."

I schooled my face into indifference and clasped my hands together between my knees to keep them quiet. My boot knife of pounded iron may be missing, but when Koanga had searched me and taken away my knife, he had missed my Sailor's Curse, a wicked little blade that fit between my fingers and always remained tucked in the pocket seam by my buttons.

I tried to match her tone. "It's a strange world we live in, Willow. At the beginning of the Dry, the West Islands ambassador was murdered in the streets of Kerek City and his wife was executed for inciting treason against the Kerek King. Now everyone is looking for the ambassador's children because the ransom would be rich enough to risk the hanging. And here I find myself in the company of two West Islanders. While you are too old to be the children yourselves—Koanga tells me they are 'little'—there are not so many West Islanders, I think, trying to flee the country. You are too poor to be traveling for enjoyment." I leaned forward ready to jump to my feet if Willow took a run at me.

Koanga poked her angrily. "Enough! We made promises— no harm to me or mine. We are puzzles, complex puzzles perhaps, but all puzzles have a solution even if that solution is time and trust. Now behave yourselves. I have work to do." Koanga stood up, grabbed his travel bag and the bundle of clothes we just purchased, and stalked off.

Willow smiled at me, and the tension disappeared. I wondered how she was able to do that so quickly. "Koanga is right. We all have work to do. I'll let you clean up after our meal. Koanga has tasked me with finding more aritha. I also need to find sage and annatto. Make sure the pots and pans are scrubbed out and filled with water." She shook out a seagrass bag from her bedding and disappeared into the trees in the opposite direction as Koanga.

I was alone in the campsite. For the first time since I had been found on the road to Aldi, I was alone with the West Islanders' belongings. I would like to say I hesitated for a moment. That I actually considered Koanga's words of "time and trust." That I possibly reached deep into my past and considered my future actions ignoble and unkind to those who had rescued me.

Not a chance. I was in Willow's bag and had dumped it over her open bedroll before I had time to think twice.

I didn't expect the three books. It's true I couldn't read, but I knew enough to recognize only one of them had the flowing script of the Wester language. None of them had pictures, but I thought one could have been written in Keresh—maybe. The paper was smooth and white, like nothing I had seen before. I held them upside down by the spine and fluttered the pages quickly. Nothing drifted out and the endpapers were secure.

I set those aside and rummaged through the clothes. Willow had been wearing the same Kereki style trousers, shirt, and tunic as Koanga—it was one of the reasons I had mistaken her for a boy when they first rescued me. But in her bag was a frilly white petticoat like a Kereki woman would wear, a drawstring blouse in a lighter brown than her traveling cloak, and small clothes that I had never seen before. As soon as I realized what they were, I dropped them on the petticoat and rolled them back up again. I pawed through the small pots and packets—lots of colors—but I wasn't sure if it was face paint or artist workings. I hadn't seen Willow use either, so I shoved them aside.

I couldn't imagine Koanga would have left her without coin or maps or traveling papers while he and I had gone to Aldi this morning. I could imagine too many scenarios in which we wouldn't have returned to her, but her belongings carried nothing more. I even checked the seams of her bedroll. I reached for her traveling cloak. Unlike Koanga's, hers was a deep, rich brown. As I searched the seams for hidden coins or papers, I realized it wasn't only a traveling cloak, it was a woman's skirt with tied pockets and a hood that could be tied on or off. How very clever. Willow would be able to change her appearance from boy to woman and back again with nothing more than a swirl of fabric. Was this how she traveled about?

For a moment, I considered what was before me. Either the West Islanders were as destitute as they said they were, or all of their riches were in Koanga's pack. Unfortunately, he had taken his bag with him. I stood up and carefully replaced and arranged her belongings as I had found them. I pulled one of the discarded branches and swished it around their lean-to erasing my steps in the dirt. Then I grabbed the two pots and headed for the bubbler in the rocks east of the campsite. I hadn't learned much more about them, but I had learned enough. I was not in immediate danger.

## CHAPTER 5

## WILLOW

By the time I returned, Koanga was back sitting cross-legged on his open bedroll, the shopping all around him. One of the dresses had been completely cut apart, and the other had metal pins and white strings tacked through the cloth. I set the pots of water by the unlit fire, walked over, and sat down beside him. I carefully touched one of the metal pins.

"Do you make these in the West Islands? Because all these would cost a King's ransom here in Kerek."

Koanga raised an eyebrow. "Is this true? Then I shall be more careful where I pull out my tailor's kit." He motioned to the shears, threads, and tape around him. "I don't fancy being murdered for a packet of pins." He smiled at me. "In the West Islands, I am a tailor and a good one. In Kerek, I am a rescuer of those who need my assistance—but my skills are not so accomplished." He shrugged. "Willow is not back from her foraging?"

"She barely left. I don't know what she was looking for, but I could have helped her find it." I paused. "Why does she have a Kereki name—Willow—if she is also from the West Islands? Is it because she is misbred?"

Koanga looked at me, shocked. "I don't even know what that means, and I am not sure I want to." He carefully threaded a needle and began sewing the cut pieces together. "Willow has a proper Wester name, but it isn't in her best interest to use it now. She uses a Kereki name in Kerek. Whether she uses Willow or Will, both have served her well."

Eyes on his work, he began more gently, "In the West Islands, people marry those they love. No one is 'misbred' no one is made to feel 'less than.' I could tell by your face you meant no harm by your unkind words. But they are words that should never be said or thought." He looked hard at me. "Do not use it again."

I watched him sew the pieces together. It was comfortable and soothing. I wondered if it was something I could learn. But then I wondered what I would do with that knowledge. I certainly wouldn't be able to buy so many metal pins as Koanga had poking through everywhere. I sat quietly watching, and then he spoke.

"Yesterday, in Aldi, you were different," Koanga began, "You hardly looked at the shops, but you looked in every alley and doorway we passed. You stepped off the boardwalk every time we met someone or when others approached. If we stood still, you put your back against a wall, a trader's wagon, or to me. When we reached the market cross, you barely looked at the notices, as if you knew you wouldn't be there. You dropped your eyes if anyone addressed you. None of that would be how I would act in the West Islands. So I thought, as we walked home, that you have recovered yourself and do not trust us enough to know who you are." I protested, but he raised a hand to silence me, "or we are not traveling together as friends, and you mean harm to me and mine." He looked at me steadily. "Please do not let words fall out of your mouth unless they are the truth."

I dropped my eyes, rubbed my neck, and scratched my head. I could tell him the truth as I knew it, or part of it, or lie—except my face wouldn't let me. It was clear to me Koanga was out of his depth in Kerek, but I wasn't sure of Willow. She was like a mist, just out of focus enough I couldn't form a distinct shape of how she should be treated: cautiously? As a threat? An enemy? Or an ally? Koanga was easier. He was kind to me because he seemed kind to everyone. He treated me with all the courtesy and respect he accorded Willow, even though he had met me three days ago, and he had sailed across the sea to help Willow return home.

I blew out a noisy breath. "All right then, this is what I know to be true. I do not know my name, except people I knew called me 'Red.' I do not remember what happened immediately before you met me on the road to Aldi. I do not have woodsmen skills, but I am really craving rabbit right now, so obviously I bought my meat instead of hunted it." I saw Koanga flinch. "What?"

"I don't eat flesh in the West Islands."

I rolled my eyes. "Of course not. That wouldn't be kind. How did you survive in Kerek until now?"

Koanga gave a wry smile. "Mostly by hiding like rabbits." He returned to his questioning. "So what happened yesterday?"

I thought for a moment. "Well, here's the most truthful answer I can give. It just felt right. I don't need to know anything about myself. It's like my body just knew what to do to take care of me...and you. Look Koanga, I obviously don't belong here anymore than you do, but either I was raised here long enough to gain some survival skills, or I came from a place as violent as this one." I held my breath, would he believe me?

"But didn't it feel like someone would call your name? What name were you listening for? I do not think people called you 'Red' as a kindness. And I can't just keep calling you, 'my friend.'"

I grinned. "Actually, you can."

Koanga looked startled and then gave me that amazing grin I had only seen on his face once before. "Thank you, I will."

I waited for a long moment, and then when he didn't say anything else I asked, "So what happens next?" I was genuinely curious.

Koanga looked over my shoulder and I heard Willow cross into the campsite. She crouched down beside me. "What happens next is Koanga will work his magic on a secondhand dress and tomorrow I will go into Aldi with you as my guard and carry boy. I shall find us a West Islander who knows how to move us from here to my home without coin, power, or a life debt owed."

Willow crossed over to Koanga to inspect his work. "You're going to do that one first? I thought the blue one would be easier."

"It will be. But we need to make them as different as possible so if anyone fingered them earlier, they won't connect the dresses with you." He glanced at her bulging bag. "Did you find what you needed?"

"Most of it. I'll get started." She gave me an indecipherable look, but spoke to Koanga, "What shall we do with the lordling?"

I bristled. "I'm right here." I poked a small stick into the dirt.

She raised an eyebrow but said nothing. I thought I saw a twitch by her mouth, so quick I wasn't convinced it had actually happened.

Koanga began apologetically, "My friend, Willow will need the campsite, and I must stay and finish the dress before tomorrow. Would you be able to find us two walking sticks—one no taller than what Willow would need, and the other for yourself? It may take you quite some time."

I smiled. I truly liked his old-fashioned way of talking. "Shall I just magic these sticks home with me?"

Willow was already digging in her seagrass bag and pulled out a blade with edged teeth and a wooden handle. It was as broad as my palm and the length was maybe twice that long. She walked over and handed it casually to me. I accepted it with both hands out—it was beautiful. On one side, the teeth were even and precisely spaced, the other side glinted with a straight edge so fine, I thought I could cut raindrops. The wood handle was carved and secure. I balanced it on the side of my hand and held it eye level.

"Where did you get this?" I breathed. "It's beautiful."

Willow and Koanga exchanged a look. "It's a maripi. It's used to strip kindling for a fire or in the kitchens to cut joints of meat. You would find one in any kitchen in the West Islands. There are some in Kerek, but not many." Willow shrugged. "I may have stolen it."

Now it was my turn to raise an eyebrow. Koanga had said Willow had been in Kerek for two years. In that time, she seemed to adapt to the lack of laws and flexible ownership as the rest of the people from Kerek. In fact, based on her resourcefulness this far, I would have guessed she would have been able to find her way home on her own. But if my suspicion was true, and if she was somehow connected to the murdered ambassador, she would be a very valuable hostage. Traveling with another, even one such as Koanga, would increase her chances of surviving her dash across Kerek to get on a ship to the West Islands.

But one of the first lessons taught to children in Lowertown was not to be too curious of strangers who had the power to hurt you. I kept my mouth shut and walked out of the campsite.

* * * * *

It took longer than I expected to find such straight limbs and strip the bark from them. Well, maybe I had to practice a little, handling the bone knife was fun after all. I had never seen anything like it in Lowertown. Finally, I was happy with my selections, and I headed back to camp. Koanga was standing and shaking out the traveling cloak in front of a West Islands woman. When I realized who it was, I dropped everything: the bone saw, the staffs, and my carry bag.

Willow was no longer Willow. I walked around her trying to take in all the changes. Her greyish white skin was now a rich, deep brown as dark as Koanga's. She no longer wore the black glove on her left hand. I picked up her hand and inspected it closely. There were no scars, burns, or cuts. All the fingers were there, and it was the same dark brown as the rest of her. I couldn't see what she had tried to hide by wearing the glove. I reached for her hair. Instead of the white nimbus of three-finger-width fuzz, it was now a brown so dark as to be black, braided and twisted tightly about her head.

Koanga stiffened and flinched when I put my hand on her head. I brushed my hand over the many tight braids. She smirked at me, watching the expressions I knew must be running across my face. "How did you do this?" I wondered aloud.

Koanga answered sharply, "I know we are in Kerek now, but in the West Islands, you do not touch another person, especially their head, without asking permission."

"I'm sorry." I waved my hand. "But how did you do this?" I repeated.

Willow looked me in the face. "That is not the question you want to know the answer to at this moment. But you must be patient with us as we are patient with you—while you wait to get your memories back." She gave me a half smile, and I felt in that moment she knew I had been lying all along, and she also knew a lot more about me than she was willing to share.

And for the rest of the afternoon and evening, Koanga and Willow were cheerful, talkative, and ignored any question I asked about her.

## CHAPTER 6

# RED

While Koanga had walked up to the market cross in the center of the green to read the notices posted there, and thus announced to everyone he was a stranger in town completely unaware of danger, Willow ambled from side streets to shops to push carts.

Our plan was simple, Willow had said. We were to appear wealthy enough to be taken seriously about ways to reach the West Islands, but not so wealthy she was a target for thieves and pickpockets. I was to be her carry boy and male protector as demanded by Kereki culture and lawlessness.

"The strangeness of the concept of a male protector in Kerek," Koanga had said that morning in his funny way of talking, "is the male can be a boy of ten, a man with no more wits than a bowl of porridge, or a grandfather who needs two canes to get about." He had shaken his head then, "I cannot begin to understand Kereki custom."

Willow had just smiled and said it was part of his grand adventure to learn such things. But if he looked closely, he would never see a woman in Kerek walking alone without a male behind her, ahead of her, or beside her. She had slyly added she thought it was to give younger brothers a purpose in life. Koanga had just laughed at that.

I had shrugged my shoulders. I grew up this way, it was just the way it was. But before we left camp, Willow had given me two daggers made of West Islands steel. She might have seen the greed in my eyes as she handed them to me because she had said they were only for show and not a gift. Then she smiled and told me to wear them like I knew how to use them. I tucked them into my belt.

Once we were in Aldi, I could feel more than one person's interest in my weapons as I walked behind Willow. Maybe it was a bit flashy, but I felt taller and stronger with them about my waist. That morning, I had finally convinced Koanga they were not as destitute as he thought they were if they would be willing to sell some of their metal workings.

The man behind the counter in the dry goods store was Kereki. Pale, overfed, and doughy looking, his eyes narrowed as Willow moved up to the counter, and I sauntered up on her left.

"Good morning, sir. Could I have the price of a packet of pins, please?" she said demurely.

"You speak castle Keresh." His country accent was heavy and thick-tongued, but he didn't make a move towards the sewing notions. "You are Wester and you speak castle Keresh without an accent," he repeated.

"I am, sir, and thank you for noticing. I am from the West Islands and I speak Wester as well as Keresh. The packet of pins? A price please?" Willow carefully kept a blank face.

He named a price nearly double which he had charged the woman three places in line ahead of Willow. Her eyes flashed hurt and then resignation.

"Thank you, sir. Good day." She marched so quickly out of the shop, I bumped into someone as I pushed my way through behind her. Instinctively, I threw out my elbow and connected with a Kereki woman taller than I was.

"Sorry, sorry." I didn't look up to her face but continued out into the street. Willow was waiting for me under the shade of a canvas awning outside of the next store.

"We have a price range," she said briskly. "Let's head to the store owned by the West Islander Koanga was telling me about last night." She looked away from me down the street.

"Willow, I'm sorry. All people are not like him," I tried to apologize.

She leveled a look at me. "I have been in Kerek for two years and on my own for a season. Every day I meet people and watch as their prejudices dance across their face until they give me a label of their choosing. Yes, people *are* just like him."

She exhaled loudly. "I'm sorry. You did not deserve that. You're right. Not all people are like him. Some are worse, some are better. Let's go. We have a lot to accomplish."

The morning passed quickly. Willow was able to sell two of Koanga's packets of pins at the dry goods store owned by the West Islander. He was thrilled to see real West Islands steel and showed several customers the quality difference between the iron pins of Kerek and the West Islands steel pins which were much finer and didn't snag the cloth.

At the print shop, she talked with the owner about Matasi. He had sailed to and from both Salisport and Vesaport which trafficked to and from the West Islands. Unfortunately, he said, the ships also trafficked to less savory places, such as Kerek City to the north. He told her he had never sailed out of Kerek City, even though it was closer. Kerek was not kind to those with an honest heart, but not born within its borders, he lamented.

"I have heard the same said of Matasi," Willow questioned.

The West Islander scoffed, "Those in Matasi believe everyone in the known world wants what they have. Even if you showed them all the wealth of the West Islands, they would cling to the belief 'they and theirs are better than you and yours.' Of course, that may be due to timeless skirmishes along the Kerek border." He glanced at me and leaned in to whisper, "A man in Kerek will spend twice the time and effort to thieve as he will in honest labor."

Willow said noncommittally, "The Traveler would find a hard road in Kerek."

The printer laughed and slapped the counter. "And the Seafarer would come once and never again!" They switched to Wester and started talking about timetables, and maps, and lodging. That's what I thought anyway. I took up a place at the window to watch the people outside until she had her information and it was time to go.

Before we left Aldi, Willow cut across the village green and drifted over to the notices tacked to the market cross, looking for all the world like just another housewife looking for news and gossip. I looked out at the boardwalks and pushcarts and saw again the tall Kereki woman I had stumbled into at the dry goods store. Her face was away from me, but she was wearing such an awful dress in every color, I could hardly take my eyes away. Something tugged at my memory, and I wondered if I had seen her before today.

I knew I had been getting better each day as we had walked south. It was true, I had remembered almost everything as soon as Koanga had found me, but I could not remember the reason I had been in the carriage in the first place. My headaches were gone. I no longer needed to squint against the light. My muscles remembered my past life and my instincts were returning. I thought if I could just drop in the one missing piece, the puzzle would snap together, and I would know why I had been on the road to Aldi.

"I'm ready to go if you are." Willow appeared at my elbow.

I took one last slow scan about the square. Nothing seemed out of the ordinary. "Fine, let's go." I took her carry bag of bread and vegetables and we headed north.

*  *  *  *  *

Koanga was tending a low fire when we returned. I smelled spices and the handful of vegetables he had purchased yesterday while we were scouting in Aldi. He dished up two bowls as soon as we entered the clearing, and Willow exchanged her carry bag for one of them.

I reached for the other bowl, sat on one of the logs surrounding the fire, stretched out my legs, and began eating. Willow too, was silent as we savored the rich soup. I held up the metal spoon I was using to eat and examined it closely. "Did you know, Koanga, we received enough coin from selling two of your packets of pins to buy that carry bag of food. I may have been the one wearing lordling clothes when you found me, but I am beginning to think you have a dragon's treasure in those traveling bags of yours."

Koanga smiled warily. "It's good to know we have enough to buy our passage home. It's hard to know we must sacrifice the metal workings of our country to do so." He turned to Willow. "But I would do that and more to return you to those who love you. You have been missed so."

Willow snorted and then smiled into her bowl but said nothing to Koanga. Instead she looked at me. "You have been to Aldi before."

"Of course I have. I went with Koanga yesterday." I was confused at her words.

"No, before us." She turned to Koanga. "There were two people in Aldi who thought your friend was the most interesting item in the marketplace. One was a tallish man dressed as a woman in one of the most garish dresses I have ever seen, and the other was a strong looking fellow, maybe twice as wide as you, Koanga, and maybe a head and a half taller. Solid. I couldn't get close enough to see his hands, but if I saw him at home I would assume he worked a forge in a remote village, or at one of the foundries near the smelters. That kind of strong."

Koanga looked surprised. "Why didn't you ask them if they knew him? Willow, we could have found our lordling's family and returned him to his table and his bed. Now you bring them up?" He turned to me. "Did she say anything while you were in Aldi? Or on the way home?"

"They weren't my family," I reassured him. "I remember bumping into someone wearing an overly bright dress at the dry goods store. It could have been either a man or a woman. I don't remember meeting a smith at all. But I did feel like someone was watching us at the market cross in the square."

Willow nodded decisively. "This may be the night we part then. Koanga and I will continue on to Matasi and a ship home, and you can return to Aldi and determine if your friends can help you get home." Willow tipped her bowl up and slurped up the last of her soup.

Fear slammed into my stomach. I needed her to take me with them. What could I say to change her mind? "I'm not so sure they were my friends," I began slowly, just as Koanga blurted out, "He can't go home without knowing his name!"

Willow rolled her eyes. "Fine. Let me make this perfectly clear to both of you so there is no confusion. Koanga, here was your motivation to come to Kerek and rescue me," she held her thumb and forefinger an acorn's width apart. "And your plan to have a grand adventure," she held her arms shoulder-width apart. "Here's your grand adventure. You picked up a stray who has slowly regained his mind and memories without breathing a word of them to us these past days because he is not a lordling, but a thief. We encounter his fellow thieves in Aldi where they try to meet with him, but I am sticking to him like a fly on a spider web and they angrily watch us drift out of town." She turned to me, "Your name is 'Red.'"

CHAPTER 7

## KEREKI METAL POISONING

The next moments were so confusing, it took me most of the night just to sort it all through in my head. There was a crash—at first I thought it was Koanga—but it was actually from behind me and I found myself laid out in the dirt. I tried to roll to my feet, but there was a heavy boot in my lower back that kept my face pinned down. I heard a shout—Koanga? Willow?—abruptly cut off and a distinct struggle. I tried to twist my head, but then I heard an old familiar voice.

"Red, Red, Red, what have you found for us now?"

The boot lifted and I rolled over on my back, then brushed the debris and dust off my face. The tall woman of Aldi was not a woman at all. Worse, I knew the man now standing over me dressed in Kereki trousers and tunic, long brown hair tied back in a leather thong, his mocking eyes laughing at me. I breathed heavily.

"Goblin."

He nodded. "I sent you out to capture a wealthy lordling and when I finally find you four nights later, I only see a pair of West Islander refugees for my coin."

I've heard sailors talk about storms in the seas between Kerek and the Spice Island. Waves so high and hard they crash over the bow of the ship and smash anything not tightly lashed down. My memories were just as destructive, overwhelming me, overturning my fragile sense of self I had carefully constructed in the past days. The last piece of the missing puzzle fell into place.

I turned my head to the upper limits. "Brick."

The big man nodded, "Red."

Koanga's legs were trying to gain purchase on the ground and relieve the pressure of his arms pinched tight across Brick's chest. Willow lay in a crumpled heap at his feet, her skirts tangled about her dark brown knees.

I licked my dry lips. "Is she going to be all right?"

I looked at Willow and then Brick, but it was Goblin who answered, "Brick just gave her a love tap. But we'll keep an eye on her to make sure she doesn't scarper off like you did. Get me something to tie them up with so we don't have to keep hitting them to make them docile."

I carefully rolled to my hands and knees. First dizziness, then nausea rolled over me. I bit back and then reconsidered, emptying the contents of my stomach near Goblin's leather boots.

"Bah! I didn't hit you that hard." He kicked at me to wipe his boots on my shirt. "Stand up and talk before I do some real damage."

I fisted my hands and pushed myself to my feet. Goblin stared at me. "Well? Ropes? I can't imagine your little friend is going to grow enough to reach the ground on his own."

I looked at Koanga's face pinched with fear and fury. Brick had lowered him enough that his toes rested on the ground, and he could breathe a little easier.

"The fabric scraps, where are they?" I asked him harshly.

"In the lean-to, wrapped in the tunic we bought in Aldi," he spat at me.

I found the long strips Koanga had cut from the bottom of the tattered blue dress. I tied his hands, then his feet, pushed him down on a log and tied a short leash between the hand ties and the feet bindings. Brick inspected my work closely and nodded his approval.

I crouched next to Willow. She had her eyes closed but she was breathing normally. I leaned over her face, blocking Goblin's view with my body, and whispered, "I will get us out of this, I swear it. Continue to play dead, and when I ask, use your dagger as if your life depends on it—because it does." I wrapped the blue fabric around her wrists. I gathered her skirts together and tied them within the binding about her feet. She would only have to pull her skirts out to have the binding so loose it would be worthless. I used a length of fabric to link the hand ties and the foot bindings together, but this time I used a false knot she would be able to twist and it would fail.

Brick and Goblin had both settled themselves at the fire and were devouring the contents of the fast-cooling soup pot with their bare hands. I walked to the fire and sat down across from them. Goblin looked over at Koanga and Willow, saw that they were sufficiently trussed, and stared at me. "Now talk. Tell us what went wrong with Primo Resoro."

"Believe me or not, Goblin, but until just a moment ago, I didn't even know my name. Why don't you tell me what happened?" I looked away so he couldn't see the lie in my face.

Goblin snarled at my tone of voice. "That's a little more spirit than I would anticipate from someone who just cost me enough coin to last a fortnight."

I waited.

He stared back, and just as I thought I had pushed him too far, he began, "So ten days ago, you saunter into Kerek City in your fancy clothes and pick up a new friend in Primo Resoro, the oldest son of the King's Treasurer and a wealthy young man in his own right. You two gamble at the tables, drink your way around town, and just when I think you are going to spend all my flash without a payback, he invites you to his ranch where we believe gold and goods are waiting to be shared with us. The night before you leave, you give him a bit of ah... sleeping assistance... in his drink and the three of us carry him back to his rooms in the city. Brick gives you a light tap on the side of the head, and we tuck you in the lordling's bed as a little token of our appreciation. The next morning, I watch the two of you stumble out to the carriage, your bags are loaded, and I take off to catch up to Brick who is waiting on the road at Vingt to intercept you."

My throat goes dry. Now it comes back to me. The new lordling in the city for the first time, the wide-eyed wonder, the easiness in offering him my guidance, my purse, my friendship all for the greater payoff of the lightly guarded country house or ransom of the young lordling himself. *That* was why I was riding in a carriage far away from Lowertown.

"We waited the entire day along the road to Vingt, and nothing. So you can imagine my surprise when I get back to Kerek City and I hear the lordling, the coachman, and the hired guard, have all returned safely to Kerek City, and our Red has disappeared into the wind. If Brick and I had not been in Aldi today trying to learn when the military garrison was going to get its next payroll, we never would have stumbled upon you." He waited for me to tell my version of the story. I stared back at him because I had no idea how to begin.

I did remember the events. In fact, at that moment, I felt more myself than at any time in the recent past. That was a relief to me. I remembered how Brick, Goblin, and I had worked together to set up the young lordling. I was the youngest, the prettiest, and had the best command of castle Keresh. But during the days and nights of winning the confidence of young Lord Resoro, I learned I genuinely liked his company. He was funny, very funny, and he looked at everything without the cold measure of power or purse. He was kind to those without position or strength, a concept completely at odds with everything I knew. And while I didn't fall head over heels, there was a genuine fondness I wanted to continue. And so, thinking his feelings were the same as my own, I had told him what Goblin had planned.

Primo had diverted the carriage south as soon as we reached the first ring road. I hadn't even finished telling him all of our plans. Once we were traveling to Aldi, he asked me to tell him everything again. I told some, but not all, and when he realized I was not telling all the truth he struck me with his beautifully carved and nearly lethal walking stick. Primo had never been quite as helpless as I had supposed.

"I am still waiting, Red," Goblin spoke in a quiet deadly voice. I winced. "What happened after I saw the two of you leave for Vingt the next morning?"

I gave an embarrassed shrug and looked at Koanga. He wasn't looking at anyone, just staring at his feet with an infinite look of sadness. His grand adventure indeed. "When we left the lordling's place, I thought we were going on the Vingt road. We were chatting about all the things we were going to do at the ranch—he wanted to show me how they gathered in cattle— when I realized we were on the ring road. I started to argue with him that we needed to go back to the road to Vingt. He said he wanted to show me something on the road to Aldi and it wasn't far out of the way, we would just come to the ranch from the south. But I got too insistent, and he's no fool. He thought something was wrong. Primo threw the first punch. It was pretty weak, and we were fighting. Then he used his walking stick on me and the next thing I know, I am on the side of the road being rescued by these two." I waved my arm at Koanga.

"Did they steal your purse? I had just refilled it before we tucked you into bed with the lordling." He gave a sneer towards Willow lying quiet and still on the ground.

"I lost it in the carriage while we were fighting. Lord Resoro must have it." I dropped my eyes to the ground quickly.

"So we lost the feast and now we have only dry bread and water to content ourselves with." Goblin looked over at Koanga and Willow. "Any chance these two could be more than refugees? Ransom from the West Islands would be difficult, but not impossible."

I hesitated. "No," I said sadly. "In fact, we were just separating our belongings. I was going to go back to Kerek City and rejoin you and they were going to the...military garrison at Pagta."

Goblin looked at me steadily. "You're a fool, Red, to think you can lie to anyone. If that were true, how come you didn't acknowledge us in Aldi? And why did she," he threw his hand out towards Willow, "return here—nearly a decon north—if she was headed to the fort southeast of Aldi?" Goblin crossed his arms. "I'm going to give you one more chance to tell me what truly happened, or someone is getting hurt. That someone... being you."

I looked down at my feet and then up at Goblin. "I can't change my story from true to false to make it more pleasing to your ears. We fought in the carriage, Lord Resoro threw me by the side of the road, and I was found by these two." I lifted my hands in supplication. "What I failed to mention the first time, is when they found me I had no recollection of myself. It has only been as the pain has decreased, there has been room for my memories to return. I did not acknowledge you in Aldi because

I did not see Brick at all, and you were wearing that awful dress and I thought you were planning some trickery. However, you must have said something in the girl's hearing because she called me 'Red'—as did you—and it brought me back to myself."

I gave him a wheedling smile. "For which, I am well and truly grateful. It has been difficult these last four days to know only a part of myself and not the whole." I was proud of my dramatic flourish at the end of my story.

Brick looked skeptical. "I've never heard of such a thing."

Goblin tugged at his ear. "Fine. Red, go through their bags for anything we can use or sell. Brick, kill them quietly, and let's be on the road. It's a long way back to Kerek City."

"No!" Koanga snapped to attention. "You ate at our table. You cannot break the roaming regles like that."

Goblin stared at him. "Roaming regles? You think I am worried about roaming regles?"

Goblin turned his back to me and started walking towards Koanga. Brick pulled his dagger and walked toward Willow.

I threw myself at Goblin and yelled, "Now, Willow, now!"

Goblin and I fell to the ground in a tangle. He was bigger and stronger, but I was close enough to Koanga for help.

"Koanga, pull your knife out of your boot!" He leaned forward, tugged it out far enough with his fingertips so I could reach it. But Goblin's arms were longer, and I yelled in frustration for Koanga to roll out of the way before Goblin grabbed it. A dark hand reached down, pulled the knife away from both of us, and sliced across the back of Goblin's neck like baling twine. Goblin twitched still. I rolled up to my knees, struggling to get out of the way. I watched in horror as Willow pushed him over and dragged the dagger deep across his throat to be sure he was dead.

I scrambled up to see Brick, already dead, the dagger shoved to the very hilt through the soft part of his chin upward into his head. I was stunned. I didn't realize Willow was that strong. Koanga rolled to all fours and then collapsed in the dirt.

I walked back, dazed at what I had just witnessed. My stomach lurched as I pulled Willow's dagger out of Brick and without wiping it clean, went to cut Koanga free from his bonds. He flinched.

"Shush. I'm only going to cut you free." I wanted to tell him he was going to be a mess for a while because I was sure that was the first time he had watched someone killed nearly in his lap. Not that I was any expert. My weapon of choice in Lowertown had always been to run away from Trouble.

Willow came and sat down beside Koanga. He cringed at first as she put her arm around him and then he leaned into her. She looked up at me. "Are you a threat to me and mine?"

I shook my head mutely and backed out of the clearing. I walked in circles trying to find out where Goblin and Brick had hidden their supplies before crashing into our campsite. It really didn't matter, I knew they wouldn't have much. It was more to get away from Willow and her too knowing eyes. She hadn't even stood up when she asked if I was a threat. She knew I wasn't. My hands were shaking so hard I had to stuff them into my armpits to still them.

I wondered what Willow was thinking. If she could tell Goblin and Brick were never my friends, just a wall of protection in Lowertown from other bullies. It never saved me from being bullied by them in return. I wondered if she and Koanga would abandon me now and what I could do to survive until someone else came along for me to hide behind.

It was Goblin's garish dress that finally gave the hiding space away. I unwrapped their travel packs and found a small spade head. It wasn't West Islands metal, but it would be sturdy enough to dig two shallow graves. If I was useful enough, I thought to myself, she wouldn't harm me. I took the travel packs with me and headed to the campfire. I would get Willow's walking stick and carve the end into a handle for the spade's blade.

Koanga and Willow were silent and watchful. Koanga was carefully turned away from the bodies and there were traces of tears on his face. She kept an arm around him, but I doubted he even noticed. Mentally he was far away from us.

I threw the packs at their feet. "Go through these bags and anything that can tie back to Goblin and Brick, we will need to bury with them. Anything else, split between our three traveling packs. I will go with you to Matasi and get you on your ship home." I tried to sound confident.

"You treat your friends so well?" Willow began.

"They were never my friends," I interrupted. "They would have killed me after they killed you." I dipped my head to Willow. "You saved my life. Truly."

"Do we need to find a Justice? Two men have been murdered." Koanga hiccupped.

"Hold it right there, Koanga. Let me give you a lesson in Keresh vocabulary. If you skulk about the streets and stalk your human prey, and then, when he or she is alone, without friends or weapon, then you kill that person—that is murder." I leaned on Willow's walking stick. "If you see something somebody else has, and you don't have the coin to buy it, or they refuse to sell it to you, and you take it at the point of a dagger or a knife—that is 'forced barter'—unless someone dies. Then it's called 'death by dispute,' and you're as likely to swing for that as outright murder."

I smiled at him. "But if someone loses their breath when you remove your knife or dagger from their body while you were defending you and yours?" I scoffed, "That is nothing more than 'Kereki metal poisoning.'"

I crouched down in front of Willow. "I haven't quite figured out who you are, but I have a pretty strong suspicion you have a connection to the West Islands ambassador murdered in Kerek City at the beginning of the Dry. If you were part of his household, you would have been expected to defend his family to the death. You were trained for this. What you did for Koanga and me today? This was not a casual thing. Koanga, on the other hand, is only on a grand adventure," I threw her words back at her, "and needs your help." I paused. "I will take care of the bodies."

I left the two alone in the clearing while I dug two shallow graves in the soft sand far beyond the bubbler in the rocks. I dragged Goblin first, and then Willow helped me drag Brick out to the holes in the earth. I searched their pockets, emptied their purses, and kept their daggers, before tipping them in and refilling the holes. When I came back to the campfire, Koanga was telling one of the great tales of the West Islands to the empty air. He continued while I sorted through the packs. There wasn't much there: no food, a change of shirt, and some papers with writing on them. It didn't look like the flowing script of Wester or the spiky letters of Keresh. I shoved them at Willow. "What language is this?"

She reached for them absently. "It's Mata. Looks like travel papers for someone. Landed in Vesaport and traveled to the Kerek border on the Coast Road. But they are dated in the past." She got up and took them away to examine them more closely.

Worthless then. I snorted and kept looking. Goblin had a purse with coins enough for a night of gambling—two if he was lucky—but it was clear he would have had to steal more soon. Brick had no coins, but he did have a handful of lucifers dipped in beeswax to protect them. He also had a Sailor's Curse—a small blade that could be held between the fingers. I slipped it between the fingers of my left hand and threw a punch into the air. Koanga faltered and fell silent. I looked up to see him watching me.

"Sailor's Curse." I held up the tiny, curved blade for him to get a better look. "You place the small wooden end against the 'v' of your fingers so you don't slice yourself, and let this curved, sharp edge stick out between your knuckles. Kerek's docks don't attract the best and brightest. Sailors from strange lands are sometimes set upon, emptied of their pockets, and given a 'Kereki kiss'—a scar from one of these. Just more of that forced barter I was telling you about earlier."

Koanga swallowed hard. "Willow had told me not to get off the ship in Kerek City until I could see her and the ambassador's guard from the gangway. I thought she was just treating me like a child." He paused. "I'm glad she was there."

"So am I." I needed to distract him so he didn't realize his slip of mentioning the ambassador's guard. I had suspected the pair of them were connected somehow, but I just couldn't figure it all out. Until I did, the West Islanders were like a pot of gold I couldn't spend. "No Kereki kisses for you," I teased. "Your face is far too pretty." Koanga colored and I enjoyed his discomfort for a moment.

"Thank you for saving my life today." Koanga looked away.

"Willow saved us. I had to tie you securely because I knew Brick would check your knots. I also knew Brick was lazy and wouldn't walk over to Willow to check hers, if he knew you were secure. But, truly, Koanga, it was your words earlier that saved us. You said Willow had better survival skills and I needed to know that, if my life was going to be forfeit. Neither Goblin nor Brick expected Willow to be anything but a useless faint. In Kerek, a woman would never be expected to be able to fight. None of us could have stood against both of them, but with the three of us? Working together? Goodness prevailed."

I threw down Brick's steel knife in front of him. "What can you tell me about a knife from the West Islands?"

Koanga picked it up carefully and turned it over and over as Willow came back into the clearing. He turned to her. "Do you recognize this?"

Willow stood over him and he handed it up to her by the hilt. She pulled out her own dagger, clean now, and laid them side by side on the log next to him. "The blade is more curved. It is a slashing knife. See how mine is narrow and straight? It is a woman's defense knife, meant to go in and deep. This one," she pointed to the new knife without touching it, "that would belong to someone who thought to fight their way out of trouble. A West Islands sailor, perhaps, or a soldier... or a guard. Although there are no West Islands soldiers on Kerek soil."

"Could it belong to one of the guards from the embasado? Either your ambassador or another?" I asked gently.

Koanga looked up quickly. "You think it belongs to the guard who took all of our coin to secure our passage and never returned for us?" He glanced at Willow and she smiled at him. How odd, I thought.

I shrugged, adding Koanga's tidbit of information to the others he had let slip. "I don't know what to think. I would like to know if there is anything identifiable on the blade that carrying it will get me hung for murder."

Willow handed it back to me. "No, nothing like that. Some smiths will mark their blades or a hilt may be decorated by an owner, but that one is unloved. It can be used or traded or sold without a trail back to its beginning."

She looked at Koanga. "Right now, we need to get packed up and out of this site. I would like to get down the road and camped on the far side of Aldi before dark tonight. We need to put a lot of time and distance between us and this dance with Trouble." She turned away from us, and we began to tear down camp.

## CHAPTER 8

# A WEST ISLANDS CONSTELLATION TALE

When we reached the crossroads beyond Aldi, we turned right on the Old Vikland Road. It would lead us to the Coast Road to the Matasi border. Until now, most of the journey had been in silence, everyone lost in their own thoughts; the only sound was water sloshing in Willow's steel flask. I muddled over my news. I wasn't happy to have Koanga and Willow learn I had only been a thief—and not a very good one—in Kerek City. As we continued on the road, I wondered what Willow and Koanga were thinking as well.

Before we had left, Willow had washed off the blood and changed into her trousers and tunic, but with her hair and body stained dark, she only looked like another West Islander boy. When I asked if she wanted to wash it off, she had muttered it didn't come off that easily. I had asked her if she thought that would be a problem to travel the Coast Road if none of us looked Kereki. She had shrugged and said there wasn't anything different we could do about it now. We would dance with Trouble when she showed up, she seemed to find us easily enough.

Without Koanga's stories to pass the time, the decons came slowly. Once we passed the crossroads, and I knew we were on the less traveled road to the coast, I began to look for a clump of trees or a waterway a little distance from the road. At one point, we could see the campfires of other travelers through the woods. I looked at Koanga and motioned to the firelight dancing through the leaves and bushes.

"In Kerek City and the near countryside, that is a campfire of thieves and outlaws. They have nothing to fear from other travelers, so they build a big fire to draw in the unwary or the desperate. Or it would be the fire of fools who draw attention to themselves and make themselves victims. In either case, it's important to stay away." I gave him a half smile. "What would a fire like that mean in the West Islands?"

Koanga cocked his head but kept on walking. "It would be the fire of a Storyteller who is telling other travelers here is warmth and comfort, and the telling of the great tales to lull us to sleep on the hard ground. If the fire is immediately outside the village, it means no one is able to honor the roaming regles due to sickness or death. Or it means the Traveler has been disfigured because he has broken the roaming regles in his or her travels and is denied the hospitality of those he once harmed."

"Ahhhh. So it's possible not everyone treats the Traveler with open arms and open hearth. I was beginning to think all West Islanders were everything good and kind in the world, and Kerek and Matasi had to fight over the leavings." I smiled so he knew I was teasing.

Koanga gave me a wry look. "I did not mean to sound so provincial as all that."

I had more questions for him. "Earlier, you had said Goblin couldn't break the roaming regles. What did you mean by that?"

"Mmmm. It's probably easier if I tell you a story," he began, dropping his voice into the storyteller voice I remembered from the first day they had found me.

*"A long time ago, and not so far away, the West Islanders were at peace. The Smith had come and gone, and now looked with fondness on his people from the constellations in the sky. But the West Islanders were not forgotten. Mother Earth would send her daughters, Grains, Gems, Fruits, Flowers, Medicines, and Metals, out with her bountiful gifts.*

*One day, a new person came and stood by the well in the center of the village. Slight of frame and built close to the ground as all West Islanders are, the person wore a woven cloak of bright green. The hood was drawn up and the voice that called out was neither high nor low.*

"*Greetings! I have no coin, but I seek food and lodging and in exchange I have news, and song, and a gift from Mother Earth.*"

*Now in those days, the oldest woman in the village that could walk from the village well to her home and hearth was the one to guide the people. Grandmother Marama came out to meet the traveler. "Well, what's your news? What's your gift? Then we shall see what food and shelter we have to offer."*

*The traveler chuckled. "News has value only in the first telling. After that, it becomes merely gossip to be bandied about over weeding and gathering."*

*Grandmother Marama smiled. "True. At least let us see you, so we know no one shall come to harm."*

*"A pretty boy or a plain faced maid can hide Trouble in their hearts, you must accept me as I appear and let not your generosity be based on beauty."*

*"How shall we call you?"*

*"You may call me 'They' or 'Them' or the 'Traveler,' for we go from place to place seeking our fortune, returning to family, or singing our songs in a new hearth."*

*Grandmother Marama considered. "Well, I won't let anyone in the village suffer by your hand, so come along to my home where you shall have food and shelter for one night and no harm shall come to you."*

Koanga paused in the telling and smiled at me. "And this was the beginning of our roaming regles. Anyone may exchange song or substance for food and shelter in the West Islands. No one may cause hurt to host or guest." He gave me a sly smile. "It appears not to be the same in Kerek."

I snorted at his understatement. "So what happened to the Traveler?"

Koanga continued, *"The Traveler sat at Grandmother Marama's table and told all the news from up and down the roads they traveled. After the meal, she called the village together and songs and stories were shared until the stars pinwheeled across the sky. The next morning, the Traveler continued on their journey. The Traveler is neither young nor old, male nor female, but comes bearing peace and reminds us always to be kind to strangers in a strange land."*

Koanga fell silent. We continued walking while I struggled with how I could ask him all my questions without making fun of his innocence in Kerek. I sighed. "So tell me, truthfully, Koanga. If you were following West Islands roaming regles when you first arrived in Kerek— how long before you were robbed of everything you owned?"

Koanga's head snapped up. "You have a very poor opinion of your fellow man."

"I like to think I have an accurate assessment of those who thrive in Kerek," I responded. "Truly, did you even make it one night?"

Koanga looked indignant and glanced back to Willow walking behind us. I turned as well and saw her nod at him. He looked back at me. "Of course. Willow and the ambassador's personal guard came to meet my ship. They had a traveler's cloak with them and told me to keep my face covered. I had packed lightly—just my tailor's kit and a spare shirt—since I thought we would buy passage on the next ship out. We stayed at a quiet home with others whom Willow said worked in the embasado. I helped Willow pack her belongings. Our guard offered to take them to the dock, secure passage for us, and have them loaded. We were to eat the food prepared for us and sleep as we could, since the ship would be leaving on a night tide. We slept deeply and long and when we woke the next morning, the house was empty, our belongings were gone, and no ship in the harbor had passage booked for two West Islanders. And this is the truth as the stars bear witness."

"Oh for...so you just handed over enough coin to buy passage to the West Islands to someone you had just met? You deserved to be swindled!"

Koanga stiffened, but it was Willow who answered, "I had known him for two years. He and his wife both worked in the ambassador's household. Perhaps the guard took the coin, feared for his family, and disappeared as a crime of opportunity. Perhaps he was murdered for an act of kindness, and I owe a life debt."

"But I don't know," Koanga said. "I don't know anything except I made a vow to the King to bring Willow home to the West Islands."

"The King?" My ears perked up.

"Koanga likes to make this grand adventure sound much more important than it is. Truth? I am the daughter of a tailor. Koanga agreed to bring funds to get us home to the West Islands. We no longer have all those funds," Willow parsed out carefully.

I smiled to myself. Willow was only giving me enough words to tell me the truth without answering the questions. Every child in Lowertown knew how to do the same.

"So what happens next?"

"We either walk all night and Koanga tells us another story to pass the time, or we find someplace to curl up and sleep. And I for one, would prefer to sleep," Willow announced.

I ignored her. "Truthfully? I would like to put a little more distance between that fire we passed not long ago and where we bed tonight. Fool or foe—I don't want them as neighbors." I tried to remember some of the stories Koanga had told me the first day. "Don't you West Islanders have a god called the guard or something? I thought I remembered Koanga telling me so. It was while we were waiting for you to return from your shopping, Willow. On the first day you found me," I clarified.

Willow shot me a scornful look. "He's not a god or a guard. It's another of the constellation stories. The Soldier is a constellation at the eastern edge of the night—the opposite side of the sky as the Traveler. The Soldier stands ready to protect us from enemies to the east—that would be Kerek," she said drily. "He stands ready to protect you and yours, and me and mine, from all who would do us harm." She paused. "Stop for a moment. I'll show you where he is."

We stopped. "May I touch you?" She asked, and I nodded. She turned me to the east and lifted my arm a hand-width above the horizon. "It's barely dark, so it's a little hard to see, but see those four stars close together in a line straight up and down? That's his soldier's pike. To the left of that are three more stars a little more widely-spaced. Starting from the bottom star, that's his foot, the brightest one in the middle is his dagger, and the top star is his head. His pike is upright because he is on sentinel duty. His dagger is the brightest star in the constellation because it is made of West Islands steel. He is one of the first constellations our children are taught, because we must be ready to help and keep from harm you and yours, me and mine."

I laughed. "So even your Soldier is good? A sentinel against evil?"

Koanga looked startled. "But of course! What is a soldier in Kerek? Or Matasi?"

"In Kerek, soldiers are not paid well enough to defend with their life. They are just one more layer of bribes and bureaucracy standing between what I have and what I want. In Matasi, the soldiers believe they are 'God's Fist'—the army of their Lost God—so anything done is a righteous deed. And if a commander or two goes crazy with power and zeal?" I shrugged. "In Kerek City, I heard of entire villages burned, with every person in the village down to babes in the cradle, gutted and piked."

Koanga went pale and I reached to touch him. "Truly, Koanga, that's just a scary story we used to tell each other in Kerek City to frighten the little ones. I didn't think you would believe it. The Matasi's military is huge compared to Kerek's, so our soldiers make up stories about how awful they are. At least that's what I've heard in Lowertown. Truthfully, I have not seen a Kereki soldier on duty, or a Matasi soldier at all."

He pulled back. Willow looked carefully at Koanga and narrowed her eyes at me. None of us spoke until Koanga gave a long shuddering sigh. "I'm fine. Perhaps a bit hungry and definitely ready for my bed. Do you think we could find someplace soon to stop for the night?"

Willow inserted herself between the two of us, radiating displeasure. I wasn't sure what I had done wrong now, or if she was just unhappy with me and the day. We tucked ourselves in the next deep bramble hedge, ate the last of our bakery bread, and rolled ourselves into our cloaks. The events of the day, as horrible as they were, did not keep us from exhausted sleep.

# CHAPTER 9

## A CONROSAN FAIRY TALE

The next morning, the sun danced through the leaves as if it was delighted to make my acquaintance. I woke first, pulled my thoughts together, and realized with a start today was the first day I knew everything. Better than that, no one else knew how I was whole again. With Goblin and Brick dead, and Willow and Koanga soon to be on a ship to the West Islands, there was no one who could prevent me from reinventing myself.

I looked at Willow and Koanga rolled up in their cloaks, and a nasty thought skittered through my mind. If they never left the clearing, I would have enough coin and West Islands metal workings to set myself up in any small village. Not so much to cause tongues to wag, but enough to make a home without sleeping in stables. I daydreamed for a moment, imagining what it would be like to live in a tidy house, have coin to pay for my needs, and a skill to earn the respect of others. I could choose a new life as easily as I chose a new name.

The daydream ended as I realized with a sinking feeling I had no skills for village life. I couldn't run a shop, or a forge, or a bakery. I was a slice of Trouble who had done whatever I needed to live. I had stolen food from the street carts, worked as a message runner for the shops, and for the promise of a safe place to sleep, I had agreed with Goblin to rob Primo Resoro.

Now I had found two West Islanders, or they had found me. They knew how to travel, to find their way, to cook and care for us. I thought about the stories they had told me last night. Koanga and his story of the Traveler and the roaming regles, and Willow pointing out the Soldier constellation in the night sky. Suddenly I realized they had told me the stories of themselves. It wasn't that Koanga didn't understand Kerek, it was Kerek didn't follow the rules Koanga used to live his life.

Every time I thought I had stuffed Willow in a tidy little box, she seemed to be standing beside it with a mocking smile. I knew now I had been putting her in the wrong box and she didn't fit. She was a soldier, but she was more than that. She was only revealing what she needed in order to get us all to safety.

Somehow, I had to convince her that Goblin and Brick had nothing to do with who I wanted to be, and that she needed me more than I needed her. I sighed. Well, that wasn't possible, but maybe, I only had to convince them they needed me just a little longer.

I blew out a hard breath. Might as well see if I could find water. We needed to fill Willow's and Koanga's steel flasks and the waxed waterskin they had given me for my use.

The water was farther away than I expected, considering how green the bramble hedge had been. I dug four seep holes with my hand in the loose soil before I found the angle of the water flow. Like yesterday, this one was a bubbler—an underground stream occasionally forced to the surface by rock formations.

I pulled off my shirt, beat the blood and dirt out of it, and then used it to wash myself from tip top to belt knot. I washed out the shirt again, drank my fill, and then filled my waterskin. I could show Koanga and Willow where to fill theirs as soon as they were up. On the way back, I took my time to pick up a few broken branches for a fire. Maybe Koanga could make that oats and berries porridge he had made the other day before we set off. That was tasty.

"Hey! I've been working away and found water and wood while you have been..." I ambled into the clearing to find it deserted. My cloak and traveling pack were still as I had left them, but Willow and Koanga and all their belongings were gone. I walked around their footprints, tracing their movements. Koanga had walked to my bedroll and now I could see he had placed the pants from the rag and bone man in Aldi, a handful of small coins, and the bone saw there. They hadn't been taken then, they had fled. I stood up and angrily jabbed my long stick in the dirt. Of all the stupid... I didn't have to worry about getting lost—there was only one way to the Coast Road. What they didn't realize was the closer we got to Matasi, the greater danger I thought we were in.

I was more upset about me. For years, I had skulked along the edges of Lowertown streets trying to stay alive. There was never enough food. And there was always someone bigger than me who tried to take it away from me. I wasn't much of a thief, well, an untended cart begged to have its load lightened. And I never would have dreamed up the plan to rob Primo Resoro. Brick had hunted me down and threatened me if I didn't turn over all my coin, then when Goblin heard me speak castle Keresh, he had intervened and offered his protection if I "helped him with a little task." What choice did I have? I was trapped in an alley with both of them, and there was no way I was going to be able to run fast enough to escape.

Then, when Primo Resoro threw me out of the carriage, the first one to find me was a West Islander who believes in roaming regles, kindness, and grand adventures. I couldn't imagine any greater fortune, and I thought I had found a way to leave my past behind forever.

And then Aldi happened, and today they had left me to fend for myself. I knew exactly how long I would last on this road. The first people that passed me would look me up and down, smile at my small size, and I wouldn't live to see the sunset.

It was true Kerek was the frontier, and everyone preyed on everyone. But, I had heard stories of the Matasians among the other street children. They would say even the missionaries who came with their heavy wagons were nothing more than monsters who tried to lure children away with promises of food and stories in order to eat their flesh and crunch their bones. I shivered in spite of myself, and here I was nearly full grown.

I sighed deeply and looked at my bedroll. Willow had all the food in her seagrass basket in her traveling pack and she had left me nothing. I was already hungry.

But bless Koanga and his roaming regles, the clean pants, and gifts would be appreciated. Koanga's sweet view of a grand adventure had turned into a long monotonous trek interspersed with moments of sheer terror and little food. He had learned I was not a lordling, he had been tied and threatened, and witnessed two metal poisonings. And yet, he still had left me coins and clothing and the maripi. I had never met a man like him before.

I had no idea what Willow thought, but as part of the ambassador's household, she had to have been aware of what a rich ransom target those children would have been. All of the West Islanders working in the ambassador's household would have been trained to protect the children. Now that I knew so, I was not afraid of Willow. No, that wasn't it, I was not afraid of what Willow would do to me. I was not a threat to her or the children.

In Kerek City, I remembered hearing of the children's disappearance and the uproar as the rewards for their return—or their bodies—steadily climbed. It wasn't just the West Islanders seeking them. Everyone was hunting them—for greed or good. The Vikland embasado had posted rewards as well as the Matasi Triune and Kerek King. Everyone had been talking about it. Even in Lowertown, there had been the tall Vikland warriors with the single long black braid, their dark close-fitting clothes, and the tahn bongs or crossbows strapped casually on their backs searching the streets. The Matasi mercenaries and missionaries also sought the children. Dressed similarly to the Kereki, but with their olive skin, close-cut curly brown hair on both women and men, they would offer food to the orphans in Dockside, Lowertown, and the Sinner's District and ask for news or sightings of West Islander children.

Of course, I had dreamed with the other street children and orphans of finding and befriending the West Islanders and winning enough coin to escape Lowertown forever. But somebody had to know where the children were and was sitting on a shipload of gold with the information.

I would bet a season's winnings at the gambling tables, Willow knew something.

I packed my travel bag and stood. My mind was made up. I would not survive by myself, but it was not too late to catch up to them. I had nowhere to go, and no one waiting for me. I would see this adventure through to the salt spray of one of the Matasi ports. I had days and days ahead of me to convince them to take me with them to the West Islands. Life would be better there. It had to be. I pulled my travel pack on my back and headed for the Coast Road.

The sun was high overhead when I finally caught a glimpse of them far ahead. I stretched my legs and picked up my pace. Willow saw me first. She touched Koanga's arm, he turned and stopped. As I pulled closer, I watched them carefully, wondering how they would accept me.

Koanga was Koanga. He rocked forward on the balls of his feet and grinned widely, but Willow seemed to shift and change in front of me. She looked wary, but it was more than that. Somehow, she transformed herself from the Kereki boy on the edge of childhood I had first imagined her to be. It was different from the well-to-do West Islands woman she had pretended to be in Aldi, but I wasn't sure what. Something more, something hidden.

When I caught up with them, they said nothing about my decision to join them. Willow moved over a bit, made room for me to tuck myself in the middle, and we walked on as if we had started out the day together all those footsteps ago. I shared my water, Willow gave me a piece of stonebread, and we walked in companionable silence.

"I have a story," Willow announced suddenly. "Some call it an origin story of the folk hero, Zren Janin. Others say it is only a pretty tale from Conrosa, and our Zren Janin was nothing more or less than a changeling in love with the humans. But I believe everyone can have part of the truth, and Truth will look different to everyone. So, I will tell you the story and you can decide for yourself." She took a deep breath and began,

*"Once upon a time, in a place not so far away, a family of the fae decided to live in the world of man. Perhaps the decision wasn't entirely theirs, but that's not the story I will tell today. One daughter, two parents, and three sons. Beautiful in the way of the fae— cinnamon-hued and dark-eyed as juncos—and clever! The parents could plant anything and it would grow and thrive while the sons were artisans with wood, metal, and cloth. But the daughter's talents lay with numbers, and their holdings increased under her care.*

*Decades passed. The fae remained strong and fair of face as their playmates married, tarried, and buried. The sons of the fae did not look for mortal wives but served their exile lightly, convinced soon they would return to their birthplace.*

The daughter, Ennesh, dealt daily with the shopkeepers, the gold lenders, the traveling tradespeople. She spoke the language of gold as if it were her mother tongue. And perhaps for her it was—all of commerce sang together buying and selling. She was the master singer.

Word of her family's success and eternal youth and beauty spread beyond the borders of their valley and over the long plains. And when words fly so high and fast, Trouble is soon to follow.

His name was... but does it really matter? He was a trickster: beautiful, charming, and spoke the lies of men with a grace and ease the fae had never known. He arrived in the village one spring morning with a dozen personal guards and another half dozen pack horses.

Knowing that mortals lie is no protection if one doesn't know the lie itself. Ennesh heard the nobleman call her beautiful and knew that it was true. All fae are beautiful. To be praised for being clever and financially astute, was only a recognition of her talents and hard work. And when the words slid into murmurs and soft kisses and touches that left shivers, well, Ennesh wouldn't be the first woman, or man, or fae, to be beguiled by a trickster's silver tongue and a black heart.

And then, like smoke on a winter's morning, he was gone. The village awoke to find their goods had been paid for with empty *promises. The innkeeper nursed his throbbing head and wondered how he could have slept through a dozen men creeping out the door without payment. And while the hostler had been paid for housing the horses and pack men, she had not been paid for the missing feed, tack, and three extra horses that had followed the trickster out of the valley and to the north mountains.*

*Everyone had something taken—except for Ennesh. But her gift was not welcome and all too soon, she was beginning to show the fruits of the trickster's talents.*

*The family of fae was disheartened. To have the child born and raised in the village would subject it to a life of hatred and cruelty by anyone who had felt wronged by the trickster. They regretfully agreed that to protect the child from the villagers, Ennesh would need to leave.*

*On the spring day Ennesh left, her brothers hitched four horses to their largest wagon. They loaded her bed, her kitchen things, loom, and ledgers for her to set up house. They added food in baskets tucked in with cages of ducks, chickens, and rabbits. The brothers would settle her in and then return.*

*Seven days and seven nights the wagon trundled through the steppes. Long views of endless plains, ice blue lakes, wide skies. At last when Ennesh thought she couldn't stand one more day of the jostling of the wagon, one more day of listening to her brothers argue who would fetch water, or gather wood, or cook the food, one more day of sleeping on the ground around a dying fire, when she thought she would scream if they said one more word... they came to the forest.*

*Ennesh could feel the magic. And like any fae, a long way from home, she and her brothers fell silent, walked within the shadows of the trees, and let the memories of a birthplace far away wash over them. They were still and the woods restored them. Ennesh had found her new home.*

*While she built the campfire, her brothers hung the canvas between the trees for shelter. They walked deeper into the woods and found a cold stream, deep and clear. Her youngest brother followed it upstream to the source tucked into a crevice on the hill. They would build the spring house there.*

*The oldest brother was gifted with a talent with wood in all its forms. On the first day, he shouldered a heavy bag from the wagon, staggering a little under the weight. He dropped the bag in the midst of the clearing, cut a corner of the bag, and then dragged it along the ground spilling sawdust along straight lines and square corners. After he drew the lines of house and rooms, he picked up the bag and made another set of lines and corners across the yard for barns and stables and pens. When he was finished, he was sweating heavily, his shirt was damp across his chest, his brown hair curled at the nape of his neck.*

*Each brother and Ennesh knelt at the corner of the house and laid a hand on the four corners of sawdust. At a word from the eldest brother, the sawdust solidified and built the house around them. The four siblings then walked to the second design on the ground, again knelt to touch the sawdust. Again the brother spoke a word, and the barn rose up around them. Each time, the design was repeated until the buildings and pens were built.*

*While the oldest brother rested, Ennesh and her youngest brother unloaded the crates of chickens, ducks, and rabbits into the pens and coops. While she scattered feed about, the second brother returned with buckets of water, pouring carefully in the wooden troughs and taking care of the horses. They all unloaded the wagon of Ennesh's goods into the house.*

*That was the end of the first day.*

*After breakfast on the second day, the second brother pulled a dark chest from the wagon. The contents of the wooden chest clinked and clanked as he struggled to carry it to the house. His gift was metal workings for hearth and field. While her older brother cut the windows of the buildings, and her youngest brother made the marks for gates for the gardens and pens, the second brother could be heard within the house, magic crackling and popping.*

*After caring for her animals, Ennesh walked out of the barn and into the golden afternoon. She could see the metal stovepipe pumping smoke into the air, so she walked into the house to see her* second brother's efforts. The stove kicked out heat and newly crafted pots and pans hung in a row on hooks on the wall. On the table, there were knives for butchering, forks for eating, and spoons for stirring. He had even built a metal shelf above the oven where bread could rise—warm but not too warm.

The chest was thrown open on the wooden floor and Ennesh could see it was still half full of metal. Her brother pulled off his shirt and wiped the sweat from his face and arms. "I'll rest a bit before I make the tools I need for the barn and gardens. I will need our older brother's help for that."

That night she slept in her bed in her fine house, and her brothers laid out their swag on the front room floor.

And that was the end of the second day.

After breakfast on the third day, the youngest brother watched as his brothers combined the wood and metal to make a hoe for him. And such a hoe it was! It drew straight furrows in the earth and turned the soil as gently as a mother opening a newborn's blanket. While the first and second brothers worked together to create axes, hammers, fence workings, and gates, the third brother drew out the rocks in the soil, made mounds ready for planting and created gardens of sun and shade, ready for vegetables and fruit and flowers.

Then when they were finished, the brothers took another item out of the wagon and brought it into the house. It was a small chest *made of clever drawers—each no bigger than a hand. Each drawer held a muslin bag of seeds and the largest drawers on the bottom held roots and bulbs.*

*The oldest brother spoke, "Our parents asked us to give you this chest. As long as this chest stays intact, the drawers will never empty. The seeds and plants will always grow with soil and sun and water, and the harvest will be sufficient for you and anyone you choose to care for." Then all of them went out together and planted her gardens. They carried water for the plants, the animals, and themselves.*

*That evening her brothers planted two rowan trees at the entrance to the clearing for protection.*

*And that was the end of the third day.*

*After breakfast on the fourth day, all the brothers carried in a long flat wooden chest. Carefully the third brother opened it. "My gift to you, Ennesh, was woven for you ahead of time." He showed her the chest, and oh my! There were textiles and fabrics of every color and type. And nestled safely in the folds were glass panes for the windows. The brothers carefully set the glass in the window frames and then took all the long panels of brightly colored fabric and hung them on the wayfarer trees on the far edge of the clearing. The third brother explained, "The weavings hung on the wayfarer trees will make this place invisible to anyone who wishes harm to you and those you care for. And the textiles we hung at the windows will keep prying eyes from seeing that this is a place of refuge for women and children."*

*Ennesh said nothing but walked into her house and returned with four small bags of boiled wool tied tightly at the top. "My brothers." She paused, took a deep breath, and started again, "My dear brothers, my gullibility in the lies of men now means I must live away from you until we can all return to the land of the fae. It would have been easy for you to turn your back on your sister, but instead you have shared your gifts with me. I also have a talent, and as long as you mix these coins within your dealings with man, you cannot be cheated in coin or commission. You will always have enough funds for food and shelter and to buy the labor of honest men. Your holdings will increase."*

*Ennesh then gave each brother a bag of gold. "Please take this fourth bag to our parents, for I recognize their gift in the seed cabinet and cling to their forgiveness."*

*The oldest brother reached out for the parents' bag. "Our gifts extend beyond this labor. I leave the bag of enchanted sawdust. If you ever need to expand your home, create the boundaries with water from the spring and draw the lines with sawdust. The buildings will grow overnight." He paused. "I also have a gift for your child." He turned and left the room.*

*The second brother stepped forward. "I am also leaving the chest of metal pieces. To create any tool, or to mend a broken one, select the proper metal pieces and bundle them with the broken one or the one you want created. In the morning, the second piece will be there, whole and complete." He smiled. "I also have a gift for your child." He turned and left the room.*

*The third brother gave Ennesh a tight hug and stepped back. "I have woven a cloak for you and one for your child." He held them out to her. "It will grow as your child grows and both cloaks will protect you from the weapons of others, those you feel, and those you hear. You cannot be harmed."*

*The second brother returned and presented Ennesh with a wicked looking dagger, laying it across her open palms. "A sword is for a soldier, but a dagger is for defense. Whether son or daughter, fae or other, this dagger shall protect the wearer from the evil in men's hearts."*

*The oldest brother brought in a short bow and a quiver full of arrows. "Whether son or daughter, fae or other, this bow and arrows will ensure food will always find your child's table. Your child will never go hungry in the land of men or fae."*

*The second brother looked at her thoughtfully. "The path ahead of you is not an easy one, but it is not an overwhelming one. Those who need your help will find you, and we will not return to Fairyland without you."*

*The youngest brother smiled at her. "Our father has asked, that whether son or daughter, fae or other, this child shall be called 'Zren Janin.'"*

*Ennesh felt her eyes fill with tears and spill down her cheeks. She hugged each of them tightly and waited by the door while they grabbed their swag from the front room and headed out into the afternoon sun. The youngest brother led the horses from the barn, and together they hitched the team to the wagon. She followed them out of the clearing and all the way down to the main road. She watched them until they faded beyond her eyesight, and then she returned to her home in the clearing."*

Willow smiled in satisfaction and thumped her walking stick on the ground. *"And that, my children, is the beginning of Zren Janin, a fae so enamored with the humans he stepped in to be their champion."*

## CHAPTER 10

## A GRAND ADVENTURE

Koanga scoffed. "I've never heard of such a silly story—magic and fae and lost homelands."

"It's not a tale from the West Islands, that's why. Our great tales are drawn from the sky because the West Islands are scattered about, and we are seafarers and travelers and metal workers who wander. We use the stars to find our way, to mark our place, and to tell time and distance." Willow gave me a strange look. "This was a tale from Conrosa, a land far to the north of Kerek. From books I have read, it has deep forests so big people can get lost in them, ice and snow, and more seasons than just Dry and Wet. Stories of the fae and their dealings among men are told around the fires in the Season of Rest when the nights are long and cold." She paused. "Do you know of such a place, Red?"

I snorted. "Imagine a place without the seasons Dry and Wet. Even the sailors in the gambling places wouldn't tell such tales."

Willow shrugged and looked at the road. "Red, I have heard of such a place and read the tales in the ambassador's house. He had never been; it is so very far to the north. But, his wife had met people from there when she was a child and had exchanged books with them. There were children's books as well, and I taught myself to read the language so I could read those lovely stories." She gave me a questioning glance. "There is a Conrosan embasado in Kerek City. It has been empty for many years, but it exists, Zren. And I have heard there are Conrosans in Vikland teaching at the academies. Did you know this? I would love to meet them and learn more."

Koanga poked at the dirt. "Another country I will never be able to travel to. Sometimes I feel my grand adventure is nothing more than a toddler shaking a stick at an old dog and thinking I am challenging a tiger. I am such a foolish boy."

Willow turned around and walked backward in front of him. "You are brave, resourceful, and loyal to those you love. Do you see my father here escorting me home? Did you see soldiers from our King or council arriving at the embasado and providing us safe passage through the streets of Kerek City? No."

Willow glanced at me and then looked at Koanga and continued talking, "What I see is one of the great Storytellers of the West Islands who knows all the great tales and has used the lessons in them to get me this far. I see one who has been trained as a good tailor who can take rags and tattered lordling clothes, and magic them into dresses and trousers and whatever else we may need. Your skill with the needle has made it possible for us to slip through a country so wild and without mercy that monsters wear the faces of men and women." She smiled at him. "I see a man who can look at the food I gather and buy and make a meal that nourishes our bodies with nothing more than a pot of water and a lucifer. Think on that as you sleep tonight."

Koanga gave a wry grin. "You have a storyteller's tongue, but today I am grateful for it. Thank you." He smiled. "Sometimes it is not so easy to stand in your shadow, Willow." He paused. "Perhaps you could tell us another tale from Conrosa?"

"I will but not tonight. It's late and we need to sleep." She looked about us and pointed west to a small shelter of trees along the river we had been following. "Can we stop there? We should be close to water, and we have left those other campfires far behind us."

I agreed and the three of us left the track and walked to the far side of the small scattering of trees. Our fire would be seen from the track, but it was late and there should be no others still on the road. Koanga built a very small fire for our soup, and Willow and I put up the canvas lean-tos. We ate quickly and then each of them took turns slipping away from the campsite to take care of night business. Even after they rolled themselves into their traveling cloaks and drifted off to sleep, I stayed by the dying fire and continued to think about my traveling companions.

Willow had said there was a Conrosan embasado in Kerek City. I thought I knew which one she meant, the one closest to the castle. But it was knowledge that hadn't helped me survive in Lowertown, so I hadn't given it much thought. I wasn't sure how it would help me now either. Today, when I had caught up to them, they had said nothing about my decision to continue on with them, but Koanga's smile had warmed me with its pleasure.

So much had happened in the past days. For four days I had worn any disguise I chose because in those moments, any of them could be true. When Goblin and Brick appeared, I could have chosen a life with them, murdered the West Islanders, taken their goods, and returned to Kerek City and laughed and lived until the coin ran out. But I didn't. I had never considered Goblin and Brick friends. I had been convinced I would die by their hand, it might not have been yesterday, but it would have been someday.

I also didn't consider Koanga and Willow as friends. That they broke camp and ran this morning convinced me they felt the same. I wasn't sure how I felt about that. I was surprised I felt a little sad, but I wondered if it was more about how I watched how they interacted with each other.

I was not an expert on West Islanders, but it was pretty clear to me that they were not a couple or desired to be one. There were no shy glances, no contrived opportunities to touch each other, no conversations heavy with double meanings. They were clearly fond and protective of each other, but it seemed more like the orphans in Lowertown, or street runners for the gangs and docks, who looked out for each other.

Willow also had started me wondering. Why *hadn't* her father come to Kerek? Surely, he knew women were not permitted to travel alone anywhere in Kerek. Why hadn't the King of the West Islands sent soldiers to bring home the ambassador's household after the ambassador had been murdered in the street? Now the world was looking for the ambassador's children for good or ill gains, and the children's lives were only as valuable as the first ones who found them. Did the King of the West Islands care so little for those who served him?

In two days we would reach the Matasi border, Willow had said, and then another six or seven days before we would reach Salisport, the closest port city. When I asked Willow how she knew she could be smuggled out of Matasi, she explained Matasi had four ports scattered about its long, narrow coastline. It gave more flexibility to the ship's captains when the weather was poor, but it was also easier to move goods and people in and out of the country. With only one port in Kerek, the Kerek King had a miser's grasp on the taxes and tolls of Kerek City.

The last of the ashes faded to grey. I poked about to make sure everything was out, stretched, and headed for my canvas lean-to. Tomorrow was another day.

* * * * *

Willow was missing when I woke up in the morning. Koanga was at the firepit, carefully feeding a tiny flame. There were twigs and dried cheatgrass at his feet and small broken branches on his other side. I nodded to him and then walked into the trees to take care of morning business.

When I came back, I noticed one of the metal pots on the fire smelled like stewed vegetables. I cocked an eyebrow.

"Willow is going to be away for a while. I thought as long as I had time, I would make stonebread and fix us a sturdy meal." Koanga didn't look at me but watched his tiny flame carefully.

"Is she all right? Is this about what happened yesterday?"

He wobbled his head from side to side. "Yes...and no. While you were in Aldi, she said she had noticed your friends."

"They were never my friends," I interjected quickly.

"Your previous acquaintances," he continued smoothly. "In Aldi, we don't know if they asked about you, or if their attention drew others to look more closely at you. Since we cannot change you, we will change the people you are traveling with, and no one will wonder what happened to the West Islands woman seeking passage and selling metal workings. I'll have to see if I can clean and repair the dress she wore yesterday when Brick died, we don't have coin for another."

I noticed how carefully he worded Brick's metal poisoning by Willow's hand. I shrugged. It was a forced barter gone wrong. It happened all the time in Lowertown. Someone misjudged as they sized up their victim. This time it had been Brick who had underestimated Willow and paid with his life.

"So who am I traveling with?"

"A Kereki boy and a West Islander looking for day work in the orchards of South Matasi." He looked hopeful, "You wouldn't happen to have experience with harvesting fruits would you? Speak the Mata language?"

I shook my head.

"No matter. I just thought it would help us talk more authentically when we tried to cross the border." Koanga continued kneading the ball of dough on a white cloth on the large rock. Slap, thunk. Slap, thunk.

"I have some questions for you." I paused, waiting for him to look at me.

"I may be able to give you truthful answers. I may tell you a story and let you learn your own truths. But I will answer nothing, before I lie to you." He raised his eyes to mine. "You may want to consider that before you ask."

I held his gaze. "Was it your idea or Willow's to flee my company after you learned who I was?"

Now it was Koanga's turn to raise an eyebrow. "That is not the question I thought you would ask. But I will tell you the truth. Finding out who you were was not a great revelation. I had thought you dressed like a lordling when we first recovered you on the road to Aldi, but then you seemed easy with the rough camp and food. As you became more aware of yourself, we noticed you did not share that information freely with us and instead became more...watchful. I thought this was just from living in such a wild frontier as Kerek, but Willow assured me it was more. In Aldi, she knew those men were watching you. She told me she feared for her life every moment of that walk back to camp." He looked at me soberly. "I would find it hard to forgive you for that, if you had not also saved our lives later."

"Willow saved us."

Koanga cocked his head to the side. "Violence does not come easy to a West Islander."

"Violence does not come easy to anyone. But if violence is all you have known, then violence becomes the answer to everything. You didn't answer my question: Was it you or Willow that wanted to leave me behind?"

"It was clear you were recovered to yourself."

"If you would not have stopped on the first day we met, the very next traveler would have slit my throat with my own knife and stolen my purse. You said it yourself, Koanga, it is better to travel with another on the road to anywhere within Kerek. I have nothing waiting for me in Kerek City. I would like to go to Matasi and see a port city. I would like to go on my own grand adventure...with you." I grinned at him.

Koanga's hands stilled over the dough. His skin was too dark to tell for sure, but I thought a blush was creeping up the side of his face.

"Look at me, Koanga." His face stayed down, and his black curls fell forward. "The bone saw was from you wasn't it?"

"It was the most valuable thing we have," he said. "When Willow said we had to go, I said 'no' at first, but then she said there was no reason that you would not kill us to cover up your friends' deaths."

He finally looked up at me. "Red, I have never seen her look afraid before. Willow is the bravest person I know, and she was afraid. So, I did as she said. She laid the coins on your bedroll, and she said to leave the canvas lean-to for you. She was already out of the clearing when I laid the bone saw on your cloak. We nearly ran for the first mile and then I realized I had not filled my steel flask last night and we still had two days left to get to Matasi. I had left the bone saw to say 'thank you,' but perhaps what I was really saying was 'please.'"

I smiled. I was so happy looking into those beautiful dark brown eyes. I felt I could just stand there smiling and looking stupid until the stonebread had been baked.

Willow pushed her way into the clearing and the moment popped. She looked from Koanga to me and back to him again. "What's going on?" she demanded.

Koanga recovered first. "We are just happy your new disguise is done. Truly, Willow, your skills are formidable."

Willow had scrubbed the dye from her skin but had left her hair and eyebrows the deep rich brown of Matasi almonds. She was wearing the long sleeved light grey shirt with the brown trousers and tunic. The bottoms of her pants were tucked into her boots with the bright Kereki ties wrapped about her calves to keep the dust and bugs out and the pants in tight. The black glove was back on her left hand and I could see the dark fabric underneath her shirt nearly to her elbow.

"The first batch is hot and ready. Come take them so I can use my stone to make more." Koanga waved at the stonebread. All of us sat down and ate. Koanga and Willow shared a bowl and I kept stealing looks at her. Her face was flushed from scrubbing, but where Koanga had tight curls framing his face, Willow had brushed out her dyed hair into a soft nimbus that haloed her head. Anyone looking at her casually would believe her to be a Kereki boy tagging along with two young men looking for unskilled work.

We took our time packing up. We knew the Old Vikland Road would connect to the Coast Road sometime today, and then going forward we would see a lot more travelers. This would make us both more and less safe. Our packs and bedrolls had shifted in size and weight as we used different items. I saw Koanga wince as he slid his pack over his shoulders.

Willow gently picked up his hand and held it to his face. "See those calluses on your fingertips? Your fingers bled from your needle pricks until your hands became those of a good tailor. Your shoulders are learning to be the strong body of an adventurer. It takes time."

Koanga laughed briefly under his breath and gently pulled his hand from hers. He glanced back once at me and then set the pace out of the clearing, back to the road, and westward to the coast.

## CHAPTER 11

## A FLOWER AND A WEED

We were walking three abreast, Koanga in the middle. We had been quiet with our thoughts although I noticed Willow was more alert of her surroundings than I had ever seen her before.

"Tell us a story to make the distance go by more quickly. One of the tales of the Seafarer," Willow said decisively. "It will put us in the proper frame of mind for our upcoming journey."

"What! You'll have me too terrified to put my foot on the gangway," Koanga teased.

"You've told me of the Smith, the Traveler, and pointed out the Soldier in the sky, but you haven't said a word of the Seafarer," I mused. "I wonder if I should be worried."

Koanga laughed and began, "The Seafarer is a constellation which appears to travel across the sky during the season of the

Dry. She spends so much time chasing waves and sunrises she can't appear in our night sky as constantly as the Soldier.

"The bow of the Seafarer's ship points to the double star—the fixed star of the navigator's night. The constellation has nineteen stars, more than any other in the West Islands skies, although most of us can only see half that many. There is one star for each of the distant shores the Seafarer has visited and returned to tell the tale."

Koanga paused for a moment. "I shall tell the story of the Seafarer and the Spice Island, and how flavor came to the West Islands stew pot." He cleared his voice and dropped it into the storyteller's cadence.

*"Long, long ago, and not so very far away, the Seafarer was at home fixing her nets on the shore. She was restless, for the harvest was in and the clouds that brought the rain to the islands were nearly upon them. She was ready and eager to set sail again, to travel north out of the Wet and into the counter currents where the winds were fresh, and the skies were blue and bright.*

*Her youngest daughter brought her a bowl of salt fish and yams—the same thing she had brought the meal before and the meal before that and the meal before that. "Ayah!" said the Seafarer, "My tongue is ready to fall out of my mouth and run away to another's stewpot. This is food only to feed the belly, not to make the senses sing.*

*I could eat this if I was lost on an island." Her daughter heard her words and ran back to tell the grandmother what the Seafarer had said.*

*The grandmother said nothing. She knew the best way to teach someone was through deeds and not words. The next morning, the youngest daughter brought the Seafarer a bowl of greens. The Seafarer took one bite and cried out, "I feel like a poor goat that I must eat the pasture in my bowl! And not even a saltfish to give it flavor!"*

*The grandmother said nothing, but for the next meal, the youngest daughter brought a bowl of ground nuts mashed flat and thick at the bottom of the bowl. "Ayah!" The Seafarer cried, "This is like eating the mud pies I made as a child! How can I eat this and live?"*

*At last, the grandmother came out to where the Seafarer was loading her ship to sail the seas. "My child, you are the greatest of the seafarers. You have traveled east to the Kerek frontier, south to the Matasi grain fields, and north to so many countries I cannot name them all. But my love, this time I would ask you to sail to a land where even the air is perfumed with flavor. Capture those things which will make your senses sing my praises, your feet to rest under my table, and your children to smile to their friends with generosity in their hearts."*

*Well! Who could resist such a request as that? The very next tide, the Seafarer set her sails, skimming over the gentle waves, aided by the southern breezes.*

*Now even during the Wet there are crops to plant and tend: rice, sweet potatoes, kang kong, and amaranth. There are chickens to chase out of gardens, nets to make and mend for fishing, and all the tasks that make a well-run home.*

*At last, it was time for the harvests. Although the day's work flowed into the evening with everything that needed to be done, there was still time to cast a glance to the sea, to walk at the beach at sunrise, to look for a sail on the horizon. Each day the rains started later and ended earlier. At last the day came with the cry, "Sail!"*

*All the children ran down to the shore. At first the sail was so tiny, the Seafarer's mother thought there had been a mistake. But then, it grew large enough to know for sure—it was the Seafarer! Everyone ran to get the party ready. Chickens were sacrificed to the cooking pots, yams dug and put in the coals of the fire to roast. Children dashed about picking kang kong and other greens.*

*Suddenly, the islanders stood still and stared! Such a sight they had never seen! Behind the Seafarer's boat was an island! And not just a coral atoll, but one with vines, and trees, and plants everywhere! The Seafarer jumped off her boat and on to the sand and dropped a small bag into her mother's hand. "See if those spices will make your senses sing! Each of those spices has a plant on the raft behind me. We will grow them and cultivate them and scent the air with the smell of flavor!"*

*And so it was, my friends. And that is how all of the spices came to the West Islands."*

I laughed at Koanga's sly grin. "That's a little fanciful."

"But that's why I like it," said Willow. "The child complains, the mother sends her out to make it better, and the child comes home successful. What's not to love?"

"Well, when you explain it that way, I can see why *you* would like it," I teased Willow. She gave me a lopsided grin and whacked some cheatgrass alongside the road with her walking stick. We passed the rest of the afternoon in easy conversation, eating leftover stonebread along the way.

We reached the Coast Road crossing with two decons of daylight ahead of us. The crossing wasn't much: an inn, stables, a place selling food, and a handful of houses for the people who supplied the services.

We thought we would continue on to get closer to the Matasi border crossing, but the thought of a hot meal that wasn't stewed vegetables sounded incredible to me. It wasn't hard to convince Koanga or Willow either.

We walked in and found a table. After waiting a bit, I thought perhaps this was one of the places where you had to ask for the food with the barkeep since there was no one walking about the tables bringing food or drink. I walked up and waited to be noticed. When the man refused to meet my eye, I called out, "I want to buy food and drink for me and my friends. What do you serve?"

The man turned his back on me and walked away to the other end where a group of Kereki workmen were sitting. All of them silently watched me.

"Hey, I'm talking to you. I want to buy food," I repeated a little louder. Could he not hear me? I wondered.

A harried looking woman came out of the back. "Hush now, put your purse away. We aren't going to serve the likes of you. Go on now, be gone with you."

"We have coin. We want to eat," I insisted.

She looked exasperated. "Look around you, fool. You are in Kerek. Every person in here is Kereki, except for... oh look, you and your friend sitting with a half-witted Kereki boy. Now get out."

"Wait! I was born and raised in Kerek City," I protested.

She raised an eyebrow. "I'm not blind, boy. Now get out before the men in this place throw all three of you out. And they won't be gentle." She crossed her arms over her chest and waited.

There was no help for it. I walked back to Koanga and Willow and tipped my head towards the door. Willow grabbed my pack along with hers and we all headed outside. I shrugged my shoulders and tried to explain, "You know, I expected something like this in Matasi, but not here in Kerek. I can't see anyone turning down coin in Kerek." I took my pack from Willow.

She knocked her shoulder against Koanga's arm. "Ah well, whatever they had wouldn't be as good as what you make, Koanga. We'll just go a little farther and then stop for the night and a good meal. At least the countryside is getting greener."

Koanga was silent. Head down, he plodded on the other side of Willow. I leaned forward to catch his eye, and Willow put out her hand. "Not now," she mouthed silently. I looked ahead, shifted my pack, and we left the crossroads behind us.

* * * * *

The Coast Road was fine and broad. Willow said, according to legend, at one time Matasi and Kerek were friendly neighbors and they cooperated on building the road from Thodport, the southernmost Matasi port, through both countries and north to Kerek City and beyond to the Cold Mountains. Then she smiled and said, another legend told of a race of giants who built the road before either Kerek or Matasi was a country. When the first settlers came, they found a long, smooth road already in place and no inhabitants. Both stories were fanciful, but if I was a betting man, I would place all my coin on the disappearing giants, before I claimed Kerek and Matasi got along, now or in the past.

I could see a wagon and a few walkers far ahead of us, but no one near. It would only get busier. I stole another glance at Koanga, but he was still oblivious to everything but the hurt within him.

The good thing about the Coast Road was the number of rivers, creeks, and streams that crossed the road on the way to the sea. Wooden bridges, stone bridges, and corduroy roads, the sheer variety was interesting to me. While I was distracted with the bridges and roads, Willow remained watchful. She had reacted so quickly back at the inn, I assumed she had been denied food or lodging before. Which made me wonder, was that part of the reason she had been in Kerek?

"Willow?" I waited until she looked me in the eye. "How are you treated in the West Islands?"

She looked at me a long moment considering. I was starting to regret the question when she responded, "Truthfully, Red, I don't believe that is the question you are asking." She paused and then continued, "The difference between a flower and a weed is someone's opinion. It does not matter to the flower what it is called, but to be called a weed? It could mean life or death. The only home you say you remember is Kerek. You think of yourself as Kereki—or so you told the woman at the inn. But when the people of Sion Inn didn't see the Kereki pale skin— you became 'someone else' to them. And for a moment, you became Trouble—not by *your* actions, but by *their* judgment."

I considered her words. "Yes." I nodded.

Willow started walking again. "But to answer your question, I am a child of the West Islands. I am known and I am loved. I am treated well, Red, I am treated very well."

We walked in silence for a long while, and so I asked Koanga for a story. He turned and walked backwards for a few steps. "Stories are fine, but we didn't get any food at the last place, and I am more than hungry. Any chance of stopping soon?"

Willow looked out at the sun hanging low in the sky. "We're off kilter. Kerek has way stations and inns a day's walk apart, but we are going slower than most travelers, so we end up just short, or just beyond. If we keep walking until we find an inn, it will be full dark. If we stop now, it will mean sleeping rough. What's your choice?"

"Sleeping rough," Koanga replied. I shrugged in agreement, and we began a search for water, trees, and safety away from the road.

## CHAPTER 12

# TROUBLE ON THE COAST ROAD

I woke instantly. My instincts were screaming at me, and although I wasn't sure what had startled me awake, every muscle clenched in readiness.

I listened. Nothing. The fire was out, grey ash only. A soft breeze wafted through the canvas lean-to like the night air breathing. There. A soft footfall on dry sand...a serration, a slipping that didn't belong. I rolled to my hands and knees and carefully pushed myself up. Another footfall. This one across the fire on the other side of Willow's lean-to. I slid backward out toward the trees. I heard the sizzle of a lucifer and saw a spill of cheatgrass bloom with flame just as a man shoved it into Koanga's face.

I pulled the knife from my boot and flung it hard. It hit the man in the back near the shoulder and fell harmlessly to the ground. He turned, I launched myself forward to knock him down, and yelped as I fell to my knees. I saw Koanga roll away from the flame.

Another man stepped out of the shadows to my left twirling a huge staff like a katana. The staff had caught me across the stomach, and that was what had knocked me to the ground, winded and gasping for air.

"If it isn't our friends from Sion Inn. Good of you to amble along so slowly, not to get us all tuckered out following you. You are a thoughtful bunch, but somewhere you missed a thing or two. Point is, Festus and I own this part of the Coast Road, and there is the small matter of a traveler's tax you need to pay. Now I'm willing to take a look through your bags and see if you might have something I want. I'm sure a little barter will clear up this misunderstanding."

Festus picked up the knife that had glanced off his shoulder. "This looks like West Islands steel. That's a fine start." He shook Koanga. "I'll start with your bag."

Koanga pulled his arm away angrily. "I'll get it. Just take your hands off me."

The man waving the staff looked around. "Where's that Kereki boy traveling with you? There were three of you at the inn. What happened to him?"

My heart sank. It was true. Only Koanga and I were in the clearing. If Willow was out taking care of night business, she would be too far away to rescue us. She wouldn't have taken a weapon either. All I could hope is that these two would be content with only hurting us and not killing us and she could mend our battering.

"Gone," I wheezed. "He realized at the inn no good would come to him traveling with us. The first wagon of Kereki folk passed us by and he whistled off with them." I spat on the ground. "Not even a coin to us for feeding him for two days." I was glad it was too dark for him to see me closely.

"Ah. He liked your food. We like your coin. What can I say? Kerek likes you." The man with the staff chuckled at his own humor.

Festus had dumped out Koanga's bag on his bedroll and poked about. "By the Lost God and those who seek him, Rusty, take a look at this! There's enough West Islands steel in here to make us both rich." Festus reached for the bone knife at the same moment Koanga shouted something in Wester and danced towards the fire. Rusty raised his staff, Willow stood up behind the lean-to and dropped the loose canvas on Festus.

Koanga grabbed the burning torch from the ground. I rolled into Rusty's knees. He fell forward toward the fire, and Koanga shoved the torch toward us. Rusty threw up his hands to protect his face. Koanga touched the burning end to his palms. Rusty squealed in pain. I knocked him as hard as I could on his head, dropping him at my feet.

Willow was still struggling with Festus. He was tangled in the ropes of the canvas lean-to, but the knives were tangled in there with him, and it would only be a moment before he would cut his way free. Koanga took the burning torch and held it to Festus's trouser legs and leather shoes. Festus jackknifed inside the canvas and cried out as he burned his hands beating out the flames on his legs.

I cut a length of rope and bound Festus below the knees before I helped Koanga and Willow carefully unroll the canvas from the rest of him. He was gasping in pain and holding his red blistering palms. I looped his hands together as Koanga poured cold water over them to cool the burns. The rope I tied between his wrists and knees could have been longer, but I was in no mood to be kind. I was beyond angry. I bent over Rusty and trussed him the same way: ankles, wrists, and a short rope between the two. "Why did you follow us?" I kicked at Rusty when he didn't answer. "Why. Did. You. Follow. Us?" I repeated slower.

Koanga placed his hand on my arm and spoke softly, "Red, he's still out. He can't hear you."

I picked up Rusty's staff and walked over to Festus cowering on the ground. "What do you want to say, or do I get to beat you first?" I let the staff smack in my palm. Ouch, that hurt.

Festus cringed but spoke clearly enough, "Rusty's right. This is our territory. We sit in the Sion Inn, pick out our victims, and follow you down the Coast Road. We like families—slow wagons and most likely, all their earthly goods—but you caught our eye. You demanded to be served and claimed you had coin. We couldn't figure out what a Kereki boy would be doing traveling with a West Islander and a Conrosan. Maybe we thought you might be running your own game. Maybe we thought your little Kereki needed rescuing. In any case, we were wrong." He pulled on his ropes. "What happens now?"

I startled. A Conrosan! I thought about the fairy tale Willow had told us earlier and wondered how Rusty and Festus would even know of such a thing. I shook my head. I didn't have time to think of it now. I pretended to consider Festus's words.

"Well, by the rules of forced barter, I could strip you of your goods and leave you here alive. You would be free to prey on someone else, and we would have free passage through your territory." Festus nodded in agreement.

"But I don't believe you were only interested in forced barter, Festus. In fact, I distinctly felt you intended to leave no witnesses. And if later, our bodies would have been discovered in your territory, you would have merely claimed 'death by misadventure.' After all, to your eyes, only that one," I pointed to Willow, "was a Kereki."

I paused for effect. "And that was your mistake. You can call me anything you want, but every memory I have is here in Kerek, every lesson about how to survive was learned in Kerek, every fight I have fought, every crime I have committed was here in Kerek. You look like you and I are about the same age—but your master was Rusty—a lazy thief at best. My mistress was the Kerek City streets—and she shows mercy to no one."

I twirled Rusty's staff to point the dagger end down and slammed it into Festus's temple. His body spasmed in death and stilled. The anger and adrenaline rushed out of my body. I felt sick and wobbly about what I had just done, and I crouched down using the staff to balance myself.

I heard Koanga gasp beside the lean-to, but neither he nor Willow said a word to me as I pulled myself to my feet and walked back over to Rusty. He was either still unconscious or faking it well. I felt like my legs were going to go out from under me and I swayed as I slipped to my knees.

That's when Rusty exploded forward. He reached for the knife hidden under his side and kicked forward with his legs, knocking me on my buttocks. Panicked, I rolled to my side and kicked out with my feet into his face. He twisted his head away. Willow shoved a long piece of wood between us and Rusty's knife sank deep. Without that piece of wood, a direct hit would have killed me. Stupidly, I realized he had cut his ropes while we were distracted with Festus. As he pushed himself to his feet, he winced as his burned hands made contact with the ground.

That was all the hesitation I needed. I grabbed the wood and slammed it into his throat. He collapsed. I threw down the piece of wood and looked up to see both Koanga and Willow staring at me.

"You heard them. This is what they did. This was their territory. If we did not end it now, next time it would be a family, or children, or someone else. I had no choice. It was a forced barter gone wrong." I cringed at the disgust and horror in Koanga's face. "Tell me you understand."

Koanga pulled his eyes away from Rusty's body and looked at me. He nodded numbly but said nothing. His face crumpled as he looked away and I couldn't decide if he was going to be sick or cry. I realized I didn't want him to do either. Couldn't he understand I had just saved us?

"I understand." Willow's voice grew stronger as she continued, "We need to leave." She put her arm round Koanga.

"We had no other choice. We did what we had to do and now we have to pull ourselves together and live with this." She looked about the campsite. "We need to leave," she repeated. She absently rubbed his arm and then looked at him closely.

I agreed. I wanted to put as much space between this and us as possible. I stared at Koanga and wondered if he could walk. I looked at Willow and she gave me a grim look and nodded as if she understood my question. I needed something to focus Koanga's attention on something other than what had just happened.

I looked up at the night sky, at the stars overhead—more than I could ever count—sparking off against the moon. "Can West Islanders tell time by the stars? How long until morning?"

At first, no one answered me. Willow gently pulled herself up and away from Koanga. "Koanga. We have to go and you are the best one to lead us. Explain to Red how West Islanders tell time at night."

Koanga pointed to a cluster of stars about two hands width from the horizon. "It's the Dry, so the Seafarer's boat is visible in the sky. It appears to lead westward across the night sky settling at the horizon a decon before dawn." He used his shirt sleeve to wipe his face. Willow and I pretended not to notice.

"So we have two, three decons before the Coast Road starts filling with travelers," Willow clarified.

"Good. Light a fire, Willow, a fairly big one. Koanga, pack our bags—be sure to get everything." I had already bent down and started untying the ropes around Festus's body.

Within the decon, we were ready to leave. Rusty and Festus were propped up around a lively fire. I had already stripped them of their coins and weapons but left their empty purses and Rusty's distinctive staff. Willow had filled our water containers and helped Koanga roll up the canvas lean-tos and pack our bags. We washed ourselves carefully and swept the campsite of extra footsteps.

"I'll do that robber bird whistle if I need you, and you do the same," she touched Koanga. "Understand? We must be two small groups, but it increases the danger." I helped Willow put on her pack.

He nodded. "We'll be just behind, but still keep you in sight." She smiled at him and was gone.

I put both my hands on Koanga's shoulders. "Are you going to be all right?"

He snorted. "I will never be 'all right' until I am back on a ship to the West Islands." He glanced at the bodies propped by the fire. "How have you lived here and survived?"

"This is all I've known. For seventeen years, this is all Kerek City has taught me: act quicker, think faster, or be dead." I picked up my pack and shouldered it. "Come on. I want to keep Willow in sight. Travelers need to see us as too harmless and too small to take on these outlaws, so we aren't blamed for this. But that doesn't mean I want to put Willow in danger. We'll regroup at the next watering or whenever we see her turn off the Coast Road."

We walked the morning in silence. I knew Willow was confident about traveling in Matasi, but I wasn't happy she was the only one who knew what we would need to get through such a huge country. I wanted to know what might happen to us. "Hey, Koanga? Do you know any stories from Matasi?"

He looked up at me warily. "I don't know any stories, but I do know Willow was confident we would be able to travel safely through the country and sail to the West Islands." He kicked at a stone. "I know that it is different than what you have heard in Kerek City." He shrugged. "But if I am forced to believe only one of you, it must be Willow. No offense meant."

I shrugged. "I only know what I am told." I grinned at him. "So tell me what you know, so I am told differently."

"Mmm. Matasi is ruled by a Triune. Do you know what that is? It is different than a King such as Kerek and the West Islands or an Empress like Vikland. The Triune is three leaders: the Voice of God—that is the church; the Rule of God—that is the law and the courts; and the Fist of God—the military. The Rule of God is always a woman, Willow says, and the Voice and the Fist can be either man, other, or woman, but there cannot be three women as the Triune. These three work together to create a land in which all people are safe, treated fairly, and live in peace in service to the Lost God."

"The Lost God. Right...How did they lose him or her?" I smirked.

Koanga shot me a withering look. "He preached a message of kindness and demanded the meek and the weak should be cared for by those who had more. He was lynched by a mob of the wealthy and the strong for his troubles." He cut his eyes at me. "I am assuming they were Kereki, since they were so fond of purse and power. Then during the night, some of his followers cut him down from the tree and took his body away. Soon the stories started how he didn't die, just disappeared, and he will return when all people honor and respect him by honoring and respecting others."

"So he's not misplaced? Merely hiding?" I wondered how you could hide a god.

"Don't mock another's religion, it doesn't become you. He's not 'lost' as in 'missing.' He's 'lost' as in 'all men must seek him.' The Matasi believe living fairly and honestly will bring the

Lost God to appear on their doorstep at any time. So they treat everyone well, because they do not know what stranger will be their Lost God come to reward them for following his ways."

I kicked a stone along the road for a while. "That's very similar to your West Islands Traveler tales."

"I thought so too when Willow first told me of it. I would never have wished her misfortunes upon her, but now we find ourselves here, I am pleased to see Matasi for myself."

"What? You don't like Kerek? That's my home you know, I'm crushed!" I jostled next to him to bump shoulders and cast a sideways smile.

Koanga stopped in the middle of the road and looked at me gravely. "My friend. You heard Rusty back at the campsite call you a Conrosan. Willow told you the stories of your homeland to see if it would bring back a memory. No, my friend. A grave injustice has been done to you. Somewhere in the land of Conrosa someone weeps for you and longs to claim you as family."

I tightened my hands on the straps of my traveling bag. "Don't, Koanga. I'm Kereki. I only knew of Conrosa as a deserted embasado in Kerek City. I have never met anyone from there. I don't know what a Conrosan would look like. How can I be somebody from Conrosa if all I have ever known is Kerek City?" I stared at the road and watched Willow get smaller and smaller in the distance. "Willow says she is West Islander yet her skin is as fair, or fairer than most Kereki. Is that why she was chosen to accompany the ambassador's family to Kerek?"

Koanga stepped around and waited until I dropped my eyes to look at him. "You do not wish to talk about your homeland, Conrosa? Fine. But don't insult my intelligence by changing the topic to Willow and think I'm fooled." He turned back to my side and we started forward again.

Koanga explained, "Willow's story is her own, and she will tell you what she wants you to know. But let me tell you this. Willow is highly respected in the West Islands as a person of learning. Men and women are educated equally in the West Islands just as they are in Vikland. But Willow is one of many in her family, and she has been out on her own for seven years— ever since I started my apprenticeship as a storyteller. Her family loves her very much, but it is not her father who came to escort her home nor is it her father's coin which pays my way. But she is loved even when the coin wears thin."

I felt my heart crash into my boots. "So you are what? Trying to win her hand? Her future husband, her..."

Koanga whooped. Bent over his knees and laughed so hard he choked. I pounded him on the back, and as I started to feel more and more foolish, I started pounding a little harder.

Finally, he held up his hand. He stood up, and tears and snot were running down his face. He wiped his face on his sleeve and started laughing again. I scowled and kicked the dirt.

"My friend, my friend, my friend." Koanga tried to squish his features into a serious face, failed, and started snorting. I turned back to the road and started taking longer strides. Koanga scrambled to catch up and soon I could hear him puffing and half skipping, half jogging to keep up. "I am sorry, Red, I am truly sorry. I was unkind and the only thing I can say is I was caught unaware by your questioning."

"Yeah, well, I thought it was a reasonable question. You two are very protective of each other."

"Red, stop and look at me."

I stopped and turned. Koanga looked so serious.

"Red, I am a Storyteller of the West Islands. I have completed my apprenticeship and for three years I have held a home and hearth as my own. I must keep my home open to any Traveler who comes to our village. I will have neither wife nor children. I have told you already Willow is a scholar and a traveler. She has chosen a life in politics moving from court to Triune to whatever country our King or future Queen will send her. I came to rescue her in Kerek—and you see how well that is working out—but I came because Willow is my oldest sister, and I owe her so much."

"Your sister." I gave him my most skeptical look.

"My oldest sister—she convinced our father to let me apprentice when I was ten, even though it will bring him no coin, but only prestige as the father of a Storyteller. And say what you will about family pride—you can't feed a family on it."

I crossed my arms in front of me and looked down my nose at him. "And you expect me to believe that?" I grabbed his hand and laid it on my forearm. His touch warmed me, and I fought to ignore it. "Your skin, my skin, different colors. Your skin, Willow's skin, different colors. Your sister? My ear." I threw his hand off.

Koanga turned and started walking again. "And that part of the story is Willow's to tell." He picked up the pace, and soon I could see an inn ahead.

## CHAPTER 13

# AN UNWELCOME TRUTH

We caught up to Willow filling her waterskin outside the inn. Since there were other travelers around, she kept her steel flask in her seagrass bag. As we walked up, she struck a conversation with the others at the well, how far to the next town, any settlements along the way, how many days to the first port city in Matasi, and on and on. She flicked her eyes to us once, and then entered the inn with some of the other travelers. Koanga and I waited comfortably outside by the well. A stable hand came out and stared hard at us for a moment, but I just tipped back my filled waterskin and pulled a long drink.

Willow came out then, her seagrass bag a little fuller, and still chatting with the man and woman she had gone in with. We could easily overhear their conversation. They had been traveling in the wagons we had seen trailing along the way. They must have driven all night to get ahead of us. Not surprising, really. The wagon was clearly not full, but it was foolish of them to have just the two of them take so many goods through bandit territory.

Willow looped us easily into her conversation. "Hey! Conrosan! West Islander! I have learned today this road has bandits and outlaws. I did not know I traveled under such lucky stars. Perhaps West Islander, you have been lucky too!" She laughed and looked back at the waggoneer. We walked up to them until we were all gathered at the side of their wagon. "Perhaps we should all travel together," Willow offered. "The waggoneer says I can ride in the back in return for taking over sentry duty when we stop for the night."

Koanga picked up on her acting before I did. "Surely, it is not as bad as all that." He tipped his head to me. "My friend and I have traveled since Aldi with no trouble at all."

The woman pulled herself up onto the wagon bench and looked down at us. "Then you have been truly lucky indeed." She considered us carefully. "You don't have the height or breadth of my man, but the five of us could get Trouble to change her plans."

Willow looked to the woman. "Well, Kereki or no, I know I am no match for bandits. I take your offer of a ride in exchange for sentry duty and offer you my pledge, 'I mean no harm to you and yours.'"

Koanga pretended to dither. "There are three of you, and only two of us."

The man looked at Koanga and then at me. "My friend, we are Kerekis from Pagta. We know these roads. To not travel with us will only bring harm to you. I know in the West Islands, there are hospitality laws. I have heard some of your stories from other travelers. I know nothing of Conrosa except it is a place of learning and has four seasons. Please join us. I would hate for ill to befall you, and we had stood by and done nothing."

I threw my pack in the back of the wagon and scooted in, resting my back along the side. Koanga did the same on the opposite sideboard, but his feet didn't reach across and when the wagon jerked forward he nearly tumbled out.

"Whoa!" The waggoneer called. I jumped out and helped Willow up. She clambered over Koanga's legs next to the covered goods, then Koanga and I braced her in. The rocking motion was stronger than I anticipated and soon I saw Willow's eyes close, and then Koanga's.

Rusty and Festus had stumbled through our camp less than a day ago, but it already seemed part of the distant past. Killing them had not been my choice. In Kerek City, when Trouble came to dance with me, I either froze in fear or ran away. But this time, the moment I had backed into the shadows of the lean-to, I knew I would do whatever I needed to keep Koanga safe. It was a strange feeling to want to take care of someone else.

Willow must have rolled under the edge of the canvas as soon as she heard footsteps, or the lucifer strike, and realized it was not Koanga or me coming back from a night trip to water the trees. Her quick thinking to drop the tent on Festus made our escape possible. Koanga, my lovely Koanga, had stood by while Festus had dumped out his traveling pack. Was he truly so helpless? Or just drawing attention to himself so Willow and I could act unseen?

I thought about Koanga's revelation he and Willow were siblings. I searched their sleeping faces. Willow's features were finer but not soft. Both had the strong nose and the full brows of the West Islanders. I looked at Willow's left hand still encased in the cloth glove. Her shirt and tunic and trousers were all baggy enough to hide her body. She wore her trousers tucked in tight to her boots with the brightly colored Kereki ties about the tops— just as a young man in Kerek City would do.

I thought about how Willow and Koanga and even Rusty and Festus had called me a Conrosan. I was confused. How could others know this and I have no understanding of it? How could I be from a place I could not remember? If I wasn't a Kereki, what would this mean? I felt myself getting sick in my head and my heart and pushed the thoughts away. For now we were safe and I let myself drift off to sleep.

* * * * *

It was much later when I awoke. I watched the waggoneer's wife pass food to her man and my stomach rumbled. I knew Willow had food for us, but she was still asleep. I certainly couldn't grab her bag. That would only convince the waggoneer I was a thief. I waited until both were facing forward on the wagon seat and then I gently poked Willow's foot. She pulled it out of my reach, but opened her eyes.

"Hi, my name's Red. I know, I know. Red from Conrosa, how original." She blinked rapidly and for a moment, I thought she wouldn't catch on. I nodded once to the waggoneer's wife. "You probably didn't notice, but my friend and I weren't served back at the inn. I was wondering if I could buy some food from you."

Willow smiled. "I have bread and meat pies to share. Save your coin, it will be your muscle that will save my life tonight." She sat up and rustled about in her seagrass bag. She handed me a fat meat pie. I bit into it and nearly moaned in pleasure, it was so good. I nudged Koanga awake.

"Our friend is offering meat pies. She says she likes my muscles. I don't know, Koanga, you may have to charm her with a song or a story." I laughed at my joke, but everyone around me froze in horror.

Suddenly, I realized what I had done. I called Willow 'she.' A woman does not travel alone in Kerek—ever. Not only did I reveal her disguise, but I endangered her life. The waggoneer hauled back on the reins and stopped the wagon.

Willow pushed her way over our legs and jumped off the back of the wagon. Still holding on to the meat pie, she shoved it at Koanga. In the time it took the waggoneer to climb off the bench and come around to the back, Willow pulled out the string bag of food, dropped it in Koanga's lap, and started running.

The waggoneer caught her easily and dragged her back to the wagon and his wife. He twisted her arm behind her and waited for his wife to walk around to the back to meet them. She looked at Willow with hatred in her eyes. "You know it is not permitted for a Kereki woman to travel alone. And to dress as you are! You know this! You are an abomination. My man would be within his rights to kill you where you stand."

Willow looked at her feet, her halo of hair shielding her face. I was frozen in the wagon. I can't believe I thought this woman was kind. Her face was so contorted in anger, I barely recognized her. "How dare you, how dare you! A Kereki woman traveling as a man. How dare you!" She slapped Willow across the face, but it was Koanga who flinched.

Willow raised her head defiantly. "I'm not."

"You're not what?" The waggoneer's wife stopped mid-swing.

"I am not from Kerek and I am not traveling alone." Willow yanked her arm away from the waggoneer and pulled off her glove to show us brown skin as rich and dark as Koanga's, a perfect hand, pink-palmed. Willow reached down and pulled off her boots and linings, first one and then the other, and we were all staring at brown toes, brown feet, and brown ankles. She pulled at her Kereki ties around her legs and lifted the hems of the baggy trousers to her knees, her dark brown knees. She dropped her pant legs and looked at the waggoneer and his wife.

"I am from the West Islands, traveling in the care of my brother, and his friend, Red. I travel with a white face because we are hungry and will not otherwise be served. I wear trousers because we have walked from Kerek City. You have said it yourself, these roads are full of thieves and outlaws, and yet you want to punish me for disguising myself to travel safely. I said it before and I will say it again, 'I mean no harm to you and yours.'"

The waggoneer and his wife looked at each other and he led her away to talk to her out of our hearing. Willow bent down to put on her linings and her boots. I reached down and grabbed the second boot as she sat on the back of the wagon to put them on. She replaced her Kereki ties about her calves and carefully replaced her glove over her hand. She kept her face down and I could see a few white strands in her hair where the dye had not taken. I reached forward and took her now idled hands. "Willow, I am so sorry. I am so very, very sorry."

She looked at me, chagrined. "How could you do otherwise? This entire journey we have done nothing but improvise on the moment. I am only glad it was you and not Koanga."

"It's true then. Koanga is your younger brother."

She gave a half-smile. "Your mind never goes where I think it will, and yes. He would take care to say he is my younger brother. I am twenty-eight and he is but twenty. He is already a Storyteller on the West Islands, a man in charge of his own hearth."

The waggoneer and his wife approached us. I saw her staring at my hands still holding Willow's. I dropped my arms to my side, embarrassed. The waggoneer looked at me briefly, and then to the front of his wagon at his horses. "I think it is best if we part here. Now that I know the three of you are traveling together, I don't like you riding behind my back where the missus and I can't see you. We wish you no harm or ill, I just don't think we need to be carrying on together."

His woman pressed her lips tightly together and stared at Willow's boots. "It's still two more days to the Matasi border. I'm not sure what you are," she glanced at Willow's face, "but I know there are wicked men in Kerek who would find you to be a curiosity to be broken. Be careful."

They walked up to the front of the wagon, and he helped his woman up to the wagon bench and took his place beside her. He picked up his reins and without looking back, slapped the reins and called, "hiyah!" The wagon lurched forward.

Koanga and I scrambled to recover our traveling bags from the back of the wagon. I grabbed the string bag with the food and let it dangle for a moment as the wagon continued down the track. Willow shifted her own pack on her shoulders and looked about. She pointed inland.

"There's a string of trees, a bit far off the track, but the trees mean there is probably water. We could stop there for the night. I don't want to be eating their dust until sundown. I don't want them anywhere in my sight." She huffed, "'Be careful.' As if that could be an apology."

It was really too early to stop for the night, but Willow's site had an artesian spring pumping into a deep circular pond. There was enough water movement so the pond was clear and weed-free. We set up camp, washed our clothes, and took turns taking long baths in the pond. Willow had purchased vegetables, spices, and rice at the last inn, and Koanga simmered those into a dish that he said had "flavor dancing in the air." We sat about the fire, dressed only in shirts or tunics, all the rest of our shirts, skirts, trousers, and small clothes washed and drying on the bushes, or over the ropes of the canvas lean-to tied between the trees. I had thought tonight would be difficult with Rusty's and Festus' death, and the waggoneer and his wife's betrayal, but it seemed we were more relaxed with each other than we ever had been.

I watched Koanga. He had his tailoring kit out and was remaking the second dress he had purchased in Aldi. He separated the blue skirt from the top and asked Willow to wash out the gathers and wrinkles. I watched as Willow crossed behind the fire dressed only in a dry shirt which billowed about her bare brown thighs.

With Willow at the spring washing the fabric, I stood up and crossed over to Koanga. He glanced up once and went back to pinning and tacking.

"Where did you learn to be a tailor?" I asked.

"My father. He is very particular, very precise. He taught my brothers and I to be good tailors as well." He smiled at me. "He would have taught my sister, but she always had her nose in a book."

"You've saved us a lot of coin by changing and altering our clothes. No one in Kerek City would recognize us." I stared at his hands—needle flashing in and out.

"Well, we are not on a boat to the West Islands yet." Koanga gave me a half smile.

"And then what happens? You and Willow just get on a ship and wave to me standing on the shore?" His hands stopped, and I forced myself to look up at his eyes.

"Red, I owe you a life debt, many times over, I know this. Finding you on the road was my greatest blessing in Kerek. But I can't begin to fathom how your mind works." He paused for a long time. "I watched you kill Rusty and Festus. It was as if…" He tilted his head back and I could see unshed tears reflected in the sunlight. "It was as if they were no more than a scorpion or a snake that had gotten into a house and needed to be killed before it hurt the children."

I reached out slowly and put my hand over his. He didn't flinch, but he didn't turn his palm over to grasp my hand. "You are older than I am, Koanga, and neither of us are children," I said gently.

He snapped his eyes to mine. "And that is the first thought that comes to mind when I describe your talents for murder?" He jerked his hand away, and my hand dropped to my side.

Koanga took a deep breath and let it out slowly. He put aside his sewing and looked me full in the face. "Red, I care about you. I care for you. But not the way I believe you are interested in me. There is no harm or shame in that. The heart loves whom the heart loves."

He waited for my reaction. I had none to give him, so he went on, "I have my role to play on the West Islands. One I have spent years preparing for. You are not suited for the West Islands and neither is Willow. I wish you had spent more time with Willow. But you still can..."

"Wait, you're pushing me on your sister? Are you stupid?"

Koanga blushed. Even under his dark skin I could see how deeply he blushed, he was so embarrassed. "Red, say nothing until I am finished. Do you agree?" Again, he waited for my nod before he continued, "This is a conversation I wished you to have with Willow, but for whatever reason you are afraid of my sister." I protested and he looked at me sharply. "No talking, you agreed." He patted my hand. "That's understandable, sometimes she frightens me too." He grinned.

"Willow is a very rare gift on the West Islands. She is a dual soul. She is neither male nor female, black nor white, but all. She has a gift for many languages. She can dance with a man or dance with shadows." Koanga looked at me soberly. "When we found you by the side of the road, it was my West Islander heart that made us stop. Willow had already lived in Kerek for two years. She had failed to stop the assassination of our ambassador, or the death of his wife— a sister to our King—at the command of the corrupt Kerek court. She said you were a trick, a ruse to rob us. She only agreed to stop if I agreed she could abandon you by any means necessary throughout our trip. Instead, you have adapted to any role she has asked us to play. You have defended us, stole for us, you have lied and not fallen for your own lies. You have an interesting face that keeps others from looking too closely at Willow."

I laughed, and Koanga fell silent. He picked up his sewing and soon the needle flashed in and out, in and out.

I had a million questions, and I didn't know how to ask any of them. I had never heard of a dual soul but, as Koanga explained, it was the perfect description of how I saw Willow from the moment I met her coming back from the river near Aldi. Her greatest success depended on people seeing and believing what they wanted to, and not what was in front of them.

"Red? Could you ask Willow to bring me the fabric she is washing?" Koanga never lifted his eyes from his needle, and after a moment's wait, I rose and walked to the pond.

## CHAPTER 14

# A GIFT OF THE STARS

I saw her light shirt laying on a shrub so I thought I knew what I would find. Willow was facing away from me, standing up to her hips in the clear pond, her arm slowly sweeping the deconstructed dress back and forth in front of her. She was naked. Across her back I saw dark brown skin from left shoulder to right hip and down into the water line. Above was mottled greyish white. It wasn't a straight unbroken line—there were inkblots of color above the waist, as well as white skin like melted candles dripping into the rich dark brown.

"I know you are there, Red. You didn't exactly softfoot in." I could hear the amusement in her voice.

I cleared my throat. "Koanga says he is ready for the cloth."

"Did he now? And what else did he say?" Another slow sweep of the fabric across the top of the pond. She didn't turn. I was dressed and on the shore above her, and from that illusionary position of strength, I finally had the courage to put my thoughts into the air.

"He says you can do anything, and you are brave, and you worked for the ambassador, and you are very important to the King of the West Islands." I paused. "Actually, I figured that last part out a while ago." Another pause. "Everyone is looking for you, aren't they? When I was in Kerek City, everyone in Lowertown was talking about what happened when the ambassador was murdered. But it is not just the children missing, is it? The Viklander soldiers walking the streets of Kerek City are also asking about a West Islands softfoot called Ngahuru. The Matasi missionaries will give food and coin to any child who tells them where any West Islanders are hiding." I paused. "I think you know where the ambassador's children are. But until I saw you baring your legs before the waggoneer and his wife, I didn't see what was right in front of me."

"I wouldn't believe everything that falls out of my little brother's mouth. For example, he thinks you are very clever, and would be a valuable asset to the King of the West Islands," she commented dryly.

I snorted. "Can I ask you a question?"

"Red, you can ask me any number of questions, but before you begin, let me answer the one question you do not know how to ask. I was born this way. It is not a disease. It is merely a change in pigmentation. On the West Islands, we call it 'a gift of the stars,' or a 'kiss from the constellations.' In the oldest of the West Islands stories, souls who pass too close to the constellations on the way to earth are sprinkled with stardust and are born like me, or with some variation of this."

I could hear a smile in her voice. "I'm sure the great libraries of Conrosa would have another reason. Perhaps your stories would say I am fairy-touched and the fae have stolen the color from my skin. In Matasi, they call it, 'coal and ashes.' In any case, my small size, my dual skin, my boyish body, and everything I hated about myself when I was your age, has saved my life any number of times, as I have been able to hide in plain sight of those who hunt me."

She gathered the fabric together and twisted it free of water. "Now the next move is yours, Red. We have two days before we reach the safety of Matasi. In that time, you could probably sell me, as the waggoneer's wife said, to men of Kerek who would find such a curiosity worth their coin. You can travel with us to Matasi and the West Islands where you could find a home much safer than the one you left, or I can help you travel to Conrosa and find your people."

I said nothing. I didn't think I could keep my voice in control. "Why do you think I am from Conrosa? I remember nothing except Kerek City."

Willow stopped and turned her head over her shoulder. "Red, I believe one or both of your parents were Conrosan based only on the color of your skin. I know the Conrosan embasado has been deserted far longer than you have been alive. I believe you do not remember because your mind is protecting you from remembering. I think I can help you, but it is your decision if you want this."

Willow was offering safety, a home, even a family I didn't know I missed. What could I possibly say to that?

"You're a smart man to stay silent when you have a lot to think about. But, Red, I would truly like to get out of this pond, and I don't want to crawl out with you gawking at me."

"Stars! I am sorry. I am so sorry. I'm going, I'm going!"

I stumbled back into camp. Koanga looked up. "Did she decide to weave the dress herself?"

Willow came up the path behind me once again dressed in the billowing shirt. "Did you want to stitch it wet?"

"I do. It will make the seams look as weathered as the fabric. Lay it on my bedroll. I can sleep damp tonight. The weather is still warm enough."

Willow sat down at the fire and looked at me. "The clothes are still drying. Koanga is trying to stitch me into something beautiful for when we cross the inspection point into Matasi. I think, Red, you could teach me how to throw a knife like you did to try to stop Festus, or you can bake stonebread for our dinner tonight."

I looked at her. "You've noticed I haven't cooked a meal yet on this trip. I grew up in Kerek City, I stole my food, or I went without."

"A knife lesson, it is." She stood up and rummaged in her pack. "I have three to choose from. All are different."

I stood up and walked over to her bedroll. For the first time, we were close enough to each other, and I realized she stood just below my nose. I was lean and slight from growing up in Kerek City, but she was so small she would never be able to muscle her way out of a fight to stay alive.

"Willow, put down the knives for a moment." I waited until she did so and then quickly snatched her off the ground with her hands pinned to her side. She twisted and squirmed and then went limp.

"You can't fight your way out." I set her down gently and looked at her sadly. "Neither could I, it is why I learned to run so fast."

She bristled. "There's not a lot of demand for either while gathering secrets. I know how to hide, to evade, and how to act a part." She paused. "I only need to kill those who threaten me and mine."

"You were going to kill me if I was a problem on the road to Aldi."

Willow wheeled on Koanga. "You told him?"

He shrugged. "I had my reasons."

"Koanga." Willow fell silent and Koanga kept his head down, cutting fabric along a pinned line. The only sound was the snip of his shears and the snap of the fire.

I cleared my throat. "If you want, I can go for a walk or something and you two can, ah, talk things out."

"That might be a good idea, Red." Willow never even turned to look at me.

I wandered off north to the edge of the tree line and beyond. We were too far west to be easily seen so I walked parallel to the main track keeping my eye out for other travelers in the distance. The sun was drifting down fast, and stragglers would be hurrying towards shelter at crossroad inns or easily defended campsites. We hadn't set up watches on our journey so far. Until yesterday I felt I could outrun our attackers, depending on the fight. Few, very few, carried steel like the West Islands knives Koanga and

Willow carried so casually in their packs. Even the steel shears Koanga so nonchalantly used for his tailoring would command two handfuls of coins in Kerek City.

I thought of the few iron or copper blades I had seen—beaten metal mined from shallow pits. The blades could hold an edge for a fight or two but then turned more claw than blade, or snapped off in mid-fight. Koanga and Willow carried enough steel to turn any fight into a rout.

Mmm. They had already gifted me the blade from Brick. I touched the handle now hidden in my boot. I wondered how they could gift me another.

I threw myself down in the sand and looked up at the clouds. Koanga, my lovely Koanga. The sand was warm and soft, and I pictured Koanga sitting on his bedroll, knees out, ankles crossed, pins, shears, tapes, and threads rainbow-shaped around him, reaching without looking, confidently cutting, stitching magic for our next act. I remembered as he had walked back to camp after his bath in the pond, tousled curls drying, red lips smiling. "Ah, Red! I forgot how great it feels to be clean again!"

I wondered what it would be like to live on the West Islands where you could be kind to anyone, where you could walk to the next neighborhood, the next city, the next crossroads, and know you could buy a meal and receive a smile for your business.

Was that why Koanga was so kind to me? Or could I hope for something more? When he had said he didn't care for me the way he thought I cared for him, did he mean not at this time? Or never? I decided I wasn't ready to examine that puzzle too closely.

I wondered what Conrosa would be like. If I still had family there, would they know me? Could I be a lost prince with a castle, like a fairy tale Willow had told us on the first day on the road together? I wondered if we could go together, Koanga and I, not like this, but better somehow. I wondered what was happening in Kerek City. If I never returned, how long before my hiding place was looted, my name forgotten? I tried to remember a time when I wasn't living on the streets, trying to hide my way out of danger, steal my way out of starvation. What would it be like to go to Conrosa—to have people look at the color of my skin and try to speak with me? If I didn't know the language would they get angry? Think me simple minded? Would they assume I was mocking them, and I would come to harm? I couldn't read—not in any language—and Conrosa was known for education and knowledge. Would I be thought a fool, or worse?

A wave of despair washed over me. I didn't have a name I remembered. I had only ever been called 'Red' for the color of my skin. How would I even begin to find a family that had lost me? What if I hadn't been lost at all? What if I had been stolen or sold or...

When I finally walked back to camp, the sun was no longer overhead, and the day had a golden glow about it. Willow was standing in front of Koanga, her arms straight out, wearing the dress he had been working on all afternoon. It looked nothing like the bedraggled, tattered thing we had bought from the rag and bone man in Aldi. There was lace and ribbons Koanga had conjured up from somewhere, scraps of fabric inserts on the sleeves I recognized from the lordling clothes I had been found in, touches and ties from other clothes worn earlier. Willow's body was not womanly, but Koanga had cinched the waist and ruffled the neckline to add the illusion of curves. He peeked under her arm and asked, "Well?"

"Koanga, you are incredible!"

Willow scowled, and Koanga burst out laughing. "Red, my friend, you are to say, 'Willow, you look lovely!' All you've done now is praise my work, which needs no further praise." He shot me a wicked smile. "And insult my sister. All this, after I just spent the better part of the afternoon cajoling her into better spirits!" He twitched the skirt one final time and said, "There. You're done. Take it off and try not to turn it into wrinkled laundry before we need it."

I turned my back and Koanga came to join me. Behind us, we could hear Willow slithering out of the dress and back into her other clothes.

"Did you get everything all sorted out between the two of you?" I asked softly.

"Of course. We are siblings. We cry foul, we fight, and then we admit no one has so many friends they can afford to throw away family." He put his hand on my shoulder. "And you? You were wrestling with yourself, I wager."

"I was, but no one has declared a winner," I said sadly.

Koanga patted my shoulder and dropped his hand. "You have time. Two days to the border and another seven days, maybe eight, before we reach the first of the Matasi ports."

"Just ten days?"

Koanga paused and then lowered his voice as if he was telling me a secret. "She won't have an easy meeting with the King and his advisors when she gets home. I think she'll post out quickly if she can. I won't be able to join her again, as I have my own duties to attend to when I return home."

"I'm right here. You don't need to talk about me as if I'm dead." I flinched at the sarcasm in Willow's voice.

Koanga turned swiftly and grinned at her. "My dear Willow, I am so accustomed to women taking ages to dress I must serve finger sweets in my tailoring rooms."

"Then you spend far too much time with father at the palace." She stepped over to the fire. "What are you making for evening meal anyway?"

"I was the only one working all afternoon and now you expect me to cook as well?"

"Yes, I do. Because you see these little feet of mine? They are walking to the pond to gather up and fold all the laundry we did today. You want a kitchen boy, you ask that pretty face standing next to you!" She waved her hand over her head and walked down the path to the pond.

I looked at Koanga. "You heard her. Tell your kitchen boy what to do."

## CHAPTER 15

# TITIRO MAI KI AHAU

The time at the pond had been good for all of us. I didn't know my life, but I finally felt I had one. I still thought of myself as Kereki, but now every time I said the word, "Conrosan," it felt…less strange. From the moment the West Islanders had found me, I had grabbed on tight and hoped they would take me with them away from Kerek City. Now, Willow had given me three futures, two I considered possible. If she was the great softfoot, Ngahuru, everyone was looking for—she hadn't truly said one way or the other—she had power to make those futures happen.

As we swung along the road the next morning, I could feel her lightness. With her secret in the open between the three of us, there was an easiness that hadn't existed before. We talked of what we might find in Matasi. I said I was worried the stories I had heard in Kerek City of how strangers to Matasi were treated did not match Willow's stories of what we would find.

She asked about rumors I had heard in Lowertown regarding the ambassador's children, and Koanga asked questions about Conrosa.

"So you've never been to Conrosa?" Koanga asked one more time. "And the only language you speak is Keresh—castle Keresh, no less. Who would have taught you, Red? Someone protected you for a time, and then they didn't. If you were old enough to remember words, you should remember your protector. How can you not remember this person? Why would that be?" He blew out a breath. "And why not call you by your name? To call you 'Red' or 'Conrosan' is not a kindness, it is an insult. It says you are nothing but the color of your skin."

I was tired of him trying to puzzle it out. I was still trying to puzzle it all out and until then, I was Red. That was all I knew for certain. I looked at Willow in exasperation.

She cocked her head, and then gently asked, "Koanga? Why don't you tell us one of the great tales?"

Koanga looked up in surprise. "I was just thinking I would like to hear one from you. Do you know any from Matasi?"

Willow considered. "No, not that I can think of. But I do know another one from Conrosa, if you wish." She dropped her voice into a storyteller's cadence and began.

*"Long, long ago there lived a wise and thoughtful Queen who lived in the land of Conrosa. Now Conrosa borders the land of the fae to the north and to the west. The great ocean lies to the east and the Shale Mountains keep the rains from escaping to the south. It is a tidy land with strong borders and no wars.*

*Now one night a fluttering of fairies (for that is what a group of fae is called) crossed into Conrosa to cause mischief. Alas, this wasn't an uncommon occurrence. Many of the fae are long lived, and when too much time and too little work abounds, Trouble is sure to follow.*

*The first farm the fae came to had a tidy little barn with a cow and a calf, a snug little pen with sheep, and a lovely little house with a garden of ripe and ready vegetables. Well, first the fairies milked the cow and drank all the cream, then they magicked the wool from the sheep, threw it in the river, and scattered the poor naked beasts into the hills. Finally, they trampled the garden and nibbled on all the vegetables. Once they had done all the damage they could think of, they ran down the road laughing and giggling to think what the farmer would say when he woke up.*

*The moon was still high in the sky when the fairies reached the village mill. Oh! This was going to be as much fun as the farm! They tossed the bags of corn, wheat, and barley about so it fell like fairy dust around them. They pushed the millstone to the floor and tied the waterwheel to the weeds below so it would not turn. Then once again, they ran laughing into the night, over the border and safe to their beds.*

*Now the next day, the farmer and the miller saw the damage that had been done and called the village to witness. The villagers clicked their tongues in sympathy and helped the farmer gather his sheep from the hills, pull the wool from the river, and harvest his vegetables that could be saved. At the mill, they put the millstone back on the hob, dove in the river to untie the wheel, and swept up the grain for the livestock.*

*As they worked, the villagers planned what they could do to prevent this from happening again. Finally, they decided this was not a neighborhood dispute, but between the kingdoms of Conrosa and Fairyland. So, they sent a message to the Queen.*

*Now the Queen was already training her two daughters to be wise and kind queens in their own right. So when she received the request from the village for help, she called in her daughters and asked what should be done. For while the fairies merely regarded their antics as a night's mischief, to the farmer and the miller this was a grave and costly injury.*

*The princesses retired to the castle library and began to read and study the great legends. At last, they had a plan. They sent out word to Zren Janin, the son of a fae who was a champion of the humans. If he would share his wisdom, they would be able to live in peace with their neighbors.*

*One day, while they were waiting to hear from the great Zren Janin, a weaver came to the castle and asked to speak to the princesses and their mother. He offered his services to visit the King of Fairyland for a year and a day, and to see if they could not come to some sort of agreement so no more Conrosans and their livelihoods would be harmed.*

*"Oh, but we have asked for Zren Janin, the great hero of Conrosa, to be our champion and prevail against the King of the Fairies," the youngest princess announced. "It shall be a great battle!"*

*"Oh my!" the weaver said. "Well, I do not think this is such a large problem we need to ask the great Zren Janin. Let me muddle about and see the King of Fairyland. If I do not return, then please, send for Zren Janin in all haste and have him bring me home."*

*Now the Queen cautioned him that fairies could be tricksters and to be careful in his words and actions. But she granted his request. She sent the weaver to the border with a letter of introduction, stamped with her great seal of her Queendom so he could meet the Fairy King to share wit and weavings and to see if there could be peace between the land of fae and men.*

*At the end of a year and a day, the Queen and her daughters stood at the edge of Fairyland to greet the weaver as he returned. He drove up to the border crossing in a wagon, heaped high with fabrics of every color and texture. The ropes used to tie the fabrics down were so long they could drop from the castle ramparts to the road below.*

The Queen's guard circled the wagon and the weaver jumped off and bowed before the Queen.

"Were you treated well, my weaver?" The Queen smiled at him.

"Yes. For a year and a day, I wove blankets of pleasant dreams and spider silk, tunics of bravery and flax flowers, gowns of beauty and meadow rue. I thank you for the honor of trusting me to work on your behalf with the fae. For this honor, I have brought you a gift as well. This wagon is full of a fabric which is beautiful to look at but creates a magic barrier that anyone with ill intent, fae or human, cannot cross. Let us hang these banners together and hide Conrosa from the eyes of Fairyland."

The Queen considered him and then nodded. "It will be as you say. But what boon do you ask for yourself?"

The weaver smiled wryly. "You remembered me, my queen. And yet you kept your secret, so that the King of Fairyland was content to indulge me at his table and his castle. If he would have known me as Zren Janin, he would have been difficult, just to prove he could. There is power in a name, and not all power must be displayed. The best perfumes are subtle, my queen."

"They are indeed, my child." And that is why, even to this day, many a person in distress is aided by a hero with no name. And only after he has passed, do they realize they have met Zren Janin." Willow smiled at me, a wide-open smile of friendship.

I smiled back. It had taken me days to figure it out but both Koanga and Willow, who I now knew for certain was Ngahuru, used stories to teach me the how and the why to the questions I asked or needed to ask. I wondered if all children were taught this way in the West Islands, or even Conrosa. I wondered if I would ever know what it would mean to be a Conrosan.

We walked in silence for a moment, and then Koanga said, "That's a good fable. Now that I know Conrosa doesn't have constellation tales, I can understand it better. Each country uses their own knowledge to create their culture. It's up to us to take the time to understand the stories that make their lives, and not wish their stories to be like ours." He paused. "I would like to go to Conrosa and learn more of their stories, but not if it is like Kerek."

Willow shot me a glance. "I think it's more than possible. Conrosa is so far to the north of us, they have four seasons. If I remember them correctly, they are the Season of Hope, the Season of Life, the Season of Harvest, and the Season of Rest. I for one, would like to know what that is like. They value learning and education. They create paper—so much paper that they can export it to other places. I think you would find stories from many lands written there, and I would hope you could share many of the West Islands tales as well." She chuckled. "From what I have read, my little brother, it is *nothing* like Kerek."

I looked about us then. The road had gotten busier. There were more people from Matasi riding horses and in carriages on the road. They would turn off on side roads, over bridges to large estancias we could see inland in the far distance. There were also walkers dressed for working in the citrus groves and fruit orchards. Their hats were funny looking to me: a covering of the head with a long hard bill in the front to shield their dark eyes, and cloth at the back which draped down to their shoulders like a woman with her hair unbound.

I had seen Matasi traders and their bodyguards at the docks in Kerek City, their dark eyes, olive skin, and fine clothes, in sharp contrast to pale and dirty dock workers. But Koanga was staring openly whenever a horse and rider would go past with the richly decorated saddles and silver trappings, enclosed wagons embossed with letters and pictures. The men wore their hair chopped short, like the street fighters did in Kerek City to keep their opponents from grabbing them by the tail or braid, although I doubted the Matasians did it for the same reason. There were women workers as well. Their skirts divided like oversized trousers, and they wore their hair in short curls or wound about their head, but the rest was the same.

No one paid us any attention. As Willow said, it was harvest season. The season was so short and the need was so great, itinerant workers came from all over to work the fields and groves and orchards.

That night, we could see campfires blazing all up and down along the streams and main road. We had trouble finding a place with enough distance from the others. Once we did, other workers came along and camped nearby, crowding us. But Willow had already built our fire, and it was too late and too dark for us to move, so Koanga shrugged and started cooking.

We had finished eating and were still relaxing in front of the campfire when we heard horses approaching. All three of us jumped to our feet when we heard a man's voice call out in an unfamiliar language. I looked to Koanga and he shook his head at me, but Willow confidently stepped forward and replied in the same language. She said some reassuring words and a dozen horses and their riders stepped into the fading light. She said a few words more, raised her hands to show they were empty, and without turning away from the riders, spoke to us in Keresh.

"He says he owns the estancia that borders this road. He and his workers patrol to ensure no harm is done to travelers. I said we were passing through and grateful for his oversight. He asked our destination and I said Alenti, the capital city of the Triune."

The man broke in again, and Willow replied in Mata. The conversation continued for a short while, and I didn't know if we should continue standing, or sit down and look relaxed. The men and women with him didn't look menacing, but they all had thick wooden canes, longer than the cudgels I had known in

Kerek City. Some had short bows with a small quiver of arrows over their backs. On one woman's saddle was a knife handle sticking out of a sheath as long as my forearm. I couldn't imagine what the rest of that knife would look like.

By the tone of the conversation between the estancia owner and Willow, we must have been deemed to be non-threatening. She smiled as she said a few more words, he said what obviously seemed like "goodbye and good luck," and nodded to Koanga and me. His group moved off down the road into the gathering darkness to greet the next campers.

"I thought we wouldn't reach the Matasi border for another two days?" Koanga questioned.

Willow nodded. "We won't. While I was working in Kerek City, I heard rumors Matasi was buying up a lot of the orchards and farms around the border. The Kereki farmers and merchants visiting the city boasted the Matasians were overpaying for the farmland, but the payments were in cash, and who were they to cure the buyers of their foolishness?" Willow trailed off, lost in thought. "I think this show of benign force is to let travelers know they are safer under Matasi rule than Kerek. If it is so, then no one will challenge the Kerekis losing their homeland, once the coin runs out and the Kerekis learn they have sold their birthright. Meanwhile, the Matasi move the border northward with little harm to their outlying settlements." She tapped her chin with her forefinger. "I wonder who is actually paying for the farms. The Triune? The grain traders? I doubt the farmers. Their cost will be in labor—and in blood—if it comes to war."

I stared at her. "You got all that from a moment's talk with a farmer?"

She smiled at me. "No. What I got from him was a lot of questions. He had met a Conrosan once before many years ago, so he knew what you were immediately. I told him you and Koanga were friends from the academies in Vikland. That the three of us were traveling to Alenti to find work as translators and in the trades in the Trader's Hall. We had heard so much of the bounty and beauty of Matasi, we couldn't wait to see it even though I was the only one who spoke Mata at the moment. I thanked him for his watchful eye over the travelers and the quality of the road we traveled. He said if we did not find work in Alenti to return here, he would like to talk more with the Conrosan about his country. That's what I got from the moment's talk with the farmer."

Koanga only said, "*Titiro mai ki ahau.*"

"Yes." She turned back to the fire. "We're safe here, and I am ready for an early bed."

"Wait! What did Koanga say? I only recognized it as Wester."

"I said, 'Look at me.'" He paused before continuing, "I meant nothing more or less than that."

I squinted at him and scowled, but he just gave me a benevolent smile and started picking up the campsite in preparation for bed.

## CHAPTER 16

# THE ORPHAN MASTER

When I woke, I could hear Willow and Koanga talking softly in Wester. I realized suddenly how much they had spoken Keresh in all our conversations to keep me included. That they had switched last night and this morning into Wester meant something—even if I didn't know what that something was. I lay there with my eyes closed, trying to pick out words in the swoop and dance of the language of their home.

I wondered how hard it was to learn another language. Koanga obviously spoke Keresh and Wester, Willow had spoken Mata last night, and said she had taught herself to read enough Conrosan to enjoy a book of children's fairy tales. Maybe it was something I could do. There were always sailors coming off the docks in Lowertown nattering in their own tongue. I laughed to myself. I had survived Lowertown by running faster and hiding from anyone bigger than I was. To confidently stroll up to a sailor who was a head or two taller than I was, or had forearms the size of my thighs, would be the height of foolishness. No, I was better off where I was. I couldn't imagine Koanga devising any amount of Trouble I couldn't survive.

Soon, I could hear the sounds of a fire being set, and the clang of empty pots being carried out of the camp, presumably towards water. I rolled out and made a show of stretching and wiping my eyes of sleep before walking into the shrubbery a ways to relieve myself. It was only Koanga at the fire. Willow must have gone to get water.

"Any chance we get oats and berries for breakfast? Or is it stonebread again?"

Koanga cocked an eyebrow. "For a man who refuses to cook, you have developed some fancy eating habits. But yes, we can have oats and honey. Maybe I can find a few dried berries at the bottom of the food bag." He looked at me soberly, "Willow says we have not traveled as far as we should. We won't reach Matasi tonight. This will be fine. We can wear our traveling clothes today and then change to our finery tomorrow just before we reach the border crossing and beg for admittance."

"Will it be hard? I just thought you walked up to the border and over. I thought that's what the people did when they walked off the ships in Kerek City."

"We don't know for sure. Willow and I have travel papers, but she expects they are searching all West Islanders. You are a

Conrosan without papers. She had an idea to get you through, but now with the heavy Matasi presence this far north, she is not sure they will be so casual about visitors to their country. Remember when you searched the pockets of Goblin and Brick? You had found a travel pass and papers from Matasi and gave them to Willow. It was probably from one of their victims, but Willow has studied it and it looks like we need to be questioned at the border. She says once we are in the country, we will need to have a travel pass everywhere we go. She also says there is an extra tax for Kereki citizens, so you must be a Conrosan in word and deed, and Willow will dye herself again before we present ourselves."

He smiled at me. "We will spend today trying to find out who you are. You must have a name to enter Matasi. I do not think 'Red' is allowed."

Willow came back with the kettles filled with water and two ripe mangos. "There was a small tree by the water. It looks like it has been heavily picked but these two were overlooked."

"Excellent! Our friend here has decided that nothing less than oats and honey will do for first meal. We will add these and be able to walk all day on the results."

I stood up. "I'll tear down camp. Let me know when the food is ready."

* * * * *

Now that we, or Willow rather, had gathered information from the estancia owner last night, she was more deliberate, more thoughtful, in sizing up those we encountered on the way. We all noted more Matasians traveling north in wagons, men on horseback looking more like soldiers than farmhands. After a few decons, both Koanga and I were getting fidgety with her slow pace and silent assessments. He muttered something in Wester just loud enough for her to hear, and she snorted in response.

She turned to me and spoke Keresh, "Forgive my brother his bad manners in speaking Wester in front of you. He didn't want you to know how impatient he was with my information gathering. He believes all I do is go in to see the King and his advisors, curtsy well, and they throw a bag of coins at me. But Red, you have survived by the knowledge you see around you. Does this not look like a peaceful occupation?" She waved her hand about. "The only Kerekis we see are farmhands or itinerant workers. How have the people not realized they have sold their country away for a few bright and shiny coins? Where are the owners? The men of business or trade?"

Koanga muttered in Wester again, and then repeated himself louder in Keresh. "They are eating their midday. Just as we should be doing. However, we have traveled such a slow place we must eat as we walk...again."

I smiled. "I thought our oats and honey was going to keep us walking all day?" I sighed loudly. "It appears once again our cook has overpromised his delicacies." We all laughed, but Willow guided us off the track to a clear running stream and some shade. We sat down. She filled our containers with cold water, and we drank and ate stonebread and honey and a bit of hard cheese Willow had tucked away in her carry bag from two days ago. Koanga stretched out and was asleep almost instantly.

"We'll reach the border tomorrow," Willow began. "Did Koanga tell you there is an extra tax on those from Kerek? It's going to be a problem because Keresh is the only language all three of us speak in common. I can't afford the tax, Red, it's expensive."

I picked up and tossed a pebble in the air. "Why the tax? Is there one on West Islanders?"

"No. West Islanders get along with everyone." She gave me a big grin. "Truthfully, the other countries covet our steel and metal workings. They are nice to us because of what we have, not so much who we are. But Matasi borders two countries. Kerek, with which it has had a very unhappy history—think of siblings that cannot get along. They have the same alphabet, and the languages are similar. At one time, generations ago, they both worshipped the Lost God. But the rich in Matasi got richer, and poor Kerek got a succession of bad kings in Kerek City. Matasi sniff their noses and says Kerek just needs to work to build a better country and they could be wealthy too. Kerek just looks at the broken pieces of their country and wonders where to start."

"And the other country is...Vikland?" I guessed. I knew the Spice Island was across the sea. I had seen their sailors in Dockside with their many gold rings on their fingers and ears. I had seen Viklander soldiers in Lowertown. Truthfully, I didn't know of anyone else.

"Yes." Willow nodded. "Vikland is a huge country with lots of natural resources but surrounded by mountains with no seaport. It is straight north of Matasi over the Silver Mountains, and straight east of Kerek. Have you seen Viklanders in Kerek City, Red?"

I nodded. "Tall. Men and women wear their black hair in a single long braid down their back. They have unmarked faces, no tattoos, no jewels. They look very different than Kereki, and I don't just mean the golden skin color. The women don't hide their faces or drop their eyes when you meet them on the street." I stopped and tried to think of how to describe it. "It's how they carry themselves. Men and women dress the same and carry either a crossbow or a..." I tried to use my hands to explain the long wooden thing as thick as my forearm and nearly as long as my leg.

"Tahn bong. The short ones are called tahn bongs and the long ones—longer than we are tall, Red—are called jeong bongs. It's a weapon used in pairs. It is said 'two Vikland warriors, skilled in the jeong bong, can hold off a dozen fools.' Vikland and Matasi are allies and have been for years. Vikland values courage and strength—it is a warrior culture. And Matasi values the purse and their religion. Because Vikland is a country surrounded by mountains on three sides, generations ago it negotiated free passage from Vikland to the Kerek City port, on the Northern Track and the Old Vikland Road, from one of the last honorable Kerek Kings."

She huffed. "In reality, *this* Kerek King seldom enforces any laws along the free passage. The Viklanders and their wagon trains are often preyed upon by outlaws and thieves. So, the Empress met with the Matasi Triune to arrange for Viklanders to cross over the Silver Mountains by guides through the mountain passes. However, that way is also difficult. It can't be done during the Wet season because there are mudslides and heavy mists. It is also impossible to carry many goods or to travel with the very young and the very old."

Willow smiled sheepishly. "I find their language is impossible for me to learn, they have a completely different alphabet and diphthongs, and as beautiful as their country is, I will probably never be skilled enough to be posted there."

"Is it a beautiful country?" I looked around us at the scrubland and cheatgrass.

"It is so beautiful, Red, the youngest princess of the West Islands went to the academies in Juisiti, fell in love with the country and one of its people, and remains there to this day."

"Mmmm. Is that one of your great stories, too?" I squinted at her.

"Oh no," she laughed. "It all happened before I was born. But it is a story still told occasionally. Her only brother, the oldest in the family, sits on our throne now. His oldest daughter will follow him as Queen when he dies and sails the Seafarer's ship across the skies. But when the King was young and new upon his throne, he tried to rule his sisters' affections as well as his country. He had other younger sisters, and they married as he bid them, but the youngest one had to renounce her claim to the throne before she could marry the Viklander she loved." Willow flashed me a mischievous smile.

"As the newly appointed tailor to the king, my young father hid his new wife along a passageway, so they were able to see the couple after they married, and before they sailed back to Vikland. When my mother told me this story, she said the Viklander was the most beautiful man she had ever seen, and swore me never to tell my father. Now if that isn't going to put ideas in a young child's head about the beauty of the Viklanders, then I don't know what will."

I laughed along with her, and Koanga sleepily opened an eye. "Tell me you weren't laughing at me," he yawned.

"We weren't laughing at you," Willow said deadpan, and we both started laughing again.

Koanga scowled and sat up. "Well now that the princess is awake," he muttered, "I suppose it's time to pick up and carry on." Willow pushed herself up and reached out her gloved hand to pull up Koanga.

"Why black?" I blurted out. "You could wear a white or greyish white glove and most people will never notice. By wearing a black glove, it's like you *want* them to focus on your hand."

"I do," Willow said simply. "If they look at my hand, they do not look closely at my face. If the next time they see me, they see a West Islander who looks familiar, but they can't remember where, and they see my hands are both brown and bare, well then perhaps they think they are mistaken. In Wester, we call it 'titiro atu' or 'look away.'"

"That's not what you called me last night, after the estancia owner left us."

"Ah, no. We said, 'titiro mai ki ahau,' which means 'look at me.' In Aldi, we saw notices and rewards for my capture and live delivery to the King. In the Sion Inn, and the Coast Road inn where we met the waggoneer and his wife, there were written descriptions posted of me as a female West Islander, and the Matasi guard accompanying me. By focusing people's attention on you, a rare and unusual Conrosan, or on Koanga, a Storyteller who is always talking," she smiled at him, "they see what we want them to look at, rather than what is in front of them."

"Was there a Matasi guard?" I wondered what happened to him or if he was the one who had taken the coin and their belongings to the ship.

"Yes and no." She bobbed her head. "At the embasado, there was a Matasi guard who often accompanied me when I had to go out. But he is not here today and more than that I cannot say."

I led out of the clearing and back to the track. I huffed along in silence for a while and then slowed down. I didn't need to be mad at Willow, she had just said she couldn't tell me, not that she wouldn't. But she should know how that feels.

"Hey, Koanga. You got a story for us? I'm tired of listening to my feet complain."

"I have one," Willow called out. "See if either of you have heard of this one."

"*Not so long ago and not so far away, the Orphan Master of Kerek City ruled his domain with a benevolent eye. Since the King had only the one harbor, all of the ships of all of the countries wanting to trade and travel within Kerek, had to come to Kerek City.*

*Not only was the Orphan Master a friend of the King (he paid the King well for the privilege) he was a very important man indeed. It was the Orphan Master's responsibility to meet each ship and learn who had not survived the passage. He would take charge of any children from the ship who could not make their way alone in the world. Sometimes, if the child could speak, or if a sibling was old enough, he could get a name, a location, of someone in Kerek who could come for the children and take them away—after they had paid the food and shelter costs of his benevolence. For everyone knew, the Orphan Master had not become a wealthy man known to the King due to his charity towards his charges.*

*Sometimes, if the parents on the ship had taken a long time to die, they would be considerate enough to write down who the children were, and where they should be sent. But the Orphan Master could only read and write Keresh, and if the parents had the misfortune to write their instructions in the language of whatever scrap of land they called home, well he could hardly be expected to understand their wishes.*

*So, the Orphan Master would meet with the captain to gather the children. He would settle with the captain for the costs they* incurred and bundle his new goods down the gangway and to the holding house. There would be food and shelter and a quick visit by the healer to ensure the child did not have the misfortune of harboring the same disease which had carried off the parent. Then there was all the trouble of going through the children's and deceased's belongings to see if there was anything of value to be kept to pay for all these expenses.

At last, it would be Market Day. All the good townspeople, and farmers, and tradesmen, could come to the holding house and pay the costs plus a little extra—because the Orphan Master couldn't feed his family on good wishes—for a boy or girl to help out at home, or on the farm, to help the journeymen fetch and carry, and perhaps to learn a trade. Infants, who were well formed and healthy and not ugly, could be raised in place of one or more that had been lost.

It was a difficult job for the Orphan Master. Sometimes there were runaways, sometimes children died quickly after they were taken to their new home, sometimes children were obstinate or inconsolable or not trainable, and the generous caretakers thought they should have their coin returned. And of course, the longer a child stayed at the holding house, the more expensive he or she would be on Market Day.

But the most difficult decision was to determine when a child could not command the price the Orphan Master had expended on his care. From profit to liability, the children who were too small, *too weak in mind or body, who had stood on the Market Day block and had been overlooked for too long were released into the streets of Lowertown to survive, die, or find a protector a little less brutal than the streets themselves."*

Willow paused for breath, and Koanga jumped in, "I don't like this story. You make the people of Kerek sound like monsters, a thin veil of respectability to cover the selling of children without anyone to speak for them."

"Koanga, what do you think happened to the children before there were Orphan Masters? At least this way, the captain receives some coin for the trouble of keeping the children alive. Otherwise, the infant would just go overboard with the corpse." She stared at him. "You've *been* to Kerek City, Koanga. You saw the throwaway children on the street, not just Kereki, but children from all countries. They didn't just grow out of the rocks on the road."

"Fine. I'll tell a story," Koanga argued. "Anything I tell would be better than the selling of children." For the rest of the way until we stopped for the night, Koanga entertained us with stories of a Seafarer and a village of never ending wants.

I heard Koanga's stories with my ears, but it was Willow's tale of the Orphan Master that troubled my heart. Some memories should never be taken out of the grave and claimed.

## CHAPTER 17

# MATASI AND THE KINDNESS OF STRANGERS

And so, on the third morning, we arrived at the Matasi border. Willow's skin was now dyed a rich walnut color, and she was wearing the blue dress Koanga had made at our campsite with the pond. Koanga and I had also put on fresh clothes that morning. The lordling trousers I had torn and stained on the road to Aldi, were now cleaned and retailored to dress Koanga. Willow had shown me how to brush and buff all our boots, and we had used Koanga's shears to cut my hair as short as the Matasi would wear it. She had practiced what she called her 'hello speech' so often, I could hear the Mata words in my head. She told Koanga and me what she would be saying so "you two can look reasonably intelligent and interesting." When I protested at her tone of voice, Koanga just shook his head at me. Any one of us being denied entrance to Matasi was not an option we could accept.

In Kerek, if you can get over the Silver Mountains, arrive on a floating object from the sea, cross the broad high desert, or the northernmost forests of west Vikland, you are in Kerek, and your survival and existence is your own affair. In Matasi, we were met at a gate as wide as two houses, with a low fence in either direction as far as the eye could see.

The guards were a little older than Willow, but all business. "Identity papers, please." One of them held out his hand and Koanga placed his and Willow's papers in his hand. As the guard started rifling through them, she spoke.

"I am Willow of the West Islands, daughter of the tailor to King Tane. I am traveling under the care of my brother, Koanga, a Storyteller of the West Islands who has his own hearth and home in Puna Mawhero. We have as our honored guest, Zren Janin from Conrosa, a country so far to the north of us, they do not have the seasons Wet and Dry. He has no papers because he was robbed in Kerek City and the Conrosan embasado has been closed for many years. We had hoped to gain help and assistance for him from our own embasado in Kerek City but as you may know, it was closed and looted after the death of our ambassador."

The first guard raised his hand to stop her and looked me over carefully. "I have never met a Conrosan before. You have traveled a far distance."

Willow translated from Mata to Keresh, and the guards' eyes narrowed. She saw the look and hastened to explain—still in Keresh, "Dear sir, it is like this. I speak Wester of course, and some Mata, forgive me for my clumsiness in your beautiful language, and I speak Keresh because it is always necessary to know the words of the thieves who will rob you. My brother, the Storyteller of the West Islands, has traveled to other countries as is his custom, to learn and understand the great tales of other places. So although we have wisdom and knowledge in our own right, it is only the Keresh language which we three carry in common."

"And yet, you come from Kerek," the second guard cocked an eyebrow, and I had no difficulty translating that as 'sure, go ahead—explain that one away.'

"Yes. Well. My brother, Koanga, has finished studying the fairy tales of Conrosa. Since his friend, Zren Janin, also studies the great epics, Zren wished to come to the West Islands and learn our great tales of the constellations. I was working as a servant in the house of a wealthy merchant in Kerek City. The two had heard of the lawlessness and wickedness of Kerek, and my brother was concerned for my safety. The two traveled from the academies in Juisiti through Kerek to see me, and we made plans for the three of us to sail immediately for the West Islands. Unfortunately, my brother booked passage on a ship captained by a Kereki thief. My brother paid our passage, delivered our trunks, and the captain sailed off in the middle of the night with the tide, leaving us slumbering in our beds on shore, now bereft and destitute." She bowed her head for a moment, then raised it and pasted on a watery smile.

I stood there with my mouth open and wondered if the guards had any idea what an incredibly gifted storyteller Willow was in her own right.

Willow made a brave sigh and switched back to Mata. "Thankfully, our Conrosan friend is a man of great talents. He has brought us safely through Kerek, knowing that Matasi is a just and fair country, and he would be able to draw upon his many resources in Alenti to see us safely home to the West Islands." She dropped her eyes to her skirts and blushed. "I confess, I am quite taken with him. He is pretty, yes, but a brave and true friend to my brother as well."

The guards laughed and Koanga and I exchanged a look. Whatever she had said had disarmed them. "Well, then, let's take a look through your bags, and we can see if you can be on your way," the first guard said easily.

Willow looked at us and then over my shoulder at the road behind me. "They want to go through our bags. Red, you go first. Then Koanga."

As I bent down to open my travel pack, I saw what she had seen, a wagon of Kereki workmen approaching from the north. Farm workers, most likely. They had their hats drawn over their faces as they slouched deep into the wagon bed. Instantly, the guards tensed, and the first guard whistled sharply, drawing more guards out from the shelter nearby.

The second guard briefly touched my rolled up lean-to, bedroll, clothes, and waved at me to close my pack. He handed Willow three travel passes, and in a low voice, in Keresh said, "Go quickly now. The nearest village is still a short walk away. We will delay these men as we can, but you need to be in the village and not on the track if you should meet them. We can only guarantee your safety here at the gate."

Willow answered, "Thank you for your kindness. We shall hurry." I shouldered my pack and we three stepped into Matasi.

I had never crossed a country's borders before, and I was disappointed. I had expected a more dramatic change, I don't know, maybe citrus groves and orchards right up to the fence. The guards had been Matasian, olive skinned, dark-eyed, short dark brown hair, and they had been brightly dressed in red and sand colored clothing. They were much kinder to us than I had expected. I *had* expected the unwelcome they were preparing for the Kereki farm workers behind us. It felt odd to be on the benefiting end of their scorn for Kerek. I wasn't sure I liked it.

We hadn't gone far along the track before the first neatly lettered sign appeared. The sign was simple with only the words,

"Ribelo - 560 Rods." We stared at it for a long moment, then Willow brightened. "It's the name of the village. A rod is a unit of measure. It will be a quick walk after all."

Koanga snorted. "Named, labeled, measured, and weighed. Our Matasian friends like their world orderly and tidy. Good fences, good borders, good neighbors." He chuckled malevolently. "Kerek must drive them crazy."

We swung along the track making good time. We came over a little rise and I stopped hard. There, in a little valley, was Ribelo. Straight-lined wide streets, houses with all the same stone façade. There was a square of green grass in the middle of the town. But where the market cross in Aldi had been plastered with tattered notices, lost items, and things for sale, this one was polished to a high sheen and surrounded by neat and colorful flower beds. Across the street from each side of the square had one building, a round one on the west side facing east, a long narrow rectangular one to the south, an ornate square box to the east facing west, and directly below us was the biggest building I had ever seen. There were no pushcarts or stands of vegetables, fruits, dry goods, and resellers. People walked in and out of buildings, string bags on their arms or carry boys behind. I was confused. This was *nothing* like the people of Lowertown said it would be.

"It's so clean!" I squeaked.

Willow and Koanga laughed, and Koanga touched my arm. "If you think this is beautiful, wait until you see the West Islands."

"Truly?" I turned to him, astonished that anything could be more beautiful and clean than this. "Truly?"

"Let's go!" Willow smiled and we nearly flew down the hill path.

We were met in the green square by another guard who had watched us come down the hill. He looked at our border passes and directed us to the largest building to be registered in the country and get accommodations for our stay. He gave us instructions in a rote voice: Sleeping rough was not permitted anywhere. Traveling through without passes was not permitted. Our passes could be inspected at any time by any guard, and we were to keep our own passes on our own person at all times.

I had never seen so many signs. There were signs to tell us where to go to register our presence, another to tell us where to pay our travel taxes, another set of signs to direct us for our interviews on why we were in Matasi—in which Willow completely dumbfounded our clerk by telling her we had come to Matasi for nine days just to visit the country, no family to visit, no business to conduct, no final destination.

"I've never heard of such a thing!" the clerk had exclaimed. "To travel all this way just to see a place you've never been!" But she stamped our passes just the same, and soon we were back out in the sunshine, looking for our assigned place to rest and to store our packs.

I was silently trying to reconcile how all the stories I had heard about Matasi, the monsters wearing the faces of men, could be the same place as I saw in front of me. I had heard these stories for years. How could they have lied so long? Why would they?

We made our way along a street and all of us grinned at the shops, the neat and tidy gardens in front of each house, the tall trees providing welcome shade over us. Even the houses had signs with numbers and names on them. Through it all, Willow kept up a steady stream of talking in Wester to Koanga. I just hoped he could remember it all to tell me once we were safely behind locked doors.

It wasn't long before Willow had found our building. It was two stories high and filled up the entire space between two streets. We pushed our way through the gate, up the walk, and knocked. The door was opened by a woman wearing a dress of the brightest shade of orange I have ever seen.

I blinked twice, but Willow just introduced herself and showed her stamped pass. The woman smiled, greeted us all, and then Willow explained "the boys" didn't speak Mata but she would interpret for all of us. At least that is what I assumed she said, for while Willow looked at me, she translated into Wester, and when I started to speak, Koanga put his hand on my arm, and showed his pass. I pulled mine out as well, and when the woman had examined all of them, she turned, and we followed her in.

The front room was filled with a long table and various comfortable chairs set about in groupings. There were a handful of people visiting—mostly Matasian, but I saw two other West Islanders, and a Viklander with golden skin and the long single black braid. He turned to greet us, and I thought he looked startled when he saw Willow, but the expression came and went so quickly, I doubted myself. Then he smoothly turned to Koanga and greeted him in Wester. Koanga gave him a large smile back, and I felt a flash of jealousy. But before I could think anything more, Koanga was tugging my arm and following the woman down the hall. Willow started up the staircase, and when I turned back to her, Koanga touched his fingers to his lips and motioned me onward.

The woman chattered in Mata, impervious to our inability to understand her. She unlocked a door with a huge iron key and ushered us into a tidy room with two narrow beds stacked on top of each other, a small table, and two straight backed chairs. She gestured us to put down our bags and follow her. Koanga put his on a chair, trusting fellow that he was, but I kept mine close. We walked down to the end of the hall where she showed us a room with a huge copper tub and a long-handled spigot.

She took a pot of hammered copper from a shelf behind me, hung it on the end of the spigot, and pumped the handle. Three, maybe four pumps later, water came gushing out! I dropped my jaw in surprise and Koanga laughed at the expression on my face. He said something in Wester, but she caught his meaning well enough and smiled kindly at me.

She walked us back to our room and gave Koanga the key. He shook her hand, like the ship captains did with the businessmen in Kerek City, and so I did the same. Then we locked ourselves in and Koanga started talking. "Willow doesn't want us talking Keresh any place where we might be overheard. We don't look Kereki and there is no reason for us to be from there. There's a Viklander here, but he greeted me as a fellow West Islander so I don't expect trouble there. Thank goodness, Conrosa is so far away, you won't be expected to converse with anyone."

"Where did Willow go?"

"This is mixed accommodations. Men on the first floor and women on the second. We can only meet Willow in the open room or outdoors. She said we must carry our passes everywhere. They show anyone who asks we are registered here, and we have coin enough to spend the night."

"It's only morning, we are going to waste the whole day here?" I was surprised.

"It's not wasted. We are going to have to sell most of our West Islands steel to afford our passage home and Willow needs to learn how we can do that. I doubt it is as easy as bartering in Kerek...or as dangerous." He smiled at me.

"She also told me to tell you they've changed the rules of passage. She learned this while we were registering. The only way a Kereki can now be in Matasi is on a worker's pass, or a business conduct pass. Both of those passes carried a large down payment in coin for good behavior. We don't have that extra coin. They take their religion very, very seriously, Red. The Voice of God, the Rule of God, the Fist of God. We can't afford any fines, or to pay the fees to stay in their jails if we break any of their rules. You have to be convincing as a Conrosan. Oh, and your name is Zren Janin. That's how Willow registered you."

"Zren Janin." I tasted the name on my tongue. "Like the fairy tales?" I grinned at him, and he grinned back. Then I thought of another problem. "Koanga, I know *nothing* about Conrosa. And for a country that prides itself on education and knowledge, just how likely is it I would not be able to read, write, or speak my own language?"

"Red, you've lived in Kerek City for seventeen years and you said you don't read or write Keresh."

I turned and walked to the window. "Yes, but Kerek City demanded a different set of skills. Reading and writing were a luxury most people could not afford. Look! There's Willow heading down the walkway. Are we supposed to follow her or stay here?"

"Follow her. It's good our room faces the street."

I felt naked without my pack, but Koanga insisted I leave it on the other chair. Koanga carefully locked the door behind us, and we headed out to the street. The front room was now empty as we passed through.

Willow was fumbling with a little drawstring bag on her wrist when we reached her. "So you have your passes? We don't go anywhere without those."

I patted my stomach. Earlier, Koanga had made little cloth pockets for us that tied around our waists. We wore them over our shirts and under our tunics. Not as accessible as Willow's little bag but a whole lot safer from pickpockets and thieves.

"What's that in your hand?" Koanga looked over her shoulder.

"It's a map of the town. The dommastrino gave it to me to use since this is our first day in Ribelo. This is the first town over the border so lots of people have to stay the night unless they have paid for a travel through pass. Red, did Koanga tell you your name is now Zren Janin? You need to learn as many Mata words as possible. We can't risk talking Keresh where we can be overheard, and I don't want you not understanding what we are going to do."

"I will. I am also smart enough to follow Koanga around like a little lost puppy." Koanga blushed, and I felt a little better. I cocked my head and asked him, "What did that Viklander say to you anyway?"

"He said it was good to see a face from the West Islands and bid me welcome to Matasi—the land of many rules."

Willow looked up distractedly. "We are going to have to watch what we say in Wester as well. I saw the two Islanders in the common room, but there could be others like the Viklander who speak Wester as a second or third language. I should have taken a better look at him. Come on. I don't want to stay standing here. Let's go be strangers in a strange land."

We followed Willow like Lost Girls behind their protector. She read the signs out loud in Mata, then murmured a translation in Wester—or in Keresh—whenever possible. She and Koanga continued a steady stream of words in Wester whenever we were around others, but Koanga assured me it was a lot of empty conversation about what they were seeing, to distract those about us.

I caught sight of the Viklander again that afternoon, once when we were touring the round building on the green, which turned out to be a church, of all things. The person giving us the tour reminded us services were held every day to hear the voice of God, and he would be looking forward to seeing us in the benches. The large ornate building across from the church was the Justice building, and while it was open to the public to tour as we wished, none of us wanted to dance with Trouble by wandering around inside.

There were signs saying "no spitting," "no littering," "no loitering." Signs to say where to cross the street, where to sit and rest, and where to bring your horse. All the shops had signs on them as well. Koanga said that in addition to saying what was sold inside, the signs also said when the shop was open and closed.

I thought he was teasing me. "You mean the people can't tell the shop is closed when the iron grates are pulled down and locked?" I whispered.

"What iron grates?" he murmured back.

It was true. There were no bars on the windows and no iron grates high over our heads to be lowered down over the doors at sundown. We wandered in and out of shops, and there was no Patron at the door with a heavy cudgel to look through our bags and make sure we didn't walk out with anything not paid for and wrapped. Even so, I always walked through the doorway with my palms open.

I assumed Willow was getting her questions answered. She didn't translate any of her conversations with the shopkeepers, and I was content to walk around goggle-eyed at goods for sale I had never seen before. Just the amount of paper—fresh, clean, used-only-once—had me silenced.

We hadn't eaten since breakfast. I was starting to feel very hungry when I had a creepy feeling on the back of my neck telling me I was being watched. The three of us had just stepped out on to the street and I took a slow look around to see who it might be. There were people walking up and down the boardwalks, chatting together, arranging their string bags on their arms. I was just about to give it up as the unease of being in a new place, when I caught a sudden movement disappearing around a corner. There!

I put my arm around Willow and drew her close. She looked at me, startled, and I whispered in her ear. "We are being watched. It might be a good time to find a place to eat and get off the street." She nodded and stepped quickly out of my arm.

We found a noodle shop. The bowls were big and full of fat noodles, vegetables, and different spices than I had known before. I slurped noodles while Koanga and Willow talked easily in Wester, and Koanga made a big deal about saying please and thank you in Mata to the person who brought the food to the table.

The woman came to look at our passes and said something to Willow. She fumbled in her bag then pulled out and laid unfamiliar coins on the table. The woman nodded and took the coins and our dirty bowls away.

"You paid for our food after we ate it?" I was so shocked I forgot I wasn't supposed to speak.

"Shhh!" Both Koanga and Willow shushed me, but I was sure it was so noisy in the shop, no one had heard us. Willow rushed us outside and pushed me into the nearest alley. She put both hands on my face as if for a kiss. Instead, she whispered furiously, "Watch and learn, Zren, watch and learn!"

I pulled away angrily and Koanga murmured something to Willow I didn't catch. I gave him a pointed stare. He tipped his head to the boardwalk, and I saw the Viklander standing there watching us.

Koanga stepped in front of Willow and said something in Wester with a very pleasant voice. The Viklander answered with a question, and both Koanga and Willow walked toward him. I followed. It wasn't like I had any other options—the alley was a dead end. We walked to the green and two benches that sat at right angles. The Viklander gestured for us to sit down. He said something to me, but it wasn't Mata or Wester, and I didn't think it was Vik. He smiled and tried again in Keresh. I recognized the words even though his accent sounded more like Koanga's than any Viklander I knew.

"Ah, I see we found a common language! Don't look so surprised! Vikland has no port of its own and we must go through Kerek or Matasi. Kerek is an uncivilized country with an uncivilized language, but every Viklander learns it if they ever wish to travel." He looked at Willow. "You are new to Matasi." It wasn't a question.

"Yes. It's our first day and we are traveling to the port cities. Is it true it will take us about six days to walk to the closest one—Salisport?" Willow questioned him.

"It's true. Matasi will track your movements. You will either need to pay a travel through tax or pay for accommodation fees in each town you come to. They are about a day's walk apart but there are many tracks so you can take different ways to your final city. Don't leave the track, ever. It's all private property and you can be jailed for trespassing, or not going through a checkpoint on your route. You're safer in Matasi than anywhere else, but the safety comes at the cost of your freedom."

"Why are you here?" Koanga asked accusingly. "You speak Keresh with a Wester accent."

The Viklander gave a shrug, but I could see his eyes were assessing Koanga. "I have spent the last year in the West Islands at the palace of your King Tane. I am now waiting in Ribelo for a caravan to join so I can cross Kerek and return home to Vikland."

He turned and smiled at Willow. "I could not believe my good fortune when I saw you enter the boardinghouse. I followed you this day to be sure. Do you not remember me, Ngahuru, child of the West Islands, sister to Koanga the Storyteller of Puna Mawhero?" He reached for her hand and held it in both of his. "Because I have never forgotten you since we met at the ambassador's..."

"...dinner on the holiday celebrating the beginning of the Dry," Willow finished weakly.

I looked at Koanga, and his eyes were the size of noodle bowls.

## CHAPTER 18

## UNEXPECTED GIFTS

Miyamoto Suki was not as tall as the Viklanders I had seen in Kerek City, though he was a good hand's-length taller than I was. He had the easy posture of a fighter, balancing on the balls of his feet, and the gracefulness of one who knew his body and its capabilities. He told me, he was like Ngahuru and trained in international politics. She stiffened at this but didn't say anything. Listening to him, I had the impression he was more diplomat than softfoot. I had never met anyone like him before and didn't know how to act or talk. I wasn't jealous of him exactly, it was just watching him talk with Koanga and Willow, he seemed so...so fancy.

He had lived for two years in Matasi several years ago and was telling us of things to do and see while we were here and what we could do to make our travels easier. We continued to speak Keresh, very formal Keresh, although it wasn't as old-fashioned as Koanga's speech.

Miyamoto was oblivious to the odd looks we received from passersby. He congratulated me several times on escorting the West Islanders safely through Kerek and down the Coast Road. He insisted we call him "Miya" as his friends did. But I was distrustful of his friendliness, and Koanga noticed it.

"Miya, my friend," Koanga said smoothly, "I am pleased beyond measure our paths have crossed, and I hope we may speak with you again, but I believe my sister and you would like to talk about politics and events that are not for my ears. Zren and I will part from you now. If you would see my sister to our accommodation whenever she wishes this evening?" Koanga looked as pompous as he sounded. I looked away to choke back my laughter.

Miya jumped to his feet as we stood. "Thank you for entrusting your sister to my care. I have so many stories to tell her. I appreciate your thoughtfulness."

I saw Willow roll her eyes, but she smiled. Before we had even walked out of hearing distance, Willow had switched to Wester, and Miya answered her.

"So, what's truly bothering you?" Koanga asked without preamble. "He seems like a nice enough fellow. He's been in the West Islands for the last year, so there's no way he's mixed up in the murder of our ambassador. Willow would have signaled me if she did not want us to leave her alone with him."

I snorted. "Nice enough? He's traveled everywhere. He's dined with ambassadors and kings and spent years training in Viklander politics. He speaks four, no wait, five languages, and..."

"He's very handsome," Koanga added, "And sophisticated. He talked so formally, like a prince, or one who is used to talking with princes." He tipped his head down to hide his face away from me.

I turned to glare at him and saw him smirking. "You're *trying* to make me upset. I don't even know why I am upset. But I am." I ran my hand through my short hair in disgust.

"Red—Zren," he corrected. "You are my friend, and I tell you this to cause you neither hurt nor harm. Your world has exploded in the last few days. For seventeen years, you lived in a box this big," he pinched his fingers together. "And now, within a handful of days, you learn you are from a beautiful country called Conrosa, you hear of the great tales of the West Islands from one of their famous Storytellers, you travel to a new country with new food, and language, and things you have never seen or done before." He took my hands in his. "It's too much, Red, it's too much. The box is gone, and you feel afraid and excited. You want to experience everything, and you're confused because you don't even know where to start."

I pulled my hands away. "I'm glad you are such an expert on my feelings." I crossed my arms over my chest and started walking. Koanga said nothing but fell in beside me.

For the rest of the afternoon we walked. We probably walked up and down every street in Ribelo, but I could tell you nothing of what we saw or who we met. Koanga walked silently beside me. He just greeted those we passed, guided me as we crossed streets, and steered me around obstacles.

It was the magic time of twilight when I finally walked down the street to our boardinghouse. Koanga stepped in front of me as I turned to go up the walk.

"Any winners?" he said gently.

"I wouldn't bet on any coin under the cup just yet." I paused. "Koanga, what should I call your sister?"

"That's a very good question." Koanga considered. "In front of Miyamoto Suki, we should call her 'Ngahuru.' That is what he knows her by, and there is no reason he would ever see her travel passes with her other names." He shrugged. "She'll tell you, if she does not wish it to be so." He opened the front door and we found Miyamoto and Willow—no, I needed to remember to call her Ngahuru— sitting together alone in the front room.

"Good! You're back!" Ngahuru jumped up to greet us. "I hope you are hungry. Miyamoto wants to take us to his favorite place in Ribelo."

Koanga groaned. "I hope it is not far. I feel as if I've walked all the way to Salisport already."

Miyamoto stood. "It's not far and we can go as we are. We will also be able to speak Keresh there, so no one will be left out."

I bristled at his comment, but Ngahuru leaned into me. "Make an effort, Zren Janin, he's trying to be nice."

* * * * *

It was a baboy. The place was loud, the drinks were cold, and the roasted pig was carved in front of us. After days of eating nothing but vegetables and fruits and grains cooked over a campfire or raw, just the smell of the roasting pig made me want to drool. It was delicious! Koanga and Ngahuru told funny stories about their family. Miya added some tales about his year in the West Islands and his two years in Matasi when he first started as a diplomat for Vikland. He wasn't that old—maybe a few years older than Ngahuru, but I had nothing on which to base my instincts. Miya asked about the hospitality laws in the West Islands and shared stories about visiting some of the other storytellers. I had not known each island within the West Islands had their own storyteller. Miya also congratulated Koanga on his role as the Storyteller on the King's island, a very prestigious honor. I hadn't understood that either.

Miya told us how he had been at the palace in the West Islands when the King heard of the deaths of the ambassador and then his wife—the King's sister, Hana—in Kerek City. The Viklander said he had been worried for Ngahuru since he knew she was still posted there but didn't know how he could ask anyone of news of her. I watched as he touched her hand lightly with his fingertips and his face grew sober.

I tipped my glass up and drained my drink to hide my face, but I wondered how we were going to leave the next day if Miyamoto and Ngahuru had just found each other. It made me wonder how Koanga and I would part. As much as I tried to kill my growing feelings for him, I knew the best I could hope for was just to stuff them so far down they would slowly die from suffocation and neglect.

And then the music started, and all sad thoughts winged their way to the stars.

The first singer was female with a voice so joyous, you couldn't help but smile back at her. She waved her hands in the air, taught us the chorus so we could sing along, and stomped her feet to the beat. Koanga leaned over and laughed. "This is how we will learn Mata! We will just sing our way through their country!"

Singer after singer took their turn. Some taught us the songs and we all participated, some stood and sang alone. We danced in place, we threw our hands in the air, we stomped, we made a joyful noise. Sometimes the music was lively and fast, sometimes slow, sometimes somber. I loved all of it.

At last, a big man stood in front and boomed out a few words in a respectful tone of voice. He paused, looked at all of us, and then smiled and held his hand out over us. He said a few more words and then left the stage. Ngahuru leaned over. "That was the prayer and benediction. Now there will be a last song and they will be closing for the night. Stand up and mouth some words. It's their nation's hymn." A woman came out again, and Ngahuru gave us a stern look. Koanga and I stood quickly and followed her lead. I had expected a military march like I had sometimes heard in Lowertown, when the King sent his soldiers to cure us of our worst excesses. But this was another boisterous anthem ending with fist-pumping cheers.

We spilled out into the street and walked towards the boardinghouse. There were a lot of people walking arm in arm, some still softly singing, but for the most part everyone was moving fairly quickly out of the shops and streets.

"Curfew soon," Miya observed, "but we are close by so no need to rush much."

I saw a string of lanterns walking towards us from the long low flat building right across from the round church. "What's that?" I waved my arm.

Miya looked. "Those are the village soldiers. They form a human square on the green facing outwards, and then when curfew is sounded, they walk down each of the streets looking for people who are not where their passes say they should be."

"Are we going to be all right?" Koanga asked.

"Yes. But we probably shouldn't stand here and watch them much longer." We hurried home and as we latched the gate behind us, the door opened. Our dommastrino stood there, just pulling in the lantern from its hook by the door.

"Hurry now," she called. "The whistle will sound any moment." She pulled the door shut after us. The dommastrino made pointed remarks at Miya. He smiled, pushed out his hands in a placating gesture, and answered smoothly in Mata, trying to calm her. Ngahuru translated softly in Wester, and I saw Koanga duck his head to hide his smile. I heard a shrill whistle then and the dommastrino gave Miya a triumphant look. I didn't need to know any Mata to know that the whistle had just proven the landlady's argument about our close call with curfew.

Our host was clearly waiting for Ngahuru to go up the staircase to her room, so she scampered off with a quick "dream well and the stars will watch you" to all of us, in Wester, of course. I followed Koanga down the hall and watched Miya as he turned left at the corridor. He looked back over his shoulder, saw me watching him, and nodded his head just once as he spoke. I wondered in what language he wished me a good night, and then I wondered if that was truly what he had said, or if his gentle smile had hid words threatening my life.

We slipped in our room. Koanga locked the door behind us, and I started in immediately, "What was that all about? The dommastrino was clearly unhappy with Miya. I know your sister translated it for you. Or part of it anyway."

Koanga smiled wickedly. "It seems our Miya likes to come in at curfew most nights and she is worried he is corrupting her newest travelers." He sobered then. "She also said he is to report to the administration building tomorrow. His pass is expiring, and he cannot stay any longer."

"What did he say in return?"

"Only that he loves Matasi so much he cannot bear to miss a moment of it. He also said he will go tomorrow to the administration building, but for him to travel alone in Kerek is a death sentence." Koanga looked sad.

"So what can he do?"

"I don't know. Get his pass renewed? Find a caravan traveling through Kerek? Find a mountain guide to take him over the Silver Mountains this late in the Dry? Go with us to Salisport and take a ship to Kerek City and try to find a caravan or wagon train of supplies that will go across the Northern Track? Vikland is surrounded by mountains and Kerek. He has no good choices."

I groaned. "He's going to come with us, isn't he?"

"Would that be so bad? His first posting was to Matasi—he has two years of experience here. He was a diplomat from his own country when he met Ngahuru in Kerek City, and he knows more languages than you and I put together. He's not a bad person to have travel with us."

"He's going to be making eyes at Ngahuru for the next seven days and I have to watch!" I groaned.

Koanga gave me a quizzical look. "I don't know what that means."

I gave him my most adoring look and he barked out a laugh. "Ah, Zren, you will never make a King's Player. In Wester, we call it 'karu kurii,' puppy eyes or..." He gave me a wicked grin. "...maybe 'tummy trouble.' I wasn't sure what you were doing." He laughed at his own joke, and I gave him a pointed stare.

"Red—Zren—I had to apprentice five years before my King gave me a home and hearth of my own and named me as a Storyteller. Ngahuru has been studying languages and cultures and countries almost as long as you have been alive so she can enjoy a position like that of Miyamoto Suki. He said tonight he is following in his mother's and his grandfather's footsteps, so he has probably been training his entire life for this as well. They may think kindly of each other, but there certainly isn't going to be days and days of 'making eyes.'" Koanga looked out the window. "I'm sorry, Red, but Ngahuru granted my wish when I asked her to stop and save you. I am disinclined to tell her 'no' if she asks tomorrow to add Miya to our travels."

I went down the hall to wash up and when I returned Koanga had already undressed and taken the lower bed. I threw my clothes on the second chair and climbed up to the top. Soon I could hear him softly snoring, but I laid there, staring at the ceiling, wondering what was wrong with me.

* * * * *

In the end, I sacrificed my sleep for nothing. We walked Miyamoto Suki to the administration building immediately after our dommastrino had fed us, prayed for us, and inspected our rooms to ensure we weren't walking off with the candlesticks. In front of the brick steps, Miya had looked at Ngahuru's new map and together they selected the easiest track for us to reach

Salisport. He told us what he could remember of some of the villages along the way. Then Ngahuru looked at the map with the route and villages marked and circled, folded it between her hands, and bowed to Miya. I watched as he returned the bow and said some words in Vik. Then he turned to Koanga and me and gave us handshakes like I had seen between the ships' captains in Lowertown. With one last wave he walked up the steps of the administration building. We shouldered our packs and turned west.

I felt happy and small all at once, so I kept my mouth shut until I figured out my feelings. Koanga and Ngahuru also didn't feel like talking and so we plodded along silently.

Just past midday, we found another painted sign, this one for a wayside rest. There were little tables and places for us to sit and deep pits with wooden lids for us to throw down our scraps. Everywhere there were more signs, "No littering," "No cooking," "No sleeping." It was a peaceful spot, shady and cool with well-tended flowers. Down the track, I just made out a checkpoint shelter and the movement of a soldier or two. "Think they're watching us?" I tipped my head to the checkpoint.

"Absolutely," Ngahuru replied, "but they can't hear us, so listen carefully." She reached in her pack and took out three guavas and two small bags of coins. She handed each of us the fruit and a bag of coins in one hand. "Miya knew of a private dealer in Ribelo who handles delicate transactions. Yesterday while you two were off sightseeing, he and I converted all of the West Islands steel in my pack to coin. I will continue to carry most of our coin, but those purses carry enough for food if we are separated. I couldn't get into your room, Koanga, so we still have your tailor kit, the bone knife, and two daggers left." She looked at me. "Three daggers if we count the one we gave you, but I would rather not beg for that one's return, unless there is no other way for us to cross the sea," She continued, "Miya and I both agree the coin we have now is enough to get us home, I think. We will have to sleep in lesser accommodations and eat lightly, but Miya said it is not worth the risk to sleep rough. Not for our safety, but the fines are high. The Matasi love their laws and love enforcing them as well."

She grimaced. "If we dance with Trouble, the West Islands have an embasado at Alenti, but I would wish not to travel so much further into Matasi. It would be better for us to make the first port—Salisport. But if we are desperate, or destitute, Miya said Vikland has a main embasado in Salisport and a secondary one in Alenti. We can appeal for help from the Vikland embasado. He says he is not so important that clerks quake at the mention of his name, but someone should be able to help us."

"Ah, that explains why your pack is so light! I wondered why I did not hear the pots clanking about," Koanga mused.

"I took the chance we would not need them again. Miya said there are collectors of West Islands and Vikland artifacts, but it is officially discouraged. Hence, the private dealers and the sinner's market."

"So...what about Miya?" I asked.

"Miya is still officially traveling under his diplomatic pass. It is nearly worthless in Kerek, but carries quite some weight in Matasi. His plan is still to travel to Ahni in Kerek, and then cut cross country on the Old Vikland road to reach home. It's a long hard journey and not a common one, but it is too late in the season to find a reliable guide to go over the Silver Mountains. He needs to get home soon and report. This idle time is not good for him or Vikland."

Koanga hummed, "Mmmmm. So, I'm just going to ask the wrong question. Why didn't he come with us and sail out of Salisport to Kerek City?"

Ngahuru shot a look at me, but answered Koanga, "He would be backtracking. He loses another seven days heading southwest with us, takes a ship to Kerek City, and then still has to find a wagon train or caravan, or Kerekis honest enough to travel with him across the Northern Track. He can defend himself, he said, but he's never seen a Kereki fight yet where it was even odds." She paused. "I told him about our experiences outside of Aldi and then again at the Sion Inn. He wasn't surprised. He thought our three to two odds were closer than he would choose." She smiled mischievously at Koanga. "I told him everyone underestimates you, and you are my biggest asset."

"I agree. You underestimate my intelligence all the time." Koanga reached over and opened Ngahuru's and his packs and dumped half of his contents into hers.

"Hey, what are you doing?" Ngahuru grabbed for her pack.

"If you sold all our West Islands steel yesterday, that means you walked this entire morning carrying nothing more than a dainty dress and three guavas. I think the packs should be a little more evenly distributed," Koanga pointed out.

"Pah! I had the canvas lean-to."

"Well, take all the clothes and I'll take the canvas lean-to, otherwise I will leave them here and you can pay the littering fees." Koanga gave her a half smirk.

"Fine. Just fine. Trust my little brother to prance along carrying only tailor's shears and complain about the weight."

I sighed and rolled my eyes. "Come on, you two. Let's start walking. We still have a long way to go before nightfall." Inwardly, I smiled. This was the first time since I had met them, the siblings had actually acted like brother and sister. I wondered if it was because they were comfortable with me, finally felt safe now we were out of Kerek, or could sense they were actually going to both make it home alive. Or maybe all of it.

To make time pass on the track, Koanga tried to teach me my Keresh letters and memorize Wester words. Ngahuru tried to teach both of us Mata phrases she thought we needed to know to be respectful travelers. The three of us created these ridiculous conversations of Mata, Wester, and Keresh gibberish. I couldn't remember a time I had laughed so much.

I felt so at ease without having to worry about bandits and thieves. After the third checkpoint, where the soldiers had shown us where to fill our water containers and had given us a piece of fruit—Ngahuru called them figs—I told her I could see myself living here.

Koanga snorted. "You would sell your freedom for a little food?"

I tried to explain my thoughts. "Freedom to die in Kerek? We have freedom here in Matasi. Look at us. None of us are Matasian and we are just walking along. No one is lying in wait to do us harm. That's not what I heard it would be like when we were in Kerek. In Kerek City, even in Aldi, people would talk about how awful Matasi was to outsiders. Remember? But here, no one passes us and looks us up and down to see if we are weak enough they can take what they want. In Matasi, there is food and safety and music and living without fear. I could go out every night and find a place to sing and dance like we did last night, and not worry about being stabbed as I was followed home. Look around us. It's beautiful here, no trash, no lost children trying to beg or steal your food, no squatter homes of broken boards."

"You would have to worry about curfew," Ngahuru said, "and you know all the music last night was religious songs and praise hymns? All the live music you will hear in Matasi is only praise and prayer and parables of the Lost God. Nothing else is tolerated. You could not go somewhere to hear the tales of the Constellations, or even Conrosan fairy tales, if you wished."

"Huh." I paused. I hadn't known that. "I liked the music. I didn't realize it was all religious. I could dance to it, the parts where everyone was singing were fun. It was loud." I felt chastised. "I liked the music," I repeated.

"Oh, Zren, I didn't mean to be discouraging. The music here is wonderful and joyful and even the slow or somber songs are meaningful. And I am deliriously happy we can walk along the track without worrying about who or what is going to jump out at us, or have to sleep with one eye open on our packs. But the Matasians pay a high price for such a sheltered existence. I like traveling here just as you do. But I think, if I was posted here for two years as Miya was, I would be staying out until curfew as well, just to assert myself."

We went back to talking about other things, but I spent a lot of time thinking about what I had said, and what my price would be for a home of my own. Koanga had been frightened for only a few days, Ngahuru for a season. But I had been afraid, and hungry, and lonely for years. Most of my remembered life. The safety Matasi surrounded me with right now wasn't suffocating, it was comforting. How could they not see this?

* * * * *

Our rooms that night were in a small home quite a distance away from the central square. When we had registered at the administration building, Ngahuru had been honest about our need for inexpensive lodgings. The clerk had narrowed her eyes a bit but had assigned us a home without further comment. I guess poverty wasn't a virtue of the Lost God.

The dommastrino was a middle-aged widow who asked us to pray with her before we went to bed. The rooms were clean and small, and the food for first meal was fresh bread and uncooked greens, olives, grains, and figs. I had never tasted olives before, and they surprised me with their saltiness. Luckily, the widow had stepped back into the kitchen to bring us water, so only Ngahuru and Koanga saw my expression. I remembered what Koanga said about my exploding world and swallowed them hastily. I was going to be bigger than the box I had grown up in.

# DANCING WITH TROUBLE

I never realized what a pleasure it was to have absolutely nothing happen. For the next two days, we would set off on a well-marked track, pass some checkpoints throughout the day, and then reach another town on Ngahuru's map before end of day. We would register at the administration building, look for a lively place with food and music to eat and enjoy, or wander about until dark, and tuck ourselves back in our beds well before the curfew whistle.

In Kaoso, we stayed with a grain trader who had lived for years in the Flower District of Kerek City, when the previous King reigned. When the new King had taken the throne, he told us he believed it was a good time to move back home. "I could see he would never be the King his father was, and I thought to sell my holdings while they still had value," he told us with a satisfied smile.

He talked about his experiences through business and trade with travelers in Matasi. He explained hosts had to apply for the privilege, and priority was given to widows and widowers, and those who had no other means to support themselves. As our host in Kaoso stated it, "Matasi will never let the old, the infirm, the very young, and those unable to care for themselves be in want of food or shelter. However, there is a smile with the charity if an effort is made to care for yourself first." He winked at us and told us he was not criticizing his government, merely stating an observation of his advanced years.

Koanga told his stories. Now that Miya had opened my eyes to Koanga's role in the West Islands, I understood Koanga wasn't just a man who "liked to talk a lot" as Ngahuru joked. His stories explained who the West Islanders were, what values were important, how people should be treated, and how the world came to be. In Kaoso, when we were in for the night and visiting with our host, Koanga told a great tale of the Traveler.

When he finished, our host said there was a similar parable of the Lost God and told the parable to us. Both stories told of a small person in a small village. When news of a Stranger/Traveler coming through town reached them, both dropped everything to go to meet the Stranger/Traveler to learn of distant places and a bigger life than their own. In both stories, the townspeople mocked the person and tried to keep him from reaching the Stranger/Traveler. Both climbed a tree to see and be seen, so great was their desire to meet the Stranger/Traveler. In both stories, the villagers laughed at the silliness of a grown man, one that was not a member of the best families, who would sacrifice the approval of the townspeople to get a better look.

In both stories, the Traveler/Stranger broke with tradition and requested permission to dine with the one who desired to meet them, and treated them with the respect of an exalted and welcome host.

"So which tale came first?" Ngahuru asked when our host was finished. "Truly, they seem so similar, I wonder which country borrowed which tale?"

Our host shrugged. "I am not sure it matters. Our stories will outlive us all. It is more important to hear the story with your heart, than to be lost in the where, and the how, and the when."

"Labeled, boxed, and buried." Koanga muttered under his breath. Ngahuru shot her brother a sharp look, and then graciously thanked our host for his kindness and his story and excused us to our beds.

On the fifth day, we walked out of Kaoso a little later than usual. Our host had fed us first meal, prayed with us for safety on our journey, and then we had lingered visiting. He looked at our map, and noted Miya and Ngahuru had circled Subversiva for the night's lodging. He suggested we stop at Malea instead, but he didn't say why. Ngahuru rolled up her map, thanked him politely, and we were on our way.

We talked that morning of the parables of the Lost God and Ngahuru wondered why she had never been taught any in the West Islands academies when she had studied the Vik sagas, the Conrosan fairy tales, and the West Islands Constellation stories. Then we talked about what I was going to do once we reached Salisport. Stay in Matasi or go to the West Islands? I knew my time was running short to decide my future, but every night I would go to sleep thinking one way and wake the next morning, deciding to do something else. I told Koanga I wished for a clear sign of what I should do. Something to convince myself I was making the right decision.

"Ah, be careful what you wish for," teased Ngahuru. "In the Conrosan fairy tales, saying such a wish out loud would only bring you a dance with Trouble, or punishment for a year and a day."

We laughed about that and swung along easily down the track. Shortly after the second checkpoint we came to the village of Malea. It was after midday. As we walked through, we noticed people hurrying about, but nothing that concerned us. Ngahuru checked her map again. "This is way too early to stop for the day. Subversiva is not more than two decons. We should push through."

"Maybe our host thought we took a nap after our midday meal rather than eat it on the way, or that perhaps we paused to buy a drink in the inns rather than only stop to refill our water containers?" Koanga offered.

I shrugged. "Doesn't matter why. Let's go on." I took a quick look around and we walked out west to the track. There were other travelers and soon we found our own pace again. People passed us, we passed others. Some peeled off on small side tracks and half-tracks heading down to homesteads and estancias for work. The closer we got to Subversiva, the emptier the track got. By the time we walked into the town, we had been the only people traveling on the road for a while. In Subversiva, the streets were empty. There was no guard on the green to tell us where to register. But we knew what we needed to do and we walked up to the administration building. The doors were locked.

"What happens now?" I asked Koanga.

"I have no idea. Ngahuru? Can you pull something out of your bag of magic?" He looked around uneasily.

"Let's stop at the church first, then the Justice..."

"Hey! What are you doing? Put your bags down and walk away from them." The voices were gruff and assured. Ngahuru translated instantly into Keresh. My first thought was to run, but where would I go? I followed the actions of Koanga and

Ngahuru, as we slowly and gently put down our travel packs and then stepped several paces away to the left.

The soldiers were older than we were. They carried cudgels worthy of the most miserly Patron in Kerek, and some had large pikes. I stepped behind Ngahuru and carefully pulled my Sailor's Curse. Speaking in Mata, she began with an apology, and then a series of questions. Or that is what it sounded like anyway. The soldiers were abrupt and curt in their responses. Koanga was as focused on her face as I was. We had to use tone of voice as our signal, as she would only be able to give us a moment's warning in Keresh if they gave a hostile command.

One of the soldiers stepped forward and held out his hand. Ngahuru gestured to her pack. He nodded once, but then the rest of the soldiers pointed their pikes at Koanga and me to hold us in place. She whispered to Koanga as she walked by him, and then opened her pack and pulled out her pass. Koanga slowly untied his tunic, holding his palms open. He pointed to the pocket he had tied about his waist. Again the short nod from a soldier, and he reached in and pulled out his pass. I followed Koanga's moves exactly, keeping my Sailor's Curse hidden in my left hand. Once I had handed my pass to the man as well, I stepped back and took a deep breath.

He looked at the travel passes and then asked Koanga a question. Koanga looked to Ngahuru.

"I am sorry, sir," she began in Keresh, "I am the only one who speaks Mata, and I speak it so poorly. You can see by our faces we are all a long way from our homes. What this means is that we only have Keresh as a language in common." She looked at her feet and shook her head slowly, "We were all taught it is best to learn the language of those most likely to do you harm. We did not know today was a special day for your faith. We would have gone to the church after this and then we would have realized when all the benches were full. We did not know the administration building would be closed early and our hosts would not be able to receive us if we came so late in the day. We did not know... and now we have deeply offended you. I cannot express my sorrow."

The soldiers conferred amongst themselves, and I could tell from the look on Ngahuru's face we weren't going to like the results of the discussion. Soon, we were told to pick up the packs and carry them with us down the steps of the administration building across the square and into the long low building. The soldier presented us to his superior, gave him our passes with a triumphant gloat, and stepped back smartly.

Ngahuru began to speak, but the superior just raised his hand for silence. He fingered through the passes several times, asked the soldiers a question, and then turned to me. He spoke at length with such a non-expressive face and voice, I couldn't decide if I was being scolded, praised, or told to prepare myself for a hanging.

In the end, we were ushered into a jail cell. Koanga and I were placed together, and they took Ngahuru down the hall and through another door.

"Will she be all right?" I whispered to Koanga.

"I don't know. But she's the only one who speaks Mata, so I'm worried for all of us."

We waited in silence and then waited some more. A long time later, a young soldier came down the hallway and set a plate on a narrow ledge outside the bars. He unlocked the flat metal flap and walked away. Koanga carefully walked to the door, lifted the flap, and pulled the plate inside. It held two bakery buns, some raw vegetables, and a handful of figs. Koanga carefully split the food in two and then offered me the plate.

"Ten days of this and we'll just be able to turn sideways and slide through the bars," he muttered.

I looked up startled. "You think we'll be here that long?"

"I have no idea. I don't know if we are being held until the church services are over, or if this is our last meal. I don't know if our crime is 'Oops, you're a little late,' as a flagrant disregard for the country's laws, or since it's a religious holiday, our actions are considered heresy and treason and worthy of a hanging."

I stared at him, and Koanga stifled a laugh in spite of himself. "Ah, Red. There's a lot I don't know in this world, but I do know all those years Ngahuru said to learn more languages than just Wester and Keresh, she was right and I was wrong."

I smiled a little weakly. "I want to be around when you tell her that." I finished my half of the food on the plate and handed it back to him.

"So do I, Red, so do I." He crunched through the raw vegetables, ate the bun, and thoughtfully chewed the figs one at a time. I thought about asking for a story to pass the time, but I knew he was worried about his sister, and neither one of us was really in the mood.

I didn't sleep that night. If this was the last night of my life, I wanted to be awake for it. I thought a lot about what had happened the last few days. If I lived through this, I wanted to be different. I would never go back to Kerek City. I would never go back to just surviving from day to day. I liked Matasi, and until our visit to Subversiva, I truly thought I would stay behind and live here when Ngahuru and Koanga sailed home to the West Islands. But I didn't know the rules of living here, and there was no one to teach me.

I looked at my jail cell and Koanga sleeping fitfully on the other bench. I lacked Ngahuru's instincts for reading a situation and knowing what to do. I lacked her talent for acting a part. I lacked her education and her knowledge of languages. Everything I had ever learned was fight or flee. I sighed. I knew I was a follower; I just needed someone worthy to follow, I decided. I was determined there would be no more Goblins and Bricks in my life.

I thought about going with Ngahuru and Koanga to the West Islands. Koanga said he wanted to show me his country, and I wondered if he just needed more time to discover his feelings for me. A little voice inside said he would never develop those feelings, and the ache and yearning I felt around him would always be unreturned.

Koanga had said Ngahuru would have a meeting with the King and his advisors and then post out again quickly. Where would she go? What does a softfoot do, except to pretend to be something she isn't? Isn't that what I had been doing my entire life? Could I follow her? Could she take me with her?

Ngahuru had made the plans, determined the route, made sure we had food and coin. But whenever we encountered others she became meek, hiding behind her brother's extravagant personality, slipping behind me to be unnoticed. She was powerful, but she was more powerful because no one knew who she was. She had taken her body—an accident of birth—and turned it into another weapon in her role. She spoke Keresh without the lilt that Koanga and Miya had. She spoke Mata. She could read Conrosan. Yet, she was sitting in a jail cell down the hall just as I was. I blew out a noisy breath and Koanga stirred across the cell. I couldn't be what she was. And I knew no other options.

* * * * *

The soldier who brought us first meal followed the same routine as the other. I walked to the door, opened the flap, and pulled in the plate. It was the exact same meal as last night. I divided it carefully, ate my half, and tried to decide if I should wake Koanga or not. The food would wait, I decided. If he could sleep, he should sleep.

* * * * *

Koanga had awakened, eaten, straightened his clothes, and wiped his face, when another soldier came to get us. We hadn't spoken. There was no need. Koanga's face was wracked with worry. We both worried for Ngahuru.

We were escorted into the same room where we had met the superior officer last night. Ngahuru was there. She looked tired but unhurt. Our three packs were there on a bench beside her.

Another soldier came out of an office with three travel passes. "Your sister has paid your fine and your hospitality fees.

In the future, please ask for advice before you willfully disobey our laws." He paused as if waiting for us. "You are free to go." He waved his hand at us, shooing us out.

I didn't need to be told twice. I grabbed my travel bag, it felt lighter, a lot lighter, and followed a soldier out the front door. Koanga and Ngahuru were close behind me. Once we were left alone, he began to speak, "Are you all right?"

"Not here, not now. I'll tell you on the track." We followed her westward out of town.

We walked slowly, three abreast, Ngahuru in the middle so we could hear her better.

"You've noticed your packs are lighter," she began. "They confiscated the canvas lean-tos we had used in Kerek. They said there is no sleeping rough in Matasi and therefore, we would have no need of them. The superior kept one of the West Islands daggers. He thought it looked 'pretty.' He didn't know what the bone knife was, so I said it was for sacrificing animals and he dropped it back in the pack. He also said we had three knives of West Islands steel and only two of us were West Islanders. It is forbidden to buy or sell our metal workings in Matasi; therefore, our Conrosan friend must have gotten his on the sinner's market—which is a crime. But, if he took the dagger away, there would be no crime because there was no dagger. He knew you would be grateful to him, Zren, for saving you from a meeting with the Justice and a jail sentence. He also charged us 80 cals for our overnight stay and our food."

"Eighty cals?" Koanga moaned. "That would buy a three day stay for all of us in some fine inn with food and drink for a crowd!" He looked at her mournfully. "Do we have any funds left?"

"We do. We have the coins I gave you both earlier and I had some hidden on my body. I believe our fine was whatever was in my purse. I am glad I shared our coins among us." She paused. "I was not searched. Were either of you?"

"No, neither of us." Koanga added, "Nor harmed. And you?"

"Left alone with my thoughts and my nightmares. At least I knew we were going to be released this morning. They didn't tell me until we had already been separated." She gave us both a sad smile. "I am sorry I had no way to tell you."

"We survived." Koanga was quiet for a while and then, in a bitter mocking voice repeated, "In the future, please ask for advice before you willfully disobey our laws." He kicked a stone. "How would we even know what questions to ask? Are we supposed to wake up every morning, 'excuse me, sir, what do I need to know today to not end up in one of your jails?' How would we even know the country closes early for religious holy days? How would we know what days are holy days? Are there degrees of holy days? Today, sir, you do not eat. Today, you spend the day in the round building. Today, you walk on your knees to Alenti." He went on and on.

Ngahuru let him talk his way out of his mood. When he finished, he smiled at her sheepishly. She gave him an indulgent smile and simply responded, "As you said, we survived."

She gave a big sigh. "But that does put us in a predicament. Either we must go to the West Islands embasado in Alenti for more coin, which lengthens our trip by an additional five days, and we do not have coin to last us five additional days, or we go to Salisport, and see if the Vikland embasado will assist us on the name-dropping of our friend, Miyamoto Suki. We could sell the rest of our West Islands steel, including your tailor's kit, Koanga, but I do not know how to find a private dealer as Miya knew in Ribelo. It is not something I can just go to the village green and announce. I wish I would have understood what a gift he had given me that afternoon to take me there and help us. I am not sure I appreciated all he has done."

CHAPTER 20

## ANARKIO

We trotted into Anarkio just after dusk. Koanga had picked up a pebble in the seam of his boot that morning and hadn't been able to work it out. Other travelers—more than usual—passed us on the track, and we knew we were falling further and further behind. After last night's stay in the Subversiva jail, we just wanted to find the next village and sleep. But of course, we couldn't find anything but half-tracks and private estancia roads on the long downward slope to the sea.

A farrier passing us had noticed Koanga's limp and had stopped to ask us what was wrong. He used a long horse pick to work out the stone from the inside. It had made an immediate improvement, but we had already lost a lot of ground by then. Again, I marveled at the kindness of strangers in Matasi. Why did all the stories about Matasi I had heard in Lowertown talk about how awful the country was? How had I lived so long without knowing the rest of the world?

Anarkio was clearly a market town for a large number of estancias and settlements in the surrounding area. The administration building was smaller than we had seen previously, but it was open, and that was our main concern. We hurried up the steps to get our passes stamped and our accommodations assigned. Thankfully, the passes we already carried said nothing about where we had spent the previous night.

I could tell the clerk was impatient to go home for the day. She looked over our passes and traced our route on the big map in front of her.

"You left Subversiva this morning?"

"Yes," Ngahuru answered.

"You reached this checkpoint at midday? Your passes are stamped so."

"Yes."

"You should have been there by midmorning. Did you go off the track?"

"No. My brother picked up a stone in his shoe. It slowed us down," Ngahuru patiently explained.

"You did not meet anyone? You did not agree to carry something for a stranger?" She was skeptical.

"No. We're slow walkers. I'm so very short you see, and with the stone in his shoe, we just fell further behind."

"You reached the second checkpoint here at this time." The clerk looked at our passes again. "Your time was much quicker. Ha! Did you deliver something to someone? You do not have a carry pass to transport goods for someone else." She looked sternly over her map at us.

"No, nothing like that." Ngahuru's voice wavered a bit and I looked at her in surprise. Everything we had been through and she was going to cry now? Just because an old lady was going to be late for her evening meal? Or was she acting again and I needed to do something? I felt the panic rise inside me.

"Do you read Mata?" The clerk snapped. "You see the signs that say, 'No loitering.' This means you. We do not stay open all night long just because you decide you want to look at every pretty flower on the track." She took out three passes and stamped them briskly. She pulled out a chart and ran her finger down. "You will stay at 15 Brohom Street. The cost will be 30 cals for the three of you."

"That's too expensive." Ngahuru sighed. "Do you have a cheaper place? We'll take one without first meal."

The clerk slammed her palms flat on the desk. "This afternoon, I had something more reasonable. Even two decons ago, I had something cheaper. But now? When curfew is just under a decon away? This is what I have: 30 cals for the three of you."

Ngahuru counted out her coins and asked for Koanga's purse. She handed it back nearly empty, but the clerk gave us our passes.

We walked out of the building and down the steps. "I don't need a full translation, Ngahuru, but what just happened back there?" I asked.

"We were behind schedule, and she thought we were transporting goods for someone else."

"Truly? Is that what all the coin was for? Were we fined again?" Koanga tilted his head.

"No. Apparently, we are staying in a very fine house tonight."

"Ngahuru."

I recognized that voice. I looked up just in time to step aside as Miya grabbed Ngahuru in a huge hug. "You made it! I've been so worried. I've been checking the administration building all evening trying to intercept you. I thought maybe you had changed the route after we had chosen this one."

"What are you doing here?" Ngahuru looked confused.

"It's too long of a story to tell now. Where are you staying? We must get you to your boardinghouse as quickly as possible." He grabbed my pass out of my hand. "Ah, 15 Brohom. I know where that street is. Hurry! The soldiers will be coming out for curfew enforcement soon."

We ran after him across the green down the street with the round church—Stars! Did every town have a round white church facing east?—and down the block. "Meet me on the green tomorrow morning as soon as your host has finished serving you first meal. I have to run, my rooms are much farther away. Tomorrow morning on the green!" He took off running down the street, the three of us staring after him with our mouths hanging open.

Koanga recovered first. He shepherded us up the walk and to the door. At his knock, the door opened, introducing us to a well-dressed man of middle years, slender and soft-looking. He was my height, but wore expensive clothes, dark trousers and a soft woven blue shirt.

"Come in, come in. I'll inspect your passes inside. The curfew whistle will sound any moment now." He pulled the lantern from the hook and closed the door. We fumbled for our passes and set down our packs on the gleaming floor. The curfew whistle sounded, and our host tipped his head to one side. "I wouldn't have wanted to scrape it any closer. Now show me your passes and tell me where you have been this day, and where you are headed tomorrow."

We turned our passes over to him, and I watched the worry on Ngahuru's face. I wondered if Miya had made it back to his rooms on time. Would having a diplomat pass help him?

"So, two West Islanders and a Conrosan?" He looked me up and down. "I've never met one from your country before. You're a long way from home."

"Yes, sir." I was beginning to feel like a talking pig.

"Ah, you speak Mata! Good manners, too! I have heard your country values learning. I am very glad to meet you."

Koanga bit back a laugh, and Ngahuru smiled weakly. "I'm afraid that's all he can say— and 'please' and 'thank you.' Between the three of us we have Wester, Keresh, and Mata—if I interpret."

"I speak Keresh. It is rusty, but I had an estancia on the borderlands for many years. My workers were mostly Kereki day laborers."

Koanga and I visibly relaxed as he slipped into words we understood.

Our host looked at our passes again. "Willow, the daughter of a tailor. From the West Islands. How interesting. Our gossips are full of news of a woman named Ngahuru who was kidnapped along with the West Islands ambassador's children. The Matasi government has offered your King help in recovering his missing citizens. We have soldiers searching in Kerek City now, I have heard."

Ngahuru gave him her best smile. "That's so wonderful of your country! Ngahuru is a very common name in the West Islands. Although our passes say we have traveled from Kerek City, I never had the opportunity to meet anyone named Ngahuru there." She looked at me and then turned to our host. "And did you know our Conrosan friend here has been named for his country's folk hero, Zren Janin?"

It was a fine bit of misdirection and successful. Even I could follow what she needed me to do. Our host smiled at me, "Is that so? Then it becomes quite the name to live up to, doesn't it?"

I smiled weakly and replied, "I am just beginning to learn how much."

I shot Koanga a look for him to start talking, but our host went on, "Well, I have three rooms here, all on the second floor, and two of them have bathing rooms attached. Did you eat this evening? Your passes show you came into Anarkio very late."

"We did come in late. I picked up a stone in my shoe I could not shed on my own," Koanga explained. "Fortunately, a farrier overtook us on his way to a farm and he had a tool that was able to work it out for me. People are so kind here in Matasi."

I smiled hopefully. "No, we have not eaten this evening."

"Ah well, if you will indulge an old man an evening's conversation, I think I can put together something to quell that rumbling I hear." He chuckled. "The rooms are upstairs, and I will let you sort yourselves out as you wish. You are the only ones here with me. Come down after you have had a chance to wash up." He turned and walked towards the back of the house.

I trailed Ngahuru and Koanga up the stairs. None of the rooms had locks on them and I cocked my eyebrow when I showed Ngahuru.

"It's fine, Red. It's just us three and I promise not to visit you in the middle of the night." She smiled.

"That's not what I meant." I blushed but didn't say anything more. Koanga popped out of the end room.

"This one has a washroom attached. One of you can have it, or I'll share with the one who doesn't have one."

We sorted ourselves out, washed, and headed downstairs. Our host came to the greeting area. "I'm sorry, I forgot to introduce myself. I am Ebla Potenco of the Olio de Olivo groves. My daughter and my grandsons run the groves now, and I entertain myself by meeting travelers from across the seas." He dipped his head to each of us.

Ngahuru folded her hands formally to respond. "I am Willow of the West Islands, daughter of a tailor. I am traveling under the care of my brother, Koanga, a Storyteller of the West Islands who has his own hearth and home in Puna Mawhero. We have as our honored guest, Zren Janin from Conrosa, a country so far to the north of us they do not have the seasons Wet and Dry."

"A Storyteller! I am so fortunate!" Ebla Potenco clapped his hands. "Come to the table, my friends, we are going to have a lovely evening."

## CHAPTER 21

## CHOICES

I woke to full sun streaming in my window. I bolted upright, heart hammering, before I remembered where I was. Our host had let us sleep in very late. Last night, Koanga had told story after story of the constellations, and our host had kept our plates and glasses full. It was such a delightful evening, I was convinced we went to our beds closer to dawn than dusk. I craned my neck listening for movement or voices from Koanga or Ngahuru. Hearing neither, I threw back the covers and padded to the door. Once I eased it open, I realized there were voices, not my fellow travelers, but Miyamoto Suki and Ebla Potenco. I pulled my trousers on and threw my shirt over my head. Barefoot, I stepped out and rapped lightly on Koanga's and Ngahuru's rooms before I tiptoed down the stairs.

"Good morning, Zren! When none of you met me on the village green this morning, I walked here to find out what had happened to you. Your host has been very kind and has invited me over his threshold." Miya had his hands wrapped around a tiny drinking cup. "And, he has coffee from the hills of Vikland." He smiled broadly.

Ebla smiled shyly at me. "You said you three were only traveling to Salisport today, a half day's walk at most. Since I was the one who called for story after story last night, I thought it would harm no one if I did not send you out at first light." Ebla turned to Miya. "I have always wanted to travel to the West Islands and hear one of the Storytellers tell the great tales. Koanga indulged me many times last night with a tale from each constellation."

"You have been blessed." Miya smiled. "I spent the last year in the West Islands at the palace of the King and was only able to hear Koanga twice. The palace halls were crowded, but he is so renowned, I could stand in the very back and hear every word. The children are that quiet when he speaks. He has held his hearth and home for three years now." He paused and then added, "The King especially likes his Seafarer Tales."

"I liked the Soldier stories best." Ebla smiled and looked at me. "And what about you, Zren Janin? What stories do you like?"

"The Traveler." I smiled at him.

Ebla nodded. "I can see why that would be so. And what are the great stories of Conrosa?"

I thought of the stories Willow had told us as we had walked our way through Kerek—when she was still trying to learn who I was. "We have wise queens and fairies who like to live with the humans and partake of human joys." I bobbed my head. "And create mischief. But Willow tells them better than I do."

"Willow?" Miya questioned. "Of course," he muttered so low, I barely heard him, "In Keresh, Ngahuru would be Willow."

I stared at him slack-jawed. It had never occurred to me why Willow would choose such a false name while she was in her Kereki disguise. Miya saw my face, smiled, and explained to Ebla, "Our friend, Zren Janin, is like a magpie who gathers every bit of shine and song around him. He shall be a map of the world when he parts from us to travel to his home."

I heard footsteps and Ngahuru and Koanga came down the stairs together. They had both bathed and were dressed in the best clothes we had with us, the ones we had worn to cross the Matasi border. Ngahuru smiled at Miya but addressed her first words to our host. "Good morning, Ebla Potenco. Thank you for the gift of sleep this morning. It was a rare pleasure to be had on our journey."

"The sleep was only cut from one end of the night and sewn to the dawn. I was greedy in my gift of a West Islands Storyteller at my doorstep." He gestured to Miya. "This morning I received another gift, a prince of Vikland, who has lived and loved Matasi in the service of his country. He says he is a friend of yours."

"Yes. That is true," answered Koanga promptly.

"Then, sir," Ebla said turning to Miya, "please share our first meal with us."

"I will, and gladly." Miya made a small bow.

Make no mistake, Koanga was a fine cook with two pots and a campfire, but the meal we were served that morning was the best I had ever eaten. Bread so soft and light, I thought it would float off my hand. Little sausages that popped with heat and flavor. Brightly yolked eggs poached in tiny bowls. Elba Potenco brought out finger sweets and served it with those tiny cups of Vikland coffee. I loved the finger sweets but tasted the coffee and found it bitter. I tried to squish my face into pleasure, but Ngahuru noticed. The moment Ebla disappeared into the kitchen to bring out more food, she swapped out her empty cup for my full one. "This is a luxury too wonderful to waste," she admonished me.

Over our food, Miya told us what had happened since we parted in Ribelo. His pass had only been extended five more days. He had given up on finding a caravan and searched for Matasi guides to take him over the Silver Mountains. But it was too late in the season. At the higher elevations, the deadly mists were already settling in. With no guides, no caravan, and no extension on his pass, he was forced to backtrack to try to meet us and travel together to Salisport and his embasado.

"But how did you get here before us?" Ngahuru questioned.

"I hired a horse and took the northern route. There are fewer villages and towns so it is not open to walkers, but only horses. Since I made better time, I arrived here yesterday afternoon. Once I learned you had not yet arrived, I decided to wait on the village green for you. I was just getting ready to go back to my accommodations, when I saw you walking out of the building with your passes in your hand."

"So what now?" Koanga asked.

"Ebla Potenco said you were going to Salisport. We will talk about all our options on the road there." Miya didn't meet our eyes. "We still have a half-day of walking ahead of us."

We pushed back from the table and in Mata, I said "Ebla Potenco, thank you." I switched back to Keresh and continued, "That was the finest meal I have eaten with the best company I have known." I imitated Miya's small bow and caught Koanga grinning at me from across the room.

Everyone said thank you and we ran upstairs to pack our bags. Miya's travel pack was already by the door.

After another flurry of good-byes at the door, we swung easily down the road to Salisport.

* * * * *

Two decons later and I was wishing myself back in Anarkio. Koanga and Miya were still arguing over the plans on the way to Salisport. Koanga wanted me to sail with him to the West Islands so he could show me his country and show me off to his friends and family.

Miya wanted me to travel with him to Kerek City and then across the Northern Track to Vikland. In return, he promised to teach me the Conrosan language and culture and take me with him when he was posted to Conrosa. If I wished, I could find my family. He would help, if he could.

"Wait, wait," I had interrupted. "You knew I was from Kerek and I don't speak Conrosan? Who told you this? Ngahuru?" I turned on her.

"No one did." Miya tried to soothe me. "I greeted you in Conrosan in Ribelo and you didn't acknowledge me. You didn't even blink like you understood the words. Then when Ngahuru and I were talking later that day, she said you had saved their lives twice on the trip to Matasi. I knew without her saying more, you had killed to protect them. I had made an incorrect assumption based on the color of your skin. Once I looked at you, truly looked at you, I saw a Kereki man of Conrosan descent." He paused, and then said, "A man I would like to travel beside from Kerek City to my home in Vikland. In return, I would like to give you knowledge of your homeland. What you choose to do with that knowledge is yours."

Then Koanga had started arguing with him again, and the two were at it once more. Ngahuru slid her pack off her shoulder and kneeled down to shake a stone out of her boot. I dropped behind to wait for her, and I watched as Koanga and Miya kept on walking and talking.

"Thank you," she said as she picked up her pack.

"Let's not hurry. It's good to have a little peace and quiet." Ngahuru said nothing, and I shortened my steps to match hers. I watched as the two ahead of us pulled farther away. "You know the funny part? In Kaoso, I wished for an easy decision on what to do."

She said nothing for a while, and then spoke softly, "It's a decision between your head and your heart, isn't it?"

I squinted up at the sky and then looked at her. "Does being a dual soul mean you see both sides of the problem?"

She snorted. "You really have to stop believing everything Koanga tells you. I choose no gender, but because the world demands I call myself something, I am sometimes she, sometimes he, to match the time and place. Dual soul? Koanga would fill your head full of fanciful stories because he is in love with his own voice and imagination."

She put her hand on my arm and stopped me. "Red, I love my brother, and I see the way you look at him when you think no one is watching. But if you choose to go to the West Islands because you think you can change his mind about you, to get him to care for you the way I think you care about him, then you will have a heartache I would wish on no one."

I stared at her face looking for an answer. "You think I should go with Miya."

"Miya is ten years older than you are, maybe more. He has been raised in a palace, not as a son or daughter of a tailor with too many children to feed, but as a son and grandson of statesmen and ambassadors. The education he could arrange for you, the doors he could open for you...but it would have to be a future you want in order for you to risk your life again."

I blew out a breath. "Does he know I cannot read or write? That I lived in Lowertown before I met you?"

"No. It wasn't my story to tell." Ngahuru looked gently at me.

"Ngahuru, if he doesn't know I am from the Kerek City streets, then he is making his offer to Zren Janin, an illusion, a figment of your imagination, and not to Red, isn't he?"

"He wishes to travel with you and repay you, based on the man you are, and not on the boy you were in Kerek City," she replied stubbornly.

I said nothing and we walked along in silence. Up ahead, words drifted back from Koanga and Miya, and I didn't recognize it as Keresh. "What are they talking about now?" I pointed my chin at them.

She cocked her head and listened for a moment. "They are talking in Wester, and Koanga is explaining why our Seafarer tales are of a daughter and her mother, and a man with a village."

"Is that important?" I was surprised.

She considered. "Some constellations are male, like the Smith. Some are female such as the daughters of Mother Earth, Gems and Grains, Metals and Meadows and the others. Some are neither—like the Traveler and the Soldier, and some are told with many genders such as the Seafarer. People need to see themselves in the stories. How can we only say 'he' and 'she' when we are 'all'? How can we ask great things of ourselves, if all we see are 'others' as heroes?

"In the stories of Conrosa, the queens are always wise, but in the fairy tales some of the fae are good, and some of the humans are. In Matasi, the parables of the Lost God preach that he may come in any form: a rich person bearing gifts, a destitute person carrying nothing but sorrow. But the parables say, all strangers should receive justice and mercy, food and shelter. The Vikland warrior sagas are all about defending the defenseless and fighting for what is right and just. Our tales, in the West Islands, teach us who we are and who to be. We—all of us—need to be present in the stories."

She paused and looked at me. "You need to create your own story. You and you alone."

I thought for a while, and Ngahuru kept an easy pace with me. I wondered why she didn't race to spend her time with Miya since they would be parting within a day or two. I tilted my head and considered her. She glanced at me, then looked again. "Oh, stars! Just ask me already!"

"Miya doesn't know you are…as you are, does he?" I said slowly.

She sobered instantly and watched her feet. "That wasn't the question I thought you were going to ask." She huffed and I waited. Finally, "No. He doesn't. He belongs to another country in which I may serve my King, or future Queen. It is a secret we cannot risk sharing across borders."

"Yet you told two strangers, the waggoneer and his wife."

"I thought they were going to kill me." She shrugged. "No one will believe them if they tell their story." She looked at me. "In the West Islands, people like me are common enough, there are stories, as I have told you, of how we are kissed by the constellations on our way to earth. Some have only a hand, or part of a face, some have more color leeched out than I do. Yet, I have not seen anyone like me in any of my travels. Which leads me to believe either I am not common in other lands, or children like me were not permitted to live."

She let that soak in for a moment, and I felt a chill down my arms. What would it be like to think the only reason you are alive is by virtue of where you were born? There was no solace I could offer her. Awkwardly, I changed the subject. "You are fond of Miya?"

She scrunched her forehead. "Sure. I admire him because he wears his titles and honors well. He is kind to everyone, not just those who hold power. But most of all, I trust his words. I believe if you can keep him safe across the Northern Track of Kerek, he will do everything he promised, and more, to give you a life worth that risk." She fiddled with the straps of her traveling pack, and finally looked me in the face. "This is hard for me, Red, really hard. Miya is offering you everything I have wanted and worked hard for. It would be so easy for me to be angry at you, to think you ungrateful for not grabbing at this opportunity, but I have to remind myself of two things: This is your life to live and not mine, and what you want may not be what I want. Also, there is a very real possibility you two might not survive the crossing from Kerek City to the Vikland border."

We started forward again, and I stepped in beside her. "Ngahuru, the story you told of the Orphan Master of Kerek City. Do you think he would know what children he has sold? And from what ship?"

"He has to keep records, Red. He pays a tax to the King on the children by country and by age. When I worked for the ambassador, our office would redeem the orphans of the West Islands. We would pay a little extra to the Orphan Master to ensure none of the children were 'lost' on the streets of Kerek City. I'm not sure how far back the records would go, but I can't think there were so many Conrosan ships."

She stopped and pursed her lips. "Unless your parents were diplomats like Miyamoto Suki and his family. Then they could have been on any ship traveling from one location to their next posting, but then your queens would have tried to bring you home...if they knew you survived." She looked up at me. "I'm sorry, I've been thinking about this for a long time—ever since I met you on the road to Aldi."

"You're just asking the same questions I have been thinking." I smiled at her. "It's reassuring to me to know I have your clever mind thinking things through." Miya looked back at us and stopped, realizing how far ahead he and Koanga had gotten. "Ngahuru, let's catch up to the others. I've made up my mind." She waited expectantly.

"I'm going to Vikland with Miyamoto Suki."

## CHAPTER 22

## SALISPORT

Miya had been delighted when I told him I would travel through Kerek with him. He didn't say anything to Koanga, but he couldn't stop grinning. Koanga had given me a sour scowl, but after a moment nodded. "It has a good future for you."

I threw my arm around him. "If I live through Kerek." Koanga snorted in response, but for the first time, he didn't pull away immediately.

Miya and Ngahuru had dropped back and continued a long conversation, first in Keresh, and then when I turned back to listen, switched to Mata, and almost immediately into Wester. I looked at Koanga and he shrugged.

"It's a whole lot of political maneuvering," he said. "She cannot be discovered and detained this close to leaving Matasi, and he says his country must receive something in exchange for assisting her. It pains her more than you can imagine, Red. Subversiva didn't just leave us destitute, it leaves her exposed." Koanga gave me a side smile. "When you and I talk, Red, people may or may not choose to listen. When those two talk, they make promises their King and Empress must acknowledge. You choosing to travel with Miya helped her immensely." He looked up at me and gave me a sad smile. "Actually, you have been her greatest asset this entire journey home."

"But I didn't help! In Kerek, I do not think Goblin and Brick would have visited our camp if they had not recognized me in Aldi and followed us back. And if I wouldn't have insisted on being served at the Sion Inn, Rusty and Festus might not have noticed you. And it was me who made the mistake with the waggoneer and his wife. And your sister had to tell a pretty story when I did not have papers to cross into Matasi. I was the one the hosts have tried to talk to and I don't speak any Mata." I ran my hand through my hair. "All I have done is make things worse."

Koanga gave me a lopsided grin. "Quite the grand adventure for both of us, huh?" He sobered. "No, Red, you have allowed my sister to escape undetected. Even as we met the Matasians within Kerek's borders, you have stood like a shield between my sister and those who would look too closely at a pair of West Islanders who may be hunted by the Kerek King. You have done this from the very beginning, and you are doing it now with

Miyamoto Suki. Do not underestimate your value to him as you two travel across the Northern Track."

And that's how we walked into Salisport.

I had lived in Kerek City all of my remembered life, and I avoided the docks and wharfs as much as possible. I was small and I was fast, but if I was ever cornered and caught, I would not have survived any encounter in Dockside. The longshoremen gangs ran the docks with muscle and bribes. I had expected the same of the port cities of Matasi, but I had not accounted for their tidy laws.

We had a checkpoint at the edge of Salisport City, another at the entrance to the trade zone where the warehouses and trade offices were located, and finally a third checkpoint before we could enter the shipping area. This was where the schedules of the ships were located and the ships' captains registered in and out of the country. There were signs and arrows for on-shore housing for the sailors, and in front of us, the large administration building to buy tickets and passage to all the known world.

Now we watched Miya as he met with the shipping officials and talked about ships, sailing times, ports of call, and travel costs. In Kerek City, passengers negotiated directly with the captains for costs and sailing times. The trick was to find a captain who was leaving quickly, but not so quickly he sailed with all your coin while you went back to get your belongings.

It was how I assumed Koanga and Ngahuru had lost their coin and baggage. They wouldn't have been the first. Most people sailing out of Kerek City would try to board the ship immediately after securing passage, just to ensure the captain wouldn't leave after taking their coin and goods. Of course, showing up with your belongings without knowing if a ship was going to sail led to another set of problems. It was nearly impossible to secure passage and keep your belongings if you were traveling alone.

But in Matasi, all the information was posted about the ships and sailings, along with the tide tables. Fees were collected at a central office to be given to the captain at the point of sailing. Before the clerks would even allow us to book passage, they needed to see our travel passes and asked for our residence in Salisport until our ship sailed. Miya gave them the Vikland embasado's name and location. It raised a few eyebrows, but he showed them his diplomatic pass and some other papers I didn't get a good look at, and everyone quickly made time for him.

Ngahuru acted shy and quiet, allowing Miya to take charge. I knew she and Miya had that long discussion as we had walked into town, but this seemed so out of character for her. I tried to figure out what she needed to hide beside herself. And maybe that was enough, as I heard Miya dismiss her as "just the daughter of a tailor I know and offered to assist," when a clerk appeared too interested in her papers and gave her a long measuring look.

Miya found passage for Koanga and Ngahuru on a direct sailing to the West Islands on the following day, and one for Kerek City on the outgoing tide after that. Tickets, boarding passes, and checkpoint passes to get to the ships' zone were printed on fresh, clean, used-only-once paper in both Mata and the language of the final destination. When Ngahuru stepped forward to collect them, Miya had put a hand on her forearm. "I have asked the tickets, the passes, and the billing to be sent to the embasado. We can make final arrangements there."

Ngahuru said nothing but looked pointedly at his hand on her arm. He quickly removed it.

The clerk stamped our travel passes and gave us new ones to get out of the restricted areas. The head clerk reminded us again the paperwork and boarding passes would be sent over to the embasado along with the invoice, and if we were sure that was our final address. Ngahuru quirked a half smile and murmured, "Quite a clever way to ensure we are who we say we are."

Miya just grinned and ushered us back out into the sunlight.

It dawned on me how quickly we were going to be separated, maybe forever.

* * * * *

There was a Matasi checkpoint and then a Viklander checkpoint outside the Vikland embasado. Our bags were inspected, our remaining West Islands steel inventoried and kept at the Vikland checkpoint. We were finally allowed to enter. Miya spoke Vik the entire time, but we could follow along, a little. We were not searched, Miya had told them it would not be necessary, and showed his paperwork. He spoke Keresh only once, when he turned to us and asked Koanga and me to give up our boot knives. I didn't know he had even known we were carrying them. I wondered if he knew what else I was carrying, but the weapons we left behind were enough to satisfy the guards.

Inside the embasado's reception hall, we were introduced to the Secondo, the woman who ran the day-to-day operations of the ambassador's staff. She was surprised to see Miya back again, but he explained—again in Keresh—how he had not been able to get attached to a caravan or find a Matasi guide to take him over the Silver Mountains. With time running out before the rains began for the Wet season, he had returned to Salisport to sail to Kerek City and attempt the Northern Track.

Miya then introduced Ngahuru and her brother Koanga who were returning to the West Islands. I saw a flicker of a muscle jump in the Secondo's jaw as she heard Ngahuru's name, but she greeted her without any indication this was the woman most of the known world was searching for. Miya introduced me as Zren Janin, an emissary from Conrosa, a friend of Ngahuru, with experience in crossing Kerek and his future guide across the Northern Track. This time she could not hide her surprise and she quickly switched to Vik and asked Miya a series of questions. Miya's smile just grew larger and larger. I looked at Koanga and realized this was what he was trying to tell me when we had been walking into Salisport. We were all quite the prize for Miyamoto Suki to bring to the embasado. Miya gave a short answer and looked at Ngahuru.

"Forgive us our rudeness in speaking Vik," he said in Keresh, "Our Secondo has underestimated your ability to achieve the impossible, Ngahuru. She has asked for a moment to prepare overnight rooms for you. Food will be brought to a small reception room for all of us immediately. We will be given time to refresh ourselves, clean clothes will be supplied to our rooms, and there will be a short reception for us tomorrow morning with the ambassador and the people who are currently here in the area."

The Secondo interrupted, asked Ngahuru a few questions in Mata. Ngahuru looked confused for a moment then responded in Wester. Miya translated. Koanga and I surveyed the opulence around us.

If Matasi appreciated power and wealth as an indication of the Lost God's benevolence, then the Vikland embasado was a very good friend to Matasi and their god. The paintings and tapestries on the walls were all of Vikland warriors, long black braids, dark closefitting clothes that defined the muscular bodies of the heroes. Many of the women warriors were shown with crossbows, but a few carried the jeong or tahn bongs on long straps over their backs. They were inspiring rather than intimidating. Anyone who came to seek sanctuary or an alliance here would feel secure in the knowledge help was near.

The Secondo summoned two junior assistants and dispatched them with tasks. She asked us to follow her into a reception room. We would be served shortly, she said, but if she could be excused to oversee our accommodations herself and let the ambassador know we were here, she would be grateful. She addressed all of her remarks to Ngahuru, and Miya left the room with her.

Koanga smiled broadly after the staff and Miya had left the room. "Wait until our brothers and sister hear about this!"

Ngahuru rolled her eyes. "What I know is that our middle siblings will hear a tale of an adventure I will not recognize as one I traveled."

We wandered the room, looking at more paintings of Vikland warriors, this time in settings I didn't recognize. There were no tidy orchards of Matasi, no open scrubland and pastures of Kerek. Ngahuru came to stand beside me.

"What are these?" I waved my hand at the paintings. "Are these imaginary lands like the fairy tales you told me?"

Ngahuru kept her eyes carefully on the painting. "That's a good question. These are the Cold Mountains of Vikland, or possibly Kerek. They are far to the north in both countries and stand as a barrier between the land and the northern seas. The Vikland sagas tell how a woman invented the crossbow, and the warriors defeated the Monsters of the Mountains through her wisdom and the warriors' bravery."

"So that is what mountains look like," I muttered. I cut my eyes over to her and she was still looking at the painting. She glanced to our right and then walked over to another one.

"Come here, Zren," she called and I walked over. "This one, I think, is telling the story of how the Viklanders defeated the Beast of the Forest. I have read the story, but I have never seen a picture of it. The Beast of the Forest was another monster who preyed on the woodcutters and loggers who cut the logs to build the homes and fire the hearth. It represents the elements of nature who strive against those who protect the defenseless and give them shelter. See how the forests are dark and forbidding and the family stands around the house, each person's jeong bong touching the next, so nothing can pass by?"

Forests. The trees were huge compared to the scrubby stands along the rivers and streams in Kerek.

"Are they real?" I whispered. "Is that truly what Vikland looks like?"

"I don't know, Zren. I have never been there. The trees look different than what I see in the West Islands, but we call the same tight cluster of many many trees a forest." Ngahuru bit her lower lip. "Zren. Don't let anyone make you feel small for not knowing something. You have a wide-open heart and a wide-open mind. You can do this." She started to say more, but the doors opened to the sitting room and Miya walked in with the staff pushing two wheeled carts of food. The scent alone was wonderful.

As we filled our plates and found places to sit, Miya updated us, "Forgive me for abandoning you so quickly. I asked to speak to the ambassador to tell him all our passages have been booked, and I needed to see him to tell him of what I learned these past few days in Matasi.

"I also learned he is entertaining this evening and will not be able to meet with you, Ngahuru, but he is honored to have your brother as a 'diplomatic staff exchange' from the West Islands." He dipped his head to Ngahuru. She gave him a sly smile and I wondered why Koanga would cause such a reaction. "I have asked to have your rooms next to each other and Koanga and Zren will share a room. I will be on the floor below with others who live and work here. Once you have been shown to your rooms, let's clean, change, and go enjoy the city as guests of Vikland. I will come to gather you, as I must return to the ambassador who has more questions for me. The Secondo has confirmed there will be a small reception for a Storyteller of the West Islands tomorrow morning before you need to leave. It is very informal, only those assigned here will be permitted to attend. Again, the ambassador is disappointed he cannot entertain you this evening." He looked at Ngahuru. "As you wished." She gave him a grateful smile and straightened. Somehow, power had passed between the two and Ngahuru was once more in command. But for the life of me, I couldn't figure out what she had done.

Miya continued, "Any clothes you wish to be prepared for your journey—washed, pressed, mended—should be set outside your door this afternoon. They will be collected and returned to you tomorrow morning before the reception. No one will enter your room, save at your invitation." He paused. "Questions? Ah, good! Let's eat!"

I did have a question, but no way to ask it. Was I sharing a room because Miya thought I was a thief and he didn't trust me? Did this mean he would abandon me at the border of Kerek and Vikland? Ngahuru said she trusted him, but she hadn't even recognized him when they had met in Ribelo until he had prompted her. He had been friendly, but the charm he had scattered over her the first night had diffused into easy graciousness. I was thoughtful as I ate my food.

After we finished, Miya left us at the doors to our rooms while he went back to meet with the Secondo and the ambassador.

Koanga and I walked into a bedroom of soft smells and bright colors. There were two beds in the room, other furniture, and two soaking tubs in the adjoining room. The two rooms were in a space larger than the entire floor of the broken-down boardinghouse where I had hidden with other children in Kerek City. While we had been eating, staff had filled the two huge soaking tubs in our washroom with hot water and scented soaps. It was far, far finer than anything I could possibly imagine. I looked at Koanga and we both laughed.

"I see this, Koanga, and I think 'I was worried about karu kurii'?"

"I know. If I would have known this was how he traveled, I would have begged him to join us!"

I felt the sour feeling in my stomach return. "Koanga, do you think he put me in the same room with you because he thought I might steal something? Does he know I was a thief?"

Koanga looked surprised. "Of course not. He put us in the same room together because he knows we are friends and that after tomorrow, it may be years before we can see each other again. Because this fancy setting may be so much, we have questions for each other we would be too embarrassed to ask someone who works here. Because we have plans to make for tonight, tomorrow, and the next time we meet." He twisted his fingers together in that box shape again, threw them apart, and rained them down by his side. "Your world is no longer a tiny box, Zren. Don't be your own enemy. I may have saved your life, but Miya can *give* you a life."

"If I survive the Northern Track across Kerek." I scowled.

"Well, there is that."

While we had been talking, we had been undressing, and now we slowly lowered ourselves into the chin deep hot water. "Aaaaaaahhhhhhhh. I am never going to leave," I moaned in pleasure.

* * * * *

By the time Ngahuru had knocked on our door, Koanga and I had washed, dressed, napped, and sorted out our packs. She and Koanga gifted me all of their remaining West Islands steel still in their possession: two daggers and the maripi, the bone knife. I still had the steel knife from my boot, now sitting at the Vikland checkpoint, which Koanga had gifted me after the death of Goblin and Brick. It had never been taken from me at Subversiva. With the trek across northern Kerek still ahead of me, I felt a little better.

"I wished we had the steel pots we sold in Ribelo, and the canvas tents confiscated in Subversiva, but if wishes were horses, we would all ride behind the King," Ngahuru mused. "You will be joining Miyamoto Suki without our supplies, but it may be, he will travel very differently than we did, and our belongings that were sold or taken would not help you. We'll see what Miya has for plans, Zren."

Miyamoto Suki had also bathed and changed before he knocked on our door. Under his arm he carried a rolled map. Ngahuru asked if she and Koanga could stay while he talked with me about crossing Kerek. She had an interest in me, she said, and wanted to learn of my journey. I was grateful to her as Miya's plans were very different than walking across the Northern Track.

"I had thought we would make a quick dash across the top of Kerek. I've taken that road six times," he laid out the map on the desk. "There are inns with fast horses at Vingt, Balza, Huk, Cloa, Sary, and Ishes. With such a change of horses we would be home in five days or less, little or no sleep, near constant movement." He looked up at me.

My face must have told an interesting story because Miya's face turned from confident to…odd. "You don't ride a horse?" He looked at me, surprised, when I slowly shook my head. "Who doesn't ride a horse?" He hummed. "You don't ride a horse." He looked down at the map with a lost look.

"Miya, neither Koanga nor I ride a horse," Ngahuru snapped. "It is not like eating or breathing. It's only a part of Vikland culture, not the rest of the world."

Miya looked up from the map, stunned. "I am sorry. I was thinking about other options and not paying attention to the words that fell from my mouth."

He turned to me. "You need to see me fight and what weapons I can use. My word is not enough. But first we will see Salisport." Miya rolled up the map but left it in the room.

I looked at Ngahuru, and she answered the question on my face. "He needs time to come up with another plan, Zren. We can go out and all enjoy tonight and leave the hard thinking to him." She smiled gently at me, and we followed Miya down the stairs and out into the evening.

## CHAPTER 23

## WEAPONS TRAINING

I groaned and rolled over on my back. The daylight spilled across my bed, and I let myself drift with my eyes closed. I heard Koanga's giggle and I opened one eye. Miya was standing over me, arms crossed, eyebrows raised.

"You are young, Zren. You are the youngest of all of us. You should be able to eat and drink, sing and dance to praise songs all night, sneak as deviously as a softfoot through the streets of Salisport evading curfew patrols, *and* be the first one up in the morning! Instead, I find you still kissing your pillow with the morning half-gone."

I opened the other eye to see Koanga still in bed as well. "I think you have had years of practice, Miya," I told him, smiling. "Years!"

He grinned back. "Come, both of you. The guards are in a weapons training session, and I want Zren to see this before the ambassador's reception."

"Your embasado has weapons training?" Koanga questioned. "Is that even permitted in Matasi?"

"We rotate our assignments between Kerek, the Islands, and Matasi. The Matasi Triune understands the need to keep Kerek within its fences and to keep our people safe in Kerek City. To be assigned here is a relaxing assignment before and after Kerek. Not as much fun as a West Islands or Spice Island posting, but we all can't live in paradise." He threw my covers off. "Up!"

Koanga and I pulled our clothes on and followed him down to the courtyard. There were three people choosing their weapons when we walked in, and Miya hurried over to make a fourth. The weapons looked like very thick walking sticks, and I recognized them from the paintings and tapestries the day before. The four paired off and held their weapons gently across their stomachs. A sharp command from the woman across from Miya and they were fighting. Sometimes the staffs were used as blocks, sometimes to trip, strike, or spear. It was like nothing I had ever seen in Kerek. I watched Miya take a sharp blow to the shoulder and while he winced, he swept his staff at the legs of an opponent and dropped him. I heard a whistle, everyone stopped, and the captain came out carrying four shorter staffs. The fighters gave short bows to each other, drank from their flasks, and exchanged the long staffs for the short ones. Miya stepped away and the captain stepped in. Together we watched the next sparring match.

"What do you call those long ones again? Ngahuru told me, but I forgot," I asked Miya.

"Jeong bong. Those are the ones that are taller than me. The short ones are called tahn bong."

"No daggers?"

Miya winced as he rubbed his shoulder. "We don't have access to West Islands steel, and our own metals make inferior weapons." He huffed. "Actually, our metals are the same, we just don't have the knowledge to build the foundries and smelters the West Islands have. But, in Vikland, every villager can learn to use some type of bong and they can be readily harvested from our trees. You use what you have." He looked at me. "Have you ever fought against someone using one of these?"

"No, but I can see how it would eliminate any height disadvantage. The woman across from you was the shortest of the four and she wiped the floor with all of you."

He laughed. "You whisper a lot of sweet nothings for someone who has never fought against me."

"They have West Islands steel flasks," Koanga pointed out.

"Yes. Every time someone is posted or travels to the West Islands, they buy as many of your metal workings as gifts as possible. We honor your demand that we not sell your steel, but your many other creations are much coveted in Vikland. And since military service is required of everyone immediately after the academies, there are many who receive gifts."

Koanga looked skeptical, and I continued to watch the guards practice. It was more about footwork and defense, and luring your opponent into making a fatal error, than it was about battering them to the ground. Mmmm. I knew I was fast, and I wondered if this might be a weapon I could fight with. "Huh. Can you teach me how to use them? On the way from Kerek City to Vikland?"

Miya smiled. "Certainly. I also have something else I would like to show you." He turned, and we followed him down a long narrow path against the outside wall surrounding the embasado. To the far left were three concentric circles a hand's width wide, the first just taller than Miya, then chest height, and finally the smallest one in the middle, waist high. To the right was a wooden table with a variety of crossbows. I had seen the Viklander patrols wearing them on their back or held in their hands as they walked the streets of Lowertown, but I had never seen how they worked. I peered closely at Miya's hand as he explained, "These are quarrels, or some call them bolts."

"West Islands steel," Koanga said accusingly. "We don't make these at home. We use short bows with quivers of arrows."

"Koanga, I am a lowly foot soldier. I know nothing except what I am told." Miya held the crossbow so we would watch him. "You load the quarrel like this, cock it here, aim, and shoot." The quarrel landed in the straw bale just to the right of the second chest high circle. "Of course, I expect both of you to do better than I do." Miya gave a chagrined smile.

Koanga reached out for it. "Did you see our hunting bows when you were in the West Islands?" Gracefully, he loaded, aimed, and shot. The quarrel leaned left but tipped the edge of the innermost circle. He gave us both a sly grin.

Miya gave a delighted laugh. "Well done! I did see your hunting bows, but I was not as adept as you must be. Our government controls the making and exporting of our crossbows so I couldn't bring one to the West Islands for a gift, but I could see the similarities. Your bows take better advantage of your steel production and are better for heavy cover in your rainforests. Our crossbows are better in our plains and open mountain passes... and defense."

I looked at the bow in Koanga's hands but made no effort to take it. "It's a distance weapon—no good in Kerek City, which favors hand to hand fighting. There is no way to recover the quarrels if the plan is to ambush someone from the rooftop or a high window." I looked at Miya then. "You could not take it in a traveler's pack because it is too large, and just carrying it would make you a bigger target as you walked from village to village."

"But in a Viklander wagon train or caravan, this is the weapon of choice." Miya plucked it out of Koanga's hands and gave it to me. "Try it, I want to see what you think."

I couldn't figure out how to aim it, even though loading it didn't seem that difficult. My shot went so wide, it even missed the circling straw bales.

"Ah, Zren." Miya clapped me on the shoulder. "It will be tahn bongs and jeong bongs for both of us."

"And West Islands steel daggers," added Koanga. "Your guards are holding them at the checkpoint, but we have gifted Zren all of our steel except for my tailor's kit. I would send it along as well, but I don't think you could turn that into a weapon as well as I did."

Miya smiled at the tone in Koanga's voice. "Your talents were as valuable as any in getting your sister home. And thank you for your gifts to Zren Janin. I know I will benefit from them as well. Let's go find Ngahuru now. We have an ambassador who wants to listen to our stories. If we tell them well enough, he'll send us home with coin and courage. You will be able to tell your father and your King you have brought Ngahuru home."

I squinted at Miya. "Ngahuru saved herself. She wasn't helpless."

"No, she wasn't," Miya agreed easily. "I think in the days to come, Zren Janin, you will learn what Vikland, Matasi, and Kerek have already learned. Ngahuru is a formidable opponent, and an essential ally. She can weave her talents into a silken thread so gentle, but so strong, one doesn't realize how well the board has been played until all the pieces have been toppled. Power is not always displayed in front of you, Zren. That is the most important lesson I have ever learned from Ngahuru." He gave me a disdainful look. "What we say, and what we know, are not always the same words.

"I know—Vikland knows," he corrected, "the ambassador's children are safe. They were Ngahuru's responsibility. I have traveled with you, and she does not display grief over their death or regret over her failure. We know ships were searched, and she would never desert them. The King in Kerek is so incompetent, and the court so corrupt, she never would have left them there. She won, against all of us," he gave me a half grin, "and I for one would love to learn how she did it."

I considered his words and what else he was saying. "Why doesn't anyone do anything about Kerek?"

"Who?" Miya looked at me closely. "The court is corrupt. The court members benefit from the King's excesses. They are piling up wheelbarrows full of coin and hiding behind walls two feet thick. The King collects taxes to pay for parties for his friends, and the honest and the poor suffer. Those who have power through the King's favor are not going to suddenly throw power away and do the right thing. And those who don't have the power have no way to make it right. To kill the King is regicide, and to kill the two princes would be murder. Whoever would succeed as King would be forced to have their first ruling be the capture and execution of the King killer. Who will make that sacrifice to save the kingdom?"

CHAPTER 24

# THE AMBASSADOR'S RECEPTION

We reached the reception room, and I stopped short. Last night Miya had taken us out to eat and enjoy the city. Today, I saw for the first time how many people called the embasado home. There were people gathering food at sideboards lined along the walls, finding open seats at the tables scattered about the room, having drinks poured, or just milling about talking with others.

Men and women were dressed in a variety of clothes: Vikland's dark trousers and shirts and black boots with laces, the brightly colored shirts and sand colored wide-legged pants of Matasi, even the shapeless tunics, billowy shirts, and baggy trousers of Kerek. I could smell more of the Vikland coffee, as well as juices and West Islands tea. I saw Ngahuru, dressed in her best dress, speaking with a young Vikland woman. We followed Miya through the line, found our seats, and before he could even sit down, he was called away to talk to some friends. Another

Viklander, this one dressed in Matasi bright colors and sand colored pants, took his place.

"*Bonan matenon,*" he nodded to us.

Koanga peered around me. "Good morning. Do you speak Keresh? My friend here is traveling there tomorrow and needs practice." I turned and gave a pointed look to Koanga, but he just returned a bland smile.

"Certainly." The Viklander smiled at me. "I heard you were going to go back with Miyamoto Suki. I came through that northern route last year with only three others. Ran the horses nearly flat out. No bandits on the road, but we were robbed at an inn in Balza. By the time we walked into the embasado in Kerek City, we owned only the clothes we were standing up in. I couldn't wait to get posted to Matasi. If I ever have to go back to Vikland, I'm crawling through the Silver Mountains," he shuddered dramatically.

"You've traveled the route? What can you tell me? I've never been beyond Vingt." I pushed my plate forward to listen.

"Actually, the closer you are to Kerek City, the worse it is. You wouldn't think so, since there is more military near the city. But the military garrisons at Earles and Ishes are well run right now with career commanders. There are pioneer families near there and lots of small settlements. Ishes is only a half day ride, one day's walk from the Vikland border, and we've provided a trading post, some loggers, healers, and teachers to help the settlers closer to our border than Kerek City. It may not be enough they would side with us in a revolt, but they know we would provide better protection than anything coming out of Kerek City. As for Vingt and Balza? Sleep with one eye open." He laughed and reached for another pastry on the table. "I don't know if Miya snores, but it would have to sound like Vikland fire explosions before I would sleep alone in any inn along the Northern Track. There are as many cutthroats inside the inns as outside."

I looked at Koanga. He had a thoughtful look on his face but was silent.

"I'm Bima Ritwik." The Viklander nodded his head towards us. "You'll get more up to date information in the embasado in Kerek City, but I would rather tell you the worst and have you be happily relieved, than to leave anyone unprepared of what they will face."

"I am Zren Janin of Ke—Conrosa," I stumbled, but Bima pretended not to notice. "And this is Koanga, a Storyteller of the West Islands."

"Ah, it was *your* sister who survived in Kerek City when the ambassador was murdered. I heard she was here yesterday, but when I came to meet her, you had left to enjoy the evening in Salisport." He looked around the room until his eyes lit on Ngahuru. "My, she's a tiny thing. Could one of you introduce me? I have some questions I would like to ask her." He pushed back his chair and Koanga joined him. I played with my fork while I watched. After a moment, I saw Koanga frown, and then he gave a false smile and started back to me. I raised an eyebrow, waiting.

"I introduced him, he said he had some questions about Kerek City, and she switched to Mata. She *knows* I don't speak Mata." He paused. "I really don't like Bima Ritwik."

I smiled knowingly. "Ah, come on. The real reason you are scowling is because he didn't fall all over himself when he found out you were a Storyteller. Is this what your sisters and brothers have to put up with when you are made known on the West Islands?"

"I suppose that may be part of it, but only a very small part." He considered his words carefully. "He's very dismissive of Ngahuru. I know that is what she wants, everyone to underestimate her, but it hurts to hear sometimes." He groused. "If we wouldn't have lost our coin and belongings at the jail in Subversiva, we never would have needed Miya's help. Vikland is being very gracious about it, but this will still cost our King." He paused before adding, "To come here was a difficult choice for Ngahuru, no matter what Miyamoto Suki thinks."

We sat for a moment watching the room. We were certainly the youngest, but the groups of people gathered about Miya were all about his age. I was startled to see that he wasn't as tall as I thought. Amongst the four of us, he had stood a solid hand's length above me and the West Islanders were even shorter than I was.

I took a closer look at the group now standing about Ngahuru. Bima had now been joined by the Secondo we had met yesterday, and two additional females, one wearing Kereki male clothes. None of them had the soft overfed look I had noticed in the Kerek officials or the Matasi clerks. Actually, the more I looked at them, the more they looked like soldiers in hiding.

"Say, Koanga. What do you know about Viklanders?"

"They're all taller than me." He scowled. "And prettier." I followed his line of sight and saw two more people enter the room and walk over to Miya and his circle. The man carried himself as elegantly as a King, and I thought of Ngahuru's remark of Viklanders' grace and beauty. His skin was darker than the others, more like burnished gold, and I wondered if he spent most of his time outdoors. His long black hair was in a thick braid down his back like the others, but he had wavy tendrils escaping while most of the Viklanders' hair was straight. I glanced from him to Koanga and back again. The man was truly the most beautiful person I had ever encountered. Koanga was staring at the woman who was also stunning...and stunningly tall. But instead of smiling, he was still scowling.

I gave him an indulgent look. "I seem to remember you saying the Kerek King's walking stick was taller than you. No, are the Viklanders fighting with anyone? Grudge matches? Royal abductions?" I found my attention straying to the beautiful man again.

"I don't know anything like that. I do know all youth must serve three years in the military, but I think you were with me when Miya said that. Ngahuru says their great tales are of warriors of all genders. She could tell you some, but I have not learned them yet. They are a country surrounded by mountains…and Kerek, but they are not poor for all that. They are blessed with many natural resources. Their people are travelers taught to speak many languages from the time they are young." He paused, waiting for me to look at him to catch on to his meaning. "Ngahuru has said they can trip over their noses looking down at other people."

I laughed. "You're still upset about Bima Ritwik? No. I meant, doesn't it seem odd how everyone looks like a soldier out of uniform?"

I watched him as his eyes slowly took in the room and then narrowed. "Well, they would have to be exceptionally strong and healthy to come over the mountain passes in the Silver Mountains to come work here in Matasi. And the Northern Track from Vikland to Kerek City isn't a stroll on a Matasi green. Then they would also have to sail to the Spice Island or to the West Islands to the embasados there."

"That would explain it and yet…" I let my thoughts trail off and continued to watch the room. It was like working the tavern rooms with Goblin and Brick back in Kerek City. Watching to see how the power and coin rocketed around the gambling tables, illegal transactions, and sinner's market trades. It was about who had power at the beginning of the interaction or introduction and who walked away with it at the end.

I watched the group with Ngahuru and the Secondo in it. Ngahuru's stance was open and her gestures wide. She was doing most of the talking with the others asking the questions. The Secondo stood to the side, not facing her. I heard Mata spoken, Ngahuru paused and considered for a long moment, then answered in Wester, and switched to Keresh. Ah, her language skills were not as deep as I thought. The entire group shifted to Keresh, and I wondered what it would be like to be able to talk in so many languages to include or eliminate someone by a word or phrase. There was a kind of power in that as well.

I shifted my gaze to watch Miya. His group had risen from the end of the table and others had joined them. Miya stood with his legs slightly apart, weight forward, and his shoulders back. A soldier at rest. He wasn't the shortest in the group, but most of the others were broader than he was. I remembered how easily he had slipped into weapons training with the jeong bong.

I wondered suddenly if he had deliberately missed the target with the crossbow, so Koanga and I would be comfortable trying it without feeling foolish. It takes power to give up power, I reasoned. If we were back in the taverns in Kerek City, I would say he was the most powerful person in his group. I wondered if it was the same here. He must have felt my eyes on him. He finished talking, crossed his arms, and looked over to me. He raised an eyebrow and waved me over.

"Come, Koanga. We're being summoned." I pushed back my chair and looked down at Koanga hastily swallowing another kolache. I grinned at him.

"What? I'm going to be on a ship for days and days. You think I am going to just look at a plate of fresh baked pastries when they are placed right under my nose?" He dusted his hands over his plate, stood, and together we made our way over to Miya and his group. The circle shifted easily, and I found myself standing next to Bima Ritwik again. I wasn't sure when he had moved from Ngahuru's side to Miya's group. My surprise must have shown on my face because Miya laughed gently.

"Forgive him, Zren." Miya smiled. "Bima Ritwik is a shadow, and we seldom pay any attention to him anymore."

I looked at Miya in astonishment and poked Bima just to make sure he was real. This time the whole group laughed, but not unkindly.

"Ah, Zren. A gatherer of secrets, like Ngahuru, that kind of shadow. A softfoot." This time I had schooled my face in time and Miya introduced me to the others. "This is Zren Janin. He is Conrosan born, but raised in Kerek. His tongue has no accent. He will be traveling with me over the Northern Track."

"Weapons training?" An older woman with a light scar near her eye asked.

"He does hand to hand fighting, owns and knows how to use West Islands steel very well, according to Ngahuru," Miya supplied.

"Ah, but can you keep secrets?" Bima asked.

I thought of everything I had learned on the trip with Koanga and Ngahuru. What I had done to survive in Kerek City and beyond. And what Miya had done and not done to get us here to this place. As long as I did not have to lie outright, my face should let me keep any secret I chose to.

"Yes." I didn't say anything more, and Miya smiled at me.

"How many languages? And I mean fluent, not just soft words to flatter someone so you don't sleep alone?"

I blushed and looked at the one who had spoken. It was the beautiful man Koanga and I had observed when he walked in before. That he had said those words made me wonder if he had noticed me admiring him earlier.

"Only Keresh—castle Keresh," I answered him. "It is not a language known for seduction. Perhaps you could recommend another?"

The group burst out laughing and Miya clapped me on the back. "Well played, Zren, well played. Solkka needs to be reminded now and then, he really is just another pretty face."

Solkka laughed easily along with the others and gave me a lazy smile which nearly melted me where I stood. The room behind us quieted, and I turned to see a middle-aged man had entered. His hair was neatly queued like Miya's, and he wore a crisp black shirt, close fitting pants, and the black lace up boots like the ones I had seen on the staff practicing that morning in the courtyard.

Everyone in the room stood a little straighter and stilled. I was right. He was used to commanding soldiers. His eyes roamed the room until he found the Secondo, he nodded once. He looked at Miya and nodded again. Then his eyes traveled to me and back to Miya. Miya nodded, and the man turned and walked out. As the room resumed the conversations, Miya took me by the elbow. "The ambassador wants to talk to us."

"He didn't say a word," I protested.

Miya quirked a small smile. "Really? Because I distinctly heard a command to bring you to his office now." We stepped away from the others, and I heard him whisper under his breath, "Tell the truth, whatever else you say or do, tell the ambassador the truth."

## CHAPTER 25

## SECRETS REVEALED AND KEPT

Bima Ritwik volunteered to walk Ngahuru and Koanga back to their rooms and I followed the Secondo and Miya up a floor to the ambassador's office. It was large and well furnished. Miya's opened travel bag sat in one of the soft chairs fronting the ambassador's desk. The Secondo ushered us instead to a table covered with maps and papers. I marveled at the amount of paper casually weighted down with glass orbs or flat metal disks. The Secondo and Miya stood across from each other and we each stood at each straight edge of the table.

"Good morning, Zren. Or do you prefer to be called 'Red'? Or even another name?" The ambassador began.

"Zren. Please call me Zren." I licked my lips nervously.

He looked at the Secondo. "You questioned Ngahuru?"

"Yes," she replied. "There are some gaps in her story. She refuses to say anything about the children. Says her brother is here on a grand adventure and she is accompanying him and his friend, Zren Janin, who also goes by the name of Red." The Secondo looked at me. "She is protecting this one a little, I think."

He nodded once and looked at me. "Miya told us yesterday you guided the two West Islanders from Kerek City to Salisport. The trip took you ten days. Are you a guide? What country do you serve?"

"Actually," I took a deep breath. "I think I know what Ngahuru is protecting about me. I better tell you everything before I travel with Miyamoto Suki."

And I did. Bima Ritwik would have been so disappointed, or impressed, as I laid out all my secrets. I wasn't sure. I told of my growing up in Kerek City. My survival in Lowertown based on theft and being faster than those chasing me. I explained the difference between metal poisoning and death by disagreement during a forced barter. I insisted I had never done a murder for coin, but admitted I had defended the West Islanders by causing the death of others. It was storytelling and misdirection, but I had spent enough time with Ngahuru to understand the part she needed me to play.

"How much did the West Islanders pay you to get them from Kerek City to Salisport?" the Secondo asked.

"It was a life debt owed. They found me by the side of the road between Kerek City and Aldi." Then I heaved a big sigh and told them about the trickery we had planned for Primo Resoro, the wealthy son of the Kerek King's treasurer. How it had gone wrong, how Brick and Goblin found us outside of Aldi, how Ngahuru had ended Brick's life in self-defense. There! I wanted to say, Ngahuru is not helpless. She does not need Vikland.

"These were your business associates?" The ambassador lifted an eyebrow. "And you were able to betray them so freely?" He cut a concerned glance at Miya.

I shook my head. "It wasn't like that. Kerek City demands you run in a gang to survive. Loners are stalked and easily murdered. As soon as you are untied from someone's apron strings, it's a constant maneuvering to find someone faster, stronger, smarter to run with, and be safe from."

"You say you are from Lowertown. Who can be bribed in the docks area? Say if a load of weapons were to come through?" The Secondo interrupted.

"Everyone. The docks are run by longshoremen gangs. They decide if and when your cargo will be unloaded. They take a cut of your shipment to sell on the sinner's market. You can sell your goods in Kerek and find your worse competition is goods stolen from your own shipment—and sold for a lower price. The ships' captains negotiate who they will take, and when they will sail. Never send a woman to the docks to negotiate, she won't come back. But you know all this already. There is no way for a Viklander to travel over the sea without going through Kerek City or Matasi ports."

I wondered why she had asked me this, and then hazarded a guess. "You asked me this to confirm my story I am from Lowertown."

The ambassador flicked his eyes to Miya again and then focused back to me. "You never met Ngahuru until you met her on the road to Aldi?"

"No."

The ambassador raised an eyebrow, and Miya coughed under his breath, "Sir."

"No, sir," I repeated.

"Ngahuru said she had been hiding in Kerek City," he explained. "We had people looking for her and the others we thought had escaped the assassination and the bloody purge afterwards. We found bodies, but not her, the children, their Matasi guard, and one other we have searched for. Yet, you say, if she was traveling alone, she never would have survived. Where did she place the children? How does a West Islander who comes no higher than my waist, buy food, drink, and shelter in Kerek City when their embasado has been looted and occupied by soldiers? How do the children and Ngahuru escape all of the Kerek soldiers, Matasi busybodies, and our own softfooters until she appears in Ribelo, Matasi and is reacquainted with our Miyamoto Suki?" He glared at me and then Miya.

I made my face as blank as possible. *By hiding in plain sight,* I thought to myself. She had turned herself into a Kereki street boy to steal and buy food. She was taller than the ambassador's waist, but not enough to attract attention if she was impersonating a skinny street urchin on the edge of childhood. She said she had her reasons for keeping her secrets from the Viklanders, and so I would give up mine before I would betray hers.

I shrugged my shoulders. "She didn't tell me how she survived in Kerek City before I met her, and I didn't ask. But she was able to evade an ambush on the Coast Road and defend her life near Aldi. She thinks fast and has courage."

"So do you." The ambassador smiled at me. "We have a different plan for you than what Miyamoto Suki offered earlier. He wanted a fighter to get him across the Northern Track as quickly as possible. I am looking for more than that. What was your price for keeping Miyamoto alive?"

This was it then. I took a deep breath. "Ambassador, I learned in Matasi it is possible to pay for your food after you have eaten it. I could ask for gold upfront, but I would be robbed of it in Kerek City before the first day on the Northern Track. I would like to be paid this way instead. I will get Miya alive to Vikland and I will stay and learn two languages, Conrosan and Wester, and learn to fight with the crossbow and the bongs. Then I wish to accompany your diplomat to Conrosa. There, I will serve at the pleasure of your court until I find my family or, as the Conrosan fairy tales have it, for a year and a day."

The ambassador's eyebrows climbed nearly to his hairline. "That is a very ambitious payment for six, maybe seven days' work."

"That's a very appropriate payment for a life that could be lost each morning of the journey," I responded soberly. I glanced at Miya and caught the laughter in his eyes before he quickly dropped them to the maps on the tables.

"Well, then I agree to your terms. But now I certainly don't have any qualms about telling you about your new crossing assignment." He looked down at the maps and put a thick finger on Kerek. "You and Miyamoto Suki and Bima Ritwik will travel from here to Kerek City on the 'Silver Boot.' It's a Kereki registered ship, but the captain and some of the crew are ours. In Kerek City, you will stay at the Vikland embasado and pick up any who need to return to Vikland. While you are waiting in Kerek City for those Viklanders who will be traveling with you,

I want you to examine the West Islands embasado." He stared at Miya. "You know what you are looking for. Don't wait more than two days in Kerek City. I would like you out of town before the..." He glanced at me. "Events."

Miya nodded. The ambassador turned to me. "Miya tells me you do not know how to ride a horse or shoot a crossbow."

"Not a lot of demand for that in Kerek City." Before Miya could remind me again, I added, "Sir."

He looked at Miya. "There will be many due for a rotation home. Pick at least two outriders good with the crossbow. You will be responsible for payments and the arrangements. Craft your story based on those who will accompany you. We have materials and goods to go from here to our garrisons. Zren can drive one of the wagons. I believe your wagon train will be two, possibly even three, wagons. It depends on what is needed and must remain behind in Kerek City. I have letters for Ambassador Lalsy in the Kerek City embasado explaining my reasoning, but she may override my choices based on her own knowledge and her softfooters' information. I would expect no less."

The ambassador tapped his fingers on the table and frowned at the Secondo. "Get them what they need. Find Bima Ritwik. He knows he is going, but I have more for him." He gave Miya a level look but addressed the Secondo, "Allow the West Islanders to make their sailing. A runner should be sent now to upgrade their cabins to the best on the ship and to secure passage for an appropriate honor guard. We will honor Ngahuru's request to slip out of Matasi unannounced. I will write a letter to accompany them as the West Islands King needs to know how 'honored we are to escort a Storyteller of the West Islands home to his hearth. We wish his grand adventure was all that he expected.' This is the story our Matasi and Kerek neighbors must hear."

He nodded his dismissal to Miya, and we followed the Secondo out. Miya stopped her in the hallway. "Bima is with the West Islanders, I will find him and send him to the ambassador. We have travel packs, but we will need fresh clothes and coin. I have nearly nothing. Zren, what do you have?"

"Nothing. I was found without coin. Ngahuru paid all of my costs." I kept my eyes on the floor to hide my lies, but Miya merely nodded absently and turned back to the Secondo. "We would like to see the West Islanders before they leave. Is that possible?"

"It should be. No big gestures, Miya. We are carrying on the illusion for Matasi we have entertained Koanga, the great Storyteller of the West Islands, and his sister. We have your map of their path from Ribelo to Anarkio. Bima will send one of his softfoots to retrace their journey to ensure there are no suspicions of her identity."

She paused. "We have been careful there will be no meetings or interactions with the ambassador that can be carried to other ears. Only the honor guard will discuss the cost of our silence." She glanced at me. "May we have permission to enter your rooms to deliver your needs?"

Miya answered, "Yes. I am in the staff room with Solkka Ulani for this stay. Zren is in the guest room with Koanga, but of course you already know that."

"Yes. Solkka returned from Alenti yesterday." She gave a half smile. "The ambassador was pleased to see him at the reception. I don't think he'll have a long stay in Salisport." She paused. "Now send Bima and enjoy your time with the West Islanders."

We raced up the stairs to Ngahuru's room, but there was no response, so we tried at my door. I walked in first, and while it was clear they had been in here, no one was in the room now. I crossed over to the window and looked out.

Miya saw the note on Koanga's bed. "We are in the formal garden," he read aloud. "That's odd. It's in Vik. I wonder why Bima would choose to write in a language you don't know, if you would have returned here alone."

I thought to myself, because then I would need to wander the hallways looking for someone to read the note to me. He wanted to remind me of how small and insignificant I was. Even if he didn't witness my humiliation, it still would have been done.

Aloud, I said, "Perhaps he wanted to surprise them. Ngahuru is so accomplished in languages, he was hard pressed to find one she didn't read. He wanted you to know where they were of course, but he wanted them to be pleased when he showed them such beauty."

Miya gave me a funny look. "Did you just try to lie to me? Your face and words do not agree…" Before he could finish, I turned and walked down the stairs.

## CHAPTER 26

## GOODBYE

We found only Koanga and Ngahuru in the gardens. Someone else had found Bima Ritwik and sent him on his way to the ambassador.

"So we have maybe two decons before you say goodbye to Matasi for a very long time." Miya smiled at Ngahuru. "Is there anything you must do before you leave for the ship?" His grin widened, "Maybe, tuck a couple of lost children in your travel bag?"

She gave him a mischievous smile. "You have been a friend beyond price, Miyamoto Suki. We both have played our parts, and if it was within my grace to grant you more of the truth, you would have it. There is nothing I must yet do on this side of the sea."

We wandered through the gardens, talking about the future, remembering the past. When Koanga expressed worry that the travel ahead would be difficult for the two of us, Miya said Bima Ritwik would be traveling with us, but said nothing of the wagon train across Kerek. I did tell Ngahuru in one quiet moment, I was not taking Miya across the Northern Track for gold, but for an education. I hoped to be able to write her a letter someday in both Wester and Conrosan.

"Better yet, I will write the letter in Wester telling you *where* to meet me in Conrosa. We shall both live there someday." Koanga turned back and saw us whispering but said nothing and didn't approach us.

She squeezed my arm in reply. "I would like that, Zren. There is so much more ahead of you. I wish to see the man you are someday."

As we walked and talked, we shifted partners again and again, and too soon I found myself next to Koanga for the last time. I thought about all of the things I would miss about him, his old-fashioned way of speaking Keresh, his smile, and his stories.

"Thank you for your stories, Koanga. But most of all thank you for stopping by the side of the road."

He considered me thoughtfully. "I have had my grand adventure and am ready to go to my hearth and home and tell the stories of the stars. It hurts me to say this because so much that is ugly has happened on this trip. You are not the only one who had to crawl out of a box to see the greater world. My sister may have taught me one or two things as well as she did you. I have learned the lessons, but, you my friend, were the far better pupil."

He took my hands in his. "When you come to the West Islands, my Traveler, and note I said 'when,' when you come to the West Islands, please spend some nights at my home. I will look for you as eagerly as the Seafarer searches the night sky for the homeward star."

Bima Ritwik came to meet us then. "It's time," he said. "I'm sorry, we need to get them to the ship."

We five walked back upstairs, Bima the only one talking. "Miya, the ambassador wants to see you again. Zren, I will go with you and the West Islanders to the Viklander checkpoint. You'll have to say goodbye there as you will not be permitted to go further. I will see them to the ship."

Bima waited in the hall while Koanga and Ngahuru packed their bags with the freshly cleaned clothes and Ngahuru's papers. There was nothing else to pack. Everything else had been sold, stolen, confiscated, or gifted away. She picked up her travel bag and adjusted it on her shoulders. "Who would have guessed this is all I would have after nearly three years in Kerek City? I certainly hope my next posting goes better!"

We walked to the ship and Bima graciously fell behind so we could continue to say our goodbyes. "Be careful, be safe." What else was there to say? In ten days, my world had been turned upside down, and now I was saying goodbye to the ones who saved me. I asked, just in case Ngahuru could make it so, "I had hoped to go on the ship with you. I have never been on one before, and I didn't want to look the fool when I stepped on one with Miya later." She glanced behind at Bima, and then looked at me sadly and shook her head.

"It is not the Viklanders or the West Islanders who make this impossible," she said quietly. "I must be sailing on the seas before Matasi ever knows I was here. I am sorry, Zren, this is bigger than the three of us."

I huffed to hide my disappointment. "I am going to ask the rude question. Is this how embasado staff acts? Because today we have not been out from under someone's watchful eye since we opened our eyes to daylight this morning." I wasn't as quiet as I could have been.

Koanga shrugged. "I just thought it was because Matasi checkpoints are so difficult. What did we have yesterday? Three? And that was with Miyamoto Suki waving about his Prince of Vikland royal ring. I can't imagine how many checkpoints we have today to actually get on board the ship."

I heard Bima's choked laughter behind us. Mmmmm, maybe we were not quite out of the hearing of our escort. Ngahuru and I exchanged a glance, and she shrugged. Bima wasn't going to learn any new secrets now.

At the Viklander checkpoint just outside the embasado, the guards brought out the inventoried West Islands steel—two daggers and the bone knife. Ngahuru signed for them and then handed them to me.

"This is a gift from me and mine to you and yours. Keep your blades sharp and your wits sharper. And when Trouble comes to dance with you, remember your friends have gifted you Strength"—she touched the one dagger, "Grace"—she touched the other, and "Maripi"—she handed me the bone knife with both hands. "Let this not be the last time we meet, Zren Janin. I do not have so many friends I can afford to throw any of them away."

"Thank you." I was humbled. "I shall treasure the steel as much as I treasure the friends behind it." I turned to Koanga. "I expect to hear a Traveler story about all of this when I get to the West Islands." I grinned.

A woman came hurrying up to the checkpoint. I recognized her as the one who had asked about weapons training at the ambassador reception. She carried a travel pack. "Bima, I am to go with you to the ship."

He raised an eyebrow. "I thought it was to be Solkka?"

. "Two. Ten days, maybe longer," she said cryptically. She turned to us. "I'm sorry. I didn't get to introduce myself earlier. My name is Ven Wila."

"Fine," Bima snapped, and then turned to the guards to hide his sharpness. "You can allow the West Islands steel to be taken to the embasado. It will be packed for a sailing later tonight. The ambassador has allowed it." He fished in his shirt sleeve and pulled out a written note for the guards to have. The guards pulled out my boot knife, checked it off their inventory, and handed it to me.

Bima nodded to Ven. "Well then, let's go." I could hear the aggravation in his voice and wondered what I was missing.

Ngahuru reached over and hugged me unexpectedly. I nearly stabbed myself with the daggers in my hands. "Be careful," she whispered in my ear. She released me and I hid my face from the Viklanders by tucking away my daggers about my waist and in my boot.

Koanga squeezed me so tight, I couldn't catch my breath. "You are so very dear to me." My heart clenched, I had imagined those words in a thousand scenarios, but not at the moment of never seeing him again. My heart was too broken for me to speak. I nodded mutely.

The guards released the gate and the four walked through. I watched them walk down the hill to the Matasi checkpoint. Just before the turn in the road, in front of fuchsia shrubs covering the high stone wall, Koanga turned and looked back at me. I can still see him now, dark almond skin, dark curls, and wide white smile against the vibrant pink blossoms. My eyes filled with tears, and I turned quickly and walked back up the hill.

## CHAPTER 27

# IN THE TENDER CARE OF VIKLANDERS

Miya was short-tempered and distracted all afternoon. We were sailing on the next tide which would be in the middle of the night, and he was hurrying from place to place, while I was left sitting around waiting. Waiting for someone to take me down to the weapons room and select a jeong bong and a tahn bong for my use. Waiting for someone else to take me to a tailor to pick out Kereki clothes: two pants, two shirts, and two tunics.

"At least they're meant to be shapeless," the tailor sniffed as she kept me trying on pair after pair of trousers trying to find some narrow enough her alterations would not be so obvious. In my boot, I carried the dagger I had taken from Brick's body, and I asked the tailor to fasten a sheath for that one. I showed her my Sailor's Curse, my lovely, nasty blade that fit between my knuckles, and asked her to make a leather pocket I could tie about my waist like the cloth one Koanga had made, so I could carry one of my blades away from my other bits and pieces I needed about me. She did so, and now I could carry it either in my cloak or over my trousers. I still had my traveling cloak which Ngahuru had bought on the road to Aldi. It was Kereki made, so I could keep it, the tailor said, but she added long narrow pockets of leather on the inside to hide my Sailor's Curses and daggers. I felt better leaving her rooms than I did the weapons room. I wondered what that said about me.

I had too much time to replay Ngahuru's last words, "Be careful." I heard those words tumble in my mind throughout the long afternoon. I didn't know if she meant "be careful through Kerek," which would go without saying, or "Be careful. Something's not right," here in the Vikland embasado. My eyes also leaked a lot, even though I wasn't bleeding or in pain anywhere. I couldn't remember that happening before, but then I had never said goodbye to Koanga before either.

Bima Ritwik found me in my room staring out the window. "Are you hungry? The ambassador has some fancy doings tonight, and so a bunch of us thought we would go out to Salisport for food and music. I am looking forward to having one last night where I can relax and absolutely nothing will happen."

"Did the ship leave? Did Ngahuru and Koanga get off all right?" I wheeled about.

"Yes. You should know I escorted them on to the ship. Koanga said to tell you 'after looking at his fine accommodations, karu kurii for an entire Wet would have been acceptable.' I assume that means something to you." Bima raised an eyebrow.

I choked back a laugh. "Yes, it does." But I didn't say anything more because suddenly I had a huge lump in my throat.

Bima repeated himself, "Would you like to go out tonight to Salisport? It will be your last quiet night for a while."

"I'm just waiting. But I don't know for what. Is this all I am supposed to pack?" I waved to the clothes on the bed next to my travel pack.

Bima crossed the room to take a closer look. "Miya will have the maps and papers. Did you pick out your bongs, both long and short?"

"Yes, Miya said he would pack those with his belongings."

"Carry your own steel," he admonished.

Wordlessly, I unrolled my travel cloak and showed him the newly added leather pockets with the two daggers tucked in their little beds.

"Nice." He paused. "And the bone knife?"

"I have it." I said nothing more.

"Trade you a steel flask for one of those knives." He touched a dagger hilt covetously.

I gave him a cool look and held up my hands. "Two hands—I need two daggers."

He laughed easily. "Come on, let's go find some others and some food." I followed him down the stairs to the entry area where three others were waiting. I recognized them from the reception earlier, but now they were all wearing the black closefitting pants and shirts. Nothing to grab on to in a fight. With their long thick braids and identical clothing, male and female blended together. They looked even more like soldiers.

"I guess we are not going in disguise," I deadpanned. "You look like muscle for a lordling in Kerek City. Guess I get to be the lordling."

Bima cracked a smile. "I'm going to like traveling with you." He looked to the others. "Let's go."

"Wait." I held up my hand. "No Miya?"

"Poor boy is still packing. Such a procrastinator, our Miya." One of the women sniggered unpleasantly.

The skin on the back of my neck began to rise. "Huh. Let's see if Solkka can come out to play. He has to teach me all those pretty words, so I don't have to sleep alone at night."

Another one spoke, "Solkka is making a delivery for the ambassador. He'll have to teach you those pretty words next time. I'm Lomes. If I would have known you were afraid of the dark, I would have volunteered to share my room…and my bed." There was laughter in her? his? their? eyes.

"No one is sleeping with Zren until they get back to Vikland and their next rotation. We need to keep his head on surviving Kerek." Bima scowled. "I can't take you three anywhere."

And with that, we disappeared into the waning daylight.

* * * * *

I expected Trouble to come dancing. I wasn't sure from where or when it would happen, but my instincts had been screaming at me since we left the embasado. I tried running scenes in my head. I knew it couldn't be a full on fight because we were in Matasi after all—the land where nothing is allowed. I thought perhaps they would leave me somewhere and I would be forced to find my way back alone to the embasado, or even the ship. Difficult for one who didn't read or write Mata, but not impossible. I started to track my journey as we ambled along.

The two women were flirtatious. Trying to distract me, I thought. When the conversation changed from how handsome I was, to how a Conrosan ended up in Matasi, to questions and comments about Ngahuru, I realized I was nothing more than a mark to them, a victim to whatever trouble they were planning.

Lomes, I couldn't figure out. Because of Ngahuru, I considered Lomes as a dual soul. Once I stopped thinking about how I should talk to them, I realized they were easy to talk to—the easiest of all of them. Suddenly I heard Koanga's voice in my head, "Don't worry so much about it. Not everything has to be named and labeled."

The place Bima picked was comfortable with lots of tables and a stage for music. The food was good, very good, and the music was similar to the same praise songs and hymns we had been hearing since Ribelo. During one especially lively number when everyone was up and dancing about, I caught a movement out of my eye and saw one of our women slip through the door. I said nothing, but as we sat back at our table, I waved our server over as I had seen Ngahuru do. "We'll pay for our food now. He will pay for all of us." I pointed at Bima Ritwik.

He grumbled, but he paid. I saw a smile in his eyes that didn't reach his mouth and I knew I had guessed correctly. They had been planning to leave me behind with the cost of all the food.

The next two songs were slow hymns and our table stayed with just the four of us. Once another 'jump-up-and-shout' refrain began, I saw Lomes fade into the shadows and then out. I decided I needed to be next. I leaned over and told Bima I needed to find a private tree. He made a face but said nothing. I imagined him cringing inside about crude Kereki street boys, but I could smile later when I beat him home.

As soon as I reached outside, I started running. We had taken a long roundabout route because I remembered passing some of the landmarks more than once. But since I didn't read Mata, I couldn't navigate my way back, I could only retrace our steps. At one intersection, I thought I caught a glimpse of Lomes darting down an alley. I hesitated, wondering if following Lomes would help with a shortcut, or if I was meant to be led astray and injured in the alley.

There weren't many people out anymore. It had to be close to curfew. I twisted and turned down a few more streets before I saw the hill with the stone wall of pink fuchsia and the street which led to the embasado. I stopped running and listened to the blood pound in my head. Then I listened to the night around me.

Trouble had come out to dance with me tonight. I hadn't been humiliated with a bill I could not pay—and I am sure Matasi had a fine for that. I hadn't gotten lost in a city where I didn't know the language. I tried to look up the hill and see what was coming next. I thought I would get jumped between the two checkpoints, where the hill curved. It made sense, they would assume I would think the danger would be over and my guard would be down. I walked up to the Matasi checkpoint and asked in Keresh, "How long to the curfew whistle?"

"Less than half a decon, you better hurry," she responded as she opened the gate.

"Thank the Lost God for guards of many languages," I muttered to myself as I hurried through.

I had just stepped into a circle of light when I heard a small voice, "Red? Are you Red?" he asked in Keresh. I looked about and saw a small Matasi boy hiding in the foliage. He was wearing dark clothes.

"Who are you?" I asked.

"Willow sent me. From the ship. She was with her brother, she said."

"I know Willow and her brother." I hesitated before saying more.

His face broke into a grin. "I am glad I found you." His accent was thick, and I had trouble understanding his Keresh.

"She said to tell you Ven Wila and Solkka Ulani are on the ship and going to the West Islands. That she and her brother are to be escorted all the way home and not just to the ship." He paused. "She said it was important you get this message, and you would give me coin."

"How could she tell you all this when she was onboard?" I raised an eyebrow.

"I help clean the cabins on the ship. I was just getting ready to leave when she said she was looking for a boy who spoke Keresh. I said I spoke Keresh, and she told me to find you at this checkpoint. That you had cinnamon skin and you would be sailing out tonight. That you needed to know Viklander soldiers were traveling with her all the way home." He set his face in a stubborn look. "She said you would give me coin because I might have to sneak about after curfew."

I reached in my tunic pocket and pulled out the coins Miya had given me earlier that day. "Here," I put them all in his open palm, "I think you just saved my life."

The boy looked at the coins in his hand and gave me a huge grin before he disappeared into the foliage. I took out the Sailor's Curse and kept it hidden in my left hand. At the Vikland checkpoint, the guards looked at my pass and checked me in. "Am I the last one?" I asked.

The guard looked at his list. *Stars! The amount of paper in this country,* I thought to myself.

"No, there are three more behind you. They better be running up that hill."

"Thanks." I passed through the checkpoint, moved out of the lighted path cast by the row of lanterns, and crept up the hill. I went around to the staff entrance instead of the front doors and found a staircase that would let me out on the guest wing floor. There was no one about.

I eased open my door. The lights were on. Miya was pacing the room. "Oh, thank the stars, you're here!" he blurted out. He froze to the spot when I slowly opened my left hand and showed him the tiny blade winking between my fingers.

"Miyamoto Suki, Prince of Vikland. Let's sit down, shall we? There is so much to talk about before we set sail."

## CHAPTER 28

## LOST AND FOUND

Miya bowed his head but kept his eyes on me. "I will tell you the truth as I know it to be, and where I cannot tell you the truth because I do not know it, I will say nothing." He squinted. "Where's Bima?" At my shrug, he flashed a quick grin, and then looked serious. "We can't do it here. I have the key to the room Ngahuru used, you can lock us in. Bima won't think to look there."

I opened the door and looked down the long empty hallway. I motioned him through and he slipped us into the room Ngahuru had stayed in. He gave me the key as he promised, and I felt the satisfying snick of the lock. The lantern flared behind me as Miya lit it and set it on the table.

"Sit down," I ordered. I hooked the other chair with my foot and sat down facing him. I held up the blade. "This is called a 'Sailor's Curse.'"

"I know what it is." Miya folded his arms across his chest.

"Then you also know that if you lunged out of that chair I would have slashed your throat or your belly before you could do anything to hurt me."

"I get it. You are more dangerous than I am." He seemed very calm.

"First question, is Ngahuru in any danger? I know two Viklanders—Ven and Solkka—are on the ship with her. She and Koanga weren't just escorted to the ship and then waved to from shore. I met both Ven and Solkka, Miya, they both look like…" I struggled for the word.

"Assassins?" He flashed a mocking smile and then shook his head. "No, Zren. The ambassador chose Ven Wila because she leads her own team of soldiers—she is a strong strategist. She is also the captain of the Secondo's personal guard. She represents power and honor, and Ngahuru should be very pleased she was selected to accompany her. He chose Solkka because…" he paused a long moment. "I'm afraid I can only tell you Solkka is more than a beautiful boy, even though we all tease him otherwise. If there is trouble on the ship or pirates on the sea, and we don't expect any," he added hastily, "Ngahuru and Koanga will be as well defended as if you were there in person." He tilted his head. "How did you learn Ven and Solkka were sent as an honor guard? That was not to be shared knowledge."

"I am asking the questions. You only get to tell me the truth or nothing. I think that is what you said. Koanga said almost the same thing once. I believed him. You still have to convince me. Is Ngahuru in any danger?" I repeated as fiercely as I could.

"No." Miya looked straight at me. "This I believe to be true. Vikland is not an enemy to the West Islands. We want them to be a strong ally if possible. It is true we had softfooters and soldiers looking everywhere for her in Kerek City. It is true we are pleased to pay her passage as an exalted guest and send an honor guard with her to be part of her welcoming home to earn grace and favor with her king. But, it is also why we have honored her request that the eyes and ears of Kerek and Matasi see all of our actions as honoring one of the great Storytellers of the West Islands, so she can slip unnoticed back into her country. It is true our honor guard want to see the ambassador's children in the West Islands—for that is where they must be—even though we cannot uncover how she made that happen."

"So what's your interest? They are not your children." I was genuinely curious.

Miya scoffed. "Would you allow children to be lost in Kerek City? If sold to the Orphan Master, they are resold to the highest bidder without regard for their welfare. If used as hostages, bits and pieces could be carved off to make the demands attention-worthy. Kerek's King will do nothing. *Nothing*. If we could rescue the children, then we can return them to their country and family."

I smiled sarcastically. "And just like that, Vikland is a friend to all, a beacon of peace and justice."

"We are already a friend to all," Miya replied.

"What you are is a country surrounded by mountains and Kerek without a seaport of your own. Ngahuru says you have the Cold Mountains to the north, Silver Mountains, and your border with Matasi to the south, and an utter failure of a kingdom to your west. You need the West Islands as your ally." I cocked my head to the side. "You didn't bring Trouble to the dance in Kerek, but you didn't mind a waltz or two while you were there."

I considered the past days and spoke slowly, "You didn't have anything to do with us ending up in jail and losing our coin and goods in Subversiva, did you?"

"No!" Miya remained sitting with his arms crossed over his chest, and I saw him quickly fist his hands and release them. "No," he said again quietly. "My first posting was in Alenti – the capital city of the Triune. I learned the punishment does not always fit the crime, especially if you are not from Matasi. There is *never* any mercy for mistakes. I am sorry you had a poor experience in Subversiva. There is truly much to love about Matasi. Remember Ebla Potenco? Remember the guards at the border? Ngahuru told me how they let you in without papers," he said in response to my look. "Remember the baboy in Ribelo, where you danced all night without understanding a single word of the songs you were singing?"

We both heard it at the same time—footsteps running down the hall. At least two people, I thought. A gentle knock on the door to my room a little ways away.

"Zren? Zren? Are you in there? It's me, Lomes." I heard the door open softly and the flick and flare of a lucifer. Miya and I held our breaths.

"He's not here!" Someone else said something inaudible.

"By the Lost God and all those that follow him, where did he go?" I looked to Miya, he held his finger to his lips and mouthed, "Bima."

"We are in so much trouble," a female voice said.

"Hey, let's have fun with Miya's new friend, he says. Let's take him out, he says. Let's play hide and seek, I bet he doesn't read or speak Mata. Let's see if we can frighten him and then rescue him so he thinks he owes us a gift of West Islands steel, he says. Bima, you lousy piece of sheep dung! We have completely lost the ambassador's prize just three decons before he is to sail away. We are as well and truly cooked as a roasted pig at a baboy."

"Oh, shut up, Lomes. I can't think with you crying like a toddler over there." Silence. "Well then, let's go down and ask at the checkpoint if he has returned to the embasado. The curfew whistle has blown so if he has not, it will just make the hide and seek back in Salisport a little more dangerous." Footsteps pounded past our door and down the stairs.

I wheeled around so quickly that Miya flinched. "That was for fun? That was just a joke? Are you crazy?"

Miya put his hands in the air. "It wasn't my idea. I've been working on our trip to Kerek City since I met with the ambassador yesterday. I will tell you Bima usually does something like this to all the new Viklanders when they arrive on rotation. I did not think he would do it to you, until I came to your rooms this evening and found you were not here. When I went to the checkpoint and learned you had checked out with Lomes, Bima, and two of his young softfoots, I started to worry. I did not know if Bima was testing you, or his new softfoots, and what the tests would be. But I knew you and Bima had to be on the ship tonight. Even Bima Ritwik would not defy the ambassador so."

"Stars, Miya! I almost killed them tonight." I put the Sailor's Curse back in my leather pocket. "I thought Solkka and Ven were on the ship to make sure Koanga and Ngahuru would not reach the West Islands. I thought Bima and the others were to lure me away from the embasado and murder me. Ngahuru sent a boy to evade curfew to tell me your Viklanders boarded the ship with her. I thought she meant she was in trouble, not telling me how fancy of an honor guard she had." I ran my hand through my hair. "This was all just for fun. Viklanders play games like this for fun." I was dumbfounded, truly dumbfounded. "Ven and Solkka are honor guards." I stared at him with my mouth open. How could I survive something so different from anything I knew?

Miya looked concerned. "Zren, only the people you have told—Ngahuru, Koanga, the ambassador, the Secondo, and me—know who you are and what your life has been to this day. That is not our secret to tell. Ngahuru told me you were a treasure worthy of a Vikland warrior saga, and to treat you as such. But Bima Ritwik knew nothing except you were from Conrosa, a land known for its learning and its peaceful ways. I didn't know Bima had anything planned, if so, I would have warned you. I think he planned to embarrass you, but I swear, no harm was ever meant to you. Zren, believe me, Ngahuru and Koanga are safe. Truly. They are safe."

I ran my hand down my face. "You better be the one who tells Bima how close he came to death tonight. I'm not sure I could say anything without rearranging that face of his."

Miya heaved a huge sigh of relief. I knew then I trusted him. A little. "Zren, Ngahuru told me how fierce you were. She said you grew up without a childhood, but I don't claim to understand what that means. I will only tell Bima, you are far too serious to play his little childish games, more than that I leave to you to say."

He paused a long time, and I could see him struggling with what he wanted to say. "Zren, our Bima Ritwik is a man of many talents. Vikland would be beyond sad to lose him to your knife over a misunderstanding. I would be grateful if you could forgive him." He smirked a little. "That's not to say, he doesn't deserve the agony he is going through right now searching the city for you. You have a talent, Zren, to best those who would underestimate you. Trust me when I say, I hope to learn from their mistakes and not make my own." He stood up from his chair. "We need to pack our travel bags, and I need to ensure the wagons have loaded our other goods for the ship."

I was a little unsettled as I unlocked the door and went back to my room to gather my travel bag. Miya went to arrange to have our belongings carted to the ship. I trusted Miya because Ngahuru had told me he was a friend. But she wasn't here, and I didn't know if she knew everything. I had known the ambassador had planned to send an honor guard, and I had assumed she had been told. Or maybe, her telling me who was the honor guard was the important thing.

Miya and I walked to the Vikland checkpoint, signed out, and waited for our escort and Bima. Since curfew had already sounded, we had to have Matasi soldiers walk us to the ship.

The soldiers arrived first. Bima raced up to the checkpoint, hair disheveled, travel bag bulging just as we were ready to depart without him.

Miya cocked an eyebrow. "Someone forget to toss you out of a bed in time? Who's going to be crying this time while you are out doing your softfooting?"

Bima scowled at him. He looked at me and started to say something, but Miya raised his hand. "Not here, not now." He tipped his head towards the Matasi soldiers.

We passed the point where the boy had intercepted me with Ngahuru's message. I wonder how long before she learned Ven and Solkka were allies and not assassins. Or did she already know and I had misunderstood her message? Or how long before I learned Miya had lied to me?

The horse and two wheeled cart clopped ahead of us in the quiet night. The Matasi soldiers walked easily in pairs ahead of the horse and behind the three of us. Both Miya and Bima were alert to their surroundings, but not concerned. I wondered why such high security for Viklanders? Was it because of who they were, or because it was after curfew?

We crossed through four checkpoints before we were delivered to the ship. A Matasi sailor in a bright yellow shirt and dark green pants came down to look at our papers and then at the three large trunks.

"Out on rotation?"

"Close enough," Miya replied in Keresh.

"Can't outrun Kereki bandits carrying fourteen dresses for your sweetheart," the sailor smirked.

"Good thing, I'm only carrying one dress each for fourteen sweethearts." Miya grinned back.

A soldier behind us snickered, and the sailor handed back Miya's papers. "I'm not going to help you with those, so you better hurry up and do it yourself. We're only waiting on another pair of passengers and then we are on our way."

"Right." Miya sighed. "Zren, stay here and keep our bodyguards company while Bima and I get us sorted out on the ship." They grabbed the rope ends on the first wooden trunk, lifted it over the side of the cart, and followed the sailor up the gangway, staggering a little under its weight. I narrowed my eyes. There were no dresses in that crate.

The four soldiers made a couple of comments, looked at the cart driver and me, and then, once they thought we didn't understand Mata, shifted in a circle, and began to talk among themselves.

I rocked back and forth, shifted my pack to the cart, and waited. I asked the driver how long he had been in Matasi. He gave me a long, long look, and then in a thick Viklander accent, said he didn't let Keresh filth cross his lips unless he was talking to idiots. He spat at my feet, settled down a little more into the seat, and stared at the horse.

One of the soldiers said something to the others, another shot me a quick glance, and they all started laughing. They went back to their conversation. It seemed like forever before Bima and Miya came down the gangway. Bima said something to the driver in Vik, and the driver and Bima took the second trunk up the walkway, grunting with the effort. I glanced at Miya, no dresses in that one either.

I heard the clip clop of another two-wheeled cart. This one held a Matasi woman wearing an old-fashioned dress with a somber looking man beside her, hunched over to hide his height. They had one trunk between them, and Miya offered to help them carry it up the gangway. No sailor came to look at their papers, and the soldiers barely gave them a glance. The woman followed the men and her trunk up the gangway, meeting Bima and the cart driver at the top. Bima motioned me to take the last trunk with him. I shouldered my pack as well and we staggered up the gangway. We had barely reached the top when the horses and carts clip clopped away, and the soldiers wandered off in opposite directions.

Within the decon, we had slipped free of the dock and followed the tide out to the sea.

## CHAPTER 29

# THE MATASI MISSIONARIES

The room we three shared was small with two beds bolted to the wall one on top of each other on each side of the narrow doorway. We had to stack the trunks, boxing in over half the narrow space in between.

"Have you sailed before?" Miya asked.

I shook my head.

"Bottom bunk." Both Miya and Bima said simultaneously, pointing me to the one without their travel bags. I sat down and then looked at Bima.

He looked at me, then at Miya's stern face, and back to me. "What?"

I tried to look fierce. "Miya tells me, this sailing usually takes three days." I waited for Bima to nod before I continued, "That's a long time for you to be looking over your shoulder every decon wondering when I am going to get even."

"Pah!" Bima waved his hand in dismissal. "It was a simple test to see if I was going to be holding your hand all through Kerek City, or if Miya and Ngahuru were trustworthy about your talents. You must remember, I had never met Ngahuru—a softfoot from another country—before yesterday. She could have been sowing trouble on all my well-laid plans." He gave me a nasty grin. "It's what we do."

He dropped his smile. "You did well." He sniffed. "Consider yourself worthy to watch my back."

I started from the bottom bunk, fist raised, and Miya threw his arm across my chest.

"Bima!" he warned.

Bima sighed and looked at the ceiling. "Oh stars! Another delicate flower with feelings. Fine. You were clever and tricksy, and I thought Lomes was going to die when we came back to your room the first, second, and third time and you weren't there. I had to dash for the ship and they were going to have to tell the ambassador you were lost in the city. Except the guard at the door to the embasado overheard us crafting our story and said you had already left with Miya to meet the wagon at the checkpoint." He gave a wry smile. "You're good. But then you should be, you were taught by Ngahuru."

I opened my mouth to contradict him, but then I realized he had given me my story. All trickery requires a good story, and if Bima built mine as a softfoot trained by Ngahuru? Well then, I already knew how the Viklanders held her in high esteem. I hid a smile as I sat back down.

"So what's next?" I said as nonchalantly as I could.

"Did you get anything from the guards?" Miya asked Bima.

"I didn't. I've been in Matasi too long. They suspected I spoke Mata. Our cart driver, however, gathered a wealth of information. The Matasi government is continuing to help landowners in the borderlands buy up additional land in Kerek. As long as the farms and orchards have a building in Matasi, all of the housing for the workers and the production can be in Kerek. He said there are only a few holdouts, but in some places, especially near the Silver Mountain foothills, Matasi owns halfway to the Old Fort Road. The soldiers were talking because they have the option of getting posted in the 'frontier'—and many are considering it. They said they heard it is mostly guarding wealthy landowners and grain silos."

"Zren came down the Coast Road to the west of where you are talking about. What is Diempf—Kerek or Matasi?" Miya glanced at me and then back to Bima.

"Diempf and the other villages around there have heavy Matasi presence: settlers with armed guards, soldiers patrolling the orchards and fields. Weapons are West Islands bows and steel. No idea how they are importing it, there is still an official 'refusal to share' from the West Islanders." Bima sounded exasperated.

"Sinner's market," Miya offered. "Private dealers."

"Has to be," Bima agreed reluctantly.

There was a soft knock and all three of us stilled. Miya nodded, and Bima gently opened the door. The Matasi woman in the old-fashioned dress stood outside. Bima quickly waved her in.

"Trouble?" he asked.

"None. Everyone was too busy grabbing the tide to fuss much with our papers. Chul is talking with the sailors now, trying to get in their way. He offered to lead them in prayer before we sailed, so we should be properly avoided for the rest of the voyage."

She looked at me. "You're the Conrosan I heard about. I came to look for you this evening when I heard we would be sailing together, but the gossips said you were out with Bima and Lomes." She continued drily, "I can't imagine that went well." She looked hard at Bima who threw up his hands.

"He's onboard the ship, isn't he?" Bima snapped.

I looked at her again. So she was part of the ambassador's staff. "My name is Zren. Are you traveling with us all the way to Vikland, or just to Kerek City?"

"Only Kerek City." She nodded her head at me. "I am Raeshon. Chul and I are just two Matasi missionaries in the castle city preaching the Lost God while looking for a pair of lost children."

"Those are some very important children," I noted.

"You have no idea. Ngahuru didn't casually tell you where she tucked them away, did she? Any clues, any tears telling us they are dead? Any tall tales from little brother disguising the travel of two nearly royal children?"

I looked at Miya. "I thought Vikland thought the children were in the West Islands? Why are you still searching for them?"

He smiled and shrugged. "I said *I* thought she had spirited them away to the West Islands. There are others who say that is not possible, and she is bluffing her way home to keep them safe until they can be removed from hiding. The more time I spend with you, Zren, the more I believe I am right. Time will tell."

Another knock at the door and Chul pushed himself into the room. It was now so crowded, we had to stand touching each other just to fit us all in. I felt the rocking of the ship, the warm closeness of the bodies, and looked at Miya.

"Right. I think we are done here for now. This is Zren's first sailing, and it looks like I need to get him up to the deck now." Chul was so tall, he nearly knocked himself out trying to get the door open, and he and Raeshon spilled out into the narrow hall. Miya hauled me out and pushed me in front of him, and we pulled ourselves up the ladder.

The cool breeze cleared my head instantly, and we moved up to the front of the ship. There were sailors moving about still arranging cargo, lashing down equipment, and tying off sails. I started to say thanks when Miya put his finger to his lips and whispered close by my ear, "Assume everything can be reported back to Matasi or sold to information traders in Kerek." I nodded and gulped in deep breaths of salty air.

I looked behind me and saw the lanterns at the end of the Matasi docks fading behind us. Everything ahead of me was dark ink below and above...Oh! The stars! Flashing and dancing in the sky, all the constellations of the West Islands. I could almost hear Koanga's voice in my ear reciting his tales of the Smith, the Soldier, and the Seafarer. I looked up and let the cooling breeze wash across my face. This was so beautiful!

Closing my eyes, I imagined Koanga beside me instead of Miya. I imagined coming back from Vikland, educated, speaking

Wester as I stepped on land at the West Islands. Koanga would be proud to meet me again. I would be an educated Conrosan who had traveled to all the known world and was as smart and talented as Miyamoto Suki. I let myself sink into my daydreams.

Miya was content in our silence. He stood at the railing, legs slightly apart, arms crossed, hands wrapped about the sleeves of his black shirt. His eyes were closed, but he had the alertness of a soldier.

We were still there, silent, when I heard footsteps. Miya never opened his eyes, just said, "Bima."

"So, the wise warrior and the fierce little boy are standing at the edge of the world saying nothing."

"You make a lot of noise for a softfoot." Miya opened one eye.

"You spout a lot of nonsense for a wise warrior. Did you know Ngahuru's brother calls you a Prince of Vikland?"

Miya chuffed. "I'm sure you were quick to tell him Vikland has no princes, only the Empress and her two daughters."

Bima shrugged. "I may have forgotten that part. I haven't figured out yet if calling you a 'Prince of Vikland' will help me or hurt me." He paused for a long time, and I could feel a shiver of tension flow between the two. Then suddenly, Bima spoke into the darkness, "Raeshon asked me if it was true you have made twelve trips across Kerek. I told her yes, and I have held your hand for three of them."

"She's made what? Six? And her first one when she was eight? That's impressive herself. If she was due for a rotation, I would travel with her without hesitation."

I considered our surroundings. No one was about, so I asked, "Why are the Matasi working with you?"

"They're not." Miya opened both eyes and looked at me. "Like you, Chul and Raeshon were bought and sold by the Orphan Master in Kerek City. Probably twenty-five years ago, or a little less. In their case, they were bought by Viklander diplomats who were coming home from their posting in the West Islands. The ambassador thought she would be quickly reposted to Matasi and intended to bring the children with her to Alenti to look for their families. She told Chul and Raeshon her plans and they agreed. They were children, true, but old enough to know they had come from a village near Vesaport. Everyone agreed it was better to go to Vikland and cross over the Silver Mountains to Matasi, than to leave the two children to the mercy of the Orphan Master and Kerek City."

"She didn't get reposted?" I asked.

"Their wagon train was attacked between Balza and Huk. The children escaped on horseback with two others—not the diplomats. They ran without stopping for the border, stealing horses along the way. The children were brave and stoic—something Viklanders cherish."

Miya continued, "They were offered a home in the palace, to be raised and educated with the royals and the near royals. They were told they could choose to go to Matasi at any time and our embasado would attempt to find their kin." He paused. "They chose to stay." He stopped abruptly. "You must ask them for the rest of their story."

We stood a while, all lost in our own thoughts. I was beginning to wonder just how bad the Northern Track was to travel. I had thought the Coast Road was lawless, but this sounded like a whole new level of deadly.

After about a decon or so, Miya asked if I thought I was settled enough to sleep. I nodded and we went down below. We left Bima staring out into the sea.

## CHAPTER 30

# BACK TO KEREK CITY

I didn't like sailing, although I never embarrassed myself by hanging over the railing like some of the other passengers. Bima said most of them were hired muscles for the grains and fruit tradesmen who negotiated at the Kerek castle for import rights. Kerek had the same climate, Bima told me, to raise everything they imported from Matasi and Vikland, but the infrastructure was so broken down, they were completely dependent on their neighbors for everything.

Bima was different on the ship than he was in Salisport. After that first night, he answered every question I asked. I learned if I asked a foolish question, or some information he thought I should already know, he would quickly drop his eyes to his feet, and then look me straight in the eye and answer me truthfully. I know that, because I would later ask Miya, rephrasing the conversation as 'Bima told me...is he telling the truth or trying to embarrass me as he tried in Salisport?' Miya would raise his eyebrows, but he would answer me. Most of the answers were the same.

From Bima, I learned most of the Viklanders were educated at home with teachers and tutors or local schools until they reached the age to attend the academies. "About your age, Zren, maybe a year or two younger." I told Bima what my price was for taking Miya across the Northern Track: Admission to the academies, and then future travel to Conrosa to find my family when Miya was posted there as a diplomat. Bima had looked at me for a long time with an odd look on his face.

"What?" His look made me uneasy. I wondered if Miya had lied about being posted to Conrosa someday.

"The academies are hard, Zren. Not everyone who starts is able to finish. Sometimes it is because their tutors and schools at home were not good enough. Sometimes it is the city of Juisiti that swallows them up, and sometimes they need the discipline of their years in the military before they return and can navigate the academies." Bima had looked away over the sea. "You'll succeed, Zren, from sheer force of will, if nothing else."

The second evening, the three of us were standing out on the deck. I could never get enough of the stars as they came out. First it was sunset, the sun crashing fast and hard into the sea as it did in Kerek, and then, and then...the stars springing into the night sky as if the Smith had thrown open the door to his forge and the sparks flashed out into the dark. Without thinking, I said the words aloud. Both Bima and Miya had stilled. I could hear the smile in Miya's voice as he replied, "Well, I am glad to know Ngahuru did not spend every moment of your journey to Salisport teaching you softfooting."

Bima asked me to tell him a story of the West Islands, if I knew any. I thought for a moment at which one I thought I could tell the best. I picked the one of the Seafarer, where the daughter brought the spices to her mother and the West Islands. I faltered a bit as I began, I didn't have the cadence Koanga had slipped into so easily, but then I found my rhythm.

I finished with, *"The Seafarer jumped off the boat and on to the sand. She dumped a small leather bag into her mother's hand. 'See if those spices will make your senses sing! Each of those spices in the bag has a plant on the raft behind me. We will plant them and cultivate them and scent the air with the smell of flavor!' And so it was, my friends, and that is how all of the spices came to the West Islands."*

I waited for their response. Miya and Bima said nothing, and I was uncomfortable with their silence, so I continued, "That one is Ngahuru's favorite."

Bima turned his head and looked at me. "Do you know why?" He paused. "I would like to know."

I thought back to what she had said that day. "It's because the daughter complains about something, the mother sends her out to make it better, and the daughter comes home successful," I added, "beyond successful."

Miya laughed. "That's our Ngahuru. She keeps all of our countries on our toes. You were given a wonderful gift to travel with her. And now I have the privilege of traveling with you."

It wasn't so much the words he said, but the tone in which he said it, which made me stiffen. I knew Miyamoto Suki regarded Ngahuru highly. Yet I didn't feel the same high regard given to Bima, who was also a softfoot. Not from Raeshon, or Ven, and certainly not from Miya. But Koanga had said Ngahuru wanted to be underestimated because it made her role easier. Was Bima Ritwik the same way? Or was it something else?

"I'm not going to tell you all her secrets," I told Miya sullenly.

Miya crossed his arms easily and continued looking out over the ship's railing. "Of course not, Zren. That's not what I meant. I only meant I get to touch the greatness of Ngahuru by traveling with someone who knows her well."

Bima snorted but said nothing more. As I stood between the two of them, again I started to feel the currents of Trouble dancing around me. It felt like those nights making deals in Kerek City when a shift of power moved too quickly. Or when

Trouble was only a knife throw away. Just like then, I needed to get away. The Trouble brewing between Miya and Bima was too big, and I was too small to survive.

"I'm going to bed," I said suddenly. "I'm tired. You'll have to tell yourselves the rest of your bedtime stories."

Both men looked at me, said goodnight, but made no move to stop me, or ask me what was wrong.

I laid in my bunk for a long time thinking while I waited for them to come back to the room. There was an undercurrent between Bima and Miya I didn't understand. It didn't seem like anything I *could* understand. The men were polite to each other, or Miya was anyway. I thought Ngahuru might be a part of it, but that didn't make any sense. I wondered if I was part of it, but I couldn't figure out why.

Both men seemed very interested in making sure I was given any information, food, and company I wanted or needed. I wondered if this was how a victim in Lowertown felt once they knew they were part of some trickery. I worried how it might hurt me, but I couldn't figure that out either. I wondered who had wronged who, and if it was something the other could not forgive or would not.

Sometime during the night I fell asleep. I woke towards morning, at least I thought it was near morning, to hear both men sleeping in their bunks. It troubled me to realize I had grown so comfortable they could both enter a room, undress, and climb into upper bunks without me stirring awake. I missed Ngahuru and Koanga very much. I had so many questions and I just wanted her to say one more time, "That's not the question I thought you were going to ask..."

* * * * *

Once we docked, Bima asked me to stay with our goods until he and Miya returned with an unloading crew and transportation to the Vikland embasado in Kerek City. While they were gone, Raeshon and Chul stopped by just long enough to wish me luck. They gave me the iron key to their room and said Bima Ritwik would pick up their trunk. They were carrying only their traveling packs. Raeshon said they were headed straight to a missionary compound to gather information and begin their own search for the children.

"Send word, through Bima, if you think of anything else of the children's whereabouts," Chul added as an afterthought.

"How old are they?" I asked.

"Ngahuru didn't tell you?" Chul looked thoughtfully at me as Raeshon explained, "Ten for the boy and twelve for the girl. But they are West Islanders so they will look small for their age to anyone's eyes."

"Too small for the stables or household help, too dark and too obvious as street runners for the gangs." I nodded. "You aren't going to find them hiding on the streets."

"You see the predicament?" Chul smiled at my insight. "Their value lies as hostages or bragging rights. We can't have that happen." They shouldered their packs and headed down the hallway.

At long last, I heard footfalls. Bima opened the door and stepped aside to let in a big, burly Kereki with tattoos and scars. He took a look at me, swore, and backed into the hall, knocking into the other longshoremen and Bima.

"Red," He muttered from the hallway.

"Cresken." I was trapped in the room. If I panicked, I would be dead before I left the ship. Cresken would kill me if he thought I would tell anyone he was working for the Viklanders. It was worth his life to keep me quiet.

I thought of how Miya would handle this. I widened my stance and acted as if it was perfectly normal for him to see me here. "Good to see you again."

"I heard you were dead. You and Brick and Goblin. Got on the wrong side of Lord Resoro." Cresken stayed in the hallway to talk.

"Partly right. Brick and Goblin are dead. Me? I just moved to where the coin is better. I guard boxes instead of lordlings." I nodded to Bima. "As did you, I see." I stretched and tried to make myself look a little taller. "So, this is how this will go. You tell no one you saw me alive, and I tell no one you work for the Viklanders."

Cresken stared at me. "Or I just find you alone on the streets and keep all my secrets safe."

"There is always that." I nodded. I wanted to make a smart remark, but my throat was too dry with fear.

"Are we done here?" Bima asked coldly. "We are going to attract attention on the dock soon if the horse and wagon wait too long."

I stepped out into the hallway and far enough away so Cresken and the other Kereki could get in the narrow room and haul out the trunks. Bima watched them as they hauled all three crates up a pulley to the deck, did the same with the one from Chul and Raeshon's room next door, and then climbed the ladder themselves to carry the crates to the wagon on shore.

Still looking at the open hatch, Bima said quietly, "You going to be all right?"

"Of course!" I tried to sound indignant.

Bima raised his hand to calm me. "You stink of fear sweat. But you sounded completely convincing." He turned and smiled down at me. "I think this is going to turn out just fine. Better than fine." He swept his arm out in front of him. "After you."

* * * * *

We reached the embasado without further incident. Ages ago, when I called the streets of Kerek City my home, I would walk up to Castle Court from Lowertown to dream of a different life than my own. From the street, I could see the high walls and heavy gated compounds of the embasados as they marched down the street from the King's castle. The embasado closest to the castle had been deserted for years—ever since I could remember. I had known it as the Conrosan embasado, but because I had thought of myself as a Kereki, I didn't think much about it. It had meant no more to me than the West Islands building with its landscaped gardens of vibrant flowers overhanging the walls and peeking through the steel bars of its gates. Next to the two of them, the Matasi compound was the largest embasado of all. Glimpses of the inside through the iron-barred gates revealed interior walls nearly as high as the street-facing ones. The location of Vikland's embasado down at the end of the street, farthest from the castle and on a busy crossroads, was the King's way of insulting his neighbors forced to travel through his country. From my point of view, it was a direct contradiction of the rule to keep your enemies closest to your eyes and ears.

The guards at the embasado gates looked over Miya's paperwork, gave me a long, long look, said something in Vik to Bima where I caught the word "cargo" and waved the wagon through. The guards and Bima took the trunks elsewhere, and the cart and driver were sent away.

Miya and I had only our travel bags as we entered the building. I could see the Secondo already walking down the hallway towards us. Miya bowed deeply to him and spoke respectfully in Vik. I had seen something like this in Salisport and remembered Ngahuru had called it the formal Vik greetings when one encountered another of higher rank.

Here in Kerek City, all pretense of a diplomatic outpost of fancy dinners and elegant evenings were gone. This looked like a military garrison. Boots stomped on the brick and stucco floors. Men and women didn't wear a variety of the local clothing as they did in Matasi. Here, everyone wore the dark trousers and shirts.

In Matasi, the Vikland Secondo at the embasado had been a woman upwards of forty, well-dressed, her long black braid streaked with grey. The Secondo here was a man in his middle years, with the look of one who could work hard all day and stay out patrolling half the night. He looked as strong and fit and solid as those half his age. Miya introduced him as First Soldier Joon, but no explanation of what that meant. Miya introduced me as Zren Janin, a Conrosan of Kerek City.

First Soldier Joon smiled. "Zren Janin." He paused a long time. "I've seen you on the streets, I believe, but if I remember correctly, one of my street runners told me your name was 'Red.' Are you one of Bima's softfooters?"

I looked to Miya who answered, "No, sir. Zren Janin will be guiding me across the Northern Track." The Secondo raised an eyebrow, but Miya pretended not to notice as he continued, "I have dispatches and instructions from the ambassador in Salisport for you and Ambassador Lalsy. The ambassador in Matasi has staff he wants to send to you on the next two ships and asks that you release those who need to return to Vikland out on rotation. He has written out his plans for your consideration. I am able to meet at your convenience to answer your questions as I am able."

"Bima Ritwik is traveling with you as well?" The Secondo asked. "We need him here."

"Bima Ritwik is to stay here until the West Islands children have been found, or properly mourned. It has been a long time since he has been home to Vikland, but there are so few with his talents and connections," Miya explained.

"How long are you in Kerek City?" The Secondo asked.

"Not more than two days. We have an assignment here to assist Bima." Miya casually shrugged. The Secondo raised an eyebrow and Miya straightened quickly. I quickly dropped my eyes to hide a smile.

First Soldier Joon looked at both of us. "I need to ask you not to go out into the city for the rest of the day. I will update Ambassador Lalsy once she is free, and we will send someone to find you in the embasado. I think we would like to review the ambassador's plans with you present."

He paused, exhaled hard, and then continued, "I am sorry to tell you this. You should know we have had no word from those who were to join us last from Vikland. By now, they are so overdue, I fear the entire patrol is lost. I had requested two softfooters and the rest soldiers. Without them...well, Bima would be an asset to me. If the Northern Track continues to be so deadly, we may soon be forced to use only the Silver Mountains into Matasi and then sail to Kerek City. But for now...for you...I will send the most skilled due for a journey home. We can talk more of this later."

The Secondo looked at me. "Are you more skilled in archery or the bongs, Zren Janin?"

Miya spoke first, "Hand to hand fighting with his own West Islands steel and other weapons. He had some training in softfooting from Ngahuru of the West Islands." He smiled broadly. "You should know she has been found. Ngahuru is on her way home accompanied by her brother, Koanga, and with an honor guard of Solkka Ulani and the Secondo's captain, Ven Wila. The ambassador in Salisport insisted she travel as our guest on the ship home."

First Soldier Joon broke into a wide smile. "That *is* good news. Found by us, I assume, since we are escorting her home. Or were the Matasians involved?"

"Neither." Miya grinned. "I met her by chance in Ribelo and again in Anarkio. She had traveled from Kerek City with only her brother and Zren Janin. In Matasi, every administration building in every settlement had a description of her and a reward posted for her 'detainment and return to Kerek.' I can only assume Kerek was just as eager to claim her before she left their borders. Yet she strolled into the Salisport embasado dressed in her best, and as easily as if she was meeting the Secondo and ambassador for a cup of Vikland coffee and finger sweets. Zren Janin comes with her full recommendation."

The look First Soldier Joon gave me now was appraising and respectful. I wasn't sure what I had done right, but Miya had smoothed over any reservations the Secondo had earlier.

"Well done, Zren Janin. There were many people looking for her here in Kerek. Some for power, some for purse, some for patriotism. I have not met her brother, but I met Ngahuru at an ambassador's dinner. Of course, her stories proceed her." He smiled at me. "It is clear none of you should be underestimated."

He thought for a moment, and then added decisively, "You should go to the weapons training and demonstrate your steel skills, Zren. Some of these new ones act as if a Kereki fight is no more than two bongs dancing."

He turned back to Miya. "You've been here before. Take Zren and go down to the staff dormitories. Find food. Catch up with your colleagues. And remember, don't leave the compound for the rest of today or tonight."

## CHAPTER 31

## SOFTFOOTING

Dawn was still three decons away when I heard the strike of a lucifer. Then I heard the soft clang of a lantern door, so I opened one eye against the light.

"Get up, Zren. Hurry." I felt a hand on my shoulder, pulling me to a sitting position. Blearily, I pulled on a shirt and then opened the other eye.

"Where is everybody?" I looked around at the empty beds in confusion. There had been six beds in the room I was sleeping in. I had briefly met my bunkmates before crashing into my bed the night before, but now I looked around and the room was empty except for me and Bima, who was holding the lantern.

"On assignment."

"Oh." I let my tired brain process this. "Why are you here?"

"I thought you might want to see the beginning of the Kereki revolt against the monarchy."

Now I was awake. I grabbed my boots, but Bima motioned me not to put them on, to bring them and follow him silently instead.

The halls were deserted. Apparently, when the Secondo says 'lights out,' all the good little boys and girls of Vikland shut their doors and close their eyes. Except for Bima Ritwik.

He eased open the exterior door in the weapons training area. He dropped a black cloth over the lantern but didn't blow it out. The light dimly lit the path below our feet without casting a wider glow. He motioned me to put on my boots, and then I followed him along the outside wall until we came to the inner wall between the Vikland and Matasi embasado compounds. He tossed a throwing hook and rope over the wall and listened for the snag on the top. He blew out the lantern, wrapped it in the black cloth, and carefully secured it on his back in his traveling pack. I felt him lean close to me. "Do what I do," he whispered.

He backed up and ran at the corner of the wall, climbing it with a foot on each side of the corner, barely hanging on to the rope. He threw himself flat at the top, and I heard a very soft thud as his feet hit the ground on the other side. The rope slid up a few feet.

I tried to do the same as Bima, but I had never seen such a thing done before. I heard Bima's grunt as he took my full weight as I dragged myself up the rope. I rolled up and over, but at least managed to drop softly on my feet. He quickly wrapped up the hook and rope and slid it on his shoulder. He paused for a moment as if he were waiting for something. Moments later, a huge explosion rocked the sky, screams followed like the call and response songs I had heard in Matasi.

Bima grabbed my arm. "Run!"

We scraped along the back wall of the Matasi embasado, nearly twice as high as the one we had just thrown ourselves over. Another explosion, this one farther down. By the docks, I guessed, on the north side where the grain warehouses were. Bima barely paused as the next interior wall came into view. He tossed the throwing hook and ran at the corner wall and was up and over. I followed him, dragging on the rope, and I heard him grab the hook on the other side to counterbalance my own slower ascent. I dropped beside him and listened for a moment.

The crowds outside on the street were still in disarray. I could hear yelling, military shouts and commands, and the chaos of frightened horses and carts colliding with people and other moving obstacles.

"Come oooooonnnnn," Bima whispered. "One more...."

BOOM! This one was the closest—on this side of the docks. I tried to remember what would have been in the way. Bima pulled on my arm, and we made our way to the West Islands embasado building. The lock was broken, and the door hung crookedly. He pushed it open and slipped inside. I could feel loose bricks underneath my feet. I made a slow slide forward to avoid tripping.

I heard another snick of a lucifer. Bima already had the lantern open and the black cloaking fabric over the top so the light would only point downward. Once it was lit, we could see the floor and our feet, but nothing higher than our knees. We wandered through the building, rooms ransacked, drapery and furniture slashed and broken. Personal items left behind in the moments trying to flee. Bima would kneel down and look at dusty footprints, press his hands in cushions, overturn and peer into desks and chairs. I thought it was a waste of time, the building had clearly been looted many times.

The family's personal apartments and children's rooms were on the fourth floor. I pushed open a door and saw pretty maps on the walls, books, and papers on the small tables. Although this was the worn, pressed and repressed paper, bleached of inks and colors sold in the Kereki market, I marveled even the children had paper to write on, to draw maps, to own for themselves.

"Ssssst." I heard Bima outside the door. He had set the lantern on the floor and the cloth now covered it completely.

"Here, take my hand. I want to show you the fires." I felt his warm dry hand take mine and lead me down the hall. He pushed open the door. Across from us three windows framed red flames. All the granaries along the north end of the docks were on fire. There were Kereki soldiers with pikes and shields trying to keep people back, but others were just using the fires as a distraction for their own looting on other streets and businesses. I saw bundles laying in the street and realized they were bodies, either trampled or murdered in the mayhem. I felt sick inside. It was past harvest, there would be no food in the city for those I knew. Even the castle would feel the pinch of this one.

"Come on. Let's see the castle's response." Bima put his hand on my shoulder and led me away from the windows. We went back into the hallway and pushed open a door at the end. It was only a little dormer window, but we could see the deserted embasado next door and the castle beyond, high on the hill overlooking the city.

The castle was lit up with lanterns from nearly every window and I could see groups of people pushing their way into the frames for a better view. I wondered what the conversations were about. Concern for the people who would starve during the coming Wet? Or worry only for the rich owners who lost their granaries and their fortunes?

I looked at the Conrosan embasado and wondered about the last time it had been occupied. Had my family ever been there?

What had the diplomats thought traveling all that way to take up residency in Kerek City? What had the previous King been like? Would they have liked their stay? When did they leave? Why didn't my family leave with them? Did they move on to Matasi, wander the West Islands, or brave the frontier to get to Vikland? I turned to ask Bima if he knew what happened, when I caught a movement out of the corner of my eye. A reflection of the fire in the wavy glass? I waited. The reflections of the fires danced and surged. There. A drapery had definitely twitched.

"Bima," I whispered. "Bima!"

"I heard you." He was right behind me.

"There's someone in the embasado across the way, top floor looking out towards the fire. You can't see a face. It's only the fire's reflection that catches the movement."

Bima slid up to me and watched out the window. I felt him slow his breathing, relax his stance, and realized he was preparing for a long wait. It reminded me of when I had picked out a fool to follow home from the gambling halls, or a drunk that needed to be separated from his coin. I was just ready to tell Bima this when I saw it again. This time it was unmistakable. Someone was in the Conrosan embasado. I looked at Bima and he just rocked back on his heels and grinned at me. "Let's go home. I've got a plan."

We went back to the hallway and picked up the lantern. Bima carried it at knee height all down the steps, but we still stumbled over the debris left by the looters. At the ground floor, he carefully blew out the lantern and hid it near the receiving room. "We'll need it later," he whispered. He hung the rope and throwing hook over his shoulder, and we eased out into the night.

I didn't get any better at running up walls, but I was still the first one back in my room at the Vikland embasado. I undressed, crawled under the covers, and thought about my first day back in Kerek City. I thought about the Conrosan embasado and how it felt different to me now that I knew I was more than the streets of Lowertown. I fell asleep before dawn.

*  *  *  *  *

My meeting with the ambassador would have occurred after first meal, had I been able to wake up in time. Instead, I opened an eye when I smelled the coffee Viklanders couldn't seem to live without. Miya stood inside my room, fully dressed in a military uniform, a tiny cup of coffee cradled in his hands.

"Waiting for breakfast in bed? I hate to tell you they stopped serving food in the dining room."

"I was counting on this lot," I flung my arm out at the empty room, "to wake me up this morning." I pushed myself up in bed.

"There's no way I slept through them coming home this morning or heading out to first meal. What happened?"

"No one expects them home until tonight. Once I found out, I came to tell you, but you weren't here." He smiled at me. "When you are not where I expect you, then I assume Trouble has come to find a playmate. So, I looked for Bima and he was also gone." He raised an eyebrow. "You two out softfooting? That's a little dangerous, when the Kerek City Secondo tells you *twice* not to leave the embasado compound."

"We stayed off the streets. I wasn't in any danger from the rioting."

"Not in danger from Kerek City, no. But I was talking about the Secondo, First Soldier Joon."

I scowled. Miya chuckled.

"Anyway, I came to tell you that you have two meetings this morning. The first one, you and I will go present our plans for traveling across the Northern Track. I met with Joon earlier this morning and he is already aware, so this is more a formality to present to the ambassador."

"Your second meeting, you and Bima are to present your plans. Bima has an idea the West Islanders are hiding in the Conrosan embasado and wants you, with him as your second, to petition the Kerek King through our ambassador to formally allow you—as a Conrosan diplomat, no less—to enter your own embasado and remove some important items. Your story is you have come from Vikland, are going to retrieve your country's artifacts, and sail away to your next posting in the West Islands. He's still working on that part."

He took a sip of his coffee. "You wouldn't happen to know where Bima suddenly came up with this idea, would you? Because we have had people all through the West Islands embasado, and I truly don't want to be part of the clean up going through massive piles of rubble looking for secret entrances and hidden rooms based on one of Bima's guesses."

I muttered something under my breath.

Miya blew an exasperated sigh. "Zren, listen to me. If you trust no one else in the Vikland embasado, trust me. I am highly invested in getting home alive, unwounded, and soon. That's not going to happen if I don't have you by my side. You tell me everything, and in return, I will make sure you have the best information available to navigate the next few days." He paused. "Please, Zren. I know I need you more than you need me right now, but let's work together on this. Please," he repeated.

I huffed. It was the 'please' that did it. "I was with Bima last night watching the fires from the West Islands embasado. We went to see the castle's response from a small dormer window on the top floor, and I thought I saw movement in the embasado next door. No. We did. We both saw evidence someone is hiding there."

Miya looked at me sharply.

"How did you get past the checkpoints? No one, except those on assignment, could leave the embasado last night. The guards were checking carefully—very carefully."

"We scaled the interior walls between the embasados. The explosions covered our noise and distracted the Matasi guards as we crossed through their compound."

Miya stilled. "You climbed the interior walls? You trespassed on the Matasi compound?"

"Well, Bima mostly just hauled me over on a rope. I'm a lot shorter and lighter than he is."

"But just as crazy, apparently." Another sip of coffee. "Zren, let Bima tell the story as if he disobeyed a command by himself. Trespassing on another's embasado grounds is a serious offense. There will be repercussions, I am sure of it. I just don't want you to get covered in them as well." Sip. "If he does draw you into the story, say you understood we were supposed to help him, you just didn't know he was not acting under official direction."

I nodded, thought for a moment, and then asked, "Just to be clear, should I ever trust Bima Ritwik?"

Miya looked away to hide his smile. "If I am ever in trouble, I could do a lot worse than to have Bima Ritwik by my side. But if I am dancing with Trouble, it is because he introduced me, and he *better* be at my side. Bima looks at the world sideways, and he and Truth do not often sit at the same table. It is a talent of his that has cost him many friends over the years. We are not friends, he and I, we will most likely never be friends, but he has many skills that help Vikland, and in that we are in agreement. You should know this, Bima Ritwik will never run away from duty. He will defend to the death those that need his protection."

He drained his coffee cup. "Now let's find something you can wear to meet the ambassador and convince her my plan will work. Oh, and Zren? No matter what you see, Ambassador Lalsy is the smartest person in the room. Like Bima, she looks at the world sideways. She will play you, if she can, to gain an edge. It is a skill that serves her well here in Kerek City. She has been dealing with this incompetent Kerek King since he ascended the throne, and if we can't get the sons better behaved, then she will have to manage them as well."

## CHAPTER 32

# BEST LAID PLANS

I am glad Miya had a plan and I am glad he is so well spoken. Before Miya took me in to the reception room, he asked me to bow as deeply as he did to Ambassador Lalsy and not as deeply to First Soldier Joon. "You've already met, so you are merely acknowledging he is part of this meeting. I have asked everyone to speak Keresh so you can understand everything. Answer any questions truthfully, Zren. No one will think less of you for what you say. They will think less of you for what you do not say." He cocked his head to the side. "Except for Ngahuru. Keep her secrets, Zren. It will let them know you can also keep mine."

Ambassador Lalsy was seated at a large formal table. First Soldier Joon stood just behind and to the left of her, reminding everyone he was watching. There were three people along the far-right wall, all younger than Miya but not as young as me. I watched them. They didn't carry any weapons, so I didn't know what they were doing there. I snapped my head forward as the ambassador began to speak in Keresh.

"Miyamoto Suki, it is always a joy to see you again," she began formally. "Where are you traveling from this time?"

Miya bowed, and I bowed a moment behind him. "It is always an honor to visit your home away from Vikland, Ambassador Lalsy." He bowed lightly to Joon, and I did the same. The ambassador quirked a half smile, but Joon just nodded his head once at both of us. "I have traveled the last year in the West Islands and have come to you by way of Matasi. I look forward to the opportunity to go home to Vikland, to study and to train before my next posting."

"And where would you like that to be?" she asked gently.

"In the best of all my dreams, I would be posted to Conrosa. But I am content to go where the Empress sends me."

"But for now, you wish to go home. Come. Show me your plans for crossing the Kerek frontier." She moved her hands to show a large map. Miya motioned me forward.

In a formal tone he began, "Ambassador Lalsy, this is Zren Janin, Conrosan born, and Kereki trained." He looked down at the map and his finger followed his words. "He guided the West Islanders, Ngahuru the Softfoot, and her brother, Koanga, a Storyteller, down the Coast Road from Kerek City to Salisport in Matasi. My path intersected with theirs twice." He tapped the map. "In Ribelo and in Anarkio. Ngahuru told me of Zren's skill in evading Trouble, but also dispatching it when Trouble came to dance. They survived two ambushes in Kerek." He paused. "There are four less Kerekis who misjudged their opponents."

Ambassador Lalsy raised an eyebrow at me. "Forgive me for underestimating your skills and courage. You looked young and slight next to our Viklanders. I won't make that mistake again."

I gave a half smile at the compliment, and then quickly straightened my face.

Miya continued, "Zren Janin has many talents, but riding horse is not one of them. The ambassador in Matasi and I thought Zren and I could lead a wagon train. He does not have archery skills, so I would ask at least two of yours to be sent home are bowmasters. I have four trunks of West Islands steel the ambassador in Matasi sent with us. Bima Ritwik has arranged for its storage. Some is for your needs here in Kerek City, and the rest is to take to Viklander garrisons. If you have enough of your own people due to return to Vikland, we could use them as outriders to protect us through the Northern Track. The ambassador also thought we should check on the military garrisons north of Cloa and at Ishes."

Miya's face fell into sadness. "I understand from First Soldier Joon the last group that was to report for duty here from Vikland did not arrive. Zren has a small talent in softfooting, and Kerekis wouldn't look past the color of his skin. He may get information about the Viklanders, or their tragedy, where the rest of us would get a blow to the head."

The ambassador looked at Joon. He spoke, "I have selected four who have been in Kerek City for three years and are overdue to go home: two are bowmasters. Rell is also a healer, Kern is one of Bima's softfooters. I would also like to send Song Yao, she is a master on the bongs, but I do not know if she has ever taken the Northern Track. I believe she took the Silver Mountains pass to Matasi, and then came to us on rotation by sea. It has probably been five years since she has been home in Vikland. The fourth," he sighed, "The fourth is injured and needs to go home for medical care. He's a firemaster, injured last night. We can't have him treated here for obvious reasons, but we talked to him this morning and he is agreed. Rell says she can care for Chul's burns on the journey and is learning how until the group goes."

"Not Chul Swyler," Miya stiffened.

Joon nodded. "It also meant we needed to pull in Raeshon because she can't work alone in Kerek City, in the guise of a missionary or no." He considered, "You said six would be coming from Matasi on the next two sailings. Do you know who they are and what their experience is?"

Miya shook his head. "Regretfully, I do not. But if you have Bima Ritwik, perhaps the loss of Chul Swyler will not be so painful."

"Perhaps. But Chul is a firemaster and Bima is a softfoot," the ambassador said drily. "And perhaps Bima will lose all my little softfooters in his 'training' exercises."

I dropped my eyes to the floor so she couldn't see my smile. So I wasn't the only one Bima liked to lead astray. I wondered what happened to lost softfooters.

The ambassador and Joon conferred quietly for a while. I recognized Vik, but Miya's face showed absolutely no reflection of what they were saying. Then they faced Miya again.

"We agree with your plans. Create a wagon train with Zren Janin as one of your drivers. Take all of the trunks of West Islands steel and Chul Swyler as your cargo. Rell, Kern, and Song will join you as outriders. Visit the military garrison at Ishes, but not at Earles; we have not received final word it is fully ours. This afternoon, First Soldier Joon, and you, Miyamoto Suki, will petition the Kerek King for an escort. Wear your uniform of course."

She looked at me. "Zren Janin, we will keep you here. I understand you have another role to play for us, but I will wait until I hear everything from Bima Ritwik."

She stood up from the table then and I saw she wore a long formal dress that didn't quite reach the floor or cover up the tops of her black military boots. I snapped my eyes back to her face and she smiled at me. "You will learn quickly, Zren Janin, all Viklanders have many talents. I am also a bowmaster and I practice daily. I am sending my best, Rell Huena and Song Yao, with you to help keep Miyamoto Suki and Chul Swyler safe on the road to Vikland. But I am also reassured your skills are just as formidable as my warriors." She nodded at Miya who had gathered his maps and papers. He stepped back and gave a short bow to Ambassador Lalsy and another to First Soldier Joon. I did the same.

"I will send a note to the castle requesting an audience and have someone find you when I have heard," Joon said.

"Thank you for interceding on my behalf," Miya said formally. With that, we walked out to the hallway where two handfuls of others waited their turn to talk to Ambassador Lalsy and the Secondo.

We hadn't gone halfway down the hall before we saw Bima Ritwik standing alone with a tube of papers under his arm. He was almost bouncing on the balls of his feet, he was so eager to meet with Ambassador Lalsy and First Soldier Joon. Miya stopped in front of him, "We are going with four. Chul Swyler was injured last night."

Bima stilled instantly. "How bad?"

"Bad enough they can't fix it here. Not so bad they think he won't survive the Northern Track. He's to be cargo, I am told, I cannot count on him to fight."

Bima scoffed. "Chul can fight blindfolded and lame. With Zren, you will be six. Your odds should be good. Who are your archers?"

"Kern and Rell. I am very happy with both."

"I will be sorry to lose Kern here in Kerek City. But it is right, she is long overdue for a journey home." Bima gave a mocking smile. "Ambassador Lalsy appreciates what a rare delicate flower you are to send such exceptional archers to protect you."

Miya just smiled back blandly. "The ambassador appreciates that she is sending all four trunks of steel with me. I'm just muscle for such an expensive shipment. Do you know Song Yao? She is my fourth."

"Three women and Chul? I know they are overdue to go home, but that's a tough run. Kerek is such a backwards country they throw away half their soldiers, half their leaders, half their brains, because they do not treat their women as we do. You won't be able to stay in inns or do horse exchanges in the stables without losing decons hiding your warriors in the woods."

"No. I am not hiding them. I thought I would just let the Kereki fools take their chances. If they don't realize what a Viklander woman is capable of, they should be part of the body count."

Both men laughed. I smiled, but there was something niggling at me. "Why do they have to go as women? I know, because you say so, all three are capable of swatting down their enemies as if they were bugs, but it's messy, and it takes time to bury bodies."

I turned to Miya. "Koanga made Kereki pants and tunics for Ngahuru. Her hair was this long," I held my fingers two widths apart. "She walked like a boy. Koanga talked all the time so people would look at him, and he made sure everyone knew he was a Storyteller newly arrived from the West Islands on a grand adventure. She made everyone look at him...or me." I scrunched up my face. "She called it 'titiro mai ki ahau,' or something like that. What if, instead of a well-protected Viklander shipment, we looked like farm laborers with camp packs or settlers with a wagon of our belongings?" I offered.

"That would only work in Matasi," Bima replied. "And you will never get a Viklander to cut off their hair. It is more than vanity, Zren. If a Viklander is a coward, or does something dishonorable, his or her braid is cut to show everyone the warrior's shame. No one will cut their hair merely for a disguise."

Miya tilted his head. "Bima's right. But, Zren, you've given me an idea. Let's meet with the others and see the best way to go forward. I also want to find Chul and see what else we need to take or do for him. He's going to have a miserable trip. I'd like to get him back to Vikland, to the healers and to his experiments, as painlessly as possible."

We turned to go when a younger cadet called, "Bima Ritwik, you're next."

Bima looked at me. "I need you for this part." He looked at Miya. "If Chul was injured, I would start by looking in the infirmary. I'm not sure where the other three are, but if they are leaving Kerek City for good in the next two days, I would check the staff rooms. They are probably packing."

Miya nodded and walked off without a word.

* * * * *

Bima's meeting with First Soldier Joon and the ambassador did not go as well as Miya's. I began to see what Miya meant when he described Bima as sideways. When pressed for why he thought the West Islanders were in the Conrosan embasado, he had several not quite plausible reasons. I noted he said nothing about defying First Soldier Joon's order not to leave the Vikland embasado last night. When asked how he thought he could dress up a young man who needed a few good meals and a growth spurt to even look old enough to be a Conrosan diplomat who had sailed halfway around the world to clean out a few closets, Bima was very amusing, but not convincing.

In the end, I wasn't going to meet the Kerek King after all.

*  *  *  *  *

After midday, Miya left for the Kerek castle with First Soldier Joon. I was outside in the courtyard when the ambassador's carriage and matched horses were pulled about, and the two, dressed in fine military brass and buttons, climbed in. Bima was standing next to me as the formal gates opened, the carriage pulled out, and turned up the street to the castle.

"Why didn't they walk? It took more time to open the gates and drive through than it would have to walk the short distance," I asked Bima.

"It's to show they are asking the King as a courtesy, as equals. Not as poor supplicants begging for assistance."

"Huh." I looked at him. "It's probably a good thing your plan wasn't permitted. I wouldn't know how to act in front of the Kerek King."

Bima looked down at me and smiled. "The plan was never supposed to be permitted. It was only supposed to draw the ambassador's attention from what we are really going to do."

His smile turned into a smirk. "You don't scream if beautiful women show up in your room, do you?" He laughed at my startled expression. "You should meet Kern before tonight. Oh, and get some rest, we'll be softfooting about after dark. Kern will wake you." He turned and walked away leaving me staring after him.

## CHAPTER 33

# SONG YAO AND KERN THE SOFTFOOT

I wandered about the embasado until I found myself at the weapons training area. There were three large circles sketched out in the dirt, and battles with short and long bongs going on in each one. Joon had described it to me as dancing, and I could see the gracefulness and quick footwork in the movements. One of the circles held a shorter woman with a jeong bong considerably longer than she was. I watched to see her skill, and I realized it was never to be, or to do, what her opponents expected. If she lunged in for a jab, she would drop her bong and go for a sweep. If she needed to block, she would spin and slide the bong along for a hit on the upper body. I watched her drop three opponents in a row, before she stepped out of the circle to drink from her flask.

She stepped back into the ring and called out, first in Vik, and then in Keresh, "I need to fight two or more. I leave on the Northern Track tomorrow." Two tall men waiting their turn at the side, looked at one another and then stepped into her circle. I guessed this might be Song Yao, our bongmaster, and so I watched her carefully. The battle was hard and fast. She was able to keep both of them in front of her, but now she was fighting defensively, rather than taking the initiative.

She was good, the problem was any Kereki would just throw a knife or a riata. Sure, Kereki knives were just hammered copper or iron, but they could interrupt the bongs enough to grab the victim and cut the throat with a Sailor's Curse. I walked over to her circle and waited. Finally, one of the men swung a short blow at her neck that would have laid her out flat if he would have connected. Instead, she blocked it and swept the other end at the other opponent, crashing him into his partner. The three bowed to each other and then turned to face me.

She nodded, tucked her jeong bong under her arm, made a short bow, and started with their funny formal way of introductions. "Conrosan, greetings."

I winced. I really hated to be called Conrosan. "My name is Zren Janin. I will be traveling to Vikland tomorrow."

"I am Song Yao. I will be returning to Vikland for the first time since I posted out, first to the West Islands, and then to Kerek. I am *very glad* to meet you if it means I can return to Vikland." She tilted her head towards me. "I have heard you are Kereki trained, and you carry West Islands steel."

"Yes," I nodded. "And I would like to show you how you would die on the Northern Track." I reached for one of the tahn bongs hanging on the wall. I pulled the dagger from my boot and untied one of the fabric strips about my calves. I tied the knife to the end of the bong, talking the entire time.

"You've noticed how the Kereki men and boys always wear their pants tucked into their boots with these fabric ropes wrapped above their ankles? We call them 'Kereki ties', and if you asked, any Kereki would tell you it is to keep the desert critters from crawling up their pant legs. But what they don't tell you is these cloth strips are long enough to tie up someone, secure a knife to a tree limb or walking stick, drop as a distraction, or tie around a piece of rubble and use as a riata—a weapon." I held up my hastily constructed pike. "Now when I fight, I can slash across legs, body, and face, as well as connect with blows. Less accuracy and strength is needed and I have also created a distraction, as my enemy now needs to keep an eye on the blade."

One of the soldiers sneered. "It is not elegant, nor does it take the skill of a bongmaster."

I bit back my retort and tossed the modified tahn bong to Song. She caught it easily in her other hand. Ah, one who could fight on either side. I would need to remember that. Then I grabbed a fist-sized vase holding dirt and a scrubby plant from the windowsill. I dumped out the plant and the dirt and wrapped the vase in my other Kereki tie leaving long trailing ribbons of fabric. "If you put any heavy object, a rock, broken pottery, even your gambling winnings hidden in your boot and then tie it like this, it is called a 'riata,' or a 'Kereki housewife.' Swing it in a circle over your head, or vertically along your side, and you have another weapon against the bongs."

I nodded to Song. "Use the tahn bong and try to disarm me or disable me. Don't hold back because I won't."

I started swinging the riata around my head in a slow lazy circle with my left hand. In my right, I had the dagger from my other boot. At her first jab, I dropped the circle and the riata intercepted the bong and knocked it away. I moved in with my right hand and slashed at her with my dagger. I caught the front of her tunic and it cut away. Those watching made a collective gasp and the room stilled. Now everyone stopped to watch us.

"I mean it, Song. Fight me hard."

She came at me again, weaving, slashing, and sweeping low to try to take me off my feet. She was good. I couldn't tell if she was stronger on her right or left side, and I was struggling to stay out of her path of destruction. If she wouldn't have already been tired from fighting all those opponents all morning, I wouldn't have had a chance. The riata couldn't change direction as fast as she could, but she didn't know how to fight against it. I took a hard hit on my shoulder, numbing my arm so completely, my knife dropped harmlessly to the floor.

With only the riata, I was able to score two heavy hits on her hip, and she fought to keep her balance. I reached for my Sailor's Curse and spun the riata at my side and let it snake about her ankles. She stepped clear with one leg, but the weight of the riata around her other ankle caused her to stumble. I moved in, trapped her bong between us, and grabbed her shoulder with my good arm. I twisted her sharply and held my Sailor's Curse to her throat, "and that is how you would die on the Northern Track," I said to the room loudly.

A single pair of hands clapped in the stillness of the room, and we all looked up to see First Soldier Joon and Miyamoto Suki standing together in the balcony. Joon clapped once more and then placed his hands on the railing. He called down, "I believe there is enough rubble in the streets from last night's riots to create many riatas. It should not be necessary to destroy any more of Ambassador Lalsy's prized trimmings. Check with the laundresses to find damaged bedding that can be used for the Kereki ties. It may not be a weapon with grace and elegance," he nodded to the Viklander who had commented earlier, "but it is one of Kerek City and the frontier. Remember, you are not fighting Viklanders." He considered for a moment. "Pad the riatas and pad your tunics while you are training, but after today they should be as much a part of your routine as the bongs. Know how to fight with them and against them. They are a survival weapon."

I looked at Miya and he motioned me to join them. I took the stairs two at a time and met them at the top.

"Any other weapons I should be aware of?" Joon asked. "Most of our people go through the Silver Mountains, since they start in either Matasi or the West Islands before posting to Kerek City," the Secondo explained. "This is not an easy assignment. Some make the Northern Track once, maybe twice in their military service. More for the diplomatic service and the softfooters and those who protect them. Any edge you can teach them to help them survive the frontier, I will be grateful."

"Show him your Sailor's Curse, Zren." Miya nodded at me.

I flicked it out of my tunic, open-palmed it so Joon could see it, then folded it between my fingers so only the blade was visible. "No one in Dockside or in Lowertown would walk out on the streets after dark without one of these tucked in their fists."

"The blade isn't deep," observed Joon.

"It doesn't have to be. The point is to slash at the face, preferably above the eyes so the victim's blood interferes with their vision. Then either run away or kill them with another weapon." I gave it over to him for a closer look.

"It's not West Islands steel, but deadly enough for all that. Where can I find them?"

"No Kereki would sell you one. You, meaning any stranger to Lowertown or the docks, are meant to receive a Kereki kiss, not hand them out. I had to get this from someone I knew for years."

"I see." He handed it back to me. "We have a complication." He nodded to Miya.

"The King has granted our request for an escort to Vikland. It appears outlaws have waylaid the military garrisons' payroll and supplies for all of the Dry season's last four attempts. The castle has not had any communication from the garrison at Ishes for over a year." Miya flashed a quick hard smile.

"Apparently, a lone soldier arrived from Earles last season saying the entire rest of his patrol had been wiped out by cutthroats during a resupply visit to Huk. I thought it an interesting fact to note he fled back to Kerek City rather than return to his post. He was the one who informed the King, payroll hadn't arrived since before the last Wet season, and desertion was high."

"What happened next?" I asked.

"Nothing," Joon sneered. "The King wasn't interested in sending out the pay wagon just to have it stolen and the military commander is not interested in sending out more troops if they are not going to get paid."

Joon continued, "When I said we wanted to send a wagon with armed outriders through the frontier to Vikland, the King's advisor thought it was an excellent idea to add a Kereki military wagon and travel together. We have to delay one day, and they will send four soldiers who will take up their new posts in Earles. Apparently, the garrison at Ishes is going to have to send their own soldiers to plead for the King's mercy and receive the coin due them."

"You don't sound happy about this," I offered slowly.

"Asking for an escort was just a formality. The King knows Viklanders are preyed upon when traveling all the roads leading to Vikland, and truthfully, he doesn't care. If we take out a few bandits and outlaws along the way, he doesn't have to expand the effort to run them down and hang them. He wins by doing nothing," Miya sighed.

"And now? Are we holding his soldiers' hands? Or do we sleep with one eye open?"

Joon answered me, "Soldiers sent to the outposts, or frontier garrisons are being punished or are too green to know better. Maybe they are bad soldiers, maybe they hold unpopular opinions. I don't think they will ally themselves with the bandits against us on the journey. They would have to be smart enough to know they would just be murdered after us." Joon changed topic abruptly. "Have you met those you are traveling with?"

"Song Yao." I waved at the training below. "Chul, I met on the ship from Salisport. But not Kern or Rell."

"Good archers, both of them. They are done with their military service and both serve us in the diplomatic corps. Kern is a softfoot. Rell is one of our healers. Both carry their own West Islands steel." He watched the sparring for a moment. "Well then. You have things to do and so do I." He nodded to both of us and walked off.

I watched him disappear down the hallway and then asked, "How upset was he about the military escort?"

"He visibly startled. It was totally unexpected. The King's eyes narrowed, and the advisors were smirking, so something is definitely going on. I would like another outrider or two along, and I know there are many people who should be going out on rotation, but now is not the time. Both Joon and Ambassador Lalsy want to keep the embasado overstaffed right now. Riots, like last night, are occurring more frequently." He gave me an assessing look. "It's time you met Rell and Kern. Come with me."

Kern was sitting, relaxed and casual, in her room talking to Bima, chairs facing each other, so close their knees were almost touching. The door was open, but Miya knocked anyway. Both looked up, smiling easily.

"Ah! You found me!" Kern laughed. "I was beginning to think we were going to meet on the wagon. I would stand and greet you in the formal manner, Zren, but it would only serve to give you a false impression of me." She laughed again and tossed her long braid over her shoulder. "So tell me, Zren Janin, who was the lover of fairy tales—your mother or your father?"

She took my silence for confusion.

"Your name, Zren Janin, is the name of a Conrosan folk hero. He has many stories about him. That your parents named you for him must mean they have high hopes for you." She smiled at Miya. "Much like our Miyamoto Suki, named for a strong warrior of a mountain kingdom far, far away. Well, Miya, what brave deeds are you going to dazzle me with today?"

I glanced at Miya and saw his eyes smile back at her. "My brilliant Kern, you chatter so much I can never get a story in between your amazing conquests of shops, secrets, and hidden lovers."

"Ah, now you have frightened the new boy!" She stood up and walked over to me. She was tall—taller than both Bima and Miya. She was wearing the Kereki tunic without the flowing shirt underneath and her bare arms were well muscled. Her baggy trousers were tucked into her boots with the Kereki ties about her calves. I realized she was the first person I had met here not wearing the dark Viklander clothes. Her skin was pale, as light as a Kereki, and she had a sprinkle of freckles across her cheeks like stardust.

"I hear you and I and Bima are going out on an adventure after dark."

Miya sighed. "Please don't talk about this in front of me. I don't want to know."

Kern looped her arm through Miya's and walked him to the door. "My dear Miya, perhaps it is best for you to go to your room and think about how brave and true and handsome you are, while Bima gets the real work done around here." She patted his cheek and pushed him out the door.

"Zren, are you coming with me?" Miya called from the hallway.

Bima answered, "We will return him when we are done with him."

Kern laughed and added, "And when we have fed him a little." She poked my ribs. "I think you might have forgotten that part, Miya."

Miya threw up his hands and walked away smiling.

* * * * *

Bima's plan seemed simple. We would travel to the Conrosan embasado by climbing the interior walls just as we had the night before. "But we won't have the distraction of half the docks burning as we cross the Matasi embasado grounds," Bima warned. Kern or Bima would break into a window on the Conrosan embasado and let me in through a door. We would need to assume there would be traps throughout the empty space. If the castle guards came to investigate, I was to declare myself as seeking sanctuary in my country's embasado.

"But truly, Zren," Kern patted my hand, "We do not want that pretty face of yours anywhere near a Kereki soldier."

Bima was convinced we would find the West Islanders and march them through the front door of our embasado. Once we escorted them home to a grateful nation, the West Islands would kindly assist Vikland as it wrestled a land corridor across Kerek to the sea. "Well, maybe not an ally. But I'd be fine with them just looking the other way while Matasi and Vikland carved the country in half," Bima smiled.

My jaw dropped and I looked between Kern and Bima. "You believe this to be true. Just like that, no more Kerek!" I ran my hand through my hair. "You can't just make a country disappear."

"I can't," Bima agreed. "But the Kerek King has so neglected his responsibilities he is already at war within his own country."

"Enough talk, Bima. You've given the poor boy so much to think about, he is going to get a wrinkle on that pretty face of his. And did we promise Miya we would feed him? Tonight is going to be strenuous enough without him fainting from hunger."

"I'm right here," I said irritably. "No need to talk about me as if I left with Miya."

"Yes, you are here. But you look stunned, and I am talking until you can recover yourself and look charming and dashing again." She laughed at her own joke.

"I need to find Rell and Chul," I protested. "I haven't met Rell yet."

"She's prettier than I am, but I am much better to have at your back. Of course she can fix you back up after she has failed to save your life." Kern gave me a sly smile.

I sputtered, "But Joon said she was a good archer. Miya said he needed at least two good archers."

"She is," Kern waved her arm. "I'm just better. It's to compensate for my lack of beauty."

"But you are beautiful," I blurted out.

"See Bima? That's how it's done. You need to take lessons from Zren."

In the end, I didn't meet Rell after all. We went down to the kitchens to find something to eat and then we were supposed to sleep. My roommates had finally returned from their assignment and were all sleeping soundly in the darkened room. I stumbled my way over their smoke-scented clothes strewn over the floor and joined them.

## CHAPTER 34

# RAUMATI OF THE WEST ISLANDS

I woke to the snick of a lucifer. I watched as Kern carefully stepped over the piles of clothing and small travel packs my roommates had dropped everywhere before they had fallen into their beds. The smell of old smoke leeched from the clothes giving the room a stale stink.

Kern shook out the lucifer and touched my shoulder. I pulled myself to a sitting position, already dressed in a pair of the same black closefitting pants and shirt the others wore. She had found them for me earlier.

One of my roommates stirred. "Who's there?" he mumbled.

Kern put her fingers to her lips, smiled, and stepped over another pile of clothes. She tenderly ran her hand down the man's cheek and he mumbled again. She pushed back a lock of his hair and whispered something. The man groaned softly, and she ran her hand down his cheek to his neck. He murmured the name

"Lansa," and Kern stood up abruptly with a scowl on her face. She motioned sharply to me to grab my boots and follow her.

Bima was waiting in the hallway, the throwing hook and rope already over his shoulder. I could see now Kern had a very small travel bag on her back.

We eased through the doors out to the courtyard and found our way to the back corner of the embasado compound. Bima tossed the throwing hook, tugged to secure it, walked back a ways and then ran up the corner of the wall. Kern followed, not as gracefully and tugging hard at the rope. I was neither as graceful nor fast, and I could feel Bima and Kern on the rope pulling me up and over. I rolled over the top and dropped softly beside them. Bima wound up the rope and we listened for the Matasian guards.

We ran across the yard hugging the dark back wall and repeated the run up and over twice more. Bima was still cautious as we ran across the back of the looted West Islands compound and over into the Conrosan embasado.

The tall wooden doors were heavily barred, and it took two circlings before Kern found a window she could be boosted up to and through. Once we heard her drop through on the other side, we walked to the back delivery door and waited...and waited... and waited. Finally, she came around the corner from the outside.

"Ssssst. This door is blocked from the inside and I can't get close enough to unbar it. I found another way." We walked around to a side door with wood lying on the ground. "This one was boarded up from the outside. It's why we never saw it. All the entrances have stacks of furniture blockading them. It is, or was, definitely used as a refuge."

Bima whispered. "From now on, hand signals only. I won't light the lantern until we know the light won't shine out to the streets. We'll start at the top and work our way down. If we have to, we can drive them out. Be alert." He smiled at me in the dark. "Defend yourself, Zren, but don't hurt anyone."

I carefully drew my Sailor's Curse and followed them.

Unlike the West Islands compound, this embasado had never been looted. Furnishings were covered in cloths, paintings still hung on walls, glass and pottery caught gleams of moonlight. I wanted to linger and look, but Kern and Bima moved swiftly through the rooms. The ground floor had been boarded up, but once we reached the second and third stories, reflected moonlight made it easier to see.

There were two sets of staircases from the third to the fourth floor. Bima took the wide public one and motioned Kern and I to take the other one. We had crept halfway up when I heard a distinctive drag, like something wooden pushed along the floor.

We froze in place and let Bima continue the ascent. He lit the lantern, cloaked it, and snuck down the hallway.

Another sound, this one the softest whisper of a door closing. Whoever it was, knew the snick of a door lock would give them away, and so we slowly pushed opened each of the doors along the hall and let the rooms tell us their secrets.

All the rooms were empty, but they didn't have the smell of long disuse. In each room, we pulled all the drapery tight across the windows, and once the rooms were dark and hidden from outside prying eyes, Bima uncloaked the lantern. We went back to the beginning of the hall and entered each room, felt over the walls of the rooms, looked in wardrobes, under desks, beds, and other furniture.

I was reaching to move aside the clothes in a wardrobe when a knife slashed across my left hand. I grabbed wildly with my right and pulled out a West Islander dressed in women's clothes. She had a large burn mark on her dark face. I squeezed her wrist until she dropped her knife.

"Stop it! Stop fighting! I am not going to hurt you! Stars, Kern! Do you speak Wester? Tell her I am not going to hurt her!" I held her away as far as I could to avoid her kicks.

Kern pushed me aside and grabbed the woman around the waist, pinning her arms to her side. She lifted her off the ground and spoke in a soft comforting voice until the woman stopped struggling, her chest heaving with effort.

"I speak Keresh," the woman gasped at me. She looked at Kern. "Not Vik."

Bima entered the room and pulled three chairs in a small circle. We all sat with Kern holding the woman in her lap. "Keresh, it is then." Bima nodded agreeably. "We want you to know who we are before we release you. You are in no danger from us. We want to help you." The woman said nothing, but she didn't struggle. "I am Bima, and the one holding you is Kern. We are Viklanders hoping to help the West Islanders retrieve the ambassador's children. We have coin and a ship to get you safely home."

The woman sat up straighter. "You can get me out of Kerek City?"

"Yes," he replied. "Once we have the children safe in the West Islands."

The woman considered. "If I told you the children were already safe at home in the West Islands, would you still help me leave Kerek City?"

Bima sighed in exasperation. "We've had people check the shipping manifests every day since the ambassador's murder.

There were no West Islands ships in the harbor the day of the murder or on the day of the death of the ambassador's wife. We know any time your ships do enter the Kerek harbor, they have been thoroughly searched before sailing out." Bima threw up his hands. "The Kerek King has offered a reward and had it posted on every market cross in every village. *Everyone* is looking for you and the children. We have had patrols and friends of Vikland at the inns and stables and roads leading out of Kerek City. We've searched everywhere. The children did not leave Kerek City."

The woman shrugged. "By your words, I know you do not know enough for me to think you can help me. But I won't run, you can let me stand on my own." Kern released her, and the woman stood in the middle of the circle.

I saw now why the West Islander had not fled with Ngahuru and Koanga. Her left foot was curved inward and down forcing her to stand nearly on the side of it. She could never have walked to Matasi, not even to save her own life. I had seen beggar children with the same. 'Kluba,' they called it. Clubfoot.

I snapped my eyes up as she turned to me and asked, "Who are you?"

"In Kerek City, I was known as 'Red.'" I paused for a long time, wondering what my next words should be. Was Ngahuru far enough away in the West Islands that she was safe? I knew

Bima knew that it was Ngahuru at the reception into the Salisport embasado, but what about Kern? I exhaled. I was talking to a West Islander, it would have to be acceptable. "My friend, Ngahuru of the West Islands, gave me the name 'Zren Janin,' who is a folk hero in the stories of my country, Conrosa. I traveled with her and her brother, Koanga, from near Kerek City until they sailed for home from Salisport, Matasi. If you are a friend of Ngahuru, you are a friend of mine. You may call me Zren."

She beamed at me. "You are the person I should be talking to. My name is Raumati."

Bima asked, "Raumati, are the ambassador's children with you?"

Raumati paused for a long moment, and I had the absurd sensation she was just going to whistle up the children out of hiding, and all the days of searching for them would be over.

Instead, she looked at me. "You know Ngahuru and Koanga are safe in the West Islands? You know this to be true? Tell me the story of your journey from Kerek City to Salisport. I will be able to know if you are saying what is true."

I glanced at Bima behind her, and he rolled his hand in a circle for me to keep talking. I hesitated, we all have secrets to redeem or bury us as they will. For a moment, I had a flashback to Ngahuru showing the settlers in the wagon her dark legs and colorless arm and face, trying to stay alive. I took a deep breath. I thought I could convince Raumati and still keep Ngahuru's secret from Bima. I parsed my words carefully.

"Ngahuru, the daughter of a tailor, as she would tell you, and Koanga, a Storyteller of the West Islands who has had his hearth and home for three years, as he would also tell you—more than once," Raumati smiled at this, "have saved my life as I have saved theirs. They found me on the road to Aldi four handfuls of days ago. They fed me, clothed me, and tended to my wounds. It would have been expected in Kerek they would rob me and leave me for dead, but Koanga taught me of the West Islands roaming regles through his words and his actions. We three fled together through Kerek down the Coast Road and into Matasi."

I paused. I didn't know how much to tell of Miya's help. But I knew if I did not tell the truth, Bima would know, and that might be worse. I sighed, Miya would have to take care of himself. "In Ribelo, we met Miyamoto Suki, a prince of Vikland." Bima snorted. "Also far from home. He is a true friend of Ngahuru, she met him here at the West Islands embasado. He took her to a private dealer he knew and helped her sell her West Islands metal workings to give us coin for our journey in Matasi." I paused to look at Bima's face. It was carefully blank, the kind of blank that told me Miya's kindness would not be forgotten… or unpunished.

"We met Miya again in Anarkio after we had spent the night in the Subversiva jail and paid our fines with most of our coin and our metal. He traveled with us to Salisport. He paid for Ngahuru's and Koanga's passage home in accommodations fine enough for those who work in the service of the West Islands King, even though their traveling papers said they were West Islanders of no notice. He did this, not for political advantage, but because when they were here in Kerek City, Ngahuru and Koanga had lost their traveling papers, their coin, and all their belongings to a captain who sailed away without them."

Raumati looked at me carefully in the lantern light. "You believe this to be true."

I nodded. "Because of the great debt we owe Miyamoto Suki, I have agreed to travel with him over the deadly Northern Track to Vikland."

She thought over my words and then asked, "You say you saved their lives?"

"This is true. Two times in Kerek we were ambushed, once near Aldi, and once on the Coast Road. It was Ngahuru's quick thinking that kept us out of danger until I could ensure the bandits would not trouble any travelers again."

"You killed for them." I saw her stiffen.

"I defended them," I corrected her. "Ngahuru and Koanga are my friends. I have defended them to keep them safe and I would do so again."

"And how do you know they are safe in the West Islands?" She smiled. "There are pirates on the seas."

"I know they sailed on a West Islands ship captained by a West Islander out of Salisport, Matasi. They had two bodyguards assigned by the Vikland ambassador."

Bima cleared his throat and interrupted us. "It was an honor guard, Raumati. An honor guard of the Secondo's captain, Ven Wila and Solkka Ulani. You are familiar with the Ulani family name?" he asked casually.

She shrugged as if it didn't matter and turned to me. "Those are very pretty words, Zren Janin. But tell me something only you and I would know before I tell you of the ambassador's children." She looked at the stricken look at my face. "Not of Ngahuru, we do not tell her secrets. Tell me something of Koanga," she said gently.

"The King loves Koanga's tales of the Seafarer the best." I grinned in relief.

She laughed out loud. "I cannot imagine what your journey must have been like with those two. When I first met Koanga, I saw someone who had never left the West Islands and I said to myself, 'This is the person who will get the children home and Ngahuru out of the country? The man who is in love with the constellations, and the great tales, and the sound of his own voice? The man who wields no weapon greater than a tailor's shears?'"

"But he did!" I insisted with a grin. "Ngahuru always said I was underestimating him. She called him her titiro mai ki ahau. It was not until I met this one yesterday," I pointed at Kern, "another look-at-me, I understood how important Koanga was to our success."

"Yes." Raumati shook out her skirts, and I saw she had made up her mind. "I am the last one to go home to the West Islands. All the others have made it safely. Please take me to your ambassador and I will tell you everything in exchange for passage home. I would also like to meet Miyamoto Suki and thank him for his help and kindness. If you wait here, I have a bag I would like to take with me to the West Islands. I am afraid I will have to leave everything else here."

She walked through the chairs with a light rolling gait and Kern jumped up. "I'll go with you."

"As you wish," Raumati shrugged. "I could hardly outrun you," she added drily.

The women took the lantern and walked down the hallway, leaving Bima and I looking at each other in a shard of moonlight. I tried to keep the smirk out of my voice. "Well, that was easy. I'm back in Kerek for two days and I have solved your biggest problem, Bima Ritwik. Anything else you need me to do before I take your position as Vikland's best softfoot?"

He stared at me for a moment and burst out laughing. "She may be as much of a storyteller as Koanga, but we will pack her back to the embasado and let Ambassador Lalsy and First Soldier Joon listen to her tales. As for me, I am not a small and petty man, Zren Janin. I am grateful you were able to convince her we truly wish to help. I also think I should look a little more widely for my softfooters than the noble houses of Vikland." He stood up and walked over to me. "Well done, Zren. Well done." He gestured to my cut and throbbing hand. "We should get that looked at. Thank the Lost God she only had a Kereki-made table knife and not a dagger of West Islands steel, or you would be learning to drive a horse with one hand."

In the end, there were four travel bags of papers Raumati said she dare not leave behind. We hauled them over the wall to the West Islands embasado and then walked out the broken front gate. The streets were clear of Kereki soldiers and pickpockets, all finding more lucrative trade down by the gawkers of the burned out docks, I guessed. We walked two doors down and into the Vikland embasado.

## CHAPTER 35

# THE FATE OF THE LOST CHILDREN

Bima took Raumati to the kitchens first in order to find her better food than she had been eating while in hiding. While she was voraciously working through vegetables, fruit, fresh bread, meat, and cheese—actually anything he could find—Kern had found the personal assistants for both Ambassador Lalsy and First Soldier Joon and had awakened the two. We were told to meet in the ambassador's receiving room in a decon. All I could think about as I cleaned my cut hand, was how much trouble there would be if Raumati's information was a disappointment.

When we presented ourselves, the ambassador and Joon were standing over an empty table, all the maps were gone. Joon waved us in, and they began the very formal introductory greetings with Raumati. I caught Kern's eye and she quirked a smile at me.

Ambassador Lalsy motioned us to the table, and we all sat down.

"So," the ambassador began. "I think it is best if you tell your story as you wish, rather than have us ask you all manner of questions. Is this acceptable to you?"

Raumati nodded and looked around the table. "I am telling you all of our secrets because of two people, Zren Janin," she gestured to me, "and Miyamoto Suki. I had hoped to see him here."

Joon turned and nodded to one of the aides along the wall and she disappeared out the door. Another aide walked in carrying a tray with tiny cups of Vikland coffee and finger sweets. Bima stood to serve everyone, but I shook my head at the coffee. Joon raised an eyebrow, and I hastened to reassure him. "Miya can have mine, we are one cup too few," I said just as Miya stepped in the door. He must have run all the way. His hair was loosely braided. His shirt hastily pulled on but crisply pressed all the same. Another aide quickly brought over a chair to the table for him.

We all stood as Raumati rose and introduced herself to Miya. "I understand our King and the West Islands owe you a great debt for your help in getting Ngahuru and Koanga home. Let me repay this debt in some small measure by telling you of the escape of the ambassador's children."

Everyone sat down again, and Raumati began her story.

"There were five of us who were assigned to protect the two children. We had titles like nanny and guard and teacher, but our primary role for the three years we were to be here in Kerek City was to protect the children, even at the cost of our lives.

"We heard of the murder of our ambassador in the streets of Kerek City moments after it occurred. Ngahuru had several street runners, Kereki orphans and those who lived in the alleys and byways mostly, who were well paid to give her information any time of the day or night. With the news of the murder, we took the children in our charge and fled over the wall to the Conrosan embasado immediately. The ambassador's wife and her guards stayed behind to arrange for us to sail for the West Islands as soon as possible. But as you already know, the harbormaster, under the Kerek King's orders, refused to let our ships dock, and Lowertown was heavily patrolled to keep us from finding a place to row out to our ships. The Kerek King was not going to let us slip through his fingers.

"Now Ngahuru does not wait for Trouble to ask her to dance before she plans and plots. From the very first days, she had prepared for the Conrosan embasado to be a hiding place. She had scaled the walls with ropes, and built a false door for us to enter," Raumati nodded to Kern, "The same one you took us through to leave. The Conrosans had planned for their departure all those years ago and had carefully boarded up the first floor.

Ngahuru used their efforts to help our own. Once we were in the embasado, we reinforced the exits and entrances with furniture.

"At first, we lived on the first floor, the windows were already boarded, and no one could see in or out. We lived in daylight only so there would be no lantern light or candle to betray us. One of our guards was Matasi born, and he would dress like a country person coming to the city to market to go out and get us food. Ngahuru would dress as one of her street runners, wearing a hood or cap to hide her face and leave to bring us news, or plan our escape with the ambassador's wife." Raumati looked at me and I knew she was telling me Ngahuru had been in her disguise as a Kereki boy.

"You know what we faced. West Islands ships were searched. Shipping manifests were taken to the King and his advisors. Our street runners told us Matasi, Spice Island, and Kerek ships were offered bounties paid for West Islander families or children who had passage. Any West Islander children. No one could get traveling papers. Kereki Tax Collectors stood on the gangways to the ships and threatened to confiscate everything in the holds and the ships themselves if the captains did not comply and turn over any West Islanders traveling with them.

"Then the ambassador was accused of inciting treason, and since he was dead and could not stand for his crimes, his wife, the King's sister, Hana, was dragged to the castle and executed in his place. We watched from the windows on the upper floors of the Conrosan hideaway as Kereki soldiers ransacked our embasado, destroying what they could not carry away."

Raumati looked at Bima, "So Ngahuru made another plan. Two of the five of us guarding the children would sail on different ships to Matasi, and then take another ship to the West Islands. We would learn what bribes needed to be paid, what traveling papers would be needed to escape detection, how thorough were the inspections. If at least one person survived and reached the West Islands, he or she would convey all that had happened to us and all our needs to the King. Thank the stars, both succeeded, and the King agreed with our plan.

"We had a long glass in our hiding place. Every incoming tide, Ngahuru would search the bay looking for our disguised ship. We knew no West Islands ship could dock, but the ship we had specifically asked for was Matasi built. A novelty—a hobby, of another of our King's sisters, Kaia. We knew she herself would not be able to sail it—the risk was too great, but the captain and crew of the ship were handpicked as our country's best and loyal to the King.

"Seventeen days later, we saw the ship in the harbor. Koanga arrived from the West Islands with two large Matasi trunks such as the missionaries use, false traveling papers made out as we requested them, coin, metal workings, and goods for sleeping rough. He proclaimed to everyone on his ship of his grand adventure to travel through Kerek and Matasi, ensuring every other passenger would think him a fool.

"A finely dressed Matasi businessman, and his steward, a short, fat Kereki," Raumati smiled at me, and I knew she was talking of Ngahuru and the Matasi guard in another of their disguises, "met Koanga at the docks, gathered his trunks and the rest of his belongings, and took him to a house in Kerek City. Since Koanga wanted to see the West Islands embasado and begin his grand adventure immediately, horses and a carriage were hired for him. They toured the city and the embasado. The carriage was parked in the shade on a side street just beyond the Conrosan compound.

"Koanga, the cheerful fellow that he is, walked down to the ruined West Islands embasado and chatted with the guards tasked with guarding the looted remains. He told them of the West Islands, the roaming regles, his role as a storyteller. He told them some of the great tales of the Smith, the Soldier, and the Traveler, and laughed with them when they joked about the Traveler's odds in Kerek City. They commiserated over the lot of soldiers and guards everywhere, and talked over things to do and see in Kerek and in Matasi that would not introduce him to Trouble.

"Decons later, when his new friends had told him the best place to buy his end of day meal, he waved as he said his goodbyes, and wandered back up the street towards his carriage and his short, fat Kereki driver. With a 'hiyah!' they clip-clopped down the street, and he waved once more to his soldier friends as they passed by.

"Back at the house, four people climbed out of the carriage heavily wrapped in traveling cloaks where only Koanga had entered half the day earlier." Raumati paused, letting our hearts listen to what our ears had just heard. While Koanga had done what Koanga did best, Ngahuru, the 'short, fat Kereki driver,' had gotten the children and the others out of the Conrosan embasado under the nose of the castle.

"Now time and tide wait for no one," she continued with a wide grin on her face, "and the ship was to cast off at midnight with the night tide. At dusk the same day, an old wagon rolled up to the dock driven by a swaggering Kereki youth with his pants tucked in tight to his boots, garish Kereki ties about his legs, a grey shirt, faded tunic, and a black glove on his left hand." I jerked my head up at Raumati's words. She acknowledged me with a sly look but kept on talking. "Our Kereki youth was driving two Matasi missionaries to the ship—a Matasi built ship—remember, praying loudly for their efforts to be fruitful in the future as they had not been in Kerek City. Their trunks were extremely heavy, but the longshoremen received extra coin and a blessing for carrying all the missionaries' worldly goods on to the ship. There were no other passengers on board, just cargo, and the harbor master logged it as traveling on to Vesaport, Matasi.

"The Kereki youth returned the horse and wagon from the cart hire stable and walked back to the house. At midnight, the three of us remaining, Ngahuru, Koanga, and I, watched from the second floor windows as the Matasi built ship set sail and gently moved out into the bay. Just before it left the shipping channel and out into the deepest waters, I saw a green lantern flash, the signal the ambassador's children had been unlocked out of the trunks and were safe and unharmed. The missionaries had been none other than our Matasi guard and his wife who were ready to start a new life over in the West Islands. In six days, the ship would dock in the West Islands, and according to the traveling papers, Ngahuru, a daughter to a tailor, and her younger brother, Koanga, would step off the ship and be met at the dock by their father."

I laughed. I couldn't have stopped if I wanted to. I laughed a deep belly laugh at how Ngahuru and Koanga had told me the truth, but had told it so sideways I had been led to the different story they wanted me to believe. I looked at Miya grinning—he had been able to fill in much of what Raumati didn't say as well. Bima and Kern just looked awestruck.

First Soldier Joon scowled. "How do you know the children made it?"

Raumati smiled at me, but answered him, "Because everyone is still looking for them, either as hostages or as goodwill pawns.

Because the couple who traveled with them and the captain of the ship would die before they would allow anything to happen to the children. Because the children are the niece and nephew of our King, and if the ship would have sunk in a storm or been taken by pirates, our street runners would have heard of it and let me know."

She paused. "Once I saw the green lantern on the ship, I was not worried for the children. They were out of the hands of the Kerek King. I was worried for Ngahuru and Koanga. Ngahuru had sent her true Diplo papers home with the children. Koanga had brought a false set of traveling papers for her, created in the West Islands and true in every sense except for the names. We knew that they would have to flee the city and sail out of Matasi. We knew the Coast Road was full of bandits and thieves and outlaws. But the road to Aldi also carried Zren Janin, and Matasi held Miyamoto Suki in her hands so he could assist us. Now I would like to hear their stories." She leaned back in her chair.

"You've already heard mine," I pointed out.

"But I haven't," said Ambassador Lalsy. "And I think it's important to hear the sequence of events to understand the entire story." She looked at the empty plates and cups and turned over her shoulder to one of the aides. "Bring more coffee and some bread, fruit, and cheese, please, and something for poor Zren to drink. He hasn't yet acquired a taste for Vikland coffee." She waved her hand at me. "Well, go on."

So I told them everything. Well, almost everything. Ngahuru's secret was safe, and I saw Raumati nod in approval as I glossed over Ngahuru. I talked about Koanga's skill with a needle and how we changed our appearances and our purpose as we traveled. How we camped rough and cooked our own food to avoid the inns and small villages and towns. I skipped over the waggoneer and his wife in Kerek, but told of the kindness of the guards as we slipped over the border into Matasi without papers for me.

"And then in Ribelo, we met Miyamoto Suki, and I'll let him tell the next part." I smiled at Miya.

Miya looked uncomfortable. "Zren, I will tell the truth now, but it will not be what you believed to be the truth until today. I am sorry, but I hope you understand."

He turned to Raumati. "I was already in Ribelo looking for a caravan to cross through Kerek or a guide to take me over the Silver Mountains when Ngahuru, Koanga, and Zren entered the guesthouse where I was staying. I was surprised to say the least. Here was the softfoot which all of the known world was looking for, and she casually walks in my guesthouse in Ribelo. I didn't want to alarm her and cause her to disappear or to be arrested and held by the Matasi, so I spoke to the other West Islander. I greeted Zren in Conrosan, but he didn't acknowledge me in any way, so I wondered what would cause a Conrosan not to know his own mother tongue?

"I had met Ngahuru a year before at one of the ambassador's dinners, and I knew the children were in her special care. No one seemed alarmed at my presence, so I spent the afternoon with Ngahuru to learn more and to offer Vikland's help. She said Zren had traveled with them from Kerek City, he was Kereki trained in rough fighting, and he had saved their lives at least twice. She did not appear to be at all concerned about the ambassador's children, nor was she mourning their loss. There was so much more that she was not telling me."

Miya looked at me. "I made the decision to change my plans to cross over into Vikland, and took a horse track through Matasi to intercept them at Anarkio. When they didn't get in until late, I was afraid they had changed their travel plans and I had lost them. But we reconnected, and I convinced them to travel together with me to Salisport, rather than travel to their own embasado in Alenti.

"Our embasado was able to host them and help them on their way as Ngahuru requested. She asked to have it be said we had been hosting a Storyteller as a diplomatic exchange since I had just been in the West Islands for the past year. The Storyteller was accompanied by his sister, a daughter of a tailor and someone of no consequence. The ambassador agreed, but to ensure Ngahuru's safety on the seas, we sent two of our own as an honor guard: Ven Wila, the Secondo's captain of her personal guard, and Solkka Ulani. I believed once Ngahuru and Koanga arrived in the West Islands the news would be shared with the world. I did not know the King wanted one more person to arrive home before he revealed the children were safe and to ensure your life was not forfeit." He made a short bow with his head. "I am pleased to make your acquaintance, Raumati of the West Islands. I bow to your perseverance and fortitude as you waited for a means to return to your homeland. I also pray when you see Ngahuru again, you convey my admiration for her well-fought battle. She is a worthy opponent for the corrupt King of Kerek."

Raumati smiled. "She is very resourceful, our Ngahuru. And that, my ambassador of Vikland, is the story of the ambassador's children—the niece and nephew of the King. You could wait for the return of your people from the West Islands, but I am not sure anyone will say anything until I am safely home."

She gave a heartfelt sigh. "And now I must beg. Is there a way you can assist me to return to the West Islands? I do not have Ngahuru's pots of paint, and Koanga's tailor's shears, or resourceful friends such as Zren Janin and Miyamoto Suki. What I am is a servant in the household of the West Islands King who would like to go home and see the ambassador's children whom I have known since their birth."

"That is a beautiful tale," said the ambassador drily. "But I find it hard to believe you hid so successfully from everyone for so long, but these three captured you the first time they entered the Conrosan embasado."

Raumati explained how it was the riots and the fires at the docks which had convinced her to come out of hiding. It would be easy for the mobs to overrun the West Islands embasado since it was already looted. If rioters went over the inner wall to loot and torch the Conrosan buildings as well, she would not survive. So she stayed on the top floor and watched out the windows. Ngahuru had left her the long glass so she could see to the docks when a ship could bring her home. But it also allowed her to look inside the embasado compounds. She had watched the Viklanders at weapons practice in the courtyard in the morning and had seen the Conrosan in the presence of First Soldier Joon. Others seemed to treat him well, certainly not as a prisoner. She wondered if the Conrosan Queen and the Viklander Empress were working together to secure her release.

"Of course, I should have known it would be softfooters, and not the diplomatic corps," she smiled wryly.

"We give you sanctuary," said the ambassador. "Raumati of the West Islands, protector of the ambassador's children, we give you sanctuary until we can help you travel home." She paused. "Do you have travel papers?"

"Yes. Koanga brought papers for all of us. They will clear the Kereki Tax Collector, but you know the docks. As a woman alone, I could not secure passage, nor travel. To ask for assistance?" She pointed to the bags against the wall. "I could not let these papers fall into the Kerek King's hands."

First Soldier Joon looked at an aide at the door who nodded, and then he turned back to Raumati. "A room has already been prepared for you. Bathe, eat, and rest at your leisure. Your bags will be carried out for you to your room and will not leave your presence. I will post someone outside your door to keep the quiet and to attend to anything you need. We will make arrangements for you to sail out with an honor guard. Once we have everything in place, we will meet with you later today."

He stood, we all stood, as Raumati was ushered out the door. Two aides picked up her bags and followed her out into the hallway. The third aide remained behind. I made to follow and Bima put his hand on my arm.

"Not so fast, Zren. We still have business here." We all sat down again. By now I could see dawn in the windows and all I wanted was a dark room and my own bed.

"Even if she is not who she says she is, I still feel obligated to help her." The ambassador began, "Perhaps the King of the West Islands will reimburse us her expenses, perhaps we will incur goodwill for the future. We can get a look at the children and confirm all is well." She looked at Joon. "Do we have anyone due to transfer to the West Islands?"

"Not at this time," Joon replied.

"Well, it will be an added expense, then." She tugged her ear, a very un-ambassadorial look, I thought. She looked at us about the table. "Well, you got me into this, you have a solution?"

"My assignment here was to find the children, as was Raeshon's," Bima said slowly. "Raeshon and I could escort the West Islander home and then take a ship to return us to Matasi. Perhaps we could accompany a chest or two of West Islands steel to Matasi to be hidden in the embasado at Salisport until it could be moved here?"

"Raeshon? Was she new?" The ambassador questioned.

"Just arrived two days ago. She and her partner were to be Matasian missionaries looking for the children through the Matasi and West Islander refugee communities. Her partner was damaged in the riots. Her value is now greater back in Matasi then here," Joon informed the ambassador.

"How is her partner?"

"Chul Swyler, a firemaster," Miya explained. "He is too damaged to continue here. He's going to travel with us to Vikland for healing." He paused. "He's leaving you many of his inventions."

"I'm sorry he was injured. I wish him health and healing." The ambassador laid her hands flat on the table. "Well, that's sorted out then. Bima, I leave it to you to find Raeshon and tell her of her change in plans. Joon, have the traveling papers prepared for everyone, and the requests for more metal workings and steel from our West Islander friends to accompany Bima back. I'll talk to the treasurer to see if we can't sell some candlesticks or something to pay for it all." She smiled as she said this so I didn't think she was serious.

"There is always the payroll we are carrying for the Kerek King," Miya joked back.

"Right, and if one coin doesn't make it, you can be sure Vikland will be blamed." Her face turned serious. "Be careful, Miyamoto, you have the best I can send with you, but each has a weakness that could be the end of you all. I don't know what the additional military guard means, they could be friends that save us, or enemies that stab us in the back. Good luck and good judgment."

We were finally dismissed to find our beds. I heard the Viklanders congratulate each other and themselves, but all I could think about as I headed back to my room was the ambassador's final warning. Friends that save us or enemies that don't. How would we know before it was too late?

# ACKNOWLEDGMENTS

Since I first put pen to paper on the Tales of Zren Janin series, I have been noting who has inspired me, pushed me, talked me off the cliff, and out of dead ends, and all around made me a better writer and human being.

The notebook of thanks was as long as my first draft of the novel.

Yes, well. The journey isn't over yet.

Thank you to the team at Paper Raven Books. Morgan, you had me at "Hello. We want to disrupt the world of traditional publishing." Who could turn down an opportunity to make the publishing world more inclusive and more diverse? All readers need to see themselves in the books. Thank you Karen, Alyssa Marie, Amanda, Gabrielle, Jesus, and Rachela for your vision, your late nights, and those early morning calls to work around my day job. Everyone should have an editor like Ashley Swanson. I am fall down on my knees grateful for your all around awesomeness!

A huge debt of thanks to my beta readers, those who started with me on Wattpad way back in 2019, and those who joined me along the way. For those of you who are anonymous or have only usernames, I hope you find this book online or in a bookstore someday and recognize your feedback. Your questions made the world building and mythology deeper and better. You showed me how to let the characters unfold in all of their imperfections, and loved them anyway. Thank you, thank you. As for Stephanie Dodge, Gary Dunker, and Florence Dunker, your concise comments, suggestions, and Zoom calls made the rewrites (and more rewrites) bearable. Thank you for keeping me on track and on the right track. I owe you all so much.

Thank you to developmental editor, Benay Stein, who helped correct a fatal flaw and made me realize that what I want and what works to make a better book is not always the same thing.

The following people are catalysts. An impact so great, your words and actions changed me for the better. Thank you for walking into my life and being a part of this book journey.

Betsy Sell – for encouraging my writing way back in the previous century right up to last Christmas when you sent me 35 Years of Minnesota Women. Friends like you are as rare as a 70 degree day in Minnesota in January. I am not worthy.

Geri Buckles – You handed me Marcus Zuzak's *The Book Thief* and introduced me to YA fiction. But most importantly, you and Mike demonstrate your beliefs. You were the foundation for the West Islander, Koanga. May your world always be in harmony.

Erin J. Mullikan – Editor, poet, and aspirational goddess. May all your dreams come true.

Nancy Swenson – Ngahuru = you. But I bet you figured that out within the first five pages.

Minnesota Naturalist and 'leetle bruther,' Mike Dunker - You know I have the social skills of an orangutan, but you talk to me anyway. Thanks for giving Koanga all of his woodsman and cooking skills. Koanga's slyly hitting the bullseye with the crossbow while casually talking to others was all you. Thanks for living the dream and showing me how it's done.

Heartfelt gratitude to David and Bridget, Ryan and Bri, Jenny and Zach, Katie and Nelson, Almond, Brandon, Liz and Riley, Kaeden, Callie, Peyton, Philip, Lauren, Ryla, Rinoa, Gunther, Lark, Hayden, Max, Nordica, Penelope, Cory, Catherine, and Hallie. You are the readers I write for. Here's your cliché for the day: There is no one size fits all. Don't let anyone put you in a box. It's a big world out there.

And finally, and most importantly, Steven. Thank you for the title of the book, ignoring the 4:30 a.m. 'wake ups' so I could write before going to work, and for creating the garden outside my window to catch the sunrises. I still do not understand how you can practice unconditional love every moment of every day. But some miracles should not be examined too closely, and I think this is one of them. The world is a better place with you in it. Thank you for everything.

*"People need to see themselves in the stories. How can we only say 'he' and 'she' when we are 'all'?' How can we ask great things of ourselves, if all we see are 'others' as heroes?"*

*"We — all of us - need to be present in the stories." … "You need to create your own story. You and you alone."*
\- Ngahuru in A Gift of the Stars

Turn the page for

*A Gift of the Stars* bonus materials

including a bonus short story: *Men of Power*

and a preview of

# *Manumina*

Book 2 in *The Tales of Zren Janin*

# READING GUIDE

**Need to write a book report?**

**Try using some of these questions as a jumping off point!**

1. From the very first chapter, we learn that Red says he cannot lie, yet he is able to keep who he is and what he has done from Ngahuru and Koanga. How does this set up the action of the first few days?

2. Koanga tells Red they are traveling to Matasi so they can sail home. Yet they take an extra day for Red to recover himself enough to travel with them. Koanga says it was his West Islander heart that made him beg Ngahuru to help an injured boy. What other reasons could the West Islanders have for wanting Red to travel with them?

3. What is your first impression of Koanga? How does this change throughout the book?

4. In Aldi, Koanga and Red act very differently. Discuss how the differences in Red's and Koanga's past life impact their actions.

5. Did your impression of Willow change when she was the one who saved the three of them from Goblin and Brick? When she saved Zren in the attack after the Sion Inn?

6. From the beginning of the book until nearly the end, Red clearly states his motivation is to do or be whatever he needs to in order for the West Islanders to take him with them. How is this different from most main characters in the fantasy genre?

7. The title *A Gift of the Stars* refers to Ngahuru's vitiligo. How is the West Islander description different than the Matasi name of 'coal and ashes'? Based on these descriptions, how do you think people with vitiligo are treated in the two countries?

8. The mythology of the West Islands is very different from the fairy tales of Conrosa. Compare and contrast the two creation/origin stories, the Smith and Mother Earth, and the origin of Zren Janin. Which do you personally prefer and why?

9. At the pond, Koanga and Willow let Red see her for who she really is. Why is this trust important so early in the book?

10. Willow tells a story of the Kerek City Orphan Master, a cruel story compared to the tales Koanga has been telling of the West Islands. What do you think she is trying to accomplish? How do you think this will impact Red in the future?

11. At the Sion Inn, the travelers are refused service. Red tries to explain it away as unusual. Not because it is the wrong thing to do, but because he can't see anyone turning down coin in Kerek. What other examples do you remember where the racism is so ingrained Red doesn't understand the depths of it.

12. How do the stories Koanga tells around the campfire reflect the setting in which he tells them? What is he teaching Red?

13. At the border, Willow takes a lot of time and effort to get Red into Matasi with her and Koanga. Why do you think they continue to take responsibility for Red? Think of a person in your life who went above and beyond to help you succeed. How did this make an impact on your life?

14. What do you think of Red's new name? Why do you think Ngahuru chose to give Red the name of a Conrosan folk hero?

15. What was your first impression of Miyamoto Suki? How did this change as he spent time with the travelers in Ribelo? Why do you think Red was having so much difficulty with Miya at first?

16. What was your impression of the baboy and the music? What did you think of the homestays in Matasi? Would you like to travel this way? Why or why not?

17. A critical component of the book series is something the author calls "otherness" defined as an unrelenting attitude towards others that says they do not deserve the same treatment or kindness for any reason – lack of wealth, skin color, tenets of belief, gender/sexuality, abilities, lack of opportunities/privilege, or even no reason at all. Think about the waggoneer and his wife and how they changed towards the travelers once they learned Ngahuru used the pronouns she/her. Ngahuru didn't change, only their perceptions changed. Can you think of a time in your life when you or others you knew, were treated differently because of what others thought. Were you discouraged/outraged/resigned? Why or why not?

18. When Zren spends the night in the Subversiva jail he vows he will be different somehow. When he meets Miyamoto Suki again in Anarkio, he treats him differently than he did in Ribelo and even agrees to travel to Vikland with him. What's changed?

19. At the Vikland embasado in Salisport, Zren meets Bima Ritwik and Solkka Ulani, two men who will have an impact on him and future events in the succeeding books. How does Koanga's impression of the two men influence Zren? How does Miyamoto Suki describe Bima? What advice would you give to Zren after meeting both of these men?

20. On the last night in Salisport, Bima and other Softfoots try to embarrass Zren many times without success. What assumptions did they make about Zren that caused them to underestimate his talents and abilities? Why do you think Zren was so successful?

21. On the ship, Zren sees a very different side to Bima as he answers all of Zren's questions or just provides companionship and conversation. Zren thinks Bima is sorry for the night in Salisport. What do *you* think is Bima's motivation? Why?

22. It took a tremendous amount of courage for Raumati to stay behind in Kerek City when she couldn't leave with the children as part of their disguise and couldn't walk to Matasi because of her clubfoot. Can you think of instances in our society where *not* to do something is harder than the alternative?

23. What did you think of Ngahuru's cleverness in getting the children out of Kerek? How did the Kerek King's prejudices and assumptions lead to his failure to capture the children?

24. Why did Raumati dismiss Bima as unable to help her? Why did she trust Zren?

25. What was your favorite scene in the book?

*Men of Power*

(This story takes place nine years
before the events of *A Gift of the Stars*)

Bima Ritwik hurried down the hall of the military barracks. Just two days ago, he had returned to Juisiti from Kerek City over the Northern Track. It had been the largest group he had traveled with - nearly a dozen soldiers and their captain, two other softfoots in addition to himself, and even a Spice Islander diplomat and his family reporting for duty at his embasado in Vikland. And *still* they had been robbed by bandits outside of Balza. Surrounded by at least twenty men on horses, the travelers had been forced to dismount. Their captain had muttered in Vik to hold their fire for a coordinated attack. And so the Viklanders had grumbled and looked resigned as the bandits demanded their valuables first. Bima grinned in remembrance. Greed was the bandits' fatal mistake.

The bandits had gleefully watched them as the Viklanders started untying pockets and traveling bags and tossing them into a pile in the middle. The bandits mocked the women soldiers, bragged about the Vik horses they would take, and crowed about the uselessness of the men that needed women to protect them. Finally, the pile was ankle high and entirely surrounded by the Viklanders. The bandits jeered that Viklanders thought they were so stupid. The leader of the bandits split his men in two. Some of his men waved their crude iron and copper knives to herd the Viklanders and their horses away from the pile of goods. As the remaining bandits dismounted their own horses to gather their ill-gotten treasures, the Vik commander had called to strike.

Within moments, the Viklanders had pulled their bongs from their backs and from their horses' scabbards. In the noise and confusion, their four archers, crossbows nocked and loosed, had taken the bandits fleeing the battle. There were no survivors.

No sense in letting the word get out, the commander said. Viklanders are always armed.

The Spice Islander had stood there with his mouth gaping like a fish on land while the Viklanders had recovered their belongings and searched the bodies on the ground. What an apt description, Bima thought. Everything the Spice Islander would see and hear for the term of his diplomatic service in Juisiti would be as foreign as the Northern Track. Just not as deadly.

And now Bima was back in Juisiti, and it was time to find more new softfoots. As Kerek continued to treat Viklanders and other strangers with such disregard, he thought there would be trouble between Vikland and Kerek sooner rather than later. He wondered if he would be able to get to Matasi before the Wet and determine what was happening there, or if this newest group of recruits would be so incompetent he would lose them all in training. Why did it seem only the military leaders understood that the tougher the training, the easier it would be to survive when the softfooting could mean life or death? Bima stopped abruptly at the dormitory door and knocked twice. He counted to twenty and then pushed open the door.

The women were sitting on chairs, casually lying on beds reading, or standing about in small groups talking. The room was tidy but not overly so, inspection had been decons ago. Bima huffed, "Bah! Someone sent me on a fool's errand. I'm looking for Miyamoto Suki or Solkka Ulani. Anyone here know where they lay their heads?"

A few of the women gave him an appraising look. One of them, a very tall woman, looked him up and down and then gave him a sly smile. "And who are you that I should speak so casually of the Prince and the Wannabe?"

Bima laughed in spite of himself, "I am Bima Ritwik. And you are?"

The woman looked interested. "The great Softfoot, Bima Ritwik? The man who appears and disappears like smoke on a stiff breeze and can be found in any bed but his own? The only Softfoot known to use his family name because he has nothing to hide and no family honor to hide behind?"

Bima stiffened at the insult, but made a mocking bow. "Of course." He straightened, "and if you know so much about me, you would also know the whereabouts of," he paused, "the Prince and the Wannabe. And your name as well," he added.

"I am Ceri, a hatchet wielder from the far eastern lands of Vikland. Normally, I would not know where two little first year cadets would be mewling about the hallways looking for their mothers, but those two? They are in dorm 11."

Bima dipped his head. "I thank you, Ceri of Vikland's far eastern lands." He stepped back out of the threshold and began to close the door. "May your blades always be as sharp as your tongue."

He heard the burst of laughter as he hurried down the hall and up the staircase.

Dormitory 11 was deserted. All of the beds were regulation crisp, the room spotless. First years, Bima sneered. Probably in mortal fear of their room captain. He turned to go and saw the two men he was looking for coming up the staircase at the end of the hall. He took a moment to assess them as they walked towards their room.

Miyamoto Suki was known to him. As the oldest child of one of the chief advisors to the Empress, Miyamoto had been trained for a life of diplomatic service to the royal family. Even his name, a great warrior and poet of a faraway land, had been chosen to set him apart from ordinary Viklanders. Raised in the palace with tutors and advisors, he had probably been friends and classmates of the Empress's daughters since they all could toddle.

Bima wondered what it would be like to be under such constant scrutiny and judgment. He knew, as everyone did, Miya had been a diligent student, above average in everything, polite and courteous and well-spoken in public with no nasty habits to be ferreted out by softfoots and gossips. He was handsome and determined and everything Bima was not, and yet Bima didn't envy Miyamoto Suki. No one would be envious if they understood the glass walls the royals and near royals lived behind. Was there any decision Miyamoto Suki could make that wasn't measured against the good of Vikland?

He had never met Solkka Ulani before. But even if Miyamoto Suki had not been standing next to him, Bima would have known it was the nephew of the West Islands King. Bima had heard the softfoot Rani say the Ulani men and women looked like they stepped from a Viklander tapestry. In Solkka's case, his mother's West Islander looks sat lightly on him and softened the Vik high cheekbones and long straight nose. His braid lacked the black sleekness of most Viklanders. His skin was the color of a Viklander who spent all their time outdoors kissed by the sun.

Both men were shorter than Bima, but it was clear to see from the graceful way they carried themselves, they trained with the bongs more than the crossbow. Bima approved. He also preferred the tahn bong. Both young men were now close enough to understand Bima was waiting for them and not just merely standing about. They hurried up to him.

Bima waited for them to start the formal Viklander greetings. When they did not, he knew they thought themselves above him. He scowled, "Do you not know who I am?"

Miyamoto Suki smiled at him. "You are Bima Ritwik. It has been a while since I have seen you. My mother has pointed you out – more than once. She told me if I have any secrets to guard them closely when I see you lurking in the palace. She says even though you are so young, you are the greatest Softfoot in Vikland." His smile grew into a small smirk. "Yes, I know who you are."

Bima made his face as bland as possible so his words would carry more sting. "Ah, Miya. May I call you Miya, my first year cadet? Let me explain something very important to you. Here, you are nobody. And all of the other nobodies do not care if your mother takes tea with the Empress. The nobodies here do not care that you have had your nose in a book since you could toddle. No one will make the formal greetings to you first because here in the military you are nothing but a first year cadet." Bima watched in satisfaction as he saw Miya's jaw tighten. *Ah, one of Miya's weak points. Good to know.*

Bima tapped his chin as if considering, "I had planned on inviting the two of you to one of my little training exercises, but I think I will wait now until you have better manners."

Miya flashed a look of distaste. "Don't bother, Bima Ritwik. I am a soldier and a son of Vikland who would never stoop to listening in at doors and slithering through women's bedrooms to earn my keep."

"Stop, you two." Solkka broke in. "I have better things to do with my time than to listen to my friend" – he looked to Miya – "and a man who holds my future" – he nodded at Bima, "argue over me."

He grinned at Miya. "You have heard our captain threaten to send us to the softfoots if we do not accomplish the tasks they put in front of us. You have heard of those who wish to be softfoots fail one of Bima's trainings and then are sent in disgrace to be soldiers. It would not do, Miya, to anger Bima Ritwik, the greatest of Vikland's softfoots."

Solkka stopped smiling as he faced Bima. "I know you know who I am. I do not say this to brag, but to ask a favor and grant you one in return. I am a son of Vikland and a better than fair hand on the bongs. I plan to serve my Empress well during my military service. After? If she and those who make such decisions consider me worthy, I would like to serve her in the Diplo.

"I have no desire to make an enemy of you, Bima Ritwik. Instead, I believe sometime in the future you may consider me 'an arrow in your quiver' as my uncle would say. I will do nothing to betray my mother's family, either the King who sits on the throne of the West Islands, or his sisters who are scattered about the known world as ambassadors and diplomats. You should know I hope to be an ambassador myself someday. But between this day and that day, I have a lot to learn." Solkka paused. "And I would like to learn it without watching over my shoulder for one of your softfoots, or locking up everything I own every time I wish to close my eyes."

Bima smirked, "Are you bribing me?"

Solkka cocked his head to the side. "I didn't mean it to sound so, Bima, truly. I will practice how I can say these words more wisely in the future. But you are a man of power. If you will consider turning your eye from us while we are first year cadets, I would be grateful for the opportunity to learn without being harassed and thwarted by anyone who is hoping to gain your notice and your favor. I could not win against so many who seek your approval."

Bima laughed. "You are more than a pretty face, Solkka Ulani." He shrugged. "It's true, there are many who will seek the two of you out in the next few years. Some will be false friends hoping to trade on your connections, some will take delight in causing you trouble because it will make them feel larger." He paused a long time and watched as Solkka fidgeted a little under his gaze. *A man of action, not used to standing still.* Bima thought. Miya, he noticed, was as silent and still as a softfoot on a night's watch. Bima decided quickly.

"I am not a small and petty man, Solkka Ulani and Miyamoto Suki. I have heard your request, and I will grant it. Your next three years will be difficult enough and so, I will do nothing to help nor harm you during your years of service here. I will not seek you out for victims, nor will I hold you out for praise. My softfoots in training will never cross your thresholds to steal your secrets to embarrass you or your families just to test their skills. And in return, it may be you will smile kindly on my requests when you are men of power…and you will grant them." He crossed his arms and waited.

Miya inhaled sharply and Solkka gave him a long considering look. Bima waited some more. Then Solkka smiled and put his hands together for the formal Vikland greetings. "It has been a pleasure meeting you, Bima Ritwik. I look forward to the end of my military service when you and I may speak again." He bowed a short bow a little deeper than equals.

Both men looked to Miya. He tightened his face, but gave Bima a stiff bow – as equals. "Thank you for your kindness," he gritted out, "Three years of not looking over my shoulder for a dance with Trouble is a gift of consequence. I shall remember this in the future."

"Oh, I am sure you will," Bima grinned. He turned away to look for other victims among the first year cadets. "But between that day and this day, Miyamoto Suki, you may wish to consider the wise words of your friend." He waved his hand behind him as he walked down the hall without any acknowledgement of their formal greeting at all.

Miya wheeled on Solkka. "Why did you do that? He is *nothing* to us. He dropped out of the academies. He softfoots, stealing secrets. My mother says he is a man who knows Truth as only a casual acquaintance and to keep my distance."

Solkka looked soberly at his friend. "Miya, I am the son of a coffee farmer. When I came to the academies, I quickly saw how the others from the wop wops of Vikland were taunted for their country accents, their lack of knowledge of Juisiti and her pleasures, and their awkward social graces. You befriended me, and by the power of your name, kept those away who would have made my time in and out of the classroom an unrelenting misery.

"We have finished the academies and now find ourselves at the bottom of the dunghill again as first year cadets. Bima, and more importantly those who seek his attention, are not the enemies we need right now. This way we can learn freely. Bima has already acknowledged someday we will be men of power by our efforts as well as by our birth. Not all power should be displayed, Miya, this is the first lesson my mother taught me."

**The adventure continues in**

*Manumina*

**Book 2 of *The Tales of Zren Janin***

Red has spent his life trying to avoid a dance with Trouble.

When Red was rescued by the great Softfoot Ngahuru and
Koanga the Storyteller, he learned life was more than just survival
on the streets of Lowertown. As they traveled through Kerek and
Matasi, the West Islanders gave him a new name – Zren Janin –
and told him of a homeland he had never known: Conrosa.

Ngahuru also introduced him to Miyamoto Suki, a diplomat
of Vikland trying to reach his own country. When Miya asks
him to travel with him and protect him over the bandit infested
Northern Track, Zren agrees, in exchange for an education at the
famed Vikland Academies and future travel to Conrosa to find
his family. It's a wealthy reward – if he stays alive long enough to
claim it.

Joining them are three Viklander women: Kern, a Softfoot,
Rell, a healer and bowmaster, and Song Yao, a renowned
bongmaster. All of them will be guarding an injured firemaster
and two wagons of what Zren suspects are illegal weapons,
although everyone pretends they are merely farm implements.

To make the trip more difficult, the King of Kerek is sending along the paychest for the garrison at Earles with only four questionable Kereki soldiers to guard it. Since the Kerek King and the Empress of Vikland are not friends or allies, and barely on speaking terms, what could possibly go wrong?